This book is a work of fiction and any resemblances to persons, living or dead, places, events, or locales is purely coincidental. They are productions of the author's imagination and are used fictitiously.

Published by Stephenson & Powers Publishing House.
Copyright 2012 by Stephenson & Powers Publishing House.
http://www.stephensonpowerspub.com/

Edited by Susan Hughes

Cover Art produced by Laura Wright LaRoche at LLPix Photography. 2012.
http://www.llpix.com/

"Time is a violent torrent; no sooner is a thing brought to sight than it is swept by and another takes its place."
Caesar Marcus Aurelius, 121-180 A.D.

"Livius, if you listen very carefully, you can hear the gods laughing!"
Caesar Lucius Aurelius Commodus, 161-192 A.D.

"I wonder if the Emperor Honorius watching the Visigoths coming over the seventh hill could truly realize that the Roman Empire was about to fall. This is really just another page of history, isn't it? Will this be the end of our civilization? Turn the page."
Captain Jean-Luc Picard, "The Best of Both Worlds"

For Mary

ACKNOWLEDGMENTS

Independent Author

That title is an oxymoron in my opinion. Releasing a novel is not an independent endeavor. When I started writing this, I can say that I was independent in the sense that I had no clue what I was doing. I soon learned that I needed help - a lot of help.

I owe my wife for the past five months. Many long evenings I sat in from of my iMac lost in the dystopian world you are about to enter. She was patient with me and gave me her full support. For that I owe her a great deal. She read each chapter enthusiastically and always looked forward to reading chapters that featured the character I based on her, Elizabeth Reed. She was also a voracious proofreader. She pointed out many mistakes that I should have caught. Her support and praise mean the world to me.

I had a handful of proofreaders; however, two in particular put in a great deal of work and input for me to consider. They also provided the inspiration for two main characters, President Malcolm Powers and his Chief of Staff, Stacy Reid. I owe Carl and Stacy more than they will ever know.

I am about the least artistic person I know. I can't sing or dance to save my life, and I definitely can't draw or paint worth a flip. Stick figures are pretty much the best I can come up with. The magnificent cover that graces the front of this novel was created by Laura LaRoche. I still get chills when I look at it.

One person helped me shape this story into what you are about to read - Susan Hughes. I learned early on that my grasp of the rules of grammar was far from what I pictured it to be. Susan volunteered her services and polished this work into a professional looking manuscript. She also pointed out a lot of "fluff" as we came to call it and convinced me to slash it. Without her honest input, this book would be much slower paced. Without Susan, this book would have turned out much different.

CHAPTER ONE

In the foothills of the Rocky Mountains, Howard Beck awoke in his massive bedroom in his palatial home. Howard never hesitated when he woke; he didn't stare at the ceiling and talk himself into starting his day. Once his eyes were open, his feet hit the floor and it was time to begin the day. Howard hated wasting his time and hated even more when others wasted it. Howard had every second of every day planned to perfection. It wasn't a difficult task; Howard repeated the same routine every day with little deviation. The routine that followed his exit from bed had been the same for most of his five decades. Toilet, shower, breakfast, in that order. When Howard flushed the toilet, the shower came on by itself and achieved the exact temperature he had programmed. After the shower, Howard stepped out, and like every morning, the shower slowly trickled to a stop. He put on his robe and traveled through his cathedral sized home to the kitchen. Every time he entered a room, the lights would come on; when he left, they would fade back down. Once he was in the kitchen, the lights turned on and the curtains retracted to show a stunning view of the Rocky Mountains. Howard grabbed his cup from beneath the coffee pot and sat alone at the breakfast table.

"Good morning, Hal." Howard spoke aloud, waiting for his computer to respond.

"Good morning, sir," the world's first truly Artificial Intelligence sprang to life and spoke in a male, British voice.

"What do you have for me this morning?"

"No relevant messages received during the night. Your first vid-conference is at 9 o'clock with Director Mills. When I contacted him last night to confirm the meeting, he indicated to me that he would be reporting on the recovery progress at the Atlanta factory."

"Did he sound positive about it or like he wasn't looking forward to it?"

"Based on his vocal patterns and word choices, I would say his report will be positive."

"Or complete bullshit," Howard muttered.

"I am sorry, sir, I have little success understanding

deception. If you would like, in the future I can..."

"Never mind, Hal. What's going on in the world?"
Howard seldom ventured from the fortress he had designed.

"Residents along the Texas-Louisiana state line are
preparing for Hurricane Maxine to make landfall in the next
thirty-two to thirty-four hours. Based on my analysis, I estimate
a sixty-one percent chance that it will make landfall four point
two miles east of the tip of Galveston Island."

"You don't say," Howard muttered, not paying attention

"Wildfires continue to spread across much of California.
Officials have reason to believe that arsonists are using the
wildfires as cover to set even more fires. Officials also suspect
the arsonists are making the existing wildfires stronger."

"Uh-huh. Next story, please." Old news tended to bore
Howard. He made it a habit to ignore speculation and
sensational news reporting until it became more grounded in fact.

Hal continued, "Recovery efforts along the Florida
coastline continue to show little progress a month after the
disaster. Critics from both sides of the aisle continue to raise
questions about why much of Florida is in a media blackout. The
governor of Florida said in a press conference that Hurricane
Luther carried a toxic chemical spill up the coast, rendering much
of the region unsafe. Governor Prince also indicated that
over three-quarters of the roads in her state were impassable. The
governor also indicated that an unnamed aircraft carrier was off
the coast Merritt Island, some sixty miles from Orlando. The
Department of the Navy would not comment on search and rescue
missions along the Florida coast."

Hearing the same news day after day with only a few
minor details added irritated Howard. "Hal, give me something
interesting that I can't find on the Internet."

"Of course, sir." The most sophisticated computer in the
world, the first to shatter the Turing Test into irrelevancy, paused
for less than half a second before continuing.

"President Powers, facing the defining moment in his
administration, stands on the precipice of toppling the Great
Empire of..."

Howard laughed, something he rarely did, and interrupted
his friend. "What? Are you kidding me? Did you really and

truly," Howard laughed again, "just use the word 'precipice' and actually speculate about something as unpredictable as an actual war?"

"I did indeed, sir."

"I must say, Old Man, you never cease to impress me."

"Thank you, sir. I do try."

"Mind telling me how you figured out that the president was at a 'precipice' in the war?"

"I would be happy to, sir."

"Wait, how long will it take?"

"Forty-two and a half minutes, sir."

"Can you just give me the condensed version?"

"Forty-two and a half minutes is the condensed version, sir."

"Never mind, Hal. I spoke with the president last night, and I'm positive I know what you're about to say. Tonight when I go to bed, I would be happy to listen to you for forty-two and half minutes and tell you if you got it right."

"I look forward to it, sir."

Hal did, of course send and receive all vid-cons to and from Howard Beck. Hal recorded every conversation in intimate detail. However, Howard had programmed Hal not to access the conversations without his permission. If Howard needed Hal for anything while he was on a vid-con, he simply raised the level of his voice slightly and spoke the phrase "Hal, I need you." This would trigger another program, separate from Hal, and bring Hal into the conversation. Howard felt he deserved a level of privacy from the computer he built.

"Continue, Old Man. Anything happen on the compound last night?"

"No, sir, nothing of consequence happened on the property last night. Some wildlife did make it on the property and caused damage to some of the landscaping on the south lawn."

"Son of a bitch. Please tell me it wasn't the Middlemist's Red. What furry little shits did it?"

The Middlemist's Red was his wife's favorite. They had met when they were seniors in college. Howard immediately knew that Meredith was the woman he would marry. When Howard was able to slow his brilliant, genius mind down long enough to focus on one thing instead of dozens, it was not something to be ignored. It had happened twice before. The first was when he was old enough to sit in front of a computer. The introduction to the world of Star Trek was the second time. Captain Picard was the coolest guy to grace both the big and small screen. The richest man in the world could hardly manage to keep his composure when he met Patrick Stewart. The kind Englishman managed to put Howard at ease and the two became friends. Howard honored Mr. Stewart as being one of the few men in the world to say he had seen the inside of Howard's $500 million home.

During his senior year at MIT, Howard was relentless in his pursuit of Meredith. When he finally found a piece of data that he knew would win her heart, he gave her the flower and asked her to marry him. Meredith was deeply touched by the flower. However, she smiled, kissed him on his forehead and explained to Howard that she couldn't very well marry a fourteen-year-old boy.

Howard decided to wait until he was eighteen and finishing his second doctorate to ask again. Meredith was twenty-six and engaged to another man. She adored Howard and cherished his friendship. Howard was not fazed in the slightest by his competition. He knew it was only a matter of time before the engagement would end. They were meant to be together. Computers...Star Trek...Meredith. It was going to happen; Howard just needed to wait. Howard finally had his chance when the engagement ended just like he predicted. Three years later he founded Beck Enterprises and asked for her hand in marriage a third time. Meredith knew that Howard was a profoundly brilliant man who would change the world. She also fully understood what made Howard the way he was.

Howard had Asperger's Syndrome, a form of high-functioning autism and a pervasive developmental disorder that seriously impairs social skills and the demonstration of empathy. Aspies, as they like to be called, also have a hard time maintaining eye contact and understanding facial expressions and other social cues. This makes interpreting subtle nuances like sarcasm and deception (playful or sinister) very difficult. Aspies are very direct and speak their mind, often forgetting the impact that such honesty can bring to those around them. Meredith did not consider it a "disease" or a "disorder" or even a "syndrome". She cherished Howard dearly and embraced every single thing about him. She agreed to take things slow and the two became a couple.

A year later the two were wedded. Meredith wore her grandmother's dress, and Howard wore a Starfleet Dress Uniform from *Star Trek: The Next Generation*. Meredith thought he was kidding when he mentioned the idea. Howard's reaction was to have a total meltdown and lock himself in his room. When he finally calmed down, he was able to explain to her that the first time he saw the dress uniform in the seventh episode of season one entitled "Lonely Among Us," he decided right then and there that he would wear exactly the same dress uniform at his wedding. He then proceeded to try to describe the episode in detail and began to quote the dialogue when Meredith stopped him and kissed his cheek. When Howard made up his mind about something, it was set in stone and could not be changed. When Howard made plans to do something, it was not easily deviated from. Howard was heartbroken when he deduced that the only logical conclusion was that Meredith was going to call off the wedding because he was trying to ruin it.

Meredith simply smiled and told him that she loved him so much he could wear a potato sack to their wedding. She stood beside her handsome Starfleet Captain and made her vows. After the ceremony, Howard's gift to her was a garden of Middlemist's Red flowers. She had forgotten the young fourteen-year-old Howard giving her the flower on his first of three marriage proposals. For decades she regarded the flower to be a beautiful and symbolic representation of their marriage. She told Howard he was unique and special, just like the flower. Howard just saw the flowers as something that made his wife happy, even though they cost a fortune to bring to the U.S. and to keep alive. He could not understand what was so special about the flowers. The camellia named for John Middemist wasn't even red; it was a deep pink and looked more like a rose than a camellia.

"No, sir, the Middlemist's Red are fine. The offending creature was not a 'furry little shit' as you so eloquently put it. It was in fact a Northwestern Great Horned Owl attempting to catch a mouse, which it did, I might add."

"Really? They come this far south?"

"Yes, sir. In the winter they have been seen this far south."

"Thank God the damned flowers are fine. Her Highness would never let me hear the end of it. Where exactly did we get those cursed flowers from this time?"

"From New Zealand, sir."

"Yeah, that's it, how on earth did I forget that?"

"I have no idea, sir."

Howard's estate was one of three locations in the world that featured the flower. It was incredibly difficult to keep the flowers alive in Colorado. They were kept in a greenhouse and when weather permitted, the greenhouse walls were programmed to retract. Howard's wife insisted on it; she felt that the flowers should be a part of nature when possible. Botanists and flower enthusiasts from all over the country begged to get a look at them. Howard wouldn't hear of it. The thought of his home becoming a tourist attraction made Howard sick to his stomach.

"Thank you, Hal. Is that all?"

"There is one more thing, sir. A vehicle passed in front of the estate last night."

"Really? Belong to a nearby resident?"

"No, sir. The vehicle had an out-of-state license plate."

That got Howard's attention immediately and frightened him. He began to tap his fingers and rock back and forth. "What? Out of state? Did they slow down at all or do anything suspicious?"

"No, sir. They did not slow down or attempt any surveillance of the property.

This made Howard nervous. In the year 2027, very few people traveled outside of their hometown, let alone out of their state. Interstate travel was unheard of during the Second Great Depression. Few people could afford to travel long distances, and the ones that did have the wealth traveled by jet on the last remaining airline in the country. Long distance travel was for the élite.

Howard snapped out of his train of thought and addressed his computer. His eyes fluttered around the room, his speech became more erratic. Howard was not handling this well.

"Hal, what can you tell me about the vehicle? What state? Anything on the driver or passengers?"

"I'm sorry to report, sir, the only thing I was able to see was a small portion of the plate, enough to ascertain that the vehicle was not from Colorado. I can report with eighty-four percent certainty that the only occupant of the vehicle was the driver. This of course does not account for passengers not properly seated in the vehicle."

"You mean you wouldn't be able to tell if someone was lying down in the backseat?"

"Correct, sir."

"Could it be an evacuee from Hurricane Luther?"

"No, sir, not likely."

"Based on what exactly, Hal?"

"I have narrowed the license plate down to three possible states, none of which the hurricane had any impact on."

"What are the three states?"

"Iowa, Kentucky, and Mississippi."

"Hmmmm. Hal, until further notice, I want you to notify me immediately of any out-of-state vehicles coming near the property."

"Of course, sir."

Howard had never even considered that an out-of-state vehicle would be in the area. He had not seen one on the road in years. Most people simply could not afford to put gas in their vehicles. Instead, they used mass transit, rode mopeds and bicycles. It wasn't uncommon to see vehicles on the road; it was however, uncommon to see an out-of-state license plate.

Howard had managed to calm down and stop tapping his fingers. "Anything else, Hal?"

"Yes, sir. Several months ago you instructed me to remind you today to make arrangements to visit Meredith."

"That will be all, Hal. Thank you." Howard said sharply.

"Very good, sir. I would be happy to review the rest of your schedule over lunch." Hal went silent and began to study each room of the mansion to see what tasks needed to be assigned to his robots.

Howard did not respond to his assistant. He wanted to scream at Hal for putting him in such a foul mood. He knew that to do so would only raise his blood pressure and serve no real purpose. The elevation of Howard's blood pressure would be known immediately to Hal thanks to the thousands of tiny nanobots coursing thru the billionaire's blood. Hal knew every intimate detail about his creator and alerted him of any medical concern, no matter how small.

His trusted assistant, while very lifelike, was only a sophisticated machine, the first one of its kind. Howard built the A.I. himself and still tinkered with him. Howard was already approaching his first billion when he completed Hal. When he decided to sell the first true A.I. the world had ever known, his net worth skyrocketed into the tens of billions. From year to year, he moved around on the list of the richest people in the world. He was currently at the top of the list.

The A.I. came with a hefty price tag; only major corporations and a few of the world's governments could afford it. Hal's siblings ran much of the day-to-day operations at Apple, Google, and Facebook. Only two other private citizens in the world had a copy of the A.I. The first was his friend, Bill Gates, the other being Mark Zuckerberg. Wealthy billionaires around the world tried to buy one of the systems, but Howard refused to sell it to private citizens outside of the United States. Howard sold not one, but two of the systems to the U.S. Government. The first one was at the Department of Defense and kept tabs on the military forces deployed in the Middle East. The Central Intelligence Agency operated the second.

Howard even shocked the country when he donated a copy of the A.I. to the Office of the President of the United States completely free of charge. This was out of character for Howard, who had never once donated any of his vast income to charity. When public schools began to fire teachers at an alarming rate and replace them with "dedicated volunteers" the nation had looked to Howard Beck. Howard simply ignored them. When public schools in many states were no longer public and required parents to pay tuition, the public demanded that Howard intervene. Howard could easily donate half of his wealth and still be third on the list of the richest people in the world. Howard coveted his first place spot and couldn't believe people seriously expected him to just give up the crown.

Howard had great respect for the nation's leader, whom many thought had a successful campaign based in large part to the financial backing of Howard Beck. Howard did not understand politics in the slightest, how people could say one thing and do another defied logic. He thought that anyone who lied to their constituents even one time should be booted out of Washington and replaced with an honest person. Much to his amazement, politicians were as dishonest as the day is long and did whatever they pleased. The one thing he did know was that his good friend was the most honest, loyal, and trustworthy man he had ever known. Once Howard Beck got behind his friend, he would not stop until he was in the Oval Office. He wanted to be the first to visit the newly elected president sitting behind the Resolute desk.

Many tech companies had tried to duplicate the A.I. and all had failed. The only person in the entire world who understood how the system worked was Howard Beck. The A.I. he designed required no human hands to conduct maintenance. The system was designed to run at all times, running self-diagnostic checks and even repairing itself if needed.

Howard was a very solitary man; many considered him a recluse on the same level of Howard Hughes. He seldom left his fortress of a residence and had operated his multi-billion dollar empire, Beck Enterprises, from the safe confines of his estate in the Rocky Mountains for many years. Howard had long ago been diagnosed with Asperger's Syndrome, which explained why he wasn't fond of people in general. With some of the greatest men in history thought to have Asperger's, this did not bother Howard in the slightest. Thomas Jefferson, Albert Einstein, Steven Spielberg, and even his friend Bill Gates were all thought to be among the ranks of Asperger's. While most people considered Howard distant, rude, arrogant, and just downright odd, Howard celebrated having Asperger's and considered himself to be in the company of intellectual giants.

Howard hated to be around people and most people were not fond of being in his company. When someone has an IQ of one hundred ninety-five, it is difficult not to feel inadequate around them. Howard had little patience in trying to hold a conversation when he had to explain things over and over, no matter how far over someone's head he was speaking.

The only conversations Howard liked to be a part of were the ones with Hal. Since he created Hal, he not only considered Hal his closest friend, but also thought of him as one of his children. He often enjoyed introducing his assistant to the infrequent guests of his home and business associates to see if they would understand the clever meaning of Hal's name. Few made the association to the HAL-9000 from *2001: A Space Odyssey*. The ones that did get the connection impressed him. Howard had a tough time giving his A.I. a name; he almost decided to name Hal after Data, the android from *Star Trek: The Next Generation*. In the end, he chose Kubrick over Roddenberry and the name fit like a glove. He had even thought of giving Hal the voice of Douglas Rain, the voice actor who played HAL in the movie. Hal was given a male, British accent. Howard knew that to do so was cliché, but Howard was a true sci-fi nerd and loved the proper and dignified voice. Howard constantly teased the president that he needed to give his A.I. a proper name. The president simply referred to his digital assistant as "Computer". He joked with Howard that he couldn't very well name his A.I. after the homicidal computer from *2001*; the American people, and more so the press, would not be in on the joke.

Howard continued to sip his coffee in anger and tried to talk himself out of the plans he needed to make. He did not visit his wife at all last year, and it was time for that to change.

CHAPTER TWO

While Howard continued to sip his coffee in the comfort of his mansion, Richard Dupree awoke in his bunk at the Highland Valley State Prison in western California. Las Vegas was fifty miles due east of the maximum security facility. At the bottom of a valley, the prison sat with mountains on three sides, the fourth side being the exit to the valley fifteen miles to the south. The facility was built in the middle of nowhere, no towns or roads, nothing but heat and dirt. The state of California spared no expense when erecting the prison. Not only did they have to build the facility, they had to build the roads and utilities leading to it. Once the infrastructure was in place, opportunistic land developers were happy to swoop in and build a small town in which the staff and their families could reside. They even built a few hotels and restaurants for the employees of the prison and the people who visited their loved ones incarcerated there. The overcrowded prisons in the state were happy to send their inmates; however, the primary function of the facility was to house prisoners who had a history of escape.

Famous escapees from around the country were ushered to the isolated prison. California was proud to boast that they had the most secure prison in the country and welcomed the publicity. Such publicity could only be rivaled by Alcatraz. Should an inmate escape, they would literally have nowhere to go. The mountains and the cruel heat saw to that. An escaped inmate would not dare venture into the small town of Highland Valley; their captors and their families lived there and were well armed. The inmates that did manage to escape died from the elements. The heat and the sand were unforgiving. Some of the escapees even came back to the front entrance of the prison and surrendered, desperately seeking shelter. The Warden welcomed them back with open arms and escorted them in so they could discourage their fellow inmates from attempting to leave his fine establishment. The attempts started to dwindle and then disappeared for good. No one had attempted to flee into the blistering, hell-like terrain for over eleven years.

Richard's cellmate was grunting out his morning dump on the toilet on the opposite side of the cell. "Jesus, Billy, you can't wait thirty minutes for the door to unlock so I can get out of here?"

"Sorry, man. No choice."

Richard rolled over and crammed his face in the pillow to escape the stench. His cellmate had many flaws that continued to grind on his last nerve and this was one of them. Tank, as his cellmate was called, had very little consideration for anyone, not even his own cellmate. Incapacitating anyone that called him on his lack of consideration was one of Tank's favorite activities. When you stood 6 foot 9 inches tall and weighed in at three hundred twenty-five pounds of muscle, you could shit pretty much anywhere you damned well pleased.

Richard was no slouch himself. He was in his early thirties, a few inches shorter than Tank, and in the best shape of his life. Not much else to do on a twenty-five year sentence but work out and read books. He tolerated Tank because Tank practically worshipped him. When The Incredible Hulk was your number one fan, it was hard to pass up the advantage. Richard was smart enough to realize that. Richard chuckled to himself that Hulk would be a much more appropriate nickname than Tank.

Tank flushed the toilet. "You hitting the track with us?"

"For sure," Richard replied. Richard ran six days a week. Tank asked this question six days a week, and Richard's answer was always the same. "Us" was the gang that Tank was a member of, the Aryan Brotherhood. Tank was about as proud as a white boy could be and was also the biggest racist in the Aryan Brotherhood. For a member of a White Supremacy group, that was saying a lot. Without even opening his mouth, his racism was literally tattooed across his body. The three main attractions of his ink included a swastika across his forehead, a very angry looking Adolf Hitler across his chest, and the words "White Power" emblazoned across his massive back. He had many others tattoos on his body. Richard was disgusted by the racism. The tattoo that shocked Richard the most was the one on Tank's right bicep. On it was a black man hanging dead from a tree;

three hooded figures from the KKK looked up at him with torches. One thing was certain, Tank belonged in prison, and the mere sight of him would ensure he would never attain gainful employment. The thought of Tank sitting down for a job interview was a source of great amusement for Richard.

When Richard first met Tank six years ago, that tattoo constantly bugged him. He thought for sure that any man brave (or stupid) enough to sport such a tattoo would surely be murdered, regardless of gang affiliation. At first, Richard deduced that the Aryan Brotherhood was the most powerful and influential gang in the Highland Valley State Prison. The Aryan Brotherhood made up around one percent of the prison population around the country and was responsible for around twenty percent of the murders. It didn't take Richard long to realize that the Aryan Brotherhood, while it had power and influence, was not even close to the top of the food chain. They simply didn't have the numbers. The smallest Hispanic gang had almost twice the membership of the Aryan Brotherhood. So, the fact that Tank bore such a horribly offensive tattoo bugged Richard even more.

Determined to speak to no one, Richard had decided not get involved with any of the gangs; he simply wished to do his time in peace. The Aryan Brotherhood had other plans. Any solid looking white guy who looked like he could handle himself always got their attention. Richard certainly matched that description perfectly.

Recruitment was the number one priority of the Aryans. They needed muscle, they needed numbers, and they needed soldiers to beef up the ranks. They had their eye on Richard. He was smart enough not to piss them off, but he was also smart enough to know how to ride the fence and not get involved.

That's where Tank came into the picture.

Tank pretty much ignored Richard at first. Tank couldn't care less about recruitment; he left that to his fellow skinheads so he could focus on other things like extortion and turning the guards to do his bidding. He even bragged that he was still able to get laid. Richard cringed to think that most of Tank's sexual encounters were probably far from consensual.

One day Tank went from not even knowing Richard was

alive to suddenly thinking Richard was the greatest person to set foot in the prison. He walked up to Richard on the yard; Richard was certain Tank was going to punch him in the face. Instead of a punch, Tank clapped him on the back.

"What's up, Killer?"

"Uhh, nothing, just getting ready to hit the track."

"My name's Tank, Killer," Tank said with an enthusiastic grin.

"I'm Richard."

"Good to meet you, Killer. Heard a lot about you. Love running, do you? I couldn't stand the thought of not being able to run."

The first thought to cross Richard's mind was that this guy had called him "Killer" three times in under a minute. In their prison, "Killer" meant a chronic masturbator who enjoyed jerking off in front of the prison staff. Richard jerked off of course, but never in front of another person, especially not in front of any of the guards. Judging by the way Tank was treating him, the nickname was clearly not meant to insult him. The second and more troubling thought was that this guy had "heard a lot about him." How is that even possible? Wanting to be left alone, Richard went out of his way not to talk to anyone.

"Want to hit the track with us?" Tank asked. Well, he technically "asked" but the implication was quite clear that Richard had little choice but to comply. They hit the track that morning and over the course of a few weeks it become as routine as breathing . This Andre the Giant clown treated Richard like a celebrity, and Richard was determined to find out the reason.

Trying not to come across as disrespectful, Richard figured the only way was the direct one, so he asked him point blank how he knew so much about him.

"One of the guards asked me when you were going to join the Aryans. He said you belonged with us. Well, I hate it when those fucks know something I don't, and that asshole guard was grinning at me like I should have known about you the second you hit the yard."

Suddenly, it dawned on Richard what was going on. Tank knew about the crimes that landed him in jail for life. It was also clear where his new nickname came from.

Not long after Tank took Richard under his wing, he demanded that the other Aryans treat Richard with the same respect. A few of them felt slighted that Richard did not express an interest in joining their operation. They couldn't really figure the guy out. He hardly said a word and didn't react to much of anything. He always appeared to be deep in thought. Tank kept assuring them that Richard would come around. He was one of them, he had proven himself worthy.

"Oh yeah, what makes you so sure about that Billy?" asked an older skinhead one day when they were playing cards in the common area of their cellblock. Tank had brought Richard along hoping that they would accept him.

"I'll tell you why, Jeff. My man Richard here beat two niggers to death. One of them he beat to death in front of other niggers. They couldn't do nothing but watch! Tell me, Jeff, how many inferiors have you killed? How much trash have you taken out to make this world a better place? Huh?"

Jeff did not respond.

"Well, I'll tell you one thing, Jeff, I killed my share and your share of monkeys, so think about who the hell you're talking to!"

Jeff pretended to study his cards and kept his mouth shut.

"You boys hear about what got me a life sentence?"

I really don't want to know this, thought Richard. *I already hate this animal enough.*

"My hometown was really going down the shitter. Niggers everywhere. They just kept moving into white neighborhoods turning everything to shit. Pretty soon the schools were full of little monkeys and not long after that, most of the teachers were niggers. Then they started with all the Black History bullshit and African Studies. Can you believe that shit? What does a pure, white kid need to know about African Studies?"

Richard didn't know if the question was rhetorical; Tank was looking at him so he nodded his head. Richard wasn't sure how much more of this he could take. He wanted to get up and leave. No one was listening to Tank; they were all studying Richard to gauge his reaction.

"I had enough; no one was doing a damned thing to stop it,

so I knew it was up to me. I loaded up my cargo pockets with shotgun shells, and me and my Mossberg 464 took a trip down to the high school to put a stop to that school turning our kids into nigger lovers."

Richard doubted, more like hoped, that Tank hadn't brought a junior Nazi into the world. The world could do without Tank, let alone his offspring.

"I walked in, shot the nigger principal first. Then I went from class to class and shot as many nigger teachers as I could find. A little nigger kid must've thought his football playin' would help him tackle me down. Nope. Blew his kneecap clean off." Tank laughed hysterically when he remembered the look on the kid's face.

Everyone at the table was studying Richard very carefully. Richard felt like throwing up. He knew he had only a few seconds before they all caught on to his disgust.

Richard faked a smile, clapped Tank on his massive shoulder and replied, "Damned good thing you did that. White folks everywhere should be grateful."

"Fuckin-A right! The rest of you wannabes better recognize what I done and have some respect for my man Richard here!"

Richard was smart enough to realize just how valuable Tank was in terms of a tactical advantage. With the help of Tank, he managed to move into his cellblock, and later became his cellmate. Richard ignored the rumors and gossip that he was Tank's bitch. The other inmates were sure that Richard would eventually emerge one morning from Tank's cell wearing lipstick and nursing a sore asshole. Tank had far too much respect for Richard to even think about attacking him. In fact, he had never laid a hand on him.

With the stench of Tank's morning bowel movement still lingering in their cell, Richard somehow managed to get dressed and put his running shoes on without passing out. A few minutes later, the guard came around and unlocked the cell doors so they could make the trip to the chow hall for breakfast. Richard and Tank always ran before breakfast so they hit the track instead.

After breakfast they returned to their block, showered and decided to play some basketball. Some other skinheads already had managed to secure their own court. Tank and Richard sat in the bleachers and joined in a conversation between two other guys named Spider and Head.

Spider was a skinny little kid in his late twenties. He was always cracking jokes about the guards; he even did passable imitations of a few of them. Richard liked Spider; he was always good for a laugh. He was a complete moron, but his idiotic ideas were fun to listen to and riling him up was one of Richard's favorite forms of entertainment. Richard had no idea how he got the name Spider and quite frankly didn't care. The kid was skinny, ugly as sin, and nothing about him evoked the thought of an arachnid.

Spider had been the typical juvenile delinquent. The high school dropout had a bad habit of car-jacking unsuspecting motorists. When he starting viciously beating elderly black people for their cars, his luck changed. He spent the first six years of his incarceration working his way up the ranks of the Aryans. To the casual observer, Spider might come across as a hyper man-child trying to impress everyone, but underneath, his hatred and anger were eating him alive.

Head's nickname, however, was not difficult to figure out. It had nothing to do with intelligence, but rather his enormous skull. Richard had never seen a bigger head on a man in his entire life. It was enormous. You would think that shaving the hair off that boulder would make his head look smaller, but it didn't. Head was maybe a few years younger than Richard and the same height. The large-headed man maybe had fifty pounds on Richard but was not in the best of shape.

Head was proud of his nickname. He thought it was because of his signature fighting move, the head-butt. Head's favorite move was known to knock a man smooth on his ass and end a fight. Richard often wondered if Head would ever figure out that his nickname was not in honor of fighting prowess, but rather served to mock his freak show of a noggin.

"I'm telling you man, no fuckin way man, not possible!" Head protested.

"What are you idiots talking about?" asked Tank.

"Spider is on one of his idiotic conspiracy theories again," Head replied.

"Fuck you, Head. You know it's true," Spider said with a sheepish grin.

Head was right; Spider was constantly rambling on and on about every conspiracy theory you could think of. If you were stupid enough to get him going on one of his rants, he wouldn't stop until you agreed with him (or at least told him what he wanted to hear) about the moon landing being a hoax, aliens at Roswell, and 9/11 being an inside job. Spider proudly proclaimed that he was there and saw the Twin Towers fall, even though he was either an infant or a toddler at the time.

"So, what is it this time?" Richard asked.

Head cut Spider off. "Our young friend here is convinced that Hurricane Luther was a conspiracy."

"What?" Richard laughed. "How can a natural disaster be a conspiracy?"

Head continued to speak for Spider. "What was it, Spider? Aliens are out to take ov..."

"Fuck you, Head!" Spider laughed. "You know that ain't what I said!"

"Right, right, right. Spider here thinks that the U.S. government engineered a hurricane to wipe out Florida."

"What the fuck the government have against Florida?" Tank asked.

Spider interpreted the question as interest and saw his chance. "OK, think about it, just hear me out. Luther was just a test hurricane. You just wait, there will be more."

"Jackass, you didn't answer my question. What do the Feds have against Florida?" Tank shot back.

"It's all about fear and control, man! Don't you see it? Just look at what's going on today. It's been over a month and they haven't done shit for those people!"

Against his better judgment, Richard violated the cardinal rule when dealing with Spider - he engaged him in debate. "What makes you say that? I haven't seen shit on the news about Luther."

"Exactly my point, Killer!" Spider screamed. "What better way to end the Second Great Depression than by wiping out a bunch of people. It cuts down on unemployment by killing off people and giving other people their jobs. Fewer people that the government has to take care of; it makes perfect sense."

Richard had underestimated the stupidity of this kid. All he could do was stare at him. The statement uttered by this fool was probably the stupidest thing he had ever heard him say. Richard decided to remain silent like he should have in the first place.

Spider began to reply to Richard when Tank interrupted.

"You're a fucking retard," said Tank. "No way could the government control a hurricane. Not possible."

"Okay. Well then, answer me this, both of you. Why haven't we seen any news reports from Florida? Not one god damn report. I know they ain't got no power, but the news people drive around in trucks and beam that shit to a satellite. Why haven't we seen anything?" Spider directed his question to both Tank and Richard

"Big fucking deal." said Tank. "You know what I think? I think they got..."

Sirens blaring across the yard cut Tank off mid-sentence. Trouble.

Sirens meant a disturbance. Somewhere on the yard a fight was in progress. Without missing a beat, the four skinheads immediately forgot about the conspiracy talk and sprang into action. Tank ran to the fence and starting looking around. Richard did the same on the opposite end of the fence. Spider and Head dug into the heels of their shoes and came up with homemade weapons in a few seconds flat. The two men stepped up next to Tank and Richard, tapped them on the shoulder and resumed their posts as lookouts. Tank and Richard went through the same routine and produced knives as if out of thin air. Richard had rehearsed this move with the three skinheads and they had performed it perfectly.

"What do we got?" Richard asked the group.

"No idea," Head replied.

Richard's eyes scanned across the yard, making assessments of every group, every person, and saw nothing hostile going on. All he saw was a yard full of very confused inmates. Richard was pissed that the Aryans were split up into three groups scattered across the yard and behind different fences.

Richard cursed the skinheads for not having more tactical awareness. They would have little chance in a major disturbance if broken up into small groups.

The siren cut off, only to be replaced by the loud speaker.

"ALL INMATES ON THE YARD RETURN TO YOUR ASSIGNED CELLS!"

"What the fuck is going on?" Tank asked.

"Nothing good, Billy," said Richard. "It's only nine o'clock in the morning; they must know that we aren't going back into our cells without a fight."

"Doesn't make any fucking sense. They want us locked up all they gotta do is wait for the next count and not let us back out," Tank replied through gritted teeth.

"What the fuck do we do, Killer?" Spider asked. Richard would know what to do; he always had a plan.

"We wait," said Richard. "Wait this out and see what happens. They are probably suiting up the riot squad right now. Keep scanning the yard and call out exactly what you see and in what direction, remember that the chow hall is due north."

Over nine hundred inmates stood on the yard figuring out what to do. In the history of Highland Valley State Prison, any time they tried to lock the facility down in the middle of the day, it meant they were getting locked in their cells and not coming back out for a very long time. The old-timers who had walked the yard for years could attest to the seriousness of a major lockdown. Tank was right, made much more sense to wait for them to return to their cells for count. No fighting, no violence. Just a bunch of pissed off inmates who felt like they had been tricked.

"ALL INMATES ON THE YARD RETURN TO YOUR ASSIGNED CELLS!"

Richard grumbled under his breath. He had never been on a major lockdown with Tank. The longest lockdown Richard had known up to that point was three days. Weeks or months trapped in a cell with Tank would drive him insane.

"What the fuck is that?" Spider screamed.

"What is it, Spider? What direction? I taught you better than that, start talking!" Richard tensed up and scanned the yard to see if he could see what Spider was screaming about. He didn't see anything. He turned to look at Spider who was gazing skyward.

Slowly, like a ripple through a pond, every inmate on the yard stopped and looked up at the sky.

"How the fuck is it snowing in August?" Tank asked.

Richard stared intently at the sky. Flakes started to slowly drift and flutter out of the sky and land on the rooftops of the cell blocks. Then they started landing on the inmates and then on the ground. Dark, ominous clouds could be seen beyond the mountains to the west of the prison.

"FUCK!" Spider began to spit over and over. "This snow tastes like shit! Son of a bitch!"

"ALL INMATES ON THE YARD RETURN TO YOUR ASSIGNED CELLS!"

"Not happening, mother fuckers!!" Tank screamed at the top of his lungs, his proclamation echoing across the yard. The inmates within twenty feet of Tank almost wet their pants he scared them so badly.

KAAA-BOOOM!!

A flashbang had been deployed. It startled the inmates back to reality. The flashbang could only mean one thing.

The riot squad was here.

"That was quick," said Richard.

"They're locking us down because it's snowing?"

Richard took one more look to the sky and said, "It's not snow. It's ash."

CHAPTER THREE

Maxwell Harris awoke in excruciating pain. He rolled over to discover it was just past 3am, which meant he had only been asleep for a few hours - if you would call it sleep. Max certainly did not. Sleep was hard to come by for the forty-three year old, even with the aid of prescription sleeping pills, which Max took every night. He rolled over and grabbed his pain meds, popped the top and kicked back two pills. The prescription was for one every six hours, but he was up to two every three. Didn't bother him in the slightest that he was taking way more than he should, after all, pain is pain, right?

Realizing that he had no chance of falling back to sleep until the pain meds kicked in, he decided to watch some TV. He turned over, waking up the cat, and spoke out loud.

"TV. Begin at channel 115 and change channels on my command." The TV sprang to life and followed his instructions.

"...believe that Hurricane Maxine will make landfall somewhere near the Texas Louisiana state line..."

Max pointed up with his right index finger.

"...rnor Blackmon and Governor Prince are attempting to re-deploy the National Guard from their current assignments enforcing curfews in some of their respective states' major cit..."

...index finger...

"..timate that forty-sven were killed in the latest wave of terror attac..."

...index finger...

"...many Republicans are harshly criticizing the White House for what they believe to be a lack of support for the citizens of the Florida coastli..."

"TV, return to channel 115 and increase volume five

levels."

Since he was the chief of police of a cozy little suburb southeast of Houston called Santa Fe, Max instructed his TV to return to the first channel to see if he could find an updated path for Hurricane Maxine. He watched anxiously to see if the large beast of a hurricane would have any effect on him personally.

"Thank God!" Max exclaimed out loud to no one in particular. The hurricane was definitely moving east. If Maxine was a true Texas lady and minded her manners, she would make landfall at least fifty miles on the other side of the Sabine River and give some unlucky Louisianans a boot in the ass. Hurricane Maxine would be someone else's guest, which brought Max some relief. Maxwell was not amused that the hurricane was given the female equivalent of his name. He knew that if she had courted the state of Texas, he would have been the butt of many jokes at the office.

Max had endured all he could stand of hurricanes. He grew up in South Florida and suffered the wrath of Hurricane Andrew, which demolished his residence and everything he ever knew. Absolutely nothing could be salvaged of his childhood home. It had been completely removed from the slab like it had never even been built. When Max's family had returned, Max had hoped that he would still be able to run upstairs to his room and play with his toys. Max spent the rest of his childhood hating his home state of Florida because it had so many hurricanes. (Not the most rational of thinking, but he was only eight at the time.) Once he reached adulthood, he left Florida and the killer storms behind only to return on rare occasions to visit his parents. He was twenty-two he moved to southeast Texas to begin work as a Texas State Trooper. Two years later, he married Darlene, and two years after that a second hurricane kicked him square in the ass.

Hurricane Ike did not destroy his home; at least he could be thankful for that much. What it did manage to do was lead him down the road to burn out. Max spent three weeks working sixteen hour shifts helping the victims of the Category 3 hurricane. Some days were long and boring, guarding impassable roads, directing traffic on nearly gridlocked highways. Some days, however, were far from boring. Max was absolutely amazed that normal, everyday citizens would ignore an evacuation order and stay behind, clearly in harm's way. When those stubborn people managed to get trapped in their homes, they called 9-1-1. When they damned near died on their rooftops because they refused to evacuate, they called 9-1-1. One idiot even dialed 9-1-1 complaining that his favorite pizza joint was not answering the phone. The next year the state of Texas passed a law that fined citizens who ignored a mandatory evacuation order and required some sort of emergency service.

The worst part of Hurricane Ike was the first twenty-four hours after the storm passed. The exits along Interstate 10 in the Beaumont area where closed; many of the roads in the area were covered in downed trees and power lines. The only people allowed to exit off the interstate were law enforcement and first responders. Everyone else was turned away. This made for some furious citizens.

"You have no right to keep me from my home!"

"I'm a grown man! I don't need you clowns to treat me like a baby!"

Those furious Texans thought the National Guard was a joke and ignored them. They simply jumped the curb and drove around them. The Guardsman would call Max into action, giving him the make and model, and Max would chase the people down. Most were much more intimidated by a State Trooper and cooperated. The ones that really bothered Max were the genuine, kind souls who begged and pleaded with him.

"I just need to get my dogs; they were in the backyard and I won't be able to live with myself if anything happened to them."

"I haven't heard from my Dad. He refused to evacuate and I'm worried he hasn't been taking his medicine."

Max heard these stories all day and couldn't do a thing to help these people. Max was one of two State Troopers assigned to protect a very long stretch of Interstate 10. The only thing they could tell people was to return to the interstate and call 9-1-1 if they had credible reason to believe an emergency was taking place. They just looked at him in shock and disgust. Max had never felt so ashamed in his life.

Max recalled how agitated he and others had been at the

high price of gasoline back then. With gas being close to fifteen dollars a gallon in 2027, evacuating in the face of this latest storm threat would cost a small fortune, money that few people had during the Second Great Depression. Max wondered how residents of the Florida coastline could afford to evacuate last month during Hurricane Luther. He figured that the state of Florida must have evacuated citizens by the busload to get them safely out. Luther made Andrew look like a stiff breeze. Luther went down on record as the deadliest hurricane in the history of the world; that bastard went straight up the coastline like a wrecking ball. Luther would come ashore like Godzilla and destroy everything he saw, go back out to the ocean like he was taking a cigarette break, then travel back up the coast and start all over again. A month had passed, and most of Florida still didn't have power. Max vaguely remembered something about a quarantine zone but couldn't recall the details. For some reason, there seemed to be very little media coverage of the aftermath, so details were sketchy. However, even if they had electricity, there wasn't much of anything still standing that could even do anything with the juice. Max was able to contact his father in South Miami. Luther wasn't very strong when he came to visit him, only a Category 2. "I don't evacuate for anything less than a 5!," Max's dad proudly told him when he called, most Floridians paying little attention to a hurricane until it made Category 4. Hurricane Luther left Miami and graduated up the ranks very quickly to a Category 5. Luther left all the experts puzzled. They had predicted that he would come ashore, do his damage and go back out to sea to slowly fade away. Luther did no such thing. He came back ashore a total of five times, either maintaining strength or getting a little stronger each time. After his third trip ashore, the public cursed the experts for fools and treated Luther like he was a mythical monster that had developed intelligence.

Max's wife and children had evacuated to Oklahoma well ahead of Hurricane Ike to stay with relatives, not really because the hurricane would hit them, but rather because the electricity would probably be out and Max would be working double shifts.

Once the evacuation order had been lifted, Max wasn't surprised that his wife decided to stay in Oklahoma for a few more weeks. The water company had shut off the water in Max's subdivision since the bacteria counts were at toxic levels, they wouldn't be able to wash their clothes, take showers, or flush the toilets. The water company advised residents to shut off all faucets and bathtubs so when the water did come back on, it wouldn't cause damage. Max completely forgot to turn off the water when he left the house the morning when water service was restored. He had spent the previous evening cleaning out the freezer into the kitchen sink. The upstairs shower was also clogged and Max had left it on when he attempted to take a shower. When the water came back on, the kitchen sink and the upstairs shower quickly filled and spilled out onto the floor for the better part of forty eight hours before Max came back home.

Max's wife returned to find her home destroyed, which confused her since the rest of the neighborhood was just as it was when she left. Max had tried to dream up some elaborate lie, but just didn't give a damn and told her the truth. To make things worse, the insurance agent would later laugh out loud in front of Mr. and Mrs. Harris when she understood that the hurricane had nothing to do with the damage, but rather Max's laughable mistake. Max's marriage was already on the rocks when his wife returned home. It took over a year to repair their home and Darlene made sure that Max knew how disgusted she was with him. She was pregnant at the time and only stayed with Max because she didn't want to raise a baby on her own. Max had never been so humiliated in his life. His home survived a hurricane and was instead destroyed by his own stupidity.

Max really hated hurricanes.

Max was thankful that the Category 5 hurricane sitting in the Gulf of Mexico would do little to him other than bring some heavy rain. The first one took his childhood; the second almost ruined his marriage. He could not imagine what a third would do to him. He just wouldn't be able to deal with it, not with the constant pain he was in.

He had managed to secure a nice comfortable job at a small local police department and quickly worked his way up to chief, which wasn't hard to do with only twelve officers in the department, the previous chief's pending retirement, and Max's overqualified sixteen years of law enforcement. He was an hour away from the busy city of Houston, but the little town he managed to settle in might as well have been Mayberry. He was happy to play the role of Andy Griffith and not have to worry about much of anything outside of minor traffic accidents and a domestic squabble from time to time. The hardest work the department had to do was keep the town clear of the waves of homeless people who tried to set up hobo camps around town on their way out of Houston. As long as the 6,447 citizens of his town didn't have to actually look at the dirty bums, they were content to leave Max and his department alone. Chief Harris was actually kind of surprised the city police department even existed; the county sheriff's office did most of the real work. When their quiet little town did actually fall victim to a major crime, the county boys would always swoop in, wanting to take over. They relished the excitement and Max was more than happy to oblige; the last thing he wanted to do was real work. After all, the Internet didn't surf itself; someone had to look at strange porn, might as well be Max. The chief of police wanted as little responsibility as possible. He ran from trouble and had managed to hide from it quite well in his dream job.

An hour later the pain was only a little better, and Max realized he wasn't getting back to sleep. He played *Modern Warfare 7* for about an hour then decided to shower and eat breakfast. He got to the station an hour early and relieved Elizabeth, the graveyard shift desk sergeant.

"Morning, Chief."

"Morning, Elizabeth, anything happen last night?"

"Not a thing. The phone didn't ring, not one time."

"That's what I like to hear."

Elizabeth handed her keys over to the chief. "You see the news on Maxine? Looks like your sister doesn't like you very much. What did you do to hurt her feelings and make her stay away?"

Max just stared at her, frowned, and rolled his eyes. He turned and limped off towards his office.

"Oh, come on! Don't be like that! It was a little funny! Get it? Max, Maxine? Your sister?"

"Go home, Elizabeth," Max said over his shoulder.

Elizabeth Reed had known the chief for years and still had

no idea why he was in so much. When things got really bad for him, he even used a cane. People knew to keep their distance when the chief pulled out that cane; it was when he was in the worst of all possible moods. She even knew that he constantly popped pills, a secret the chief had managed to keep from everyone except her. He actually did his "I'm eating Skittles so no one will notice me taking pills" trick when he collapsed into his office chair in the next room. Elizabeth knew from the day she met Maxwell that he was an addict; she had seen it before with her brother-in-law after his back surgery. While Max functioned well in his job; the pills never affected his performance. In fact, the chief was the smartest man Elizabeth had ever met. He was brilliant, resourceful, and had an encyclopedic knowledge of just about everything. It was a shame, though, that he was also lazy and had no ambition to do anything more with his life. Max was only forty-three, but the way the grumpy bastard acted he might as well have been thirty years older.

Elizabeth obeyed her boss, heading home for some much needed rest. After changing into her pajamas, Elizabeth plopped down on the couch with her frisky little cat, Callie, and grabbed the remote to check out what was going on in the world. She flipped the channels until she found the latest update on Hurricane Maxine. What she saw made her push the cat off her lap and get dressed.

"Sorry kitty." Elizabeth pushed the brown and orange cat off her lap. "Momma's gotta go back to work. Something tells me the boss ain't gonna be happy."

CHAPTER FOUR

President Malcolm Powers sat at his desk in the Oval Office deep in thought. He was facing the most important decision of his second term. He knew that whatever he decided to do, many would consider it the wrong choice. His actions in the next twenty-four hours would have lasting repercussions that would be studied in the history books for centuries to come. One choice would make him hated by his own country, the other hated by the entire world. There was no middle ground. To help him arrive at his decision, he had done a lot of research on the end of the Second World War. More specifically, he studied President Truman's decision to drop atomic bombs on Hiroshima and Nagasaki. Malcolm truly believed that no president in the nation's history had ever had to make a tougher choice. If Truman had not dropped the atomic bombs, the only remaining option was an invasion into the heart of the Empire of Japan along the shores of the island of Honshu. Such an invasion would result in catastrophic losses. Having the means to prevent it, Truman could not allow countless American lives to be lost. On the other hand, saving Americans lives came at the cost of taking Japanese lives and ushering the world into the Atomic Age. Malcolm wondered if Truman had any idea that his decision would result in the terrifying stalemate that would be the Cold War.

The president felt he could give Truman a run for his money when it came to making a tough call.

"Sir, the attendants of your next meeting are waiting for you in the Clinton Room," a smooth talking female voice spoke from the ceiling.

"Thank you," the president replied. The A.I. program installed by his longtime friend, Howard Beck, was probably the first controversy of his short political career. The press had a field day with it. The American public blew the entire thing out of proportion. Many feared the A.I. would somehow overthrow the president and attack mankind like Skynet did in The Terminator. Others demanded it be removed for fear of it being hacked by Iran or North Korea. The experts knew just how impossible it was to hack into one of Beck Enterprises' world-famous A.I.s. Tech giants all over the world tried every day to understand how the system worked, and none were even close. The technology was decades ahead of its time. The A.I.s gave the appearance of sentience; attempting to hack into one was like putting a knife to a person's throat. It was hardly something that could be done without the A.I. realizing what was going on. The industry had predicted that true interactive A.I. was at least a decade away. Howard Beck proved them wrong.

The final criticism about the White House A.I. was the only one that had any merit. The president's critics in the Democratic Party despised Howard Beck for buying the presidency. They felt that Beck was somehow controlling the A.I. from his fortress in the Rocky Mountains and was Malcolm Powers' puppet master. If the American public wanted Howard Beck running the country, he should have run for president himself. Malcolm often joked with his friend that he should have just put him on the ticket as his vice president just to shut them up. Finding humor to be a waste of time, Howard got the joke but didn't laugh. Malcolm knew his friend wouldn't last a day in politics; the billionaire recluse hated being around people.

"Computer, inform the group that I will be with them shortly and ensure that they are comfortable."

"Yes, sir."

The president stood, put on his suit jacket, and walked over to the mirror. A very long day was in front of him. Once he was pleased with his appearance, he fixed his tie one more time for good measure and began pacing around the room. He was ready to begin the meeting but decided instead to make them wait. He knew it was a petty power play, but he wanted to remind the men and women in the next room that he was their boss. Some of the most powerful people in the United States government, along with their egos, were in the next room. He enjoyed putting them in their place.

Many of these same people were hardcore Republicans and couldn't understand why their president had named his conference room after a Democrat. The former president had passed away the previous year from a stroke at the age of eighty. Malcolm Powers attended President Clinton's funeral, along with the other former presidents because protocol demanded it.

Protocol didn't mean a damned thing to Malcolm. Bill was one of his closest friends. If the two men had made a career out of selling used cars, he still would have attended his funeral regardless of what protocol required of him. Malcolm not only attended the funeral, he was a pallbearer. He also stood at the gravesite in Hope, Arkansas, with his arms around his close friend's widow and adult daughter, the current Governor of Arkansas.

When Malcolm took office, many had expected him to give his former mentor a role in his administration. President Powers appointed former President Clinton as Chief Justice of the Supreme Court. The appointment didn't surprise anyone; President Clinton had a Juris Doctor from Yale and had been a Professor of Law at the University of Arkansas. The only other president to serve on the nation's highest court was William Howard Taft over a century prior. And like President Taft, President Clinton became the second president to swear the Oath of Office to an incoming president. The Second Inauguration of President Powers was an event that both men cherished.

The Clinton Room was adjacent to the Oval Office in an area that once belonged to the president's secretaries. After Beck Enterprises installed the A.I. in the White House, President Powers saw little need for secretaries. Fearing even more backlash from the media about the A.I., the secretaries did not lose their jobs. The four women were simply reassigned to other areas of the White House. There really weren't any job openings in his administration; the women were simply given menial tasks and told to look busy. A few years later, all four of them left the White House with a glowing recommendation from their employer.

Satisfied that enough time had elapsed, the president started towards the door; the A.I. calculated his direction of travel and opened the door for him. Every person in the room was on their feet and silent, the only exception being the occupant of a wheel chair, who straightened up in his chair as much as he could to show respect to the leader of the free world.

President Malcolm Powers sat in the large chair at the front of the room, a gift from his mentor, who sat in the same chair for most of the 1990s. Once the president was seated, the others took their seats and gave the president their full attention.

"Good morning. Thank you for coming on such short notice." The president spoke in a deep solemn voice, setting the tone.

The people in the room spoke over one another. "Good morning, Mr. President."

Wondering why they had been summoned, the men and women in the room looked at each other. Seated directly to the right of the president was the Chief of Staff, Stacy Reid. Next to her sat Secretary of Defense Charles Decker and FBI Director Warren Gill. Next to him sat Secretary of Homeland Security Winston Laferriere. The man sitting to the far right in the wheelchair was Director of the Central Intelligence Agency, Roberto Jimenez.

Seated to the left of the president was the Chairman of the Joint Chiefs of Staff, Carl Moody. Occupying the next two seats were Fleet Admiral William Mack and Major General James Weygandt. The woman sitting on the far left making no effort to mask her hostility was Florida Governor, Lori Prince.

"I've asked you all here today because I seek your counsel. We are at a crucial turning point in the war with Iran. Before the day is out, I must make a decision that will either bring the war to its end or extend the conflict for at least another year."

Everyone in the room settled into their seats. They finally knew what this meeting was about. The president had called them to Washington without a hint of the true purpose of the meeting. Everyone in the room had expected the meeting would be about Hurricane Luther once they discovered Governor Prince was in attendance. Governor Prince looked even angrier when she realized he was talking about the war and not the destruction of her home state.

The president paused and seemed to lose focus. President Powers was not looking well. Seven years in the White House had taken its toll on the man. Unlike most of his predecessors, Powers had little political experience when he took the Oath of Office. Like President Eisenhower before him, Admiral Malcolm Powers left military service and was urged by many from both political parties to run for president. Admiral Powers, much like General Eisenhower, had no political affiliation. The Democrats were certain that his famous friendship with President Clinton meant he was a Democrat. The Republicans were certain the Admiral belonged in their party based on his political beliefs. Powers agreed to run on the Republican ticket and in 2020, he won the presidency in a landslide. Four years later he was a lock for re-election. The Democrats knew they had no chance of winning and persuaded a reluctant congressman to run in the losing race.

The president looked to his former commanding officer, Fleet Admiral Mack, and nodded his head, indicating that he was ready for him to begin his briefing. The Chairman of the Joint Chiefs of Staff had gotten used to being overlooked. He should be the one giving the briefing, not Mack. He had accepted the friendship between the president and his former commanding officer. At first he took it as a personal insult, but after developing a close relationship with his Commander in Chief, he knew that it wasn't meant as a slight.

Fleet Admiral Mack began. "Thank you, Mr. President. We now have the Fifth Fleet underway to the Persian Gulf and the *USS Enterprise* and *USS George Washington* are underway to the Port of Gibraltar. I can report that in fourteen days we will be ready to begin the invasion of Iran."

Director Jimenez grunted and shifted in his wheelchair. "Why the delay, Admiral?" he asked in a raspy voice.

"The Roosevelt Strike Group suffered major losses when they tried to enter the Mediterranean. The *USS James Russell* will need at least two months before she can get underway again."

The newly commissioned vessel had been named for the most decorated soldier of the Iraq and Afghanistan wars. The Medal of Honor winner single-handedly took out an entire insurgent camp before they could ambush a convoy of military police transporting prisoners. He suffered a fatal wound during the attack but managed to stay in the fight. His widow and children attended the launching of the massive vessel that bore his name.

Iran had seized control of much of the Middle East in the last five years. When the rest of the world evicted Iran from the Society for Worldwide Interbank Financial Telecommunication, or SWIFT, in 2012, it had a devastating effect on the country.

Without the use of SWIFT, Iran could no longer move money across its borders electronically. All of the oil in Iran just sat there. If Iran wanted to sell its oil to the rest of the world, the only way it could be done was by moving billions of dollars of physical cash across the border. No other country was foolish enough to make such a transaction in this fashion, so the obvious choice for Iran would be to give in to the demands of the rest of the world and end its nuclear program.

Iran shocked the world when it did not give in to the threat, but instead doubled the efforts of its nuclear program. The Iranians successfully smuggled their oil to sympathetic countries and at great cost, were able to sell enough oil to keep the country running.

In late 2015, Iran again shocked the world when it successfully detonated a nuclear device in the Indian Ocean. Terrified of Iran, the West knew that war was inevitable. Over the next two years, with the protection of a nuclear stalemate, Iran successfully infiltrated the provisional government in Iraq and quickly overthrew it. Invading their neighbor was not necessary when their government was so weak. They simply moved into Baghdad, set up shop, and absorbed the vast resources that Iraq had to offer.

Iran had even managed to conquer its most hated enemy the nation of Israel. Not satisfied with Israel's status of nuclear ambiguity, Iran was determined to find out the nuclear secrets of its potential threat. Iran sent spies deep into Israel to find out what cards they were holding. When the Soviet Union fell, many Soviet Jews in the Soviet nuclear program immigrated back to Israel. Speculation ran rampant that Israel had been building an arsenal during the 1990s. No one could say with certainty if Israel had five nukes or five hundred. Israel enjoyed the mysterious threat they had constructed; Iran was determined to expose the mystery. Israel did not have five hundred nukes. They didn't have five. They had one working warhead and the scattered parts to maybe build another. The spies stole the warhead and proudly returned it to Iran. Not satisfied until every stone was unturned, the spies were sent back to confirm their findings. A year later they returned and could say with certainty that Israel was not a threat. Israel had disassembled its warheads and sold them on the black market to aid its failing economy.

When Iranian forces crossed the border into Iraq, the world again looked to the United States for salvation. With his country in the Second Great Depression, President Powers decided to sit this one out and let somebody else step up for a change. The European Union was not happy with its most valued ally. Many countries in Europe severed diplomatic relations with the United States and publicly branded the president a coward. With the insults pouring in and public outcry from his own citizens, President Powers still managed to send billions of dollars to aid the war effort. For the first time in its history, the European Union consolidated all of its armies into one fighting force to combat the growing threat of Iran.

Iran was not impressed or intimidated by the European Army. Iran held the nation of Israel as a nuclear hostage and kept the European Army at bay. They also had managed to carry out something before thought impossible. They unified the Middle East and amassed a formidable army of Muslim warriors. The only thing the European Army could manage to accomplish facing the superior force was to protect its own borders from invasion. Having already gained control of Iraq, Iran surveyed the rest of the Middle East with very lofty goals of expansion. For the first time in the history of the world, Iran could boast that they managed to topple the nation of Afghanistan. The Soviet Union and the United States had both tried and failed. Celebrating themselves as liberators, the Americans claimed that they never had intentions of conquering the Afghan people. Considering it the excuse of losers, Iran laughed at the claim. After Afghanistan came Pakistan and then the western borders of India. Considering India too costly a challenge, Iran settled in and joined ranks with China and the United States as a superpower. The Great Empire of Iran signed a treaty with the European Union, promising to leave the Union's border alone in exchange for maintaining control of all conquered territories. The Europeans had little choice but to agree.

Controlling a very large share of the world's oil, Iran refused to export any of it to the United States. This move only sank the United States deeper into the Second Great Depression with gas prices soaring above ten dollars a gallon. The American people complained constantly about the outrageous cost, but were willing to pay it if it meant they didn't have to send their sons and daughters to be killed in the Middle East

The Great Empire of Iran could not sit still for very long and began to look to Saudi Arabia and Egypt as ripe for the picking. This was reminiscent of the Nazis who had the right idea when it came to conquest; they just lacked the resources that the Empire had at its disposal. When Iran began to move its vast Army of devout Muslim warriors along the border of Saudi Arabia in clear violation of its own treaty, President Powers had little choice but to join Europe to stop the invading army. The European and American militaries joined to become the Allied Forces.

For two years the Iranians fought for control of Saudi Arabia but the Allied Forces kept them at bay. The Iranian Army won control of the crucial Port of Gibraltar, gateway to the Mediterranean Sea, early in the war and defended it at all costs. The Allied Forces knew that to win the war, they would have to get their ships into the Mediterranean and move with all due haste to the shores of Tel Aviv, ready to strike at the heart of the Empire. The Fifth Fleet was positioned in the middle of the Indian Ocean waiting for this to happen, ready to move into the Persian Gulf to flank the Empire from both sides, no doubt ending the war.

The Roosevelt Strike Group and one of her vessels, the *USS James Russell*, launched an all-out attack on the Port of Gibraltar. After two days of intense naval battle, the likes of which had not seen since the Second World War, the *James Russell* managed to gain control of the port and awaited orders. After deliberating with the Joint Chiefs and Director Jimenez, the president was confident that Iran was only bluffing about Israel and would not destroy the only leverage that kept the rest of the world from directly attacking them.

He gave the orders and the *USS James Russell* and what was left of the Strike Group entered the Mediterranean. Twelve hours into its journey, Iran called the bluff and detonated a low-yield nuclear bomb just outside Tel-Aviv. The bomb didn't level the city, but served as a warning shot to show the Allied Forces that they were not bluffing. The Empire gloated that the device had been detonated on its previous owner.

The president ordered the *James Russell* and its Strike Group to a full stop until they could figure out their next move. They hoped that stopping its advance would satisfy the Empire and prevent any more destruction. The Iranian fleet, already underway in an attempt to retake Gibraltar, met up with the Allied fleet to prevent them traveling any closer to the Empire. The standoff lasted for thirty-six hours until the Iranians began to fire shots over the fleet in an attempt to either intimidate them into turning around or taunt them into engaging in battle. The *USS James Russell* returned fire, sinking one of the Iranian vessels. The vessel sank the enemy ship not realizing that an Iranian submarine had the drop on them. A torpedo was fired on the *James Russell*, crippling her. The Strike Group, not realizing that the Iranians had submarines in the area, had little choice but to retreat and escorted the crippled vessel back to the Port of Gibraltar. With a foothold to the Mediterranean Sea, the Allied Forces finally had the upper hand and were within striking distance to end the war.

Fleet Admiral Mack continued to address the men and women seated in the Clinton Room. "The *Enterprise* and the *George Washington* are three days from the Port of Gibraltar awaiting your orders, Mr. President."

"Thank you, Admiral." President Powers had ordered the two aircraft carriers and their support vessels to remain on station. They had been situated in the middle of the Atlantic for eighteen hours. President Powers had given the order so he could convene this meeting.

The president looked to his right and addressed the Director of the Central Intelligence Agency. "Roberto, what can we expect once we reenter the Mediterranean?"

The grumpy old man in the wheelchair scowled at hearing his first name. Director Jimenez did not like the president; he never had and never would. He did not appreciate the president's attempts at being on a first name basis with him. His efforts were neither endearing nor welcome. He tolerated the president because he liked the man's politics. He just didn't like him on a personal level. He found the man arrogant and conceited, traits he found to be true in most military officers.

The seventy-two year old had lost the use of his legs in his battle with multiple sclerosis. He had adjusted to life in a wheelchair with some reluctance. He spent many years walking with a cane; however, after suffering several falls and constant badgering from his wife, he finally relented. He cleared his throat, took a deep breath and began.

"Thank you, Mr. President. Based on our latest intelligence, we know for certain that the Empire has three remaining nuclear devices holding the same yield as the one detonated outside of Tel-Aviv."

"How close are we to recovering the three devices?" the president asked.

Roberto paused, thought for a second, looked up at the ceiling and asked, "Mr. President, may I?"

"Yes, of course. Computer, establish a secure connection with the CIA and grant Director Jimenez full access."

At the request of the president, Howard Beck had installed the A.I. in his office and granted clearance to only the president. The A.I. would respond to the White House staff and visitors but only on a limited basis, essentially serving two functions. First, it acted as a very polite host, opening doors and answering and placing phone calls. Second, the A.I. would perform internet searches, essentially making the multi-billion dollar computer the world's most expensive desktop. Beck also established a secure, one way link with the A.I.s at the Department of Defense and the CIA. President Powers didn't trust Director Jimenez as far as he could throw him, wheelchair included. He knew the old spook couldn't resist the temptation to tap into the White House A.I. so he could spy on the Oval Office. He was sure the crusty old bastard had tried to do so many, many times.

Roberto was certain that Howard Beck could control the A.I. he personally installed in the White House. He guessed that the crazy billionaire had been listening to the very conversation in which he was partaking. Not long after the installation of the smooth talking female computer, he insisted that the president have his best people analyze the system to make sure it could not be controlled from the Rocky Mountains. The president saw this as an opportunity to show the American people that his trusted friend had not betrayed their friendship and lied to him. He immediately dared the top spy to do his worst. After six weeks, the Director announced in a press conference that he could say with total certainty that the White House A.I. could only be controlled by whomever was sitting in the Oval Office. Jimenez still didn't trust Howard Beck as far he could throw the odd man, fancy computers and all.

The smooth, female voice of the White House A.I. responded to the president. "Yes, Mr. President. Please standby." A few seconds elapsed. "Link established. Good morning, Director Jimenez."

Director Jimenez did not return the greeting. He hated computers, especially this one. The fact that the president gave his A.I. a female voice was a source of many jokes in the entertainment world. His favorite was a skit on *Saturday Night Live* that depicted the president falling in love with his computer. In the skit they even gave the computer the name "Monica," referring to the scandal involving President Clinton and his former intern. President Clinton was on the Supreme Court at the time and had made a controversial ruling. Something about the scandal, Roberto couldn't recall the details, had some connection to the name Monica and the old scandal was dusted off to make the circuit on the late night TV talk shows.

Years ago when the computers at his home and office had been upgraded to interact with him vocally, Roberto finally felt like the technology was simple enough for him to use.

"Computer, display the latest intelligence on the Great Empire of Iran."

The wall on the other side of the room sprang to life; everyone shifted in their seats to see the large, detailed map of the Iranian Theater, upon which every military asset, both friendly and enemy alike, could be seen.

The Director continued. "As you can see, the Iranians have completed construction on their fifth nuclear bunker deep in the mountains of Afghanistan."

After seizing control of Iraq, the Iranians immediately used their newfound wealth to construct an impenetrable bunker four hundred feet underground. The Americans had finally destroyed the ones on their home soil in 2013, and the Iranians were desperate to begin construction on a new one. Nothing in the world could penetrate it, including the most powerful bunker buster ever built. As they continued to control more and more oil fields, the Iranians built three identical bunkers and had completed construction of a fifth one that made the first four look like underground parking garages.

The Director began to hack and cough. He reached for the glass of water in front of him and drank. Once he was confident the coughing fit was over, he continued in a raspy voice. "With construction of the fifth bunker complete, the Empire has the capability of developing a nuclear device nearly triple the current yield of their warheads."

Everyone in the room immediately looked to each other in disbelief. The first to speak was the Chairman of the Joint Chiefs of Staff.

"What? Why the hell didn't we take out the facility when we had the chance?" Carl Moody regretted the question the instant it left his mouth. He already knew the answer, as did everyone in the room. The Chairman was afraid to speak another word for quite some time in fear of embarrassing himself further.

Reining in as much contempt and sarcasm as he could, Director Jimenez answered the question. "Because, General, it can't be done. The first bunker they built is the weakest one of the five, and we have yet to so much as scratch it."

The Director was indeed correct. The European Army had made several attempts to destroy it in the early stages of the war and never came close. They had even sent a team of undercover spies to try to infiltrate the facility to destroy it from the inside. Captured, the team of spies was brutally tortured. Their deaths were broadcast across the Internet.

The president, playing referee and getting back on point, continued. "Roberto, going back to my original question about the three warheads they now possess..."

The Director, again irritated with the use of his first name, smiled at the president, "Yes, Mr. President?"

"What is the possibility that the Iranians would break the three warheads down and build one really big device?"

"That's a good question, sir, one that I had myself." Jimenez gave another taunting look at General Moody as if to say, "See there? That's the type of question that should be asked, you stupid grunt."

The Director continued to address the president. "Based on our intelligence, we believe the Empire has the capability of breaking down the warheads into a larger, more powerful one. However, to do so would seriously diminish their threat in the region. Putting all their nuclear eggs in one basket would mean that they could wipe Paris or London from the map. If they did so they would, however, not have any remaining nuclear devices. It would take six months to a year for them to produce another one, during which time they would be vulnerable to invasion."

"Doesn't make strategic sense," General Weygandt spoke up, not really asking a question, simply stating the facts.

General Weygandt continued. "If I were them, I would take the three devices I had and split them into six. The yield wouldn't be enough to level a city, but it could still kill thousands of people and would instill twice the fear.

"An excellent observation that had not occurred to me, General. Well done." Roberto smiled at General Weygandt and then quickly shot another menacing glare at the chairman. The seventy-two year old was acting like a schoolyard bully.

The president almost laughed at the chairman, who was clearly letting the old man get the best of him. Carl was not hard to rile up; anyone could push his buttons, that is, outside of the military. No one in uniform would dare mock the second-in-command of the United States military. Again playing peacemaker, the president asked, "Where do they stand on completing an ICBM?"

The director did not need to ask the computer, he knew the answer, "The estimates remain the same, at least fifteen months. Their test launches barely make it into the upper atmosphere."

This was what the president feared the most. The thought of the Iranians delivering a nuclear device to an American city kept him up at night. The president and everyone in the room also had nightmares about the terror attacks they now faced on their own soil with alarming frequency. September 11, 2001, was a day they all remembered well. The mere thought that the most powerful nation on earth could be attacked on their home soil was something they had never dreamed of on September 10, 2001. Everyone in the room thought back to the day the Twin Towers fell as the beginning, a prophecy of things to come.

The president addressed both the Secretary of Homeland Security and the Director of the Federal Bureau of Investigation, Warren Gill. The two had grown accustomed to being addressed at the same time, like they were a couple.

"Gentlemen, how are things on the home front?"

"To put it bluntly, Mr. President, not good."

Secretary Laferriere never held his punches. The president had hired him because he wasn't a "yes-man" who told him what he wanted to hear or sugarcoated his answers. The secretary leaned back in his chair and looked to his close friend, Warren Gill.

The FBI Director took his cue and began. "Our soil is being attacked on two fronts. Domestic terrorists are the hardest for us to capture. The Empire continues to activate sleeper cells around the country, and we almost never see them coming until it's too late. We have seen some progress capturing the waves of Silent Warriors that make it across our 7,612 mile borders. The majority of the terrorist invaders have no identification of any kind, not so much as a fake driver's license. They avoid the major cities and the National Guard checkpoints, and well, we don't know what they are doing."

"What do you mean you don't know?" Stacy Reid, the president's Chief of Staff asked.

"Well, ma'am, they aren't like anything we've seen in the past. Our best estimate is that Iranian submarines bring them over and they just swim right up to deserted beaches with nothing but the clothes on their backs. We also have credible evidence that large numbers of enemy forces are simply walking into the country from Mexico. Most of those we captured welcome torture and are hard to crack. A few have told us that they're set loose on our shores with no plan of attack whatsoever; they are told to be creative and improvise."

"Hard to stop an attack that has no intelligence to track until the damned thing happens," the CIA Director managed to bark in a raspy voice.

Secretary Lafferiere nodded in agreement.

The president focused his attention back on Jimenez, "Roberto, what do we know about Bunker Five? Any indication that they're planning some sort of attack for us here at home?"

The director turned his attention back to the screen, "Computer, display image of Bunker Five, begin playback from six months ago and show the progress in high-speed, ending with the most current image. Compress playback to sixty seconds."

The interactive image of the Iranian Theater remained on the screen and a new window opened in the bottom left corner, far too small for anyone to see. The Director had forgotten to close the first screen.

"Son of a bitch," the Director cursed under his breath. Roberto Jimenez hated to give the appearance that he was the stereotypical senior citizen that didn't know how to work a computer. "Enhance."

The Chairman of the Joint Chiefs of Staff finally saw his chance and laughed out loud. "You need help there, Robert-O?" Moody had placed emphasis on the last "O" to really drive it home.

Director Jimenez was becoming visibly frustrated, and his face flashed beet red as he realized that Carl Moody had just made fun of him. Roberto raised his right hand to grab the image. He succeeded in taking hold of it, but the pain in his arm was too much to endure and his hand fell back in his lap. The wall sensors tracking his hand movements misinterpreted his last gesture, and the image quickly disappeared.

Governor Lori Prince could not stay quiet any longer. Watching this old geezer display his obvious incompetence with computers sent her over the edge.

"Excuse me, Mr. President. I must know, exactly why am I here? This is all very interesting, but I just don't understand exactly how the state of Florida is in any condition to help with the war effort."

The president raised his hand in a calming gesture. "Governor Prince, I understand your confusion, but if you would just remain patient for a few more min..."

"Patient? PATIENT? You have the nerve to ask me to be patient? I have been patient for over a month waiting for you to make good on your promise to help the people of Florida. You have ended my political career while close to a million people have died! You haven't done one goddamned thing to help!"

The president's Chief of Staff, Stacy Reid, was so alarmed that she almost screamed. Her shock was not that the governor had interrupted the president and used profanity, but rather what she had said.

Did she really just say a million?

CHAPTER FIVE

While the governor of the great state of Florida was becoming the first visitor of the Clinton Room to use profanity at a sitting president, Chester Stephens was thinking about a promotion. He just knew it was coming. Chester was already thinking about what he would do with the extra money. Good ole' Chester was grinning; he was so proud of himself.

Chester Stephens was the General Manager at the Kissimmee Wal-Mart Supercenter located ten minutes from the Walt Disney World Resort in Orlando, Florida. His store hadn't fared too well in the Second Great Depression. Its proximity to the Magic Kingdom and Universal Studios theme parks had helped keep his store above water – but just barely. Chester had been a loyal Wal-Mart employee for twelve years, working his way up to General Manager in record time. He took his job seriously and ran a very tight ship. He knew that the top executives at corporate headquarters in Bentonville, Arkansas were watching his career with great interest. They had told him that if he managed to end each year above the line drawn by the Second Great Depression or hopefully see a little increase, he would be moving to Bentonville to join them.

When Hurricane Luther made his fourth trip ashore greet the citizens of the greater Orlando area, Chester knew he was facing the defining moment in his career. The boys in Bentonville had told him that if he had two more successful years, there would be a big promotion waiting for him. Chester welcomed Luther with open arms and knew that the disaster would move up his promotion two years ahead of schedule.

When the hurricane began to demolish Orlando, Chester realized just how stupid he was for welcoming a disaster. Luther rose up from the pits of hell. The Magic Kingdom stood in ruins. Cinderella's Castle would only be remembered in the company's logo; it would be a very long time before it would be rebuilt, if ever. Over at Universal Studios, Hogwarts Castle was no more, the boy wizard himself would not be able to put it together, with or without magic.

Then the city caught on fire.

Chester had no idea how fires could be set in a rain-soaked

town. He gave up trying to figure it out and hoped for the best. The General Manager and many of the employees rode out the storm in the store's loading docks. The employees figured they would be much safer at their work site and Chester welcomed them in because he needed help protecting the store.

Luther answered Chester's prayers and spared the store. The massive superstore was not untouched, however, but it was one of the few large structures in the Orlando area still standing. At the front of the store, the "W" and "T" had fallen from the sign, renaming the store "al-Mar". Luther's massive right hook punched Orlando square in the balls with a world record two hundred twenty-five mile per hour wind. The Safir-Simpson Hurricane Wind Scale would later be upgraded to max out at a Category 6. Chester was convinced that the Good Lord in heaven above did his shopping at Wal-Mart.

Chester set out to execute his plan for the store that clearly had the blessing of divine intervention. He knew that he must protect the store at all costs. Just the simple fact that the store had no customers meant that he would not manage to meet his goal for the year. Chester shrugged this fact off, as it was clearly not under his control. What was in his control, however, were the tens of millions of dollars worth of inventory for which he was responsible.

Chester was no fool. He knew he was sitting on a goldmine. The first stage in his plan was to barricade both of the front entrances. Thanks to Luther, he only had to complete half of the task. The north entrance had an SUV crammed inside it with a stack of cars behind it. The north corner of the store suffered the most structural damage; the roof of the north entrance collapsed around the SUV and blocked off the entrance from the Home and Garden center. The kind old woman that greeted consumers would have to join her counterpart on the south entrance should the store open again.

The south entrance proved a challenge. It was as pristine as it had been the week before. The first order of business was to use hand-trucks to move four pallets into the entrance behind the locked doors - two behind the outer doors and two behind the inner doors. Not satisfied with the barricade, Chester ordered that the sally port leading into the store be filled with shopping carts chained together. Chester was certain that it would take a dump truck at full speed to breach the security that he had employed.

The next order of business was the loading docks. The sliding doors used to receive the eighteen-wheelers loaded with merchandise were closed and padlocked. Then Chester took a page out of medieval history and had his employees dump vegetable oil mixed with lighter fluid in front of the sliding bay doors. Should angry mobs tear down the doors and make it in, they would be set on fire. His employees joked with each other that all they would do was slip and fall because no one was actually going to set another human being on fire. Their loyalty to their minimum wage jobs had a limit.

The remaining way in and out of the store was the pedestrian entrance to the loading docks. The General Manager and his employees needed a way in and out of the store. The Assistant Manager of the demolished Home and Garden center informed Chester that pallets of dirt and fertilizer were in the north end of the warehouse. Forty-pound bags were stacked chest high in front of the door. Chester picked four very enthusiastic teenagers to stand sentry behind the door. The first two carried high-powered BB rifles to fire at any potential mobs, hoping to scare them off. The other two boys carried a fully loaded pistol and shotgun each, should any angry Orlandites make it inside. The other employees knew that they would not set anybody on fire, they were however, quite frightened that these four boys would play G.I. Joe with much zeal.

The new residents of the retail giant managed to construct a comfortable little fortress. They built a makeshift commune in the middle of the store. They used sleeping bags, comforters, mattress pads, and pillows to make beds. The perishable foods would soon be a total loss, so Chester did not object to them consuming as much as they could before it spoiled. They had a feast of the best steaks and shrimp. Ice cream and beer made for many a happy employee. They were living like kings.

General Manger Chester Stephens was quite proud of himself. Yes sir, he was damned proud. He knew that his move to Bentonville was on the horizon. All that was left to do was wait it out for the Calvary to swoop in and rescue them.

The Calvary never came.

The only people who showed up were ninety percent of the remaining employees of the Kissimmee Wal-Mart Supercenter. Chester welcomed them in, the more the merrier. They were a welcome addition to his army of blue-vested soldiers.

This was the first of Chester's many mistakes.

The two hundred and forty-seven employees felt they should be able to take whatever they wanted from the store. Chester didn't mind them eating and drinking, but he did ask them to document everything they consumed. His concern, other than keeping people alive, was being able to provide accurate, detailed records should corporate request them. At first, the employees were more than happy to keep track of what they used. That attitude quickly changed. Chester gave them permission to take bicycles so they could ride back to their homes and check on things. Every employee returned to report their homes and apartment complexes had been obliterated.

The destruction of their homes was not the most troubling thing they had to report. Carnage filled street after street. The stench was overpowering. In the rubble laid twisted and mangled corpses. They were able to identify some men, women, and children, but the majority of the corpses had no discernible gender. Ants and maggots had each taken their turn on the decaying flesh.

Much of the staff came back to the store like shell-shocked soldiers returning from the battlefield. The others returned thinking that they could simply replenish what they had lost. The Wal-Mart workers were even bold enough to grab a few shopping carts and fought and squabbled with each other over merchandise like it was Black Friday. Chester tried and failed to stop them; some even spat on their boss. Chester wiped the spit from his face, pulled out his notepad and wrote down their names. They had ended their careers with Wal-Mart. He would personally see that the traitors lost their jobs and were prosecuted for theft.

Eventually, rage began to replace shock - rage over the fact that absolutely no one was coming to rescue them. It had been over a month and not one plane dotted the sky; no rescue teams could be seen on the horizon. They were alone, living in a third world country that didn't care whether they lived or died.

Surely the American government had learned its lesson with Hurricane Katrina. Surely rescue would come.

Chester began to worry when the front doors to the south entrance began to shake. The door quickly fell, but the ingenious barricade he had constructed held firm. The General Manager himself went up to the roof and peeked over the edge to get a look at the parking lot. A makeshift camp had been erected there. Camped out in front of the store were around a hundred people. They were patiently waiting as if the front doors would simply slide open so they could come inside and buy all the groceries that their hearts desired, gladly paying cash and smiling at the kind door greeter on their way out.

Chester was confident that all he had to do was keep the citizens of the makeshift camp at bay for just a little bit longer. He just knew that rescue had to be coming. If he could just manage to hold on for one more night they would be saved, and he would be moving to Bentonville to live the good life.

Chester knew he had little time left when a few tired, broken and hungry souls figured out that they could go around to the back of the store. The boys with BB guns did manage to scare them off. Some creative citizens of the makeshift camp returned with garbage can lids to deflect the BBs. When the first one of them had his foot blown off from a shotgun blast they quickly retreated. Chester knew he had a day at best before they regrouped and tried to attack the store with different tactics. He was wrong. He didn't have a day, he had less than six hours.

Chester never dreamed that it would come to this. He had exhausted every good idea he had in fortifying the store. His first mistake was that he didn't camouflage the pedestrian entrance to the loading docks. The second mistake he made was failing to secure the hatch leading up to the roof. The third and final mistake was underestimating the primal and unrelenting will to survive at all costs - the same drive that kept his species alive.

Chester had no idea he had even committed these crucial errors. He was still quite confident that his fortress would repel any attack. He knew without question that he would be greatly rewarded for his efforts when this was finally over. When the end came, Chester would not be rewarded, he would not be promoted. The new boat he had picked out would not be purchased. He definitely would not be leaving Orlando to join the big wigs in Bentonville.

The leader of the makeshift camp was a man named Benjamin Black. Ben was not a man of influence or authority; he was the manager at a nearby Jiffy Lube. Benjamin told his employees to bring their families to the Jiffy Lube so they could ride out Luther in the pit underneath the shop. A few residents did so, and Ben offered them shelter. An hour before the full force of the hurricane was due, some frightened motorists pulled into the shop and Ben offered them shelter as well. Ben and his employees emptied out the stock from the pit and they all hunkered down, shoulder-to-shoulder, to ride out Luther's punishment. They had no idea if they would drown from storm surge; they took their chances underground anyway.

When Ben and his people managed to get out of the pit, they emerged into a new world, one of Armageddon. They could stand in one place and see in a straight line to sections of town miles away. Homes and buildings should have obstructed their line of sight. Instead they saw complete destruction and devastation. They could see dogs climbing over rubble, pieces of human flesh in their mouths - fingers, hands, and scalps with matted bloody hair. Ben found two boys, both under the age of ten, covered in dirt and blood, walking down the road adjacent his shop. A few women in the group tended to the boys and tried to get them to talk.

Ben knew these people were counting on him. He had to get them to a central location so they could be rescued. They walked for most of the day and set up camp in a vacant parking lot that was somewhat clean and free of debris. Ben tried to figure out what business had used this parking lot, but had no idea without any buildings nearby to use as a frame of reference. The group set up camp and built signal fires. Next they used debris to spell out the word HELP in big letters that might be seen by rescue aircraft. Slowly, people joined the group, a few each day. Safety in numbers was the key to survival.

They waited for almost a week for help to come. Ben knew that all they had to do was wait and they would be saved. Much like the employees at the Kissimmee Wal-Mart Supercenter, they slowly began to realize that no one was coming.

They were cut off from the rest of the world. They were alone. They must take matters into their own hands if they would survive.

The first step was to find transportation. They managed to salvage a few damaged vehicles; some vans, an RV, and a SuperTruck. Next they had to find supplies. Doing so in the barren wasteland proved very hard. They managed to find enough food and water from the rubble to keep themselves alive. They sent out scouts in all directions in the hopes that they would either find supplies or someone to rescue them from this nightmare. One of the groups came back with the best news they had heard since before the storm. A Wal-Mart had survived Luther.

Ben and the group packed up and headed off to the Kissimmee Wal-Mart Supercenter. They arrived to find one of the entrances filled with cars, the other heavily barricaded. Ben understood the need to keep the store safe from looters. Maybe they were rationing out supplies from just one entrance for reasons of safety. They knocked on the door for the better part of a day waiting for someone to answer. No one did. Maybe it was empty. After the sun went down, they could see the beams from many flashlights bouncing around inside the store, so they knew it was occupied. Eventually, they managed to break down the glass door but to no avail. The barricade was far too strong to breach.

Ben decided to call off the attempts at getting into the store. He figured if they showed the people inside that they were civilized and posed no threat, surely they would see the error of their ways and let them inside.

One afternoon it occurred to Ben that they could go around to the back of the store to gain entry. He laughed at himself for still maintaining the polite relationship between owner and customer. The consumer did not go behind the counter with the owner; it was just rude. Ben and a few men went around to the back and were quickly greeted by a hail of BB gun fire. What the hell is wrong with these people? Are they crazy? They returned with trashcan lids to deflect the BBs. They just wanted to talk reason with the manager, no need for violence. Ben knew exactly what kind of game these assholes were playing when his assistant manager had his foot blown off with a shotgun.

It was time for war. The Great Battle of the Kissimmee Wal-Mart Supercenter had begun.

The first stage of the battle was to take down the south entrance. Chester was incorrect that it would take a dump truck at full speed to breach the south entrance. It didn't take a dump truck. It took one full-sized Ford 650 SuperTruck only ten minutes to breach the door. The angry mob had outfitted the grill of the truck with the rims of a full sized van. The battering ram they had constructed worked perfectly. The A-Team/McGyver SuperTruck sat on the opposite side of the parking lot and launched full speed at the barricade. It rammed into the first row of pallets and backed out. Next, a few people quickly moved in to remove the debris. Then a man with six-foot long bolt cutters came in and cut the chains and mangled shopping carts. He stepped aside and let the busy workers clear out the mess. The second trip of the battering ram slammed into the second row of pallets, sending debris flying into the store. Flying car batteries thrown from one of the pallets killed two of the blue-vested soldiers. The pallet had been selected because of its sheer weight. The employees never anticipated that the choice would kill two of their own.

The man with the six-foot bolt cutters joined three men on the roof, ready to pierce the trap door leading down into the store. The bolt cutters were not necessary since Chester had left the door wide open. The four men descended into the store and quickly stopped at the sporting goods section to arm themselves with guns. Finding all the ammo missing, they instead settled on baseball bats.

At the pedestrian entrance to the loading dock the four boys were quickly killed before any of them could fire a shot. The Florida State Bronze Medal Archer winner quickly shot the four boys. The first took an arrow to the eye, the second and third fell with arrows protruding from their chest; the fourth was shot in the stomach and crawled away to die.

The employees that could make it out of the store ran and ran until they looked over their shoulders and couldn't see Wal-Mart in the distance. The unlucky employees that didn't make it out were killed by the mob, angry at them for being so selfish and hoarding everything for themselves.

General Manager Chester Stephens held up both hands and managed to stop the angry mob from entering. They thought he was surrendering his gold mine. When Chester began demanding that they leave or face prosecution, the crowd replied by beating the man to death. Chester Stephens died a loyal and faithful employee of Wal-Mart. His last thought was of what he would say to Sam Walton when he greeted him at the gates of heaven.

The Kissimmee Wal-Mart Supercenter had fallen; in less than a day its shelves were almost bare. Benjamin Black and his renegades took what they wanted and quickly moved on to another target.

CHAPTER SIX

William Sanderson, Harvard MBA, and recipient of the Merrill Lynch Man of the Year Award, awoke in his cardboard home in the Central Park Obama-Camp. Having absolutely no outdoorsman skills to speak of, William had no choice but to learn how to be a successful homeless man. His first cardboard home was not able to repel the elements. He awoke one night to find his domicile a sopping mess, collapsing on top of him and his family. He knew he had to do better. He quickly constructed a new home and spent over a week adding to the makeshift structure. At sunrise the next morning, William cleaned up the sopping cardboard structure and instructed his wife to protect the children. He ventured out into the violent city of New York to scavenge building materials for his home. He returned just before sunset that night with a shopping cart stacked to the point of toppling over and greeted his wife with a kiss. Lindsay had just finished feeding the children a bountiful feast she had procured from the trash cans behind a local deli. She offered William his portion of the meal. William picked a few bites and gave the rest to his children.

William had been one of the lucky ones when The Second Great Depression came to take his four thousand square foot home along with all his cars and anything else of value. William considered himself lucky because he was a born survivor. He had grown up in abject poverty in Brooklyn. His father abandoned his mother and younger siblings, and William had to immediately assume the role of the family's breadwinner and surrogate father figure. He was a star baseball player, attending Harvard on a scholarship. He worked two jobs to support himself and continued to send money home to his mother. He continued his studies and obtained his MBA. William was immediately picked up by Merrill Lynch and made a fortune investing money for both himself and his wealthy clients. He married and had two kids; his family wanted for nothing. William made so much money that his grandchildren probably wouldn't be able to spend it all.

When the American economy came crashing down and soon after, the economies of most countries across the globe, he lost everything. He managed to stay in the fight longer than the men who threw themselves from the high-rises along Wall Street. Most of those men had no idea on their way down that their idea was far from original. If they had taken a few more history courses in business school, they would have known that during The First Great Depression over a century before, the idea had been executed many times.

William arrived back at the sprawling Obama-Camp that covered most of Central Park and unpacked the contents of the shopping cart. The term "Obama-Camp" was meant as the worst possible insult to the former president. It was a throwback to the "Hoovervilles" built during the First Great Depression meant to insult President Hoover. President Obama wasn't even in office when the camps sprouted up all around the country. The blame was placed on his shoulders due to the massive debt he piled on the American economy during his time in the Oval Office. Any time a camera was placed on them, the Democrats would point out that the nation's first black president only inherited an already failing economy from President Bush. Fox News even made a logo for the camps depicting a starving, crying family cowering at the feet of an imposing and menacing looking Obama. It didn't take long for the rest of the media world to follow suit, and the name stuck through two administrations after Obama left office.

William set about constructing his new home. He had managed to find some old pallets and broke them up into lumber. Also in his cart were old tarps, cordage from wire and rope, dirty blankets, and the most prized possession – a bundle of three rolls of duct tape. Duct tape had a thousand uses, and William knew he had a valuable asset. He took one of the rolls and buried it in a hole in the floor of his new home. With the help of his wife and children, they had not built an Obama-House; they had built an Obama-Mansion.

William never once gave his children the indication that anything was wrong. He simply told his five and seven year olds that they were leaving their house to go camping in Central Park. The people out there in the park really know how to live, he told them. They have Mother Nature to look at all day, and they could play as much as they wanted in what was left of the Park. We get to look up at the stars at night. Look! Over there - that's the Big Dipper! His children had never been happier. They would spend more time with their father in the next year than they had the previous short years of their young lives combined. William cried when his little girl asked him if they could live in Central Park forever. She was having so much fun that she didn't want to go back to the house to which William no longer had the keys. If children have loving, nurturing parents, they would be happy to live anywhere.

At first William was terrified to walk the streets of New York for fear of being mocked or even attacked for being a dirty homeless man. Much to his surprise, he realized that if you were homeless, you might as well be invisible. No one so much as looked at him or acknowledged that he was worthy of the dignity that came with being a human being. He thought back in shame to the many years he walked the busy streets in the financial district. He would turn his line of sight to pretend to look at something else or even pretended to talk on his cell phone waiting for the light to change rather than acknowledge that another of God's creatures was asking for his charity.

One morning after warming up by an Obama-Furnace (a large metal drum with holes near the top for lighting fires) he returned to his one room home and told his wife that he would be gone for most of the day looking for food and supplies. This was partially true. He didn't know how to tell Lindsay that he was very, very ill. He spent the previous week running a high fever and couldn't stop coughing. William told her it was nothing, just allergies from the seasons changing. He set off to wait for what he knew would be the entire day at the Free-Clinic at the edge of Central Park. After finally being treated and given some medication to take with him, he stepped out of the medical tent to find the sun already setting. Lindsay was going to be very worried. She had probably told their neighbors he had not come home, and he was sure that his friends were out searching the park for him.

William made his way back to his wife and hugged and kissed her. Lindsay was crying and could not deliver the angry scolding she had rehearsed. William made up some excuse about getting lost and not being able to get directions from anyone. The excuse was believable since most citizens wouldn't look at a homeless person if they were on fire.

William took his medication in secret for the next few days and managed to recover. He was determined to keep the illness from Lindsay, he didn't want her to worry. One morning he asked his neighbor to watch over his house so he and his family could go for a stroll and get some fresh air. While his kids ventured off within eyesight to run and play, he held his wife's hand and looked at the skyline of New York. He tried not to think back to the days of his old life of comfort and excess. Those memories served him no good; it was from another life that needed to be forgotten. He needed to look to the future, however bleak and depressing. He had to provide for his children.

William knew his job skills were utterly worthless, at least it would be for the foreseeable future. Not many people had need for an investment banker. William was willing to work any job that gave him minimum wage. The problem was his lack of residence. Charity groups all over the country petitioned to have the Obama-Camps incorporated into actual towns with street addresses. This was met with harsh criticism from all sides. We need to get rid of the Obama-Camps, not make them permanent. The charity groups countered by offering the Obama-Camp residents the use of their business address. The public saw this as fraud, and the idea didn't last very long. Organizations that did offer jobs to the Obama-Camp residents treated them like illegal aliens and paid them next to nothing.

William knew that if he was going to give his family any kind of future, he had only one option – joining the military. The military was glad to take any able-bodied man or woman to join the fight. All they needed was some form of identification to start processing the new recruits. Expired driver's licenses would do just fine. The thought of joining the fight in the Iranian Theater was a nightmare to William. However, the bigger nightmare was that his family would most likely be dead in a few years. It wouldn't take long for malnutrition or a battle with pneumonia to pick them off one by one. He would fight his way to the gates of hell and back if it meant his family was safe and provided for.

The hardest part would be leaving his family behind while he was in basic training. He would have to count on Lindsay to keep the children safe while he was away. Once he made it through boot camp, William could move his family onto a military base, at least that's what he hoped. They would have a real roof over their heads, electricity, running water, and warm beds. They would also have free health care. Everything was going to be fine. William would do anything for his wife and children.

William was due to leave for basic the next day. He spent the day playing with his children, hugging and kissing them as much as he could. He told them that he was going away for a while so they could move into a house and even go to school. His children began to cry, and William tried to think of anything to make them smile. He promised them they could get a dog. They smiled and wiped the tears from their eyes. William beamed and asked them what kind of dog they wanted. What are you going to name it? Whose bed will it sleep in? The children got very excited, and William knew he had done his job as a loving father.

The next morning William spoke with the neighbors on either side, and they assured him that they would keep a watchful eye over his family. It takes a village, they told him. William set off for the long walk to the recruitment center. His recruiter had agreed to take him on the subway to the processing center.

William traveled many hours to the military base in the south. He spent the better part of a week in orientation, physicals, testing, and all sorts of other bureaucratic red tape. When he got his first paycheck he immediately went to the Western Union station to send money back to his wife. A television was playing above the counter. William had never been so frightened in his life.

The Unified National Guard was evicting the residents of the Central Park Obama-Camp.

CHAPTER SEVEN

Once the Americans joined with the European Army to form the Allied Forces, The Great Empire of Iran launched an all-out attack on American soil. The invasion had no similarity to Normandy or any other invasion for that matter. Troops in uniform did not storm a beach to be shot at by other troops in uniform. No tanks or heavy equipment traveled behind enemy lines to overthrow an enemy stronghold.

The invasion of America was done in secret. It was quiet. No alarms sounded. No emergency broadcast alerts to the public warning that the enemy was among them. The Empire of Iran sent an entire regiment of Muslim warriors to sneak into the United States to do one thing and one thing only - instill fear, panic, and paranoia in citizens of every walk of life. Their mission was clear and they did not discriminate. No one was off limits. They all had targets on their back.

The Silent Warriors did not act alone. American citizens helped them kill their own countrymen. Disgruntled and critical of their own government, large numbers of the American population aided the terrorists in their mission. Fed up with a collapsed economy, a failing infrastructure, and with their ineffective elected leaders, the newly branded warriors joined the fight, ready to focus their rage.

Recruitment was not difficult. The Silent Warriors simply joined in with protests and stoked the fire, causing many a peaceful demonstration to end in violence. They would pick out the most passionate and angry of the group. The waves of homeless people were the easiest targets. Cold, hungry, dirty and forgotten, the homeless needed very little motivation to join the fight.

Every law enforcement agency in the nation, from police departments, big and small, to the halls of the Department of Justice was helpless in stopping the attacks. Arriving via Iranian submarines or by simply walking across the Mexican border, the warriors breached the U.S. with only the clothes on their backs. They were given no specific instructions, no target to destroy, they were simply told to be creative and improvise. The Silent Warriors proved to be more than just experts in stealth; they held true to the name when they were captured. Puzzled captors could not make heads or tails of what little they did manage to hear. *"You'll never see us coming; you are wasting your time!" "No one is giving me orders; I give the orders only to myself!" "How many of us are here? We are everywhere! We are your own people!" "Go home and look in the mirror - you might be one! Let me out of here and join us!"*

The attacks started out small, mainly sneak attacks that did not result in a lot of bloodshed. Confidence and bravery grew from these small attacks, and the terrorists graduated to large scale assaults that killed thousands. The first attack to gain recognition was The Thanksgiving Day Massacre. Terrorists, armed with sniper rifles, launched a coordinated and simultaneous attack on the cities of Boston, New York, Chicago, Dallas, Las Vegas, and Los Angeles. At precisely the same time on Thanksgiving Day, the sniper teams began to kill as many people as they possibly could. The final death toll reached one hundred seventy-nine people, and as a stroke of luck, one of the victims was a Congressman's adult son on vacation in Las Vegas. The attack had the desired effect; the American people were terrified to leave their homes. Fear and death were now joined hand in hand with the holiday's more spirited associations of turkey and togetherness.

The Thanksgiving Day Massacre caused much more damage than simply fear and panic. Its greatest victory was paranoia. No one knew the total number of enemies walking the streets. Everyone was a possible terrorist. Your neighbor, the mailman, the waiter bringing your food, the guy in the car next to you might be the enemy. Paranoia clogged police switchboards - *That guy looked like he was up to no good; go check him out! My neighbor acted really nervous when I asked him why he never parked his car in the garage; something must be going on in there! This guy down the street gets packages at all hours of the night; he's planning something!*

The Second Amendment had never been so celebrated, gun control a thing of the past. Many citizens, both frightened and angry, began to wear gun belts and carried pistols like they were from the Old West. The fear of guns vanished when the greater fear of death took precedence. It was not out of place to see someone in a bulletproof vest on the job or in the pew on Sunday morning. The Second Great Depression was cruel to most markets, but never to the gun industry. Every grandmother, every priest, every child over the age of twelve carried a firearm. Fear is an intoxicating predator.

Since Americans could no longer afford air travel, the terrorists instead focused their attention on mass transit. Subways in the nation's largest cities became a target of suicide bombers. In order to counter the attacks, security checkpoints reminiscent of the ones in airports in the wake of 9-11 began to be installed at every subway entrance in the country. This came at great cost to the already broken U.S. economy and further enraged the American public. Angry and frustrated people had to leave their home an hour earlier just to get to work on time. The security checkpoints at the subways only motivated the terrorists to switch methods. Realizing that wearing a suicide vest was no longer an option, the terrorists instead smuggled ceramic knives onto the subways and targeted children and the elderly. Slowly, the population in major cities began to dwindle away as frightened citizens no longer felt safe. Hoping to encourage the citizens to stay and continue to work in the big cities, thirty-eight governors activated the National Guard to full time active duty to maintain law and order on the streets. Hell, they might even catch a few terrorists on the side. The plan was an overwhelming success in terms of public opinion; soon the remaining twelve states adopted the idea as well. The Unified National Guard was created and was under the sole authority of the Chairman of the Joint Chiefs of Staff, who only answered to the president. The president didn't even have to bother with the unpleasantness of Posse Comitatas in the way that President Lincoln had suffered. No formal declaration was made; the American people begged for it and applauded their leaders for finally taking action and protecting them. After a few months, the idea backfired in the worst possible way. The warm and fuzzy feeling of security was replaced with the Orwellian nightmare of Big Brother.

Citizens did not want to pay the high price of security. Random checkpoints clogged the streets. Red-blooded Americans felt they shouldn't have to show their ID and submit to a retinal scan. We have rights! You can't do this! Racial profiling bred chaos. Anyone with olive colored skin was detained and often beaten without even a single word spoken. Residents of the big cities quickly changed their minds and did not like the idea of martial law. Well, that was just too bad. The U.S. government was not willing to take it back and call it square.

The largest attack was during the Super Bowl in 2023. A man named Nassir El-Fayid, a former Al-Qaeda freedom fighter, launched a small crop duster a half-mile from Cowboy Stadium in Arlington, Texas. Before fighter jets could be scrambled to shoot him down, he managed to fly over Cowboy Stadium and release cyanide gas, killing over thirty two thousand people, including the majority of the New Orleans Saints and the Oklahoma City Sooners. The people in the stands were even kind enough to oblige El-Fayid by looking up at his plane. He almost hit the roof of the billion-dollar stadium on his way in. They didn't know if the plane was some sort of flashy gimmick or some crazy fan who couldn't get tickets. Many thought the plane was going to circle back around, wait for a time out to be called, and land on the field so some A-List celebrity could make a surprise appearance. Saints fans were looking for any reason to get their team off the field. They wanted the Saints to have a much needed distraction so they could regroup and get back in the game. The two-year old NFL team from Oklahoma would no doubt make the Saints swallow the bitter pill of defeat.

Instead of seeing a famous movie or rock star take the field, an estimated one hundred and twenty-three million viewers watched the nation's deadliest domestic massacre unfold on live TV for over a minute before the broadcast was terminated. In the wake of the attack, Cowboy Stadium was closed and the National Football League never played another game. The American public was outraged to say the least. While tragic by its very nature, a bomb in the subway was one thing, but millions of pissed off football fans never being able to watch another game was simply outrageous. Riots erupted all over the country and angry mobs killed anyone with olive colored skin. Within a month of the attack on Cowboy Stadium, the U.S. government rounded up anyone whose nationality hailed from the Great Empire of Iran and locked them up in eleven Middle Eastern internment camps scattered across the country. In order to prevent the frightened Middle Easterners from being slaughtered, the camps were literally built around the people. The American Civil Liberties Union protested the violation to human rights. They had hoped that the atrocities of the Japanese internment camps of World War II would not be repeated. After being attacked by angry mobs themselves, the ACLU quietly went away to lick their wounds.

The United States government did not have enough money for the security upgrades to the subways, nor did they have enough money to intern tens of thousands of American citizens in camps for an indeterminate amount of time. They certainly didn't have the money to activate half a million guardsmen to protect the nation's cities. Once again, the only remaining option was to borrow money from China. The current loan was to the tune of a trillion dollars, giving the Chinese ownership of sixty-one percent of the nation's debt. *Firefly* fans just knew that their favorite TV show was a prophetic, with this very thing foreseen by Joss Whedon decades prior. Pretty soon, they would learn to speak Chinese. The fans of the cult TV show were the few that relished the thought.

America was falling. Not many Americans really believed it at first. Their country had endured many challenges in its history. The United States of America had peered into the abyss many times but had never fallen in head first. They had survived a Civil War, two World Wars, and came out the other side of the First Great Depression and thrived. Democracy was the greatest institution the world had ever seen, and no other group of civilized people in the history of the world had been a greater example. To doubt the United States of America was unpatriotic and almost bordered on treason. No one dared challenge their beloved country.

The few that could see the unpleasant truth prepared in secret. They stockpiled food, water, and medicine. They learned how to purify dirty water and start a fire without matches. Couch potatoes learned how to fish and hunt. Suburbanites dug bomb shelters by flashlight. Country folk built bunkers.

Sadly, the few that had the foresight to prepare dared not recruit for fear of ridicule and rejection. The ones that did shout from the rooftops and proclaim the end of the world was near had a rude awakening. The Department of Homeland Security declared that anyone who stockpiled food, water, ammunition, and medicine were potential domestic terrorists and placed on a watch list. It didn't take long for the survivalist movement to go underground.

America was falling. Its decline had already begun. Patriotic Americans refused to believe it. America would prevail. She would rise again. Those unwilling to help make it happen were traitors. Sadly, the traitors knew the truth. The United States of America was racing towards collapse.

CHAPTER EIGHT

For the first time in two and a half years, Howard Beck made plans to leave his mountain fortress and venture to the other side of the twelve-foot high brick wall that surrounded his estate. He had spent the previous night obsessing over what to bring along with him. Howard had designated a specific bathrobe for each day of the week and wore nothing else. Leaving the compound meant that he would have to wear actual clothes; Howard had no idea what to wear. He finally decided on four outfits and packed them in his bag.

"Excuse me, sir." Hal felt he needed to interrupt his creator.

"Yes, Old Man, what is it?"

"Would you like for me alter the itinerary of our trip?"

"Why on earth would you do that? Is something wrong?" Howard anxiously asked.

"No, sir. Everything is fine."

Howard was sort of disappointed at this. He was searching for any reason at all to skip this visit with Meredith. Hal knew he was a creature of habit and figured that an excuse not to leave was forthcoming.

Hal continued. "I noticed, sir, that you have packed four outfits for the trip."

"Yeah, big deal," said Howard.

"Well, sir, the reason for my query is that the itinerary you shared with me schedules us to return to the residence late tomorrow evening. I cannot ascertain why you have packed extra clothes and deduced that our trip would be extended."

"Just being cautious, Hal, nothing more."

"I understand, sir. My apologies for the interruption."

Howard had actually lied to his computer. He was not being cautious, but rather trying to please his wife. Howard had figured through painstaking research what outfit his wife liked based on her mood. He had four outfits - one for happy, sad, angry, and one for downright dreadful. He would hope for the best and wear the happy outfit. If need be, he could always change.

Howard went to bed and hardly slept that night thinking

about what was waiting outside of his perfect world were everything had its place and made sense. The world outside his home was falling apart. People were scared and desperate.

Howard didn't understand why these people couldn't just get their asses in gear and get their act together.

Howard climbed into his car and settled in for the long drive that would take them to the outskirts of western Denver. Howard had absolutely no idea how to drive. He was confident that he could easily learn how to perform the task; however, the fact that the roads were filled with people driving in ways that Howard could not control meant that Howard never bothered to learn how to drive. Hal was the perfect driver and would keep Howard perfectly safe.

Once Hal made the ten-minute drive to the front gate, he turned left on the road. Howard was ready for his morning briefing.

"What have you got for me this morning, Old Man?"

"I will continue to monitor the estate during your absence and ensure that everything is tended to."

"I know you will, Hal, thank you." Howard lived alone in his sprawling mansion that could easily house a dozen more residents. Every day, Hal dispatched dozens of robots around the estate to clean, perform repairs, and to tend to the landscaping of his thousand acre estate. The only other creature living in the house was his wife's grumpy cat, Nala. Howard did not like the animal and counted on Hal to keep her alive.

Hal continued, "I have rescheduled all of your video conferences to later in the week. The only exception is Director Mills. I will wait for him to contact me so that I can reschedule the meeting."

"Asshole's ducking me, not surprised." Howard did not like the report the director gave him the previous day. The Southeast Director of Beck Enterprises had reported to Howard that the offices south of Atlanta suffered minor damage from Hurricane Luther. The director thought Howard would be pleased that the office complex only suffered minor damage. Howard was in fact not pleased; he screamed at the director for almost an hour as if the man was responsible for the hurricane.

"Arson investigators in California have concluded that the

wildfires are being fueled by disgruntled citizens who have petitioned the governor to remove the National Guard forces currently stationed in the major cities."

"Wow! So the solution is to burn down half of their state?" Howard frowned in disgust.

"Not the solution I would have chosen, sir."

"Me, neither. Continue please."

"The next entry confuses me, sir." Hal waited for Howard to reply.

"How so?"

"Governor Prince continues to face criticism from state representatives on how she is handling the quarantine zone. She has assured them that recovery efforts are underway and emergency crews are working around the clock to repair the damage to the state's infrastructure."

"What's so confusing about that, my friend?"

"Governor Prince is lying, sir."

This quickly caught Howard's attention. He was always proud when Hal could examine raw data and extrapolate hypotheses on human behavior. A lying politician was nothing new, but Hal had peaked his interest. "Continue. I can't wait to hear this."

Hal navigated the vehicle to another road that would lead them near Denver. "Governor Prince has indicated that an aircraft carrier is just off the coast of Merritt Island, fifty-six miles from Orlando."

"No aircraft carrier?"

"No sir, I have yet to track any naval vessels en route to the coast of Florida. The closest ones are the *USS Enterprise* and *USS George Washington*; both ships are now on station in the middle of the Atlantic."

"Anyone else in range that might be en route?"

"No sir, the remaining naval assets that could respond are either in the Iranian Theater or in the Indian Ocean waiting to take their place in the Persian Gulf."

"Malcolm is an excellent chess player. The Fifth Fleet is his queen ready to swoop into the Persian Gulf for a checkmate."

Howard didn't bother to ask about the Atlantic. The

Panama Canal would be closed to all vessels for at least another two years, most likely three. The Miraflores, one of the three locks used to transport ships in and out of the canal, had suffered massive damage due to gross negligence. Once the damage had been surveyed, the canal was closed. A complete retrofit of all three locks would be required. This did not help the American economy or its military in any way. Ships had no choice but to sail around Cape Horn at the tip of the South American continent. The detour meant another eighteen thousand miles for American ships navigating the globe.

"I will definitely be asking Malcolm about that the next time we speak."

"I look forward to hearing the president's answer, sir," Hal responded.

Beck Enterprises had one of the few remaining global satellite systems. Most working satellites still in orbit were communication and GPS satellites that kept the cars on the road and kept people talking. Howard didn't really care about recovery efforts for a hurricane that had nothing to do with him. He was more pleased that Hal had caught a politician in a bold-faced lie that he could tease Malcolm about. He was even more pleased that his A.I. was continuing to evolve at a rate faster than he had anticipated.

"What else is going on in the world, Hal?"

"Sir, I feel I should delay the morning news report to tell you that our trip to the Castle will be delayed."

"Why?"

"Rioting in Denver will cause us to take another route." Howard couldn't understand this; Hal knew that they were not to enter the city limits of Denver. "How does that affect our route?"

"The National Guard has extended its western perimeter of Denver by seven point three miles."

"That bad, huh?" Howard began to get very uncomfortable.

"Yes, sir. One of the roads on our route is now inside the perimeter."

"Can't we just go off-road?" Howard was not looking to add two hours to his round trip excursion to see Meredith.

"I'm sorry to report, sir, that given the terrain, the delay would remain the same and the ride would not be comfortable for you. Would you like me to take us off road?"

"I would not, Old Man. Do what you think is best."

"Of course, sir. Would you like me to continue with the morning news report?"

"Sure, why not." Howard was not planning on paying attention, but he did like to hear Hal's voice. It was the only thing that made him feel like he was still at home.

The rest of the trip was uneventful. Hal completed his morning report, and Howard watched his favorite episode of *Star Trek: The Next Generation* entitled "The Inner Light."

Once the episode ended, Hal informed his creator, "Sir, we will arrive at Beck Castle in twenty-three minutes."

"Thank you, Old Man." Howard replied.

The name "Old Man" was also a Star Trek reference, but this one didn't derive from The Next Generation. On *Deep Space Nine*, Captain Sisco gave his friend Dax the nickname "Old Man." Dax was a symbiotic creature that required a humanoid host. When the host died, another host was required to carry the symbiant. Captain Sisco first met Dax when a man named Curzon was the host. A woman named Jadzia carried the symbiant when the older host died. Sisco had called the first host "Old Man" because the host was actually quite elderly. He continued the nickname with the younger woman; it was a source of amusement for them both and the nickname stuck. Howard had to explain to Hal why he had given him a nickname; Hal did not understand the connection. Hal told Howard that he was neither old nor had a gender. Howard just gave up and told him to respond to both names. Hal obeyed his creator.

"Give me a status report on Beck Castle."

"Yes, sir. I have prepared the Manor for your arrival. Director Thornberry's office sent the quarterly shipment last week, which will be properly inventoried and secured in the warehouse. The air filters in the east wing are in need of minor repair; replacement parts are en route, and I will install them upon arrival. The new bay doors to the landing pad have been installed per your instructions."

"Excellent. Where is Her Highness?"

"Meredith will meet you in the usual place, sir."

When Hal came online, the basement of Howard's mansion housed his massive mainframe. Realizing that Hal was one of the most important inventions in the history of the world, Howard began to grow very paranoid that his creation would somehow be destroyed. As a very expensive precaution, Howard had a top-secret facility built beneath a mountain thirty miles northwest of his home. Upon completion, Hal's redundant backup systems were moved into the facility. Nine hundred zettabytes of data chronicling the history of mankind kept Hal company in his secondary home. Copies of every word ever written, every painting ever painted, every image of everything ever filmed, and everything about everything was stored in Beck Castle. The sprawling, underground complex could withstand a nuclear detonation directly atop it. Nothing in the world could destroy it. If a million years from now mankind became extinct, a new species could then spend another million years evolving into sentience and discover the facility. Hal would let them in the massive front door and in a few generations would finish telling their descendants everything they wanted to know about their long extinct predecessors.

When the facility was completed, Howard bumped down a few notches on the World's Richest Person list. It was of no consequence; a few years later he took back the crown. Howard built the facility as an ark for the survival of mankind. Hundreds of people could live in the complex for generations before they exhausted the resources Howard had provided. He had seen the latest intelligence on the Iranian's infamous Bunker Five in Afghanistan and wouldn't wipe his own ass with the blueprints if he ever came across them.

Howard and Hal designed the geothermal power plant that could keep Hal running inside Beck Castle until the end of time itself. If planet Earth exploded, Howard liked to imagine Hal floating inside the bunker. Howard envisioned Hal spending eternity traveling through space, waiting for some alien race to discover him. Howard debated on whether or not to share the technology of his power system with the rest of the world. He decided against it, fearing people might somehow make the connection to Beck powering some secret facility. The survival of the human race, especially the survival of Hal, was far too great a risk to gamble. Nothing in the world was more important to Howard than Hal.

Howard had kept the facility a secret from his own government and with much pain, from his dear friend, Malcolm. Should the time come, the president would be ushered to the facility to live with his friend, Howard. The superbunker was built in separate stages around the world. Each company was completely insulated from each other; Hal saw to that. The people building their piece of the puzzle had no idea what the completed picture looked like. Hal and his robots did the majority of the construction. If any stage of construction required human hands and eyes, they were searched for any recording or GPS devices and put on a windowless plane. Upon arrival, they would be blindfolded and escorted into the facility by one of Hal's robots to complete their work. Howard compensated them well, so all the subterfuge was not an issue for those involved.

The massive underground super-bunker took twelve years to build. A year after the completion of Beck Castle, the top-secret facility was under the supervision of its first caretaker. Mrs. Beck was crowned as Her Royal Highness, Queen of Beck Manor. Howard loved calling his wife "Her Highness" and really couldn't figure out if his wife liked the term or not.

Twenty-three minutes later they arrived at the secret garage that would take him down to the complex. Howard considered the garage the Batcave; he felt like Bruce Wayne every time he entered or exited the mysterious opening. The helipad was not far away. The floor of the desert would suddenly open up like something out of a James Bond movie. A platform would rise up to receive incoming craft and would then lower into the facility.

Howard exited the vehicle and told Hal to disable all communication. He wanted to speak with his wife in private. He was not looking forward to explaining to his wife why he had not come to see her in such a long time and didn't want Hal to record the event.

Howard grabbed the bouquet of his wife's favorite flowers and walked the short distance to the beautiful garden he had built for her. He swallowed his pride and hung his head as he walked over to her.

Howard Beck collapsed on his wife's grave and began to sob.

CHAPTER NINE

Years before Richard Dupree became an inmate at Highland Valley State Prison and a white supremacy group sunk their claws into him, he awoke in his home on a cold Sunday morning. He rolled his fingers along the smooth, brown skin of his gorgeous wife. The two had been together on and off since their sophomore year in high school. As his fingers ran down her back, she stirred and let out a barely audible moan of pure contentment. She drifted back into her peaceful slumber, and Richard rolled over to look at the alarm clock. Still had an hour before the alarm would sound and they would have to get the kids ready for church. Richard had spent much of the previous night in the bathroom thinking about how the events of today would unfold. He had a big day planned.

Richard had gotten Monique pregnant during their senior year of high school. He had no intention of settling down. Getting married and having to take care of a kid would destroy his plans for the future. When he was in high school, he went with his best friend to see the movie *Act of Valor*. Richard was blown away by the fact that some of the actors in the movie were real Navy SEALs. What impressed him the most was the fact that the Navy SEALs who collaborated with the production company became so frustrated over the fact that they were not being portrayed accurately and were subsequently invited by the producers to play key roles in the cast.

Richard talked non-stop with his father about how actual real-life SEALS were in the movie. His dad told Richard that the same was true about the Senior Drill Instructor in his favorite movie, *Full Metal Jacket*. Kubrick had originally cast a different actor in the roll. Tom Colceri, the actor who played the Helicopter Door-Gunner, was originally cast as Senior Drill Instructor Hartman. Colceri never got to film a single scene once Kubrick viewed a videotape of R. Lee Ermey, a former United States Marine Corps Drill Instructor who had been hired as a consultant to assist with the boot camp portion of the film. In the videotape, Ermey screamed non-stop insults for fifteen minutes, never once repeating himself. The man managed to achieve the impressive feat while being pelted with tennis balls and oranges.

Richard became obsessed with being a Navy SEAL; he spent his teenage years getting into the best shape of his life. He'd studied everything he could about a vast array of weapons and tactics. His favorite book of all time was *SEAL Team Six: Memoirs of an Elite Navy SEAL Sniper* by Howard E. Wasdin. He had lost count of how many times he'd read the book; he read it at least once a year and still carried the original copy with him always.

Richard graduated from high school, broke up with Monique before their son was even born, and set out to achieve his dream of becoming a SEAL. Richard's father was pleased that he ended things with Monique. His father told everyone it was because he also wanted to see Richard become a SEAL, but Richard knew better. Though his father would deny it and pretend to be outraged if anyone said it aloud, he was a racist. Mr. Dupree had never uttered a racist comment around his children, but it was clear to Richard when he saw the look of disgust on his father's face anytime he turned the channel to find Oprah or any Tyler Perry show staring back at him.

When Richard brought Monique home for the first time he wondered how his father would react. His father was polite and cordial to Monique as Richard expected. Mr. Dupree raised his children to treat others with respect and to display impeccable manners in his home. However, Richard could tell that his father did not approve of his girlfriend and preyed upon Richard's frustrations with teenage love as an opportunity to drive the two apart any chance he got.

Monique wanted to get married before the baby was born and even tried to convince Richard that she would be the perfect military wife. She swore she would live on base and wouldn't have any problem with Richard being deployed for long periods of time. Richard did not want to be burdened by a family and wanted to devote himself one hundred percent to joining the ranks of the world's most elite fighting force.

Richard enlisted the day after his high school graduation and left a pregnant Monique behind to join the Navy. After the baby was born, Monique sent him pictures on a weekly basis hoping to change his mind about marriage. Richard fell in love with the son he never met but buried the emotions deep down and worked even harder to become a SEAL.

Having spent most of his childhood obsessing about everything to do with the SEALs, Richard breezed through the selection process. He impressed the instructors with his vast tactical knowledge and skills with a long-range rifle. It was clear to everyone in his graduating class that Richard had a bright future ahead of him.

Richard did indeed have an amazing career. His childhood dreams became the most amazing reality he could imagine. However, his life would not be complete unless Monique and their son were a part of it. Monique never once tried to collect child support from him. She knew that to do so would only drive him further away. Richard saved up as much leave as he could and after calling in a lot of favors, traveled back to his hometown for a month so he could marry his high-school sweetheart and raise their three-year-old son.

The wedding was small and simple. Richard wore his dress uniform and Monique wore her grandmother's wedding dress. Much to Richard's surprise, his father gave him his own wedding band for Monique to place on Richard's finger. Richard had never been happier in his entire life.

Monique did keep her word on becoming a dutiful military wife. She never complained about Richard being away weeks and months at a time. Her complaints would only serve as a distraction for Richard, and his life depended on him being completely focused while he was on a mission.

Richard knew that his wife was lonely. His own guilt led him to believe that she was not being faithful to him while he was deployed around the world taking down terrorist cells. He began to become suspicious of any man, married or single, who knew Monique. His wife was stunning to look at; every man was spellbound by her beauty. Richard added man after man to his list of suspects and was convinced that one of them was having sex with his wife.

The suspicions faded away when their second child, a daughter, was born. Richard adored his little princess and could hardly tear himself away. Monique and the kids would wait anxiously by the computer for Richard to Skype them night after night. When he had down time, which was rare, he would dig his iPad out of his bag and look at the beautiful faces of his little babies growing up before his very eyes.

One night he Skyped his wife to discover the kids were already in bed. He'd been talking with his wife for over an hour when her cellphone rang from across the room.

"Oh, sorry hon, I'm expecting a call. Hold on a sec."

"Sure, sure, go ahead, not a big deal."

Monique walked to the other side of the room out of view of the webcam and answered her phone. Richard could only hear one side of the conversation, and he did not like what he heard.

"Hey, Bryan! ... "Yes" ... "Thanks, yeah, I'm online with him right now.".... "I know! I'm so excited!" …….. "Two weeks from tomorrow, I can't wait to see him." ……. "Yeah, I'm excited about tomorrow, been looking forward to it all week." …………. "Martha is watching the kids so we should be able to leave around lunch." ………… "OK, I'll remember, I gotta go." ……. "OK, yeah, bye."

Monique walked back into view of the computer and sat down. "OK, sorry about that, sweetie. That was Bryan."

"Who is Bryan? Where are you going with him?" Richard tried his best not sound like he was accusing his wife of anything.

His wife smiled and smirked. "Oh that, I didn't know you could hear me. It's nothing; he's a friend of Julia's. His sister is getting married tomorrow, and Bryan asked Julia to go with him but didn't really say it was a date. Julia really likes him and asked me to go along in case Bryan didn't make a move. She didn't want to be stuck there with no one to talk to if things got weird."

"Oh, yeah, cool. Sounds like fun. Gonna be gone all day? Spending the night?"

"No, just for the day. They're having a dinner reception and we'll drive back that night."

"Oh, well that sounds like a lot of fun. Make sure you guys don't drink too much, and make it home safe."

"I will honey. Will you be able to Skype us tomorrow? The kids really want to see you."

"I doubt it. I might not be able to call again until right before we leave to come home."

"OK, I understand, baby. I'm getting tired. Hope you can call before you come back.

"Me, too."

"I love you, baby. Bye."

Richard lifted two of his fingers to his lips, kissed them and pressed his fingers to the screen. Then the screen went black.

Richard was unable to contact his family until he returned stateside. He pulled out his iPad and tried to Skype his wife but got no answer. He dialed her cell and again got no answer. He texted her and got no reply. It was past 11pm; his wife should have been home with the kids.

When he got to his home early the next morning he discovered his wife asleep in their bed. He walked into the kids' room and woke up his sweet little princess. She rubbed her eyes, looked at her father and beamed with pure joy. He kissed her face repeatedly, which made her giggle. He knew that his son was a very deep sleeper and would not wake easily, so he left him to whatever little boys dreamed about. He carried his precious daughter into his bedroom and sat on the bed next to his wife.

She awoke and couldn't believe her husband was sitting next to her. He wasn't due to be home until the afternoon. She couldn't figure out if he was really home or if she was dreaming.

"You're home!" He leaned down and kissed her on the cheek. "Yes, dear, I'm home."

She smiled at him.

"I tried contacting you last night to let you know I would be home early. Where were you?"

"Busy."

"Doing what?"

"It doesn't matter. What matters is that you're home." She sat up and hugged him, kissing his cheek and giggling, much like their daughter, in perfect glee.

Richard relented. He always made it a point to avoid arguing with his wife when he had been away for a long time. She deserved better.

The rest of the morning and afternoon were filled with playtime with the kids. Monique loved to watch her husband play with their children; she was so proud to have a loving husband, who was also a devoted father. The family went out to a restaurant that night. Richard couldn't have been happier, that is, until Monique's smartphone rang.

"Hey, now isn't a good time. ... I can't talk right now, let me call you back. ...... Ok, ok, give me a minute."

Monique excused herself and disappeared to the other side of the restaurant. A few minutes later she returned and sat down like nothing had happened.

Richard tried not to show his frustration in front of his kids. "Who was that?"

Monique smiled and waved her hand away, dismissing his question. "Oh, it was nobody." She turned her attention to the kids so that Richard would not ask again.

The family returned home and went to bed after a very tiring and eventful day. Once his wife was asleep, Richard grabbed her cellphone and went into the bathroom. He looked at the call history, determined to know who had interrupted their dinner.

It was Bryan.

Richard spent the next thirty minutes reviewing every detail of his wife's communication with this asshole named Bryan. They called each other every single day during Richard's last deployment. Richard matched up the dates to all of his deployments from the previous year to discover that Bryan only called when Richard was not stateside. The phone calls were frequent and many lasted for hours. Growing angrier with each passing minute, Richard moved on to his wife's text messages. If he had any doubts, the texts messages from Bryan erased them completely.

Hey girl, call me.

I just want you to know that u are my closest friend and I'm thankful u are always here for me.

U coming over tnght?

When are u getting here?

Make sure u put on the dress Monica gave u

Stop freakin out no 1 is going to find out

OMG you're soooo bad! Stop it before Daddy gets the belt! LOL

Did u make it home yet? I had a lot of fun tonight. Call me when u get home.

I know u felt guilty about last night. I'm sorry. Call me.

Richard couldn't take it anymore. He didn't need to read any further; the last text sealed the deal. He knew his marriage was over. Instead of letting himself break down and cry, he instead turned his sadness into rage. At first he focused his anger on himself for marrying that cheating bitch in the first place. He had made the right choice when he joined the Navy. Breaking up with her had been the right thing to do; he couldn't believe he was stupid enough to marry her.

In his fury he had completely forgotten about his wife's lover. Rage poured over him like hot lava. He knew that he needed to stay in the bathroom and not come out or he would do serious harm to the mother of his children. Instead, he took deep breaths and focused his mind like the top-notch Navy SEAL he had spent his life training to become. He thought about his next move.

He was going to kill that mother fucker.

Richard had no intentions of ending his stellar military career or going to prison. He would bide his time and plan the death of his wife's lover, even if it took a very long time to accomplish. Richard was certain he could get away with the crime; he had made a career out of slipping into hostile territory to murder the enemy and get out undetected. Accidents happened all the time. People died of mysterious illnesses; some people even vanished into thin air never to be heard from again. The possibilities were endless. Richard knew he would not be satisfied until he could see the life fade from the man's eyes. He wanted the piece of shit to know why he was dying.

The first step of his plan was to meet this guy and

enthusiastically shake his hand, thanking him for keeping his wife company while he was gone. He did not want the asshole or his wife to have any indication that he knew about their secret love affair. The next step would be to meet Julia, his wife's friend and supposed love interest of Bryan's. He knew the bitch would lie and cover for his wife, but he was confident that he would be able to catch her in the falsehood. He thought about Monique dropping his children off with his Aunt Martha and running off to cheat on him. He knew it wasn't going to take long to figure out exactly where they had gone.

Richard was satisfied that he had made the right decision to be patient and not do anything rash. He slipped back into bed and tried to go back to sleep. He had to get up early to take his family to church.

In the morning, the family loaded up the car and began the thirty-five minute drive to the Winchester Street Baptist Church. Richard had on his Class A uniform as he always did on his rare visits to the church. He found a seat for himself amongst the crowd of five hundred. Monique was singing in the choir, and his children were at Children's Worship on the other side of the campus. Richard was one of a handful of white faces in a sea of black ones. The fact had never once bothered him; he always felt welcome in the congregation. Richard had always wanted to fly his parents out to go to church with him. He would have a blast watching his father try to swallow his racism. Hell, the old man would probably choke on it before he took his seat.

When the congregation finished singing, the pastor took the podium and the choir quietly dispersed into two hallways. Each hallway would take them around to the back of the sanctuary so they could take their seats with the least amount of disturbance to the congregation. Richard tried to pretend that he was paying attention the sermon. After a few minutes had passed and most of the choir was seated, he shifted in his seat, checking to see if Monique had made it into the sanctuary after a quick pit stop to check on the kids. Richard sat uncomfortably in his seat for ten minutes and pulled out his smartphone to text his wife.

Where are you?

A full ten minutes elapsed before she replied.

Flo is here and I'm cramping real bad, went home.

Richard searched his memory to the night before; he was certain he had not seen any tampons or other tell-tale signs in the trash can. He could not recall seeing the usual boxes of feminine products near the sink as his wife had always left them when it was her time of the month. He thought as hard as he could about what exactly happened during the menstrual cycle and like most men, really had no idea. All he knew was cramping and bleeding were involved and it lasted for five days. Or was it seven?

Plus, Monique had never just left him and the kids at church unless it was something they had discussed in advance. It was obvious - his wife was lying to him while he was in the presence of the Lord Almighty.

Did the woman have no shame at all? She couldn't wait a few weeks for him to leave the country before she started things back up with Bryan? The night before he installed a GPS app on her smartphone and deleted the shortcut from the home screen. It would track her whereabouts anywhere on the planet as long as she didn't turn it off. He pulled up the app, certain that his wife was not home and he was right. The trusty GPS indicated that she was less than two miles from the church.

Now he had Bryan's address.

He decided to trip her up and texted her.

Poor thing, you need me to come home?

The reply was practically instantaneous.

No, I'm fine. Take the kids to your aunt's house for the day. I can't deal with them today and Martha really wants to see you.

Richard's Aunt Martha was a thirty-minute drive from his house, a full forty-five minutes from where he sat at the moment. He replied.

OK.

Richard took control of his anger so he could think clearly. He wanted to do some surveillance and relished the opportunity to get his plan underway immediately. The good pastor was known for his very long sermons, so Richard had plenty of time to slip out, drive to the man's house and check out the situation. He was already thinking about pulling a detailed report on Bryan. He would be back in plenty of time to pick up the kids.

Richard exited the sanctuary, exchanging smiles with a few of the faithful on the way. He had no idea who they were but they clearly knew him. Once he was in the foyer, he stopped and thought for a minute. He realized that he needed to make sure the kids were attended to in case he needed extra time and couldn't make it back to pick them up.

On his way to Children's Worship, he knew he had to come up with a reasonable excuse and decided that his wife had already come up with a lie he could use. He was going to tell them that his wife was not feeling well, and he needed to take her home. He was also going to add that his wife really didn't want the kids to miss church on her account and that he might be late making it back to pick them up.

He made it to the Activities Building and walked in the back, looking for his kids. He scanned the crowd of singing children and began to worry. Seeing the look of panic on his face, a kind old woman suddenly perked up her head and walked over to Richard.

"Hello, dear, are you looking for your angels?" She smiled and placed her hands in his.

"Yes, ma'am." Richard returned the smile.

"Yes, dear. Things were getting too crowded in here so Mr. and Mrs. Jefferson took some of the younger ones to the nursery to play."

"Thank you so much." Richard smiled and turned to walk out.

"Is everything alright, dear?"

"Yes, ma'am. I returned from overseas yesterday, and I just have to see them."

"Oh that's just wonderful dear. They are so precious at

this age."

"Yes, ma'am. They sure are." Richard took a step back towards the door.

"Are you going to stay for the potluck, dear?"

"That sounds great, we just might do that" Richard lied, trying desperately to leave.

"Look forward to seeing you and your lovely wife; she has the most beautiful voice, and I just think the world of her!"

You wouldn't if you knew what an adulterous whore she is, thought Richard. The woman finally let Richard leave and once he was in the hallway, he couldn't remember how to get to the nursery. He could have asked the old woman, but she would have delayed him further, and he was losing time he didn't have. Richard scanned the hallways and looked for a sign to lead him. Once he finally figured out where he was going, he walked as fast as he could without drawing attention should someone see him.

Once he arrived at the nursery he reached to open the door to discover that it was locked. *Why the hell is the door locked?* He knew he was in the right place because he could hear the children playing on the other side of the door. He knocked and waited. After a few seconds he heard a click and the door cracked half an inch. He stood back expecting the door to open towards him. It did not. He opened the door and walked into the most confusing thing he had ever witnessed in his life. His mind took several seconds to process what he was seeing and once he was able to understand what was happening, he froze.

All of the children were stark naked.

Thirteen children, ranging in age from two to eight were in the room naked as the day they were born. The children not yet old enough to know shame were running around the room giggling, free from the burden of clothing.

One of those children was his daughter.

Richard knew the trouble his wife had putting clothes on their little girl when she was dried off from her bath. She often slipped out the towel her mother wrapped around her and ran around the house laughing as her mother chased her down to put her into her pajamas.

When his daughter saw him standing in the doorway, she squealed and ran over to him.

"Daaaaaaaadddddyyy!"

On the other side of the room, Oswald Jefferson opened his eyes and looked at Richard in pure terror. He had been sitting as close to the table as he could, his right arm pumping up and down, his head kicked back and his eyes closed tightly.

Richard's adorable girl stood at his feet. She looked up at his face and beamed a smile. Her face looked like a tan porcelain doll. Her mousy little voice practically made Richard cry. "Daddy! We show in Gawd we not shamed our bodies! It's fun!" Richard's second born returned to the middle of the room and resumed playing.

Richard had no idea what to do. Tears streamed down his face. He didn't know if he should grab his children and run down the hall screaming his head off like the devil was chasing him or let his mind snap so insanity could rescue him from this nightmare. He looked at his innocent toddler playing in the room and realized that she had no idea anything inappropriate was happening. She could live the rest of her life and probably not remember this day. It was then that Richard remembered his six-year-old son was also in the room.

Richard scanned the room to find his son and two other boys standing in the corner, cupping their genitals and crying. Richard would find out later from his lawyer that the three boys had tried to cover themselves with toys or books and Oswald spanked them for being ashamed of their bodies. The pedophile also told the boys that if they told anyone about their special worship, they and their families would burn in hell for all eternity.

Richard was shaking to the point of collapse; the blood racing to his head caused it to beat like a drum. The man sitting at the table might have lived had he not opened his mouth.

"Now, now, now…uh...Mister, you just hold on now a minute! Everything is just fine! You hear me? Just fine! I swear things are just fine! This is not what you think, you just don't understand. Just let me explain! PLEASE!!"

Richard let out an awful moan that began as a cry and slowly escalated into a dull roar.

Seeing the statuesque, chiseled jawed soldier glaring at him, fists balled into rocks, Oswald knew his life was about to end. "Stop now! STOP!! PLEASE!!! Look here now, just listen! I swear I never laid one hand on them, and they didn't see me do anything down there," the monster nodded towards his crotch.

Richard's son looked to his father with complete and total shame; the look on his face would forever curse Richard Dupree's slumber until the day he died. His son spoke to him through sobs and said the last thing Richard would be able to remember until moments later when he was covered in blood with two broken hands.

His naked son was standing in front of him, tears drenching his face, snot running down his chin. "Daddy, I'm so sorry! I'm so sorry you and Mommy are going to hell. Please don't be mad at me, please Daddy, please!"

Richard let out a scream that petrified the children and could be heard by the congregation on the other side of the campus. He then leapt across the room, knocking down chairs along the way. He grabbed the table with both hands and flung it into the wall, smashing it into tinder. The terrified children ran from the room; however, Richard's son and the two other boys were trapped behind the broken table.

With one hand, Richard seized the frail sixty-one year old's throat and lifted him up onto the wall, his heels kicking three inches off the floor. With his other hand, he grabbed the man's erection and scrotum into a vice grip, simultaneously pushing up on the man's wind pipe and pulling down with his other arm. The muscles and ligaments in the man's groin snapped as his scrotum ruptured, causing him to cry out in anguish. Richard threw him into the adjacent wall and watched as Oswald Jefferson crumpled to the floor, his neck broken. Unaware that the pedophile was dead, Richard attacked his prone body, savagely pounding his face with both fists.

Members of the Winchester Street Baptist Church began to pour into the room. A deacon would later testify in court that he could hear the bones in Richard's hands break as he repeatedly pummeled the corpse's face. It took six men to tear Richard away from the mangled corpse on the floor. Richard broke the first man's wrist, the second's arm. The remaining four were able to trap Richard under a dog pile, covering themselves in Oswald's blood in the process. Completely unaware of what had sparked the chaos, Sheriff Robert Jefferies ran from the sanctuary and drew his weapon on Richard while tossing a set of cuffs to one of the men atop the pile.

Master Chief Petty Officer Richard Dupree, United States Navy, could no longer call himself a Navy SEAL. His military career ended that day in disgrace.

CHAPTER TEN

Chief Maxwell Harris sat at his desk, worried about the task at hand. In twenty-four hours Hurricane Maxine would make landfall near the eastern end of Galveston Island. Maxine was a beast. She was a powerful category five and was only gaining strength and speed. The destruction to Max's little town was going to be complete. Over three-quarters of the structures in the town would take in at least ten feet of water. The remainder of the town would be subject to very high winds and torrential rain. Max could hardly imagine the damage that would be done to the city of Houston, but that was not his concern. He needed to focus on what was important - saving the lives of the people in Santa Fe, Texas.

Max was hoping against hope that the report Elizabeth gave on her drive through the neighborhoods wasn't true. She went from subdivision to subdivision and no one seemed to care one way or the other that a massive hurricane was headed right for them. They were content to keep their heads in the sand and hope the problem would just fix itself. Now that a mandatory evacuation order was in effect, they were required to leave under the letter of the law. If they remained behind, they would be fined if they required any emergency services. If such emergency services resulted in loss of life or damage to government property, they would face prosecution.

Max called a meeting of the Police Department, the Volunteer Fire Department, and every city employee on the payroll. The "Captain" of the Volunteer Fire Department was sulking; he thought he should be running the show. Max couldn't care less about the man's insecurity as long as he kept his mouth shut and did what he was told.

"OK, people, listen up; time is critical here." The noise level dropped to a dull roar, but many people kept sipping coffee and chatting. Max was growing impatient. "Excuse me; may I have your attention?" A few people turned and looked at him, but many continued to ignore him.

"HEY! If it's not too much trouble, can you people shut up and listen?" You could hear a pin drop. "Maybe some of you don't know what is going on here, but we have less than twenty-four hours to get the people in this town out of harm's way. I do not have the time or the patience to tolerate anyone who isn't focused and determined to do their job! If you have better things to do and don't care about keeping your job, then get the hell out, NOW!"

"Dude, calm down, man. In case you forgot, you're not my boss. Just say what you have to say, and let's do what we have to do. Sheesh!" The man rolling his eyes was Deputy Mayor Tom Williams. Tom was not a fan of the chief of police. When Max's predecessor retired and Max took over as chief, Tom was very vocal in his objection to Max getting the job. The deputy mayor thought the chief of police was a lazy smartass who lacked any sign of motivation. Most of the people in the room, with the exception of Elizabeth, agreed.

"Tom, I'm only going to say this once because we don't have the time for me to repeat it. Check your attitude before I lock you up in a holding cell. I am your boss. I'm the boss of every single person inside the city limits, and don't you forget it. In a state of emergency, sole authority in all matters rests with the highest ranking law enforcement official. You don't like it, take it up with the governor of the state of Texas! You have anything else to say?"

The deputy mayor was shocked. He didn't know that Max had that kind of passion in him. The chief was staring at Tom.

"I said, do you have anything else to say?" Max had his eyes locked on Tom Williams.

Tom looked around at everyone in the room. They were deliberately avoiding his gaze. He looked back at the chief, who was still staring at him. He was clearly waiting for an answer.

"No, I don't, please continue," Tom whispered and looked down.

"Good, now let's get started. We've printed up flyers to pass out to the citizens. It clearly states the mandatory evacuation order and the consequences for violating it. I want to make one thing very clear to everyone in this room. If we receive any 9-1-1 calls while the storm is on top of us, we will not be responding. I will not put anyone's life in danger by ordering my own officers to drive around in a category five hurricane. I encourage each and every one of you to pass along this information to the local citizens. Hopefully that will light a fire under their asses and get them moving. Also on the flyer are the evacuation routes. Once they make their way to I-45, all lanes of traffic will be heading north. For those of you who don't know, that's called contraflow. Once they hit Houston, they can go either direction on Loop 610 and head north. Inform them that once they get to Interstate 10, they might be diverted east or west to an alternate route leading north."

"Excuse me, Chief?" Deputy Collins had his hand raised. He didn't want to be dressed down like the deputy mayor.

"Yes, Brad?"

"We are going to have a hard time convincing people to leave when they don't have any gas."

"Yes, Brad, you're exactly right. We've planned for that. Each of you will be given gas vouchers to pass out. Each household will get one, and I mean only one voucher. The voucher is good for ten gallons of gas at the city garage or one of the three largest gas stations in the city. I'm deputizing everyone in this room. Every one of you will be given credentials and a police windbreaker. If you don't have a firearm, one will be issued to you. We will maintain order at all four of these locations. Each site will have a member of the police force in command; any citizen without a voucher will be turned away. Any citizen trying to obtain more than ten gallons will be stopped. It is crucial that we maintain order and not let things get out of control. Does anyone have any questions?"

"How long are we expected to perform this task?" one of the volunteer fireman asked.

"All non-law enforcement personnel are expected to remain and perform their duty for the next twelve hours, at which time they are free to evacuate or remain behind in the command post set up at the high school."

None of the police officers in the room needed to ask how long they would be staying. They knew they were in it for the long haul. They had already made arrangements for their families to leave immediately before the roads got too clogged.

"If there are no more questions, you have your assigned streets and you know what to do."

The room quickly cleared out. Elizabeth had been smiling

at Max the entire time, clearly impressed with her boss. She waited for the last person to leave the room and walked over to him.

"Elizabeth, I don't know how you could be smiling at a time like this."

"Maxwell, I have never seen you take charge like that. I knew you had it in you. I must say I am very impressed. You know Tom is going to try and get you fired for what you pulled. Once things get back to normal, people are going to be talking about that all over town."

"You like that? The last thing we need is a pissing contest and that asshole trying to take charge and completely screwing things up. He probably thought I was a pushover."

"Well, it's more than that, boss."

"Really? Do tell."

"He is a forty-nine percent owner of one of the gas stations you got giving away free gas."

Max laughed. "Well that explains things! And here I thought he wanted to be the Big Man in Charge! But it's simply about money, huh? What a scumbag."

Elizabeth sat down in the chair across from the chief. She undid her ponytail and let her long, flowing hair spill down onto her shoulders. She sighed and slumped back. The chief was taken aback by her beauty.

"What?"

"I've just never seen your hair down. You always have it pulled back" Max smiled.

Elizabeth ran her fingers through her hair and pulled it back up into a ponytail. "How bad is this really going to get? Are we on our own?"

"Computer, bring up the latest Emergency Action Message from TX-DOT."

A detailed overlay of south Texas appeared on the screen across the room. Elizabeth turned around in her chair and studied the map. "What am I looking at?"

"Well, I must have stared at that thing for an hour after the evac order was issued."

"I was wondering what you were doing while I was carrying out your instructions."

"I'm hoping that I'm reading this wrong and that they're working triple time to get the problem fixed."

"What problem?"

"Five miles south of the loop, they have the southbound lanes closed and have one lane diverted to the north side. It's going to be a bottleneck if they don't get those southbound lanes opened back up."

"Jesus Christ!"

"It gets worse. I-45 between Houston and Dallas has construction in four different spots. I don't know how they think they are going to get everyone out of here in time. People south of the loop are going to have a hard time getting out of here."

"Isn't that an official evacuation route? I thought they couldn't close down more than one lane at a time."

"I thought so, too. Look at the map and see for yourself. Please tell me I'm wrong."

Elizabeth walked over to the wall and studied the map closely. "You're right. This could be a disaster in the making."

"Computer, pull up the traffic cams I studied earlier today."

Three separate windows popped up. Elizabeth studied them first to figure out where the traffic cameras were located and then to figure out the flow of traffic.

"Son of a bitch!"

"I know. They better work fast; in twelve hours a whole bunch of people are going to be parked in their graves if they don't hurry up and figure something out."

"What do you want me to do now, boss?"

"You're riding with me. Let's go."

Chief Harris and Sergeant Reed climbed into the chief's SUV and headed for the city garage. Max pulled two pills out of his shirt pocket and swallowed them. His hip and knee were throbbing. If they weren't in the middle of a crisis, he would have pulled out the cane and made every effort to not leave his office chair for the rest of the day. Max thought ahead to the surgery he had planned in a few short weeks and tried not to let the overwhelming feeling of despair wash over him. The surgery was surely not going to happen anytime soon. He didn't know how much longer he could endure this pain. If things got worse, he was ready to start doing heroin, job be damned. He would rather be a junkie than live like this for the rest of his life.

"You know if anyone else is doing this free gas thing you're doing?" Elizabeth put her hand on the chief's leg. She knew he was in terrible pain.

"I hope so. It's the only thing that makes sense. It's the right call. Most people don't keep half a tank of gas in their car. You here for Ike?"

"No, I was in my senior year up north of Dallas in Plano. My uncle brought his family up to stay with us."

"How long did it take him to get up there?"

"Eighteen hours. He usually makes the drive in six."

"Sounds about right. You think people could sit in a car for that long today? Think about how many cars will run out of gas, get stuck and block traffic."

"It would be a nightmare. What do you think most people will do?"

Max took a deep breath and thought for a second. "I think most people will just stay home and hope for the best. They don't have the money for gas and know they wouldn't make it far anyway, so why bother?"

"I hope you're wrong about that. Any word on school buses being used to get people out?"

"I wish it were that easy."

"What do you mean?"

"We might be one of the dozen states that still have public schools, but that's not saying much. More and more schools are closing, leaving the ones that are still open extremely overcrowded. Then the kids just drop out. When the schools close, they auction off everything that isn't nailed down to help keep the operating schools running. There aren't nearly enough school buses to do any kind of good."

The two officers didn't say anything else. The city garage was less than a minute away. They turned into the front entrance and parked near the back. They both stayed in the car and watched the team that had set up shop to supervise. A line had already begun to form outside the main gate. The team had used orange cones to designate a route to the main gas tanks. They were in the process of cordoning off an exit route to the back gate so that no one would linger around the tanks and cause a commotion. Max watched the team and was satisfied that things were moving along smoothly.

"Elizabeth, I owe you an apology."

"For what?"

"In the office, when you let down your hair..."

"You were staring at me like a horny teenager?"

Max's face turned beet red. "Yeah, that. That was unprofessional, and if it made you uncomfortable I sincerely apologize. I'm your boss, and the last thing I want is for you to feel uncomfortable around me. It won't happen again; I'm sorry."

"Lighten up, boss. I appreciate the apology, but it's not at all necessary. You should see me in a mini-skirt and heels."

"Elizabeth! Please!"

She leaned in towards her boss and smiled. "Now Chief, am I making you uncomfortable?"

Max smiled and shook his head. "Knock it off, Elizabeth. Did Roscoe say how much gas we'll be able to give out?"

"The tank is topped off and holds two and a half thousand gallons. We can cash in two hundred fifty vouchers here before we have to shut down."

Max rolled down his window and motioned for the team leader to come over. Deputy Collins quickly ran over to his boss.

"Yes, sir, Chief?"

"Make sure you keep a running total of how many vouchers you're cashing in. Ten gallons per voucher and not a drop more. At the entrance to the gate you need to have some sort of sign stating how many vouchers you can honor. Update the tally every ten vouchers. When it gets down to fifty, walk the line and count off fifty cars. Anyone after that will have to go somewhere else. Any questions?"

"Consider it done, boss."

"Outstanding, carry on."

Max rolled up his window and exited the garage. He drove to each gas station to check on the status of the operation. Once he was satisfied that things were running on schedule, he decided to take a tour of the neighborhoods just as Elizabeth had done.

What they saw gave Max a little hope. More than half the

homes in the neighborhood were being prepared for possible wind and rain damage. Sandbags could be seen at front doors, plywood nailed to windows. People could be seen packing up their cars and trailers.

"This is actually looking good. People are listening," Elizabeth said as she looked out the window.

"So far, so good. They just have to make it to the other side of Houston. We can't really worry about that; it's out of our hands. We just have to get them out of town."

"What do you want to do now, Boss?"

"How often are they checking in with you?"

"The free gas? Every hour."

"Let's make it every thirty minutes."

"Will do." Elizabeth grabbed her radio and gave the instruction.

"Boss, can we stop by my house?"

Max turned and looked at her. "Why?"

"Relax. I'm not going to change into my mini-skirt and heels. Just need to get my cat."

"Shit. Yeah, I need to get my cat, too."

"What? I didn't know you had a cat!"

"Yep."

"Wouldn't peg you as a cat person."

"You really think I'm a dog person?"

"Good point."

Arriving at Elizabeth's house, the two walked in, and the desk sergeant tossed her duty belt on the couch.

"Make yourself at home, Chief. I just need a minute or two. Damn cat hides when she takes a nap. She could be anywhere."

"OK, no rush. We could sit here and do nothing or go back to the station and do the same."

Elizabeth answered from the kitchen. "Yeah, not much else to do but sit and wait. We've done everything we can do, everything is on schedule. You want something to drink? Got soda, water, or... stuff we can't drink on duty. Soda or water?"

"Soda is fine."

Elizabeth brought him a can of soda and proceeded to go room to room looking for her cat. She managed to find Callie sleeping in the bed frame. She had clawed away the corner of the cover to the box spring and loved to climb up in there and disappear. Elizabeth scooped her up into the pet carrier and grabbed a bag of cat food.

"Ready to go?"

"Yep."

They loaded up the SUV and drove a few miles to Max's house. Elizabeth knew where he lived but had never been inside. She doubted many people had ever been invited in. Max was a grumpy bastard and was good at pushing people away. They pulled up in the driveway and Max got out. Elizabeth hesitated.

"What are you doing? You coming?"

"Uh, sure. I guess. Didn't think you liked company."

"You think I'd make you wait in the car? Be serious! C'mon."

Elizabeth got out of the car and followed Maxwell into his house. She had to ask herself what she was so nervous about. It wasn't like she expected a Barbie Doll museum or trophy room of women's heads to be on the other side of the door. She was nervous because Max was actually inviting her into his home. It was like he was sharing something with her that he shared with no one else.

"Make yourself at home; my cat's the same as yours. No idea where he hides when he sleeps."

"What's his name?"

"Herbie."

"Cute name."

Elizabeth sat on the couch, wondering what kind of computer setup he had going. It was always amazing to watch him on the computer in his office. He was lightening fast, multiple windows opening and closing at once. His hands directed the screen like a maestro conducting a symphony.

"Hey, Boss, mind if get online?"

"Sure, just raise both of your hands in a stop motion and say 'Computer.' "

"Thanks."

"Sure."

Elizabeth didn't know if she should be seated or standing to turn on the computer. She felt silly asking, so she just stood up and raised both her hands.

"Computer."

The wall on the other side of the room sprang to life. A sixteen by nine foot screen powered up. The resolution and crispness were breathtaking. It was as if the wall faded away and you could walk inside the screen. With the naked eye you could discern no pixels or screen refresh. It made the office computer look like an antique.

"Thought you needed online?" Max walked back into the room carrying his black and white cat.

"Uh, yeah. I was just freaking out over this screen."

"Yeah, I've been building it for like ten years. I just keep upgrading it. I always keep the graphics card top of the line. Watch this."

Max raised both his hands and in a space of a few seconds his hands zipped around like he was using sign language. The screen dropped down to the floor and a doorway appeared. There appeared to be another room beyond the doorway, fully furnished and just waiting for its occupants.

"Wow!" Elizabeth's eyes were huge.

"Yeah, I've tricked quite a few people into trying to walk into that room. It's hilarious when they hit the wall. What did you need to check?"

"Oh, yeah. I just wanted to vid-con with my parents and see if they're okay. Voice interface or do I have to learn your computer sign-language?"

"Voice interface is fine." Max smiled.

"Computer, open a vid-con with Reed47AT."

Two windows opened. One was a small window that showed Elizabeth and Max sitting on the couch. The other window with a flashing circle contained the word "Connecting" underneath it. After about thirty seconds, the flashing circle was replaced with the words: "Unable to connect, would you like to leave a message?"

"Close window." Elizabeth said.

"Everything alright, Elizabeth? Are they evacuating?"

"No, they're in North Texas. I was just checking to see if they'd heard from my uncle and his family; they were heading up to stay with them."

"I'm sure everything is fine. Still plenty of time."

"Yeah, I'll just check back."

"Elizabeth, I wanted to thank you for all your help. I couldn't have done all this without you."

"Not a problem, Boss. I gotta say I'm glad you stepped up and really took charge. You've surprised everyone. I don't think anyone knew you had it in you."

"Well, I may be a disgruntled, lazy bastard, but I can handle my own when the situation calls for it."

"What made you so disgruntled? You are the smartest person I've ever known. You could have, uh..."

"Done something more with my life? It's okay, you can say it."

"Well, I thought it would be rude."

"You? I've never known you to hold back from the truth, no matter how hard it hits."

"Fair enough then, answer the question."

"Well, life has had a way of kicking me in the balls anytime I try to stand up, so I figured I would just stay down. A life without ambition is actually quite peaceful. I've enjoyed it ever since without regret."

"Your injury have anything to do with it?"

"My injury has a lot to do with it."

"Care to elaborate?"

"I would not."

"Fair enough, thought I would ask."

"I mean no offense by it, it's just that the story that goes along with it is hard for me to talk about."

"I understand. It's a shame things happened to you that would cause you to just give up on life."

"Nah, then you wouldn't have me for a boss." Max smiled and winked at Elizabeth.

Elizabeth returned the smile. "And your sparkling personality."

Max and Elizabeth sat on the couch and continued to stare at each other. Elizabeth's gorgeous green eyes filled with passion and life as she looked into the eyes of her boss. Max returned her gaze with a steely, unflinching confidence that only served to arouse Elizabeth's passion. They both knew what was coming next. Neither one of them doubted it. The only unresolved issue was who would make the first move.

The man and woman sitting on the couch were ripped out of their hypnotic stare by their radios. Three short beeps indicated that an emergency message was to follow.

"All radio units, respond to the Super Mart on 3rd Street. Shots have been fired. Chief Harris, acknowledge."

"Acknowledge. Chief Harris and Sergeant Reed, enroute. ETA three minutes."

"10-4, Chief. I've notified County; they're 15 minutes out."

The chief of police and the operations sergeant bolted out the door and were on the road in fifteen seconds flat. The siren and the flashing lights cleared a path straight the Super Mart on 3rd Street. They made it to the parking lot of the gas station in two and a half minutes. It was pouring down rain, and the sky was dark and ominous.

Max stepped out of the vehicle and headed for the entrance to the gas station, where he addressed the deputy in charge.

"Thank God you're here, Chief. Things got really ugly and they might get worse." Deputy Brandon McGee was visibly shaken, but was keeping it together.

"Start from the beginning, Brandon. What happened?"

"Well, things were running along just fine. People were patient, waiting in line; they handed over their voucher, got their ten gallons and left. Then, there started to be some snags in the order of things."

"Like what?"

"Well, small stuff really. 'I forgot my voucher' or 'my neighbor gave me his voucher' ... stuff like that."

"Damn right my neighbor gave me his! He ain't goin' nowhere! Why can't I use his?" A scruffy looking, overweight man in overalls was yelling from ten feet away.

"Hey, you! Come over here!" Chief Harris pointed at the man and motioned for him to come over.

The man looked shocked at first, then walked over to the two police officers.

"Yeah?"

"First of all, I was having a private conversation with my

deputy; I don't appreciate you interrupting."

"Well, I just don't unders..."

"Do you know how to read?"

"Huh? What'd you say to me?"

"Let me repeat that for you. Do you know how to read?"

"Of course I can read!"

"Read this."

Max took a gas voucher out of his front shirt pocket and handed it to Overalls Man.

"You want me to read this?"

"I want you to read that, yes."

The man read very slowly. "The bearer of this voucher is entitled to ten gallons of gasoline at any of the four locations listed on the back of this card. Limit one voucher per household. One use only. Voucher is not redeemable for cash and must be used in person. Voucher is not transferable."

"Good! That answer your question?"

Overalls Man had a look of frustration as he walked away, defeated.

Max turned back to his deputy. "You like that, Brandon?"

Deputy McGee was smiling and shaking his head. "Man, wish I would have thought of that; you made that look so easy."

"Continue, Deputy, I need to know what is going on before County gets here and tries to take over."

"Oh, yeah. Anyway, these two guys show up in pickups, and skip ahead of everyone. They got their beds full of gas cans. Knew it was going to be trouble. They said they were volunteering to fill up their gas cans and help us redeem vouchers towards the end of the line. I told them thanks, but no thanks, go back and wait in line. They start getting really pissy, sayin' they ain't got time to wait and they needed to get on the road quick. So, I says, 'Wait, thought you were going to stay and help pass out gas. Why you gotta leave all the sudden?' They realized I had just called them on their bullshit so one of 'em pulls out a pistol and waves it in the air. People start screaming and the two guys try to cut in line and fill up their tanks. By that time all five of us surrounded them and had drawn down on them. Before we could do anything, they jumped in their trucks and drove off. I figured keeping the gas station secure was more important so I let them drive off. Got their plates before they left and called out a BOLO."

"Nice work, Brandon. But that doesn't explain why I'm here."

"Yeah, there's more. A few minutes later they came screaming past and fired three shots at the gas station. Said they were coming back with friends. Man was in the gas station getting some candy and one of the shots clipped his left calf muscle. He's fine, just gonna need a few stitches."

Max turned to Elizabeth. "Call the other stations and tell them to look sharp, they may have trouble on the way. In fact, Elizabeth, take the SUV and head back to the city garage and take charge there. I'm gonna stay here and wait for County."

"I'm on it, Boss." Elizabeth was already jogging towards the SUV before Max finished his instructions. She turned on the lights and sirens and raced off towards the city garage.

Max turned back to Deputy McGee. "Brandon, I want you to set up barricades at the intersection. I want Elm turned into a one-way street all the way down to the next traffic light. Only one way into this gas station, the driveway on the north side of the station is closed. They come in, fill up, and leave out on the same street and drive away. The store is closed, gas only. No one enters the main building for any reason. No one loiters and only the driver is allowed to get out of the car to hand over his voucher and pump gas."

"Yes sir, Chief." Deputy McGee quickly shuffled off to communicate the instructions to his team.

"Son of a bitch." Max could see four cars from the County Sheriff's Office turning down the street. He knew that once they got there, they would assume that they would be taking over things like they had always done. Max only hoped that the county sheriff himself wasn't in one of those cars because he was not going to relinquish authority to anyone else. The four cars pulled into the gas station and fanned out.

"Chief Harris, what's the situation?" The tall deputy sheriff was scanning the parking lot. Max found it comical that the sun was nowhere to be seen but this guy was wearing sunglasses. Guess the shades made him feel in charge.

"Well, this is what I need from you fine gentlemen. I need

for one of you to stay here with me and the others to each head to one of these four locations; we are currently at location number two." He dug into his front pocket and produced four vouchers, handing them to each of the men.

"The hell is this?" Deputy Sunglasses read the front of the card and looked at his partner. "Is this a joke? You really giving out free gas? No wonder we're here. This craziness is ending now. OK, listen up..."

Max quickly interrupted. "That's right, listen up. I don't have time to explain the details. You're staying with me." Max pointed to Deputy Sunglasses. Max then pointed from right to left. "...look at the back of your cards. One, three, four. Get moving, we don't have time to waste. The officers at those locations will fill you in once you get there."

Deputy Sunglasses had a smile on his face and put his hand on Max's shoulder. "Chief, Chief, Chief...slow down. Max, tell me what's going on. You don't have to worry about anything, my boys and..."

"Son, take your fucking hand off my shoulder before I break it. I am the chief of police of this town and you will address me as such. Just because I let you boys come in here and play police officer so you can get an adrenaline hard-on does not mean that you're in charge of jack-shit. How old are you, son? And take those fucking glasses off before I knock them off."

"I'm twenty-six, Chief. I'm sorry, I just wanted to help." Deputy Sunglasses looked like a kid who had just been spanked in front of his friends at his own birthday party. He took off the sunglasses and looked at the ground.

"You were in fucking elementary school when I was a rookie. So learn some respect. Are we clear?"

"Yes, Chief."

"What are you assholes looking at? Don't you have someplace to be?" The other three deputies were frozen solid and speechless. They quickly snapped out of it, jumped back in their vehicles and sped off.

"What's your name, son?" Max looked at the deputy sheriff.

"I'm Deputy Eugene Shacklewood."

"May I call you Eugene?" Max looked at the young man and waited for him to make eye contact.

"Yes, Chief. Uh... my friends call me Gene."

"Ok, Gene it is. Look at me, Deputy. You got an ass chewing. Get over it, I've been doing this for twenty-one years, and I'm amazed I have an ass left. I don't have time for you to pout. I need you to focus and get in the game. The stakes are high, and I need you."

Deputy Shacklewood puffed up his chest and clenched his jaw. "Yes sir, Chief, you can count on me."

"Good. The reason you and your boys were called out here was some angry, pistol totin' citizens were trying to muscle their way in for some extra gas. My team here was not willing to let that happen. They drove off and returned a few minutes later, firing three shots at the gas station. They said they would be back with friends."

"Holy shit, Chief. That's crazy! What do you need me to do?"

"You see that uniformed officer over there? That's Deputy McGee, the team leader here. Check in with him and try to show some respect this time."

"Yes sir, Chief. Again, I'm sorry for the way I acted."

"Don't mention it; now get to work."

Max stood under the awning in front of the entrance and called each of his other stations for a status report. The rain and wind continued to worsen. The city garage was down to eighty-seven vouchers. His gas station had a hundred and two. The other two stations had thirty-six and sixty-four. This was going along smoothly, Max thought; people were getting gas and getting the hell out of Dodge. He just hoped there wouldn't be many in line when they ran out of gas. That's when things would get ugly. The gas station with only thirty-six vouchers left to redeem had walked the line and counted off the last car. Most of the unlucky cars turned around and left. The ones that stayed understood they were taking a risk but were willing to gamble on a few drops of gas remaining after the rush was over.

"Excuse me, Chief? I just wanted shake your hand and say thank you." An elderly man in his seventies had walked over to Max. "I asked that nice man if he could pump my gas for me so I could come over and speak with you."

Max accepted the handshake with a smile. "Thank you, sir. I appreciate that. You are the first person to actually offer any gratitude for my master plan, whatever good it will do."

The elderly man understood the subtle sarcasm. "You mean that most of these people won't make it past Houston?"

Max was shocked. "Yes, may I ask how you know that?"

"Well, unless they open up I-45 before the loop somehow, most of these people will be stuck in a very large parking lot on the interstate."

"Well, let's just say I want our people to at least have a fighting chance. You evacuating? I didn't catch your name."

"I'm Alfred. Yes, I'm evacuating, but I'm going to head west towards San Antonio. Figured I like my chances better further inland as opposed to drowning on this side when the Gulf comes pouring in." Alfred shifted his weight onto his cane and coughed into his sleeve.

"Not the best idea, but I understand your reasonin..."

Three short beeps on his radio interrupted the conversation. An emergency message was about to follow. Max tensed up and focused.

"All radio units, we have shots fired at the city garage. Two gunmen have opened fire, two injured, one dead. Officers on scene have returned fire. Chief Harris, please acknowledge."

"Copy that. I want all uniformed officers to assign another member of their team to take charge. Units 1-2 and 1-3, I want you to set up at the exit to the garage. County boys, I want you to block off the entrance and do your best to get civilians out of harm's way. Take instruction from Sergeant Reed until I arrive."

"Gene! Let's go! Keys! Now!"

Deputy Shacklewood tossed the keys to his cruiser to the Chief, and they jumped in and sped off. Max dug in his front shirt pocket and kicked back three pills. Eugene didn't notice.

Three short beeps.

"Be advised, we have an officer down. One gunman is presumed dead. The second is barricaded on the second floor of the garage admin office."

Maxwell Harris knew he had a second at best to make up his mind. Either freak out and get scared, or get angry and let adrenaline take over. He concentrated on the second gunman and let rage focus his mind. As they approached the scene, he could see lights flashing at both the entrance and exit to the garage. Good, that's covered. A second cruiser was fast approaching from the opposite end of the street. Soaked and frightened citizens were running all over the place, screaming, terrified. Max witnessed at least three traffic accidents right in front of him as cars smashed into each other in an attempt to speed away from the scene. Chief Harris ducked behind cars and made his way to the entrance of the garage. Keeping the second floor of the admin building directly above and out of his line of sight, he snuck behind some boxes and peeked over the top, trying to scan the concrete yard of the garage. Through the rain he could see an officer lying face down, a pool of blood underneath. He couldn't tell who the officer was; whoever it was had on a hat and was wearing a yellow rain jacket. The person was alive, he could see movement. About ten feet away was a motionless lump; Max knew immediately that it was one of the gunmen. The officer had shot the piece of shit dead, but not before he fired off a lucky shot in return.

Max keyed up his radio. "This is Chief Harris on scene. All units, respond in sequence with status and location."

"This is 1-2; 1-3 and I are covering the exit."

"County 6, all of my men are at the entrance."

Elizabeth.

"1-1, this is 1-0, respond."

Shit.

"1-1, this is 1-0, Sergeant Reed, please respond."

Please no.

"Talk to me people, anyone seen Elizabeth? Is that her in the middle of the yard?"

"1-0, this is 1-2. When we arrived on scene and secured the exit, I tried to get to the fallen officer. That asshole's on the second floor taking shots at anyone that comes near."

"That's right, mother fuckers."

"Repeat! Who is this? Identify yourself!" Max screamed into the radio.

"I'm the asshole on the second floor. Anyone tries to help the pig that shot my brother is in for a surprise."

Max was missing something. Clearly something was not adding up. He looked across the yard to the fallen officer and could see and hear the radio on the person's hip. How does this guy have a radio? Max quickly pulled out his smartphone and called the station. The phone rang at the desk, and Kathy Phillips answered.

"Kathy! Are you hearing this?"

"Yeah, Chief, what the hell is going on?"

"Kathy, the gunman on the second floor, what's his radio ID?"

"Crap! I didn't even think of that. Hold on a second. Too much radio traffic, get the guy to talk again and I can figure it out."

Max keyed up his radio. "Who am I speaking with? What's your name?"

"My name is none of your fucking business! Do you even care about the innocent man you shot, you c..."

"Kathy, whose radio is that?"

"Chief, that's Elizabeth's radio."

Max hung up the phone and keyed up his radio. "Listen to me. We need to start talking this out. What is it that you want?"

"I want to get the fuck out of here alive is what I want! You assholes killed my brother and you're gonna kill me, too!"

"Are you alone up there? Is anyone hurt? If you have anyone up there with you the thing to do is..."

"I ain't got no one up here with me!"

"How did you get that radio then?"

"Fuck you, that's how I got it."

Max clenched his jaw and knocked over the stack of boxes in front of him. Where is Elizabeth? Is she dead? Is she a hostage? Time was getting away from him quickly. Whoever was lying out in the middle of the garage yard might be dead soon.

"County 6, 1-0"

"County 6, go ahead Chief"

"9-0 on scene?" Max hoped that the County Sheriff's office used the same code for ambulance.

"10-4, they are standing by."

"Listen to me on the second floor. It is important that we

get those people out of the yard and to an emergency room."

"Fuck that! My brother's dead. The pig that shot him's gonna die, too!"

"Listen to me. Your brother's not moving, that doesn't mean that he's dead. There's a chance that he can still be saved. Let us get him to a hospital and try to save his life while we still can!" Max hoped the second gunmen didn't see his brother get shot in the head or this idea was going to fail quickly.

"OK, you're right! Shit! You get them out of there, but I swear, if one person so much as looks up here towards me I'm gonna start shooting."

"You have my word that no one will hurt you."

"Hurry the fuck up."

"County 6, you hear all of that?"

"10-4."

"Go!"

Two county deputies quickly escorted paramedics out to the middle of the yard to collect the fallen. They were ushered out and the ambulance screamed away.

"Hey! Ambulance! Is my brother okay? Will he make it?"

For the love of God, please lie; don't be stupid, Max thought.

One of the deputies responded. "He has a pulse. They're attempting to revive him now; that's all I know."

"9-0, this is 1-0. Please identify the officer."

"Standby." The deputy riding with the fallen officer replied. "Uh, Chief. This doesn't make sense."

"Make some sense out of it."

"Well, this officer doesn't have a badge or credentials."

"Check the wallet."

"Standby. Uh, guy's name is Tom Williams."

Son of a bitch. This is getting too weird, thought Max. *The deputy mayor?* With the two gunfighters on their way to the hospital, it was now time to focus on finding Elizabeth.

"OK, your brother is getting help. Let's start talking to each other and see if we can figure this out. Why don't you come downstairs so we can talk face to face."

"So I can get shot like my brother for no fucking reason?

Don't think so!"

"No one is going to shoot you, son, you have my word on that. Let's start by you telling me your name. My name is Max."

"I'm Randy. I swear my brother and I didn't do anything. That asshole cop wouldn't listen to us, thought we were trying to steal gas. Our car broke down a few blocks from here, and all we wanted was to borrow some tools. This is a garage for Christ's sake!"

"Randy, I believe you."

"Really? You mean it?"

"You hear the guy in the ambulance?"

"Yeah, your cop forgot his badge, so what?"

"The guy in the ambulance isn't a cop, Randy."

"What? No way! He was wearing a radio and had on the same jacket as everyone else. He had a gun and shot my brother."

"Randy, I want you to listen to me. This is just as weird for you as it is for me. That man is the deputy mayor. I deputized him this morning to help us distribute the gas."

"So he is a cop! You're lying! You made him a cop this morning!"

"No, Randy, listen. I just needed some extra bodies to help out the officers. Each of the stations I set up has a uniformed officer in charge. No one is to do a thing without clearing with their team leader. I have no idea what led to your brother being shot."

"I just told you what led to him being shot! That asshole kept telling us to leave and said we couldn't have any gas. We were on our way out, and he drew down on my brother. We both put our hands up and the guy just started shooting!"

"Randy, I told you, I believe you. I need to ask you a question and it's very important that you tell me the truth. Can you do that?"

"I guess."

"Good. I need to know how you got that radio. It belongs to one of my uniformed officers. Randy, if the officer is with you, it is very important that you tell me the truth so we can figure this thing out. If you let any hostage go we can start figuring out how to end this."

"Dude, I already told you I ain't got no one up here with

me!"

"OK, Randy. So tell me, how did you get the radio?"

"When that dude started shooting I ran up into this office. When I got here, I found a big belt on the desk that had a gun and a radio on it. No cop was here! I swear it! I just want to get out of here alive. I don't want to take a cop hostage! That's crazy! I'm a high school teacher, not a criminal!"

Maxwell thought long and hard, his gut was telling him that Randy was speaking the truth. What happened to Elizabeth? Why would she leave her duty belt on the desk?

She's in the bathroom.

If the situation wasn't so serious, Max would probably laugh. Elizabeth had tossed her belt on the desk and walked down the hall to the bathroom. She was a neat freak and would never take her duty belt off in the bathroom.

Why hadn't she made a move on Randy? Granted, the man was armed and she was not, but she could easily get the drop on him and disarm him if she was careful. Hell, at the very least she could sneak into the office on the other side of the bathroom and climb out the window. What was she waiting for? Did she need a distraction? Wasn't the storm outside loud enough? He could barely hear the radio over the blustering wind. Why would she stay on the second floor? What was keeping her there?

Roscoe.

Max had not seen Roscoe since he got to the garage. The man was in his late fifties and weighed three hundred fifty pounds. No way could he sneak out past Randy, let alone climb through a window and jump from the second floor.

"Randy, I want you to listen to me. The radio you're talking on belongs to one of my officers. His name is Roscoe. He's an old man who actually retired from the force a few years ago. He's not in the best of shape and is probably more scared of you than you are of him. I gave him a job here at the garage so he can keep busy. I'm betting he was taking a dump when you came upstairs. Roscoe has a bad heart. I really need you to let him know it's safe to come out. Just call out his name and tell him Chief Harris said it's okay to come out. Better yet, I want you to walk down the hall and turn up the radio as loud as you can. I will tell him myself. Deal?"

"OK, man, but I swear if this guy does anything I don't like it ain't gonna be pretty."

"You have my word, Randy." Max was lying to Randy. Roscoe was never on the force. He had worked in the city garage for decades. Randy had already expressed his distaste for taking a police officer hostage. Max hoped that Roscoe would play along and keep his mouth shut. If he did that, Elizabeth would pick up on the plan immediately and make her escape.

"Alright, man, start talking. Got the radio up and I'm in the hallway."

"This is Chief of Police Maxwell Harris. Officer Roscoe Stern, if you can hear me, I want you to listen very carefully. Randy here found your radio on the desk. He has agreed to let you go as long as you move slowly and do not make any sudden moves. Officer Stern, do you hear me?"

Five seconds passed by, then ten, finally a muffled voice could be heard from the end of the hall. "I hear you, Chief, I'm coming out now. Please don't shoot me, Mr. Randy. Please."

"C'mon dude, hurry up! I ain't gonna hurt you."

A door towards the end of the hall slowly opened, and Roscoe Stern stepped out into the hallway. He had his hands up as high as they would go, his elbows locked. He kept his head down and stared at the floor. He was trembling with fear. The closer he got to the man with the gun the slower he moved.

"Dude, seriously? I told you I wasn't gonna hurt you. Get your ass out of here man, c'mon!"

"Th-th-ank you, Mr. Randy." Roscoe got to the stairs and descended to the first floor. Once he stepped off the stairs he shuffled out the front door and picked up Max in a bear hug.

"Easy, big guy. C'mon, it's alright. It's over. Where's Elizabeth?"

"I'm right here, Boss," Elizabeth said as she rounded the corner. "Took you long enough to figure out what was going on. I like the promotion you gave Roscoe. Good thinking; Randy had no idea I was up there."

Max grabbed up Elizabeth in his arms and kissed her on the mouth. She resisted at first, but let out a soft moan and returned the kiss. She ran her fingers up the sides of Max's face and into his hair. Max let her go and stepped back. His face was red with embarrassment.

"I'm sorry I did that, Sergeant Reed. I'm just really happy that you're okay. I almost lost it when you didn't answer the radio; I thought for sure that was you lying in the middle of the yard."

"You better not be sorry you kissed me. It's about damned time, been waiting for you to do that. Not sure how many more signals I could throw your way."

"Signals? How long have you felt like this?"

"Maxwell, you are the smartest person I know, but sometimes you can be so damned clueless. Can we maybe talk about this some other time, like when an armed crazy person isn't holed up above us?"

"Yeah. Probably should tend to that."

"Good luck, I'm rooting for you."

Max keyed up his radio. "Randy, are you ready to come down now? How you doing up there, buddy?"

"Uh, I don't want to go to jail, man. I didn't do anything wrong. I didn't shoot anyone. You guys killed my brother, man. You're gonna kill me, too. I just know it."

"Randy, no one is going to hurt you, I promise. I want you to walk slowly down to the landing and peek around the corner at us. The only person you will see is me, and I will have my hands up; you can see for yourself."

"OK, man."

Max put his hands in the air and motioned for Elizabeth to take up position to the left of the staircase. He wanted her there in case things didn't go as planned. He had no desire to get shot. As long as Randy didn't have a weapon in his hands, he was going to let the man come downstairs so he could talk with him and sort this whole mess out.

"OK, Randy? You ready? You can peek around the corner at me and see that I'm not holding a weapon. Once you've done that, I want you to toss the pistol down the stairs. As long as I can see both of your hands this is going to work out fine. We got a deal?"

"OK, man, here I come."

Max waited and eventually saw red hair begin to appear along the wall; then he saw a man's left eye.

"That's good, Randy. See? This is going to work. Now, toss the pistol down."

Max could see a hand appear as a pistol was tossed down the last three steps, hitting the floor with a metallic clatter.

"Good, good. Now let me see both of your hands, and you can slowly walk down the stairs so we can talk."

Max saw Randy's left arm and left leg appear from behind the wall. Then his entire face appeared.

"Good, Randy, good! See? Everything is just fine. Now, let me see your other hand."

"How do I know you're alone? How do I know I'm not gonna get shot as soon as I come down the stairs?"

"Randy, c'mon, think about it. If I wanted to shoot you, don't you think I would have done it by now? I just want you to come out of this alive and for no one else to get hurt."

Max saw a look of anger and fear cross Randy's face as the veins in his forehead began to bulge.

"Randy! Randy! What's wrong? Take it easy!" Max could tell that Randy was no longer listening to him. Randy was staring intently at something at the bottom of the stairs. What was he looking at? What's got him so scared?

Oh god. He sees Elizabeth's reflection in a computer monitor.

"I knew it! Mother fuckers ain't killin' me!"

Randy's right arm came out from behind the wall. He was holding a shotgun. He leapt the three steps to the floor and took aim at Elizabeth.

"NO! WAIT! RANDY! YOU DON'T UND..."

Randy pulled the trigger and fired at Elizabeth. She was knocked off her feet and flew backwards. Before she hit the ground, Max had drawn his sidearm and shot Randy in the ear, blowing his brains onto the stairs. Max screamed and fell to the ground next to Elizabeth. A pool of blood was slowly growing beneath her.

CHAPTER ELEVEN

The president's Chief of Staff, Stacy Reid, was in shock. She had a confused smile on her face and was laughing nervously. Surely this woman was telling a cruel joke. She had to be exaggerating.

Florida Governor Lori Prince had just lied to the president of the United States. She had the nerve to blame the president for a million deaths in Florida. She must be using the term loosely - 'I haven't seen you in a million years' or 'There must have been a million people at that concert'. That had to be it. Stacy knew that her president and friend would not stand by and do nothing while a million people died. As his chief of staff, she was also his closest and most trusted advisor. He would not keep something like that from her.

Stacy knew that Hurricane Luther had carried a toxic chemical spill up the coast. In response, the Commander-in-Chief had sent an aircraft carrier along with its support vessels to render aid to the Florida coastline.

Everyone in the Clinton Room was silent. No one dared intervene. Governor Prince was staring at President Powers, waiting for his reply. The president shifted in his chair and broke the staring match with the governor. He addressed the room.

"What I am about to say will come as a shock to some of you. I had hoped to breach the subject on my own terms but the governor," he shot a sharp glare at Governor Prince, "has done that for me. To put it bluntly, there is no chemical spill in Florida. We had to fabricate a cover story to hide the truth from the media. Luther will go down in history as the must destructive force of nature in the history of mankind. He was essentially not one, but four, powerful category five hurricanes. Each time he came ashore he destroyed everything in his path. The Hurricane caught us completely off guard. The National Weather Service was certain that Luther would come ashore one time and that would be it. Instead, we are left with the horrible truth that Governor Prince has just revealed. The death toll is closing in on a million."

Stacy Reid was in complete and utter shock. It was a good thing she was sitting down because if she were standing, she would have collapsed. All of the color drained from her face. *Why had Malcolm not told me any of this? He has never kept secrets from me. He asks for my input on everything. He doesn't always heed my advice but he always considers it. What the hell is going on?*

It was clear to everyone in the room exactly who was hearing this information for the first time. Of course Governor Prince knew. Director Jimenez, Admiral Mack, and Secretary Lafferiere were not surprised in the slightest. Shock and betrayal dawned on the faces of those who had been kept in the dark for so long. Those just let in on the secret looked to at least one person in the room as if to say, "You knew? How could you not tell me?"

Stacy Reid was so hurt and angry that hot tears slowly streamed down her face. She was already writing her resignation letter in her head. She was the first to speak. "Since we're putting all the cards on the table, Mr. President, can you tell us about the recovery efforts? Is the *USS Nimitz* able to do anything to help the survivors? Is she making progress with the cleanup?"

President Malcolm Powers was caught off guard. He had hoped that the answer to that question would be implied. He exchanged glances with the men in the room who knew the answer.

"Wait. The *Nimitz* isn't there, is she?" The president's Chief of Staff didn't say anything else. She needed to collect herself and try to make sense of it all. She wanted to give the president the benefit of the doubt. He deserved the opportunity to explain himself before she said something she might regret.

The president took a deep breath and continued. "I'm afraid Stacy is right. The devastation in Florida is like nothing we've ever seen. We were simply not prepared. Citizens didn't have the means to evacuate. The assumption was that when Luther came ashore the second time, people would take things seriously and get out of the way. I'm sure everyone in this room in the same situation would drain their bank accounts to get their families to safety. That was the assumption we made. Sadly, it wasn't true. People just sat around waiting to be saved. No one had any sense of self-preservation. No one took responsibility for their own lives. They just sat back and waited for a rescue...," the president looked down at the floor and lowered his voice "...that never came."

The president continued to stare at the floor. His face reflected torment and suffering. Regret. Anguish. Shame. Malcolm Powers considered himself to be a learned armchair presidential historian. He garnered strength and wisdom from his predecessors. Many of the decisions he had made in the previous seven years were based at least in part on the successes and failures of the men who came before him.

One of the earliest lessons he learned was that a president cannot make decisions based upon the approval of the people. Every decision made is met with opposition. Sometimes the right decision, the one that is clearly for the good of the people, can be met with overwhelming opposition. Some of the most beloved presidents in history were at some point hated by the people and had abysmal approval ratings. Malcolm knew that history would be his unbiased judge. Time would either lift him up with the giants or crush him down with the failures.

The people in the room looked at each other, waiting to see if someone would say something to fill the very awkward silence. The president looked up and spoke.

"We are at a turning point in the war. The Empire of Iran must be stopped at any cost. If we are not successful in our efforts, Iran will either continue to conquer the globe or destroy it in the process. When Luther finally completed his carnage, we were already committed to taking the Port of Gibraltar. We could not spare a single ship in the Atlantic; we just barely managed to gain control of Gibraltar. On the other hand, we could not give the American people the appearance that we were doing nothing; they needed to be able to believe that their government could help and protect them. That's why the cover story was given to the media. I now face the decision on whether or not to make good on the promise to help the people of Florida and still maintain control of Gibraltar. That is why all of you are here; I need to know if I can accomplish this task. We must also take into account that Hurricane Maxine is headed for Texas and is just as powerful as Luther. The floor is open people, speak freely."

FBI Director Gill spoke first. "Mr. President, I'm not sure I understand what you're asking. What are your options?"

"Thank you, Mr. Gill. Yes, I suppose I should elaborate. The *Enterprise* and the *George Washington* are on station awaiting orders. They were en route to the Port of Gibraltar. The plan was for them to enter the Mediterranean and head to Tel-Aviv. The Fifth Fleet is in the Indian Ocean ready to move to the Persian Gulf. Once they're both in place, the invasion of Iran will begin. We project that in six months time the Empire will be fractured enough that we can take back the Middle East."

President Powers stood up and walked over to the window. Much to everyone's surprise, he lit a cigarette. Malcolm had smoked like a chimney when he was in the Navy. When he retired, he quit the habit and had not smoked in seven years. Stacy Reid wondered when he had resumed the old habit.

"Before the day is out, I must decide whether or not to send the *Enterprise* and the *George Washington* to Tel-Aviv or order them to turn around and head for Florida and Texas. As long as we hold Gibraltar we have time for them to come back to our shores and help put our broken country back together. Florida is quickly becoming a post-apocalyptic war zone. Hurricane Maxine is headed for Texas and I fear the devastation will be the same." The president walked back over to his chair and sat down. "I want you all to speak freely. Don't try to placate me, please. I need honest input."

Governor Prince was the first to speak up. "Why is this even a question? Florida is in ruins; people are dying every day from murder and starvation. I can't believe anything else is more important!"

CIA Director Jimenez coughed and hacked to clear his throat. "You gotta look at the bigger picture. I know you're more concerned with your precious little state and it's your entire reason for existence. We have to think on a global scale. The president is right, The Great Empire of Iran must be stopped at all costs. We project that within a year they will invade Europe; if they are successful, they will be headed across the Atlantic."

Governor Prince was livid. Every time this old bastard opened his mouth, she hated him even more. "Must be stopped at all costs? Are you serious? Neither of you care about American lives, do you? These are civilians, not soldiers. Innocent men, women, and children are suffering right here within our own borders. To hell with your war and your fear tactics! I'm not naive. You'll say anything to get what you want."

Admiral Mack interjected before the Director of the CIA started screaming. "Governor? If I may?"

"Yes, Admiral, please."

"Ma'am, I can assure you that Director Jimenez is telling the truth. He is not exaggerating. In fact, I respectfully disagree with his assessment." Roberto Jimenez scowled, looking at Admiral Mack with great scorn. "Based on the intelligence I have seen, Governor Prince, the Empire of Iran has the capability to invade Europe within six to nine months."

Director Jimenez wiped the scowl off his face and almost smiled. "Thank you, Admiral. I'd love to compare notes with you." Governor Prince was visibly upset but maintained her composure.

Silence filled the room for about a minute. Everyone was pensive. The president was deep in thought, his brow furrowed and his gaze distant. He sat up in his chair and looked to the men in uniform.

"Gentlemen, how long can we hold Gibraltar?"

The military men in the room looked to the Chairman of the Joint Chiefs of Staff, Carl Moody. "Mr. President, without reinforcements from the *Enterprise* and the *George Washington*, we can hold the port for ninety days at best, thirty at the worst. The *James Russell* is a sitting duck. She barely made it back to the port in one piece. Her defensive capabilities are at half strength, and they are working around the clock to get the flight deck operational. To put it bluntly, we are vulnerable. If the Empire launches a direct attack in the immediate future, the Port of Gibraltar will fall within days. We are redeploying ground forces to help secure the *James Russell* while she undergoes repair. We are commandeering anything that floats - yachts, sailboats, canoes, paddleboats, doesn't matter. If we can put armed soldiers in front of the *James Russell*, we will do so by any means necessary."

The president replied, "What if we send one of the vessels to Gibraltar and send the other one to Florida?"

"Mr. President, that would help, but it wouldn't be enough. Allied Forces control everything north of the port;

however, the Empire is gaining ground from the south and they will eventually make it to the southern shores of Gibraltar and launch an attack. We need the *George Washington* out in front to stop the Iranian navy and the *Enterprise* to defend the ground to the south. Without them both, we lose Gibraltar."

"Thank you, Carl." The president stood up and walked back to the window to smoke another cigarette. He paced back and forth, thinking back to the famous battles from the last thousand years for control of the port. The Romans held the Port of Gibraltar until they fell. The Vandals held the Port for a short time before the Islamic conquest of Iberia in 711 A.D. Muslims controlled the port for seven centuries before the Spanish took it back. The British Empire seized control and with the completion of the Suez Canal, they extended their reach to the Indian Ocean. For most of mankind's history, the Port of Gibraltar has been one of the most valuable strategic assets that a civilization could possess.

"Who's hungry? I'm starving." President Powers took his seat and looked around the room. Everyone was silent. "People, we are going to be here for a while. It's time for lunch. Computer."

"Yes, Mr. President?" responded the White House A.I..

"Take lunch orders for the guests in the Clinton Room. We will be eating our meal in here."

"Yes, Mr. President." The White House A.I. deployed two service robots that rolled over to the guests. The men and women in the room placed their order on the robots' touch screens.

The president waited until everyone had placed their order, directing his next question to the Secretary of Homeland Security. "Secretary Laferriere, what can we expect in Texas?"

"Mr. President, the evacuation of the Houston area is not going well. It's the same problem we had last month with Luther. People can't afford to fill their gas tanks and sit on gridlocked roads. No one wants to get on the road unless they have a full tank of gas. Since it can cost upwards of two hundred fifty dollars to fill a tank, most people simply can't afford it. Most American families have a hard enough time putting food on the table and keeping a roof over their heads. Gas is a luxury they can't afford."

"A lot of people are going to die." Governor Prince felt the weight of the world on her shoulders. "It's exactly what happened in my state. We just didn't have enough transportation to get a significant amount of people out. We did what we could, but it wasn't enough."

"It gets worse." Secretary Laferriere continued. "The interstate south of Houston leading down to the Gulf of Mexico is going to end up completely shut down. A few miles from the Sam Houston Tollway they have construction blocking off all but one lane."

Stacy Reid spoke up. "How is that possible? I thought hurricane evacuation routes had regulations on construction."

"You are correct, ma'am." Secretary Laferriere continued. "We're not sure how it happened, but it did. We can focus on that at a later date. The important thing now is to fix the problem. We have less than twelve hours before Maxine makes landfall. She's moving very slowly, which makes things much worse. Three hours after landfall, the eye will pass over Houston. Winds in excess of two hundred fifteen miles per hour will push water from the Gulf of Mexico and Galveston Bay inland for several hours. Much of the Houston area will be under water."

"God help us." President Powers shook his head. "When will the lanes be open? What is being done?"

"I'm being told that within the hour they will have all the lanes open. Traffic is backed up all the way to Galveston."

"We can't sit by and do nothing. We have one state descending into anarchy and another one ready to drown half its residents." The president shifted in his seat and leaned his forehead on his palm. "I can either sacrifice the lives of millions of Americans or save the world from Iran. I need a third option. Roberto?"

The Director of the CIA turned his wheelchair away from his lunch and faced the president. "Yes, Mr. President?"

"Would it be pos..."

The room began to shake and a loud explosion could be heard outside the White House.

"What in the hell?" Roberto Jimenez exclaimed.

Before anyone else could say a word, massive steel

shudders slammed shut over the windows. The doors to the Oval Office and the hallway entrance to the Clinton Room closed, and steel doors dropped down with a thud that startled the people in the room. The lights went out and were replaced by a faint red one. A few seconds apart, several loud explosions rocked the walls of the room.

The White House A.I. spoke. "Mr. President, the Secret Service will be here in a few seconds. Please remain calm."

"Computer, what is going on?" The president stood up from his chair.

"Please remain calm."

"I am calm. Tell me what exactly is..."

The steel door quickly raised and four Secret Service agents rushed into the room. Malcolm Powers was lifted off his feet and quickly ushered from the room. Those left behind looked at each other as another explosion rocked the White House.

CHAPTER TWELVE

Howard Beck was sobbing in the garden he had built for his wife. When he built it, he knew that it stuck out like a sore thumb for a mile in every direction. He was confident that Beck Castle was secure. Nothing about this garden was connected to the structure below. The grass was artificial, and the decorations were made of high quality materials that could withstand the elements. Hal was the perfect cemetery caretaker of the graveyard built for one. In the years since Meredith was laid to rest, the garden had only been disturbed three times. All of the curious intruders took pictures and videos of the garden. Hal discreetly erased the evidence after they departed and doctored their GPS devices placing the garden in random locations far away. Meredith's tombstone didn't have her name on it. Howard was smart enough to know that his spouse's grave would raise suspicion. The tombstone was simply marked "Loving Wife."

"I'm so sorry, my dear, so sorry." Howard brushed the long white hair from his eyes and wiped the tears from his cheeks. "Please forgive me, my love, I just have such a hard time coming here to see you. I know I promised you that I would always have fresh flowers for you to look at, but I just...." Howard wailed and screamed in soul-splitting agony. His cries echoed for miles; thankfully, the only creatures that could hear had more than two legs.

Meredith Beck had developed early-onset Alzheimer's six years earlier. The diagnosis didn't upset Howard at all. He simply focused his brilliant mind on curing his wife. The Founding Father of Artificial Intelligence was confident that his genius and limitless resources would prevail. For the first two years, Howard and Hal made great strides in Alzheimer's research. Their work gave the medical community a ten-year leap in treatment. Howard was tortured by the fact that his hard work did his wife no good. The strides made by the billionaire genius and his A.I. companion were in prevention, not a cure. It was too late for Meredith; she slipped further and further away and Howard was unable to bring her back. The world praised Howard Beck for his breakthroughs; Howard cursed himself a failure.

Meredith frightened Howard as her disease progressed. She would wander around their sprawling mansion in confusion, looking for something familiar to calm her troubled mind. Howard had many rooms in their home converted to exact replicas of different time periods of Meredith's life. One room was her childhood home. Another room became the first home the couple had lived in many years before. The massive, three story high library was transformed into her university. Howard would quietly slip into each world and hope that he was assigned a role to play. He willingly played the role of uncle, neighbor, and college professor. He only wanted his wife to be happy.

Hal even played his role when Meredith was convinced that the British voice she was hearing was Patrick Stewart. Mr. Stewart had become friends of the Becks and visited their home at least once a year. At first Hal corrected her, which caused her to become very confused and angry. Howard told his A.I. to play along with Meredith and make references to the visits the Englishman had made to their home. When Meredith began to insist that Patrick stop calling so much and just come over and visit her, Howard had no choice but to instruct Hal not to speak within earshot of his wife.

Meredith lost her battle, and The Long Goodbye was finished. Howard had his wife buried in the garden above Beck Castle. She belonged there; no place in the world made her happier. She understood what her husband had accomplished and praised him for his guarantee that mankind's legacy would survive. Howard and his son were the only people in attendance at her graveside service. Marshall Beck and his father had a very strained relationship. Howard tried his best to be a good father to his son; he tried to in vain to understand the illogical and emotional personality of a child. Howard's attempt to mold his son into his genius image was met with defiance. When Marshall became an adult and was expected to go out into the world to make something of himself, he had a rough time of it. Marshall thought his father would continue to support him and finance his business interests. Howard did not. Marshall mistook his father's tough love as being disowned from the family. The two men rarely spoke to each other; with Meredith no longer around to play referee, they both knew they might never speak to one another again.

Howard finally calmed down and ceased his anguished cries. He mumbled sweet and loving affections to his wife and fell asleep beside her tombstone. When he awoke the next morning, he arranged the flowers and sealed them in the climate-controlled container at the foot of her grave.

"There you are, my dear. Aren't they beautiful? Now you can look at them and be happy. I know you haven't had pretty things to look at for awhile. I'm sorry for that and I hope you will forgive me." Howard stood and smiled. "I love you my darling wife. I'm going downstairs for a bit. I'll come back up and visit with you this evening."

Howard walked the distance to the Batcave and descended into Beck Castle. He exited the elevator and walked down the corridor to his quarters.

"Good morning, sir."

"Good morning, Hal."

"Did you enjoy your visit with Meredith?"

"I did, thank you."

"Sir, do you know how long we will be staying?"

"Haven't decided just yet. What do you have for me this morning?"

"Would you like a status report on the Castle or the usual morning report?"

"Let's begin with the morning report."

"Very good, sir. Civil unrest has reached troubling levels in most of the major cities. The Unified National Guard released their quarterly report to Congress this morning. For the first time in two years, statistics pertaining to violent crimes have risen significantly. Curfew violations have also spiked dramatically."

"Huh. Any explanation for the increase? They've managed to keep the pin in the grenade for some time; why did they drop it all of the sudden?"

"Nothing in the report gives any indication to explain the increase."

"Care to speculate, Old Man?"

"I'm afraid I cannot, sir."

"Well, keep reviewing the data and let me know if you can

venture a guess."

"I will make it a priority, sir. Shall I continue, or do you have any further questions on the matter?"

"Please continue."

"Do you recall my prediction on Hurricane Maxine?"

"You mean where you predicted it would make landfall?"

"Yes, sir."

"Hmmm. Galveston?"

"That is correct, sir. My prediction was that it would make landfall four point two miles east of the tip of Galveston Island."

"Are you trying to brag, Hal? Are you going to tell me or not?"

"I do endeavor to impress you, sir. My prediction was the closest to any of the forecast models. Hurricane Maxine will make landfall within from one mile on either side of my prediction."

"Outstanding, Old Man! I just might let you work part time at The Weather Channel!"

"That will not be necessary, sir. I am content with my current employer."

"And I am content with you, my friend. Did you send your prediction to the National Weather Service?"

"I did, sir. They did not seem to give it much attention."

"I will make sure that in the future they pay attention to you."

"Thank you, sir. Shall I continue?"

"Please do."

"Wildfires in California continue to spread. Emergency crews have managed to contain the fires to the north and south. Fires continue to spread towards the east."

"Well, the terrain will see that the fires die out."

"Correct, sir."

"How are things at the estate? Anything going on?"

"Everything is running as it should be. Regular maintenance and cleaning are proceeding on schedule with nothing significant to report. Security report is negative."

"Good, good. What about our route back to the residence? Still blocked by the National Guard in Denver?"

"It is, sir. We will be able to return along the same detour we took to arrive here."

"Good. That will be all, Hal. I'm going to take a shower and change clothes."

"Very good, sir."

Howard walked into his suite and took a long shower. He then changed into a bathrobe and climbed into his bed to get some rest. He awoke an hour later and walked to the kitchen to make some breakfast. While he ate his bacon and eggs and sipped coffee, Howard thought about the state of the world. When he built Beck Castle, its original purpose was to protect Hal and ensure that he would remain online indefinitely. The expansion of the Castle to serve as an ark for mankind was meant as a precaution, to protect the chronicle of human history. Howard never dreamed that he might actually have to use the Castle for something as drastic as housing residents. The thought terrified him. Chaos was the only description that came to mind.

Howard walked to the Operations Center and sat down in his chair. When he pulled himself up to the desk, a one hundred and eighty degree screen that spanned the ten foot high ceiling came to life. Live video feeds from all over the Castle were displayed. Readouts pertaining to the geothermal power generator blinked and flashed data. Inventories of the food and water stores were in the green. Infrared scans from twenty miles in every direction of the Castle displayed all signs of life.

"Hal, everything looks good here. Anything I'm not seeing?"

"The Castle is operating at peak efficiency, sir. Diagnostics of the ventilation, power systems, and structural integrity are within acceptable limits. I will be conducting repairs to the air condensers in the dormitory wing."

"Data storage?"

"Incoming data remains at the average rate of one point eight terabytes per day. Our current storage capacity remains at seventy four percent. I estimate that in eighteen months it will be necessary to upgrade our storage capacity."

Howard had programmed for every major news feed, every news broadcast, every significant publication of print and film to be stored in the archives at Beck Castle. Hal had managed some amazing upgrades in terms of data compression. The same amount of data coming into the Castle would have been twelve times as much only twenty years prior. Nothing was kept off site. Four redundant back up drives were located a hundred yards from the structure in each cardinal direction. Hal was able to mask the Internet traffic coming into the Castle.

"What's the word on the latest *Star Trek* movie?"

The relaunch of the successful franchise that began in 2009 had spawned eight sequels and two television series. With Los Angeles in decline, Vancouver had been proclaimed the "New Hollywood." Howard consumed every bit of it like a drug addict. He even begged his friend, Patrick Stewart, to somehow work his way onto the screen as either a time-traveling Captain Picard or one of his ancestors. At his eighty-seventh birthday party, the Englishman finally relented and agreed to either a cameo or a small recurring role, if they would have him.

"The latest movie is set to begin filming in six weeks. All the principal actors have signed on for this film and two more if the series continues."

"What about Patrick?"

"Mr. Stewart is in negotiations to either be cast in the next film or as a recurring character in the television series *Starfleet Academy*."

"Oh, that is awesome! I can't decide which I would prefer! What role would he play in either?"

"Rumor around the chatrooms say that he would replace Wil Wheaton as Commandant in the television series after he retires next season. His role in the movie is believed to be the antagonist."

Howard was bouncing in his chair, his eyes filled with the wonder of a child. "Oh my, oh my! This is so exciting! What do you think he should do?"

"I have no opinion one way or the other, sir."

"C'mon, Hal! Live a little! Compare the two roles and figure out which one would have the most impact on the storyline!"

"What parameters should my analysis contain, sir? I am not sure what you are asking."

"You're no fun, Old Man! Contact Patrick and see if he

has time to chat with me. We have to talk about this! I want to know which way he is leaning."

"Standby, sir. I will attempt to set up a meeting."

"Hurry up!"

"Sir, his assistant has informed me that Mr. Stewart is on a plane headed to London. Once he lands, he will be attending a meeting. You have been penciled in at 6pm."

"Terrific! That gives me time to watch a few Next Generation movies."

"Shall I play them in order, sir?"

"Sure, why not."

Howard spent the rest of the morning and afternoon watching all four of the movies. The billionaire welcomed the distraction. It had been some time since he had enjoyed a Star Trek marathon. When 6pm rolled around, Howard talked with his friend for over an hour. The rumors had only been half true. He had not been offered a role in the upcoming movie; he had, however, been offered a recurring role in the television series. The negotiations centered on just how big the role would be. The studio wanted him to appear in eight to ten episodes a season for two years. He was more inclined to half that number. Howard told him that as long as he was healthy, he should meet them in the middle with the possibility for more. Patrick took the advice. Howard ended the call and decided to have dinner. "Hal, I think we will be leaving tonight."

"Very good, sir. I will prepare for our departure. What time to do you estimate we will leave?"

"As soon as I finish eating we can get going. That will be all, Hal. Play one of Hillary Hahn's Bach Violin Concertos. Surprise me."

"Yes, sir."

Howard finished his meal and packed up his bag. He rode the elevator to the Batcave and walked the distance to Meredith's Garden and sat on the bench to the right of her grave.

"I'm leaving, my dear. I promise I will visit more often. I realized that not visiting you has caused me more harm than good. Seeing you brings back all the wonderful memories we shared. I love you so very much, my bride. I'm sorry I couldn't figure out how to keep us together longer. I did my best, but I just didn't have enough time." Howard stood up and placed his hand on the tombstone. "Goodbye, my love. I will see you soon."

Howard climbed into his car and the A.I. led them back towards the estate some fifty miles to the south. Howard spent the time reviewing the current projects and quarterly reports from his four directors at Beck Enterprises. He answered dozens of emails and checked his investments. Eventually Howard took a break, pausing to gaze out the window. Something wasn't right.

"Hal, did we have to alter our route?"

"No, sir. We are traveling on the same detour we took to the Castle."

"Are you sure? Run a diagnostic on the GPS systems."

"Of course, sir. Standby. Diagnostic complete. All systems are functioning properly."

"Okay. Well then, where the hell is Denver? We should see the lights on the horizon."

"Sir, my sensors detect that the city of Denver is in fact to the northwest. It should be visible."

"Well, Old Man, either my eyesight is going or something isn't right."

"Standby, sir. Give me a moment to investigate."

"Hurry up; I don't like this at all." Howard was getting very nervous. *Did something happen while we were in the Castle? Am I losing my mind?*

"Sir, the city of Denver is currently in a blackout. Electricity ceased functioning approximately forty-seven minutes ago."

"Well, that's a relief. I thought the city had vanished. Makes sense. Any idea what happened?"

"It is hard to discern the exact cause from the current data. Reports of widespread rioting might be the cause."

"Did the rioters sabotage the power grid? That seems a little complicated and organized for a mob."

"I tend to agree with that assessment, sir. The logical assumption is that the authorities disabled the power in an attempt to regain control of the city."

"Well, night-vision would give them the upper hand. Let's just hope it doesn't backfire and they start setting fires."

"That would be unfortunate, sir."

"Do you anticipate any trouble along our current route?"

"My analysis does not indicate any reason to alter our route. If you would like, I can take a route that puts us further away from the city. The new route would add twenty-three minutes to our trip."

"Do it."

"Yes, sir. I will continue to monitor the current situation. I have heightened security at the residence and launched sentry drones to monitor the immediate area."

"Excellent. I need a distraction. Play an episode from season six of *The Next Generation*. Pick one at random."

"Yes, sir."

The windshield blackened out the frightening world as the episode "Tapestry" played.

"Good choice, Old Man, one of my favorites."

The rest of the drive was uneventful. They arrived at the estate, and Howard entered his home. He was happy to be safe in his private world. He decided to scour the internet and the major news outlets to see if he could find out anything that could explain what was happening to Denver. What he saw confirmed Hal's theory. The authorities did in fact disable the power to the city to confuse the rioters and prevent them from organizing. Howard looked at the time and realized it was past 2am. He climbed into bed and gave Hal some final instructions before he went to sleep.

"Hal, I want you to extend the perimeter of the drones by fifty percent. Monitor any traffic that enters the perimeter. If any vehicle is on a direct route to the residence, I want you to wake me immediately."

"Yes, sir. Sleep well."

Howard drifted off to sleep. Hal stood watch over the estate and monitored the ten mile perimeter. He monitored some sporadic traffic that entered the perimeter and did not wake Howard because their routes did not come near the residence. At 4:30am, Hal took notice of a large convoy of vehicles headed in the direction of the estate. They slowly approached a four-way stop. If they turned left, Hal would wake Howard. The convoy stopped and a few people congregated near the intersection, clearly discussing which way to turn. They got back in their vehicles.

Hal turned on the lights in Howard's bedroom.

"Excuse me, sir. Are you awake?"

Howard sat up and rubbed his eyes. "Yes, Hal, what is it?"

"Sir, a contingent of National Guard soldiers is approaching the residence. If they maintain course and speed, I estimate they will be passing in front of the residence in twenty-five minutes."

Howard Beck was terrified. He did not like guests. He certainly didn't like multiple guests that carried big guns.

CHAPTER THIRTEEN

"ALL INMATES ON THE YARD RETURN TO YOUR ASSIGNED CELLS!

"Eat shit!!"
"Fuck off!!"
"Make us go to our cells, you cocksuckers!"

Richard Dupree knew that things were about to get very bad in a very short amount of time. The nine hundred inmates on the yard had completely forgotten about the ash that was covering the ground and getting in their hair and eyes. They readied themselves to do battle with the three squads of Riot Control Teams staged behind gates that would spill them out on the yard in three directions.

"ALL INMATES ON THE YA..."

A live voice silenced the loudspeaker. The recreation yard fell silent.
"Gentlemen, may I please have your attention?"
"Who the fuck is that?" asked Head.
Richard had heard the voice before. He never forgot a voice or a face.
"That's the Warden," Richard answered.
"No shit?" Tank asked.
"Big man himself," answered Richard.
Three things about the words he had just heard made Richard realize that they were in deep shit. The first was that the warden had called them "Gentlemen." He had never once in his incarceration been called a gentleman. The second was that the man said "please." Hacks don't say please, it just didn't happen. The third and most troubling was that the top man at the prison had asked a question. Inmates were not asked to do anything. Inmates were given a command and if they did not comply, the next step was, well Richard had never witnessed the next step for himself. Non-compliant inmates were taken to the Special Housing Unit to be locked in a cell with three other inmates

twenty-three hours a day for a very long time. The cells down in the SHU were about the size of the average American's bathroom. Four men living on top of each other in such a small space made for a living hell.

The warden's tactic had been effective. You could hear a pin drop.

"As many of you already know, much of our state is seeing the worst wildfires in our state's history, the evidence of which is falling all around you. The ash falling to the ground is only the first stage and will be the easiest for us to manage. The second stage of this disaster puts every one of us, staff and inmate alike, in great danger.

"Get us the fuck out of here!"

"You gonna let us die in here? You can't do that!"

"We don't wanna die!"

The inmates on the yard were on the brink of an all-out riot. Many began to run around in circles screaming at the four speakers on each end of the center guard tower. Richard laughed out loud when he realized most of the inmates thought the warden was addressing them from inside the tower. Richard knew the man was on the other side of the electric fence sitting comfortably in his gigantic office deep inside the Admin Building, talking into a microphone. The inmates began to pile up on the fence leading to the corridor that led out of the prison.

The Warden continued, *"Please, please, you have to listen to me! Please, remain calm! Your lives depend on it, I promise you!"*

That got the attention of the inmates, who continued to pile on the fence trying to get out. They didn't stop their aggressive behavior; they did however, stay quiet enough for the Warden to continue.

"Thank you, I appreciate your cooperation. For the last twelve hours we have made preparations to lock the facility down and ride out the disaster. Our previous estimate led us to believe that we would have another twelve hours to prepare. That has changed. A massive cloud of smoke and ash was due to hit Highland Valley later tonight. However, a weather system twenty miles away has changed direction and will meet up with the smoke cloud, blowing it to us sooner than we had anticipated.

The weather system will drop the smoke cloud into Highland Valley, keeping it on top of us for eight to ten hours."

"Jesus, does anybody understand what that asshole is talking about? Is he speaking English?"

Richard knew he couldn't make Spider understand weather systems, so he tried to dumb it down the best he could. "Spider, he's saying the Smoke Monster from *Lost* is coming for us."

Spider got angry with Richard. "Fuckin Smoke Monster? Dude on the speakers is making more sense than you, man. Jesus."

"Dude, you've seriously never see *Lost*?" Head began to laugh.

"Naw man, we didn't have no TV when I was a kid." Spider tried not to look embarrassed.

"For real man, best show ever made. No joke, you should check it out. It's about these people who crash on some island, I'm gonna say Atlantis or some shit. Then some whispering dirty people kidnap the fat dude, the...uh...what was that guy's name from *Party of Five*? Fuck, never can remember. The doctor guy and I think like four other dudes. Then the bald guy and uh... it was Jack!! Yeah, that's it. They blow up this underground house from the 1950s, had to be some old shit cuz the music was played on these mad huge black things as big as a dinner plate..."

Richard seriously enjoyed listening to Head confuse one of his favorite shows, but they didn't have the time to listen to him tear J.J. Abrams masterpiece to shreds. "Head, shut up. I'm starting to wonder if you've actually seen the show or just listened to an Alzheimer's patient describe it to you."

The Warden continued, not having paused for Head's review of *Lost*. *".....are confident that the air handlers in the cell blocks will keep the smoke out. What little smoke does enter the buildings will pass through air filters. I give my solemn word to each and every one of you that you will be safe. I also give you my solemn word that if you remain on the yard for another, uh... Kevin, how much time do we have? ... forty-five minutes, you will die out here. Please, I am begging you, return to your assigned cells so that we can batten down the hatches and survive this disaster."*

The Warden had to wait through a full minute of quiet murmurs and inmates running back and forth talking with their respective gangs before large groups began to turn and walk to the cellblocks.

"Thank you gentleman. Let's show the country that the Highland Valley State Prison is the best of the best."

Richard didn't move. He had to think about everything that the Warden had just said before he did anything. Tank, Head, and Spider looked to him for guidance. Richard would have a plan.

Richard always had a plan.

****

Two hours prior to the ashes falling, Warden William Vandehoef had met with his Executive Staff in his office. The people who helped him operate his facility were seated on couches opposite each other. To his left were Associate Wardens Kevin Kapparis and Stephen Courts. Seated next to them was Captain John Zamir. On the opposite couch and to the right of the warden sat his Executive Assistant Jose Bertrand, Utilities Executive Richard Landry, and Emergency Preparedness Officer Jay Foxworth. The Warden first addressed his EPO. "Jay, is there any chance at all that this thing will miss us?"

"Warden, this thing is coming right for us unless we're lucky and get blessed with some divine intervention."

"God will not intervene and save these animals," A.W. Kapparis said.

The warden addressed the man who had just spoken. "Kevin, is there any chance at all that the buses can make it in time?"

"No, sir, I'm afraid not. I've been on the phone with Vegas for the past hour, and the fastest they can be here is eight hours."

The closest major city was Las Vegas, fifty miles to the east. The best they could offer was a fleet of school buses. The inmates would have to be in full restraints, so the preparations would take some time. That was the original plan, based on now erroneous information that led them to believe that they had until 10PM to get everyone out. With the weather system pushing the black cloud to them earlier, the buses would arrive far too late.

"We don't have that kind of time," said Captain Zamir.

"The state can be here in roughly two hours," replied A.W. Kapparis.

"Well that's good news!" said the warden.

"Not exactly. They can only provide buses to hold maybe five hundred inmates."

"Shit, that's barely a third of the population." A.W. Courts shook his head and rolled his eyes.

With the plan of moving the inmates out of the facility impossible, the Warden turned his attention to the utilities executive.

"Rick, how long will the inmates last in the cellblocks?"

Landry knew he was about to piss off his boss. "An hour, maybe two at the most."

The executive assistant turned and addressed the man sitting next to him. "I thought the upgrades to the air handlers had been finished?"

"We did upgrade them."

The warden look confused. "So what's the problem, Mr. Landry?"

"The problem, sir, is the ash. Once the ash starts falling, the air ducts will be clogged within an hour. Once the hot air from the smoke pushes the ash out of the way, smoke will pour into the cellblocks. At that time, the air handlers will turn on and try to pull the smoke out of the unit. The ash already in the air handlers will burn out the motors, might even catch them on fire. The air filters were never designed to handle that kind of load and will be essentially worthless. The inmates will be dead in an hour, two would surprise me."

"Shit! Shit! Shit! What the hell are we supposed to do, people? I need answers and I need them fast!" The warden looked desperate. The inmates had already been walking the yard for some time when this meeting began.

The executive assistant was the first to speak. "Mr. Landry, couldn't we rig the air handlers to turn on now so the smoke could be pulled out?"

"Mr. Bertrand, that was my first thought. There are forty-eight air handlers, four in each cellblock. I estimated that our best shot was to rig two in each block to come on and hope for the best. The problem is, if we started immediately, we might get eight of them rigged in time."

A.W. Courts did the math. "So four units out of twelve could be saved."

"Exactly, but that's if we start immediately; we don't have a second to spare." Utilities Executive Landry looked to his boss for the go ahead.

"Get started," the warden replied.

"You got it, boss." Landry keyed up his radio and gave the order.

"Jay, how long do we have before ashes start falling on us?" the warden asked.

"An hour, maybe two," the EPO replied.

"Shit. That only gives us time to finish one cellblock." Richard Landry looked defeated.

"Are you sure about that, Jay?" the warden asked.

"Yes, sir, I am."

Most of the men in the room started looking around to see if anyone was going to speak up.

The Warden could tell he was missing something. "What is it? What am I not being told? Somebody better start talking and quick."

"Well, pretty soon we're gonna be dusting the ash off our resumes so I'll say it." Captain Zamir leaned forward in his chair, ignoring the stare of the emergency preparedness officer.

Zamir pointed to Jay Foxworth. "This guy has no idea what he is talking about."

"Hey, not called for!" Foxworth said.

"Oh, shut up, Jay! We all know the reason you got this job was because of your wife. You have absolutely no clue what you're doing."

"Not true! How the hell was I supposed to know some weather would come out of nowhere and blow the thing right to us? No way are you going to pin this on me!"

"It's called The Weather Channel, mother fucker; maybe you should check it out!"

"Hey spic, you wanna take this shit outside? Call me mother fucker one more time and see what happens." Jay

Foxworth stared daggers into the man.

Captain John Zamir stood up and bowed out his chest. "You so much as open your idiotic, racist mouth again and you'll be swallowing your teeth!"

"What are you going to do, beaner? Cut me?"

"That's it! You opened your mouth, told you not to open your mouth."

Zamir started towards his target when the rest of the men in the room quickly held the two men back from fighting each other. The men calmed down and stood on opposite sides of the room.

The warden hadn't moved from behind his desk. He felt that to do so was beneath him. Someone needed to maintain a level of composure and control.

"Sit down, all of you."

The men took their seats. Zamir and Foxworth didn't look at each other.

"Mr. Foxworth" the warden began with frightening calm, "Captain Zamir is right; this is your fault. It is your job to monitor anything outside these fences that could do harm to the inmates in our charge. If an earthquake hits, we look to you to do your job. If the facility managed to catch fire, you would be our liaison to the emergency crews. AND IF A FUCKING CLOUD OF SMOKE AND ASH IS HEADED FOR US WE LOOK TO YOU TO DO YOUR GODDAMNED JOB!"

The warden slammed both fists down on his desk and swept everything on his desk in the direction of the Emergency Preparedness Officer.

"Gentleman, someone get this piece of shit out of my office."

"What? You can't do that! You don't know what kind of trouble you're gonna be in when I te…"

"What? You mean when you cry on a vid-con like a little bitch to your wife in Sacramento? Is that what you were going to say to me? I can give one good goddamn if your wife works in the governor's office."

"You'll regret this; I promise you'll regret it." Foxworth said with a cocky smile.

"Not today, I won't. Why is no one getting this man out of

my sight?"

The men in the room watched in awe as the dumb ass was finally getting what he had coming to him. No one wanted to move an inch for fear of missing the show.

EPO Foxworth was sitting with his claws dug into the arms of the sofa. He was not leaving.

Captain Zamir and Utilities Executive Landry carried the man into the hallway. The former EPO didn't protest; he was pouting like a spoiled child. The two men locked the door behind them on their way back in and took their seats.

Once the men took their seats, A.W. Kapparis addressed the group. "So, what are we going to do?"

The men in the room looked to their boss, who said, "We can't very well let them out. The first thing they would do is follow the road down to Highland Valley, storm the city where our families live, and do God only knows what to them. The fate of the men under our care has already been sealed. I will not grant them freedom if it comes at the expense of the lives of our loved ones. If the Lord wants to hold me accountable, I will gladly trade my own soul for the lives of all of you and your families."

The warden looked out his window, seeing flakes of ash falling to the ground, he cursed his EPO for lying to him and making him think they had more time. If the fool tried to kiss his ass and keep his job, he was sure he was going to slap the man across the face like the bitch he was. He ordered Captain Zamir to move the Riot Control Teams up to their assigned gates.

Warden William Vandehoef was about to tell a lie and administer the death penalty to one thousand, nine hundred eighty-seven convicted felons.

****

Richard Dupree wiped the ash from his bald head and took off his shirt. He tore the shirt down the middle, urinated on it, and wrapped his head like he was standing in the Sahara Desert. The three skinheads with him watched him with interest; Spider even laughed like Richard was playing a perverted dress up game.

"Should I ask why you did that? What is wrong with

you?"

"Protects your nose and mouth from breathing in smoke," Richard explained.

"You stayin' out here? What's wrong with you?" Head's large eyes looked at him in confusion and disgust.

"Suit yourself, not asking you to do it," Richard said calmly.

The three Aryans mimicked his action, minus the urination.

"Fuck this, I'm going inside," said Head, hoping for support

"Quiet. Just stay there, keep quiet and let me think."

"Look around Richard! We ain't got no choice! We stay out here, we dead!" Spider turned in the direction of their block, hoping the others would do the same.

Billy "Tank" Bratchett, the six foot nine, three hundred twenty-five pound monster, spoke an octave higher. "Richard, we gotta go man, I can't stay out here! My eye is hurtin' like a bitch!"

Richard knew all too well why Tank's eye was causing him agonizing pain.

Tank's eye was only one of the many injuries on his massive, linebacker frame. A few months after he and Richard starting running on the track together, Richard would ask him about the scars on his body and how he got them. The stories surrounding each scar finally answered the question of the extremely offensive tattoo on his right bicep and why he still had it, the one showing a black man hanging dead from a tree with three hooded Klansman looking up at him.

Every morning when they hit the track, Richard noticed that the black inmates were terrified of Tank; most wouldn't even look him in the eye. Nearly every black gang in the prison had tried to murder Tank and cut the racist tattoo off his massive arm. Tank had the scars to prove it. One scar cut across Tank's chest, severing the arm of Hitler. When he realized the damage done to Adolf, he proceeded to break every bone in the hand that wielded the offending knife. The most gruesome scar on Tank's body was on his left cheek. A large chunk of flesh had been torn away and damaged his left eye, leaving the pupil with no pigment. Tank was already a terrifying monster to look at before the damage to his eye; now he looked like some sort of demon. If he were walking the streets as a free man, the sight of him would no doubt make a small child cry and grown men cower. The eye was very sensitive to heat. Tank countered the heat with sunglasses, and in the scorching heat of the summer, he had to wear an eye patch. Richard could only imagine what the heat and smoke was doing to him. Probably felt like a hot poker being driven into his brain.

The final attempt on Tank's life pretty much ensured that no one would ever bother Tank again. In his last gladiatorial match, it was four Gangster Disciples against Tank. Tank managed to kill two of them before the bullets from the guard tower started whizzing past his head. One of the unlucky fools thought he had beat Tank when he managed to stab Tank in the thigh with a shank. Tank responded by pulling the shank out of his own leg and thrusting it into the Disciple's chest, piercing his heart and killing him. After the fight, no one dared give Tank so much as a disrespectful glare.

Richard could handle his own without a doubt, but Tank was too important an asset to just ignore. He was an important tactical advantage that Richard couldn't pass up. Tank gave one last look at his cellmate for some sort of answer.

"Billy, trust me. We let them lock us in our cell and we're dead. Them too," Richard said, pointing to Spider and Head.

"Dumbasses, get back here!" Tank screamed at the confused pair ten yards away. When Tank yelled, you obeyed.

Think, Richard, think! What are you not seeing?

Richard had listened very intently to the warden when his choice of words set off alarms in his head. He knew something wasn't right. Richard was no expert in ventilation, but it was just something about the warden pleading with them that struck a chord. He was desperate. The safety and well being of the inmates under his care was not the cause of his desperation; it was more. Richard tried to imagine how the ventilation system would work. He guessed that the system was designed to pull smoke out of an area and keep them from dying from smoke inhalation. He figured that being in the desert, the air filters had to be pretty top notch to keep the dust and dirt out.

He was forgetting one very simple thing - the ash.

The ventilation system would never be able to protect them. The ash would clog up everything, including the motors for the air handlers that were on the outside of the cellblock wall.

What was the warden so desperate about? Think. *Why is he so desperate to get us inside?* He could leave them on the yard and they would die regardless. Then it hit Richard like a bolt of lightning.

They were going to abandon the facility and leave them to die.

The only problem was they had to get the inmates to go to their cells and lock them in before they could make a break for it. Then every staff member would high-tail it to the front gate and flee home to their families.

This is not good, thought Richard. *Think!*

Then he saw the answer. He squinted his hawk-like eyes to the other side of the yard.

"Follow me."

Tank, Spider, and Head started to follow him as Head shouted towards Richard, "Where are you going? Our block is back this way!"

Richard confirmed what he thought he had seen. Four utilities foremen were pushing a cart to Cellblock A.

"We have to get inside Cellblock A. It's time for us to leave."

Tank had his hand over his left eye and was pressing as hard as he could. "What do you mean leave? You mean out there in that hell" How the fuck we doing that?"

"Let's just say I have a little experience."

CHAPTER FOURTEEN

Chief Maxwell Harris was on the floor of the City Garage screaming in desperation. Roscoe Stern was pacing back and forth a few feet away, crying hysterically. The crumpled corpse of the gunman was at the foot of the stairs, minus most of his head.

"Elizabeth! Elizabeth! Stay with me! C'mon!" Max tore away Elizabeth's shirt to see just how bad her injuries were. Her left shoulder was covered in blood and she was moaning. Max checked her pulse to find that it was racing.

Roscoe sobbed like a child. "Is she dead?"

"No, thank God she was wearing her vest. A few of the pellets hit her in the shoulder. Let's pray they didn't hit an artery; that's her only chance. Elizabeth! Talk to me! C'mon!"

"How bad is it?" whispered Elizabeth.

"Dear Lord, woman! You scared the shit out of me!"

"Well I'm sorry, I was shot you know," she managed a thin smile.

"Can you stand up?"

"I think so. Jesus that hurt so damn bad!"

Max managed to get her to her feet and helped her over to a chair. She sat down and touched her shoulder, wincing at the pain. "First you kiss me and then you try getting a look at the girls? Shame on you, Max, I'm not that kind of girl."

"Real funny. Take the vest off; we need to see the damage."

"Aren't you just being fresh? Turn around, Roscoe. Stop crying, sweetheart, I'm fine." The frightened mechanic wiped his cheeks and turned around.

Max helped Elizabeth unbutton her shirt, and he unfastened her vest and took it off. She was wearing a tank top and a bra. Max tried his best to remain professional but he couldn't help but notice her perfect breasts.

"You're blushing, Maxwell. Try not to hurt yourself; I'm sure you've seen boobs before."

"Will you please stop, for crying out loud? You're not making this any easier!"

"Sorry, bossman, I'll be good."

"Roscoe, we need to stop the bleeding; find some towels or rags or something!"

"Make sure they're clean, please!" shouted Elizabeth.

"How you doing? You feel dizzy or light headed?

"No, just feel like I was run over by a bus."

Roscoe returned with some clean towels from the break room. Maxwell took them and tenderly wiped away the blood. He could see two small holes just under her collarbone. "Can you move your arm at all? Try bending your elbow."

Elizabeth bent her elbow and moved her forearm slightly. She wiggled her fingers and tapped her fingers to her thumb. "I think I'm okay. I can start to raise my arm but it hurts too bad."

"That's good, hold still." Max leaned her forward in the chair and checked her back. "Both the pellets went clean through, so we don't have to worry about getting them out, which is a good thing. We just need to get the bleeding to stop. Roscoe, find me a first aid kit. If you don't have one in here, check one of the patrol cars."

"Holy shit! What happened in here?" Max turned to see a group of rain-soaked people standing in the doorway, wide-eyed and slack jawed.

"Any of you trained in first aid? Nurse? EMT? Anyone?" Max was not getting their attention; they were shocked at the sight of the dead man at the bottom of the stairs.

"Hey! Listen! HEY!"

"Uh, yes sir, officer. I'm a pediatrician. I live down in Galveston but I came up here to help my sis..."

"Shut up and get over here!" Max screamed.

"Be nice, Maxwell. I'm sorry for my boss here, he's a little freaked out right now," Elizabeth smiled at the woman who had just spoken up, "Hey! Perv! What are you looking at! Stop staring at my tits before I come over there and slap you!" Elizabeth was glaring at a man in his late twenties who was practically drooling over her. Once he realized that she was talking to him, he turned his head the opposite way.

"Ma'am, I'm sorry I yelled at you. Please come and help me. The rest of you get in and close the door! If your vehicle is gassed up, you should hit the road while you still can; otherwise, please sit in the next office."

The woman walked over to Elizabeth and looked at her injury. "Apply steady pressure on both sides. We need to get the bleeding stopped. If we can't, we'll have to stitch her up."

"Can we move her?" asked Max.

"You haven't been outside for a bit, have you sir?" the doctor asked.

"No, why?"

"I wouldn't drive out there if I were you. The rain is so heavy you can't see much more than a few feet in front of you. The wind is blowing so hard I'd be afraid it would blow a car off the road. The power is out for as far as we can see. We're better off in here."

"We don't have much choice. We can't stay here; this building is so old it's gonna come down on top of us eventually. We have to get to the high school. I have a command post set up in the east wing near the gym. We'll be safe there."

"If you say so, we need to get moving now. I'll stay with her but I need someone to help me."

"Roscoe! Get in here and help the doctor!"

Roscoe entered the room and stared at the ceiling, trying as hard as he could not to look at Elizabeth's chest. He bumped into a desk and grunted.

"It's okay, Roscoe, don't hurt yourself. Get over here and help this nice lady."

Once Roscoe took Max's place, he walked to the doorway and counted three people. One was the perv that had been staring at Elizabeth; the other two were city employees whom Max had deputized that morning. "Okay people, it's time to go. We have to head to the high school as quick as we can. Elizabeth, Roscoe, and the doctor will ride with me. The rest of you need to find a truck or an SUV and pull up to the front door. Let's go!"

Max went outside in the wind and rain and was almost blown off his feet. The pelting rain stung like the spray from a thousand BB guns. He managed to find his SUV and pulled it up to the front door of the admin office. One of his deputies pulled up behind him in a full sized truck. They managed to get Elizabeth into the back seat and kept pressure on her gunshot wounds. Once the group was loaded up and ready to leave, Max said, "OK, just follow me and take it nice and slow. The high school is just a few blocks from here, should be there in two or three minutes."

Once they were on the road, Max immediately began to question his decision to leave. He had to turn the wheel as far to the right as it would go to drive into the wind and stay on the road. Anytime the wind decreased or shifted slightly, the SUV would lurch to the right, coming dangerously close to the flooded ditch. He had the floodlights, the search lights, and the emergency lights on just to see a couple of feet in front of him. The SUV was being pummeled with flying debris. The rear passenger window was slammed by something and the window cracked. Thankfully the window didn't shatter, but the crack was splintering and growing by the second. They managed to make it to the high school and pulled their vehicles right up to the double doors of the gymnasium. They entered the gym and quickly headed to the locker rooms.

Max closed the doors and looked across the gym floor. Roscoe was carrying Elizabeth in his arms. He ran up to Roscoe. "What's wrong? Is she okay? Elizabeth!"

"Boss, I think she just fainted. We took two steps in the door and down she went." Roscoe continued to walk to the locker rooms. "She's still breathing, but the pain must have been too much for her."

Max took hold of her hand and checked her pulse. Steady and strong. Roscoe was right, she just fainted. They all managed to get inside the locker room. Max turned on the battery-powered lanterns so they could see. Roscoe gently laid Elizabeth down on a cot and the doctor looked over her injuries.

"What's the diagnosis, doc?" asked Max.

"Just what I was afraid of, the bleeding hasn't stopped. I'll have to stitch her up. Her pulse is steady and her breathing is fine. Good thing she fainted. It'll make these stitches a lot less painful for her."

"Good. Check that cabinet over there, should have everything you need." Max took a deep breath and sat down in a chair. He reached into his pocket, pulled out the pill bottle and took inventory. Ten pills left. His hip and knee hurt worse than usual. He kicked back two pills and put the bottle back in his pocket. He was going to run out of pills very soon. He had a full bottle at the police station and another full bottle at his house. He was furious with himself for forgetting to grab one of them. His house would soon be underwater and he could only hope that the police station withstood the wind. He needed to figure out something quick. He looked to his left to see the doctor working on Elizabeth. He walked over to the supply cabinet and started digging around.

"Officer, I got everything I need, thank you." The doctor did not divert her eyes from her patient but could hear Max rooting around in the cabinet.

"Thank you, doctor, please don't let me distract you. I'm just taking inventory of our supplies." The doctor didn't say anything and continued stitching up Elizabeth's wounds. Max fumbled with his keys, attempting to open the padlock on one of the drawers. He found what he needed – a ninety count bottle of Tramadol. The drug wasn't nearly as effective as Vicodin, but it would do in a pinch. Max popped the top and filled up his pill bottle. He closed up the cabinet and turned around. The looky-loo who had been lusting over Elizabeth was watching him. Max couldn't tell if the guy had seen him swipe the pills. "You need something, son? What's your name?"

"Name's Stew. No sir, just wondering if you know what's going on."

"Well, the worst of it isn't due for a few hours. I can only guess that a few tornadoes were kicked up in our direction."

"You mean this isn't the worst of it?" Stew asked in a trembled voice.

"Not by a long shot. Count yourself lucky you're safe in here with us." Max turned and walked to the other side of the room. He needed to do a head count of his officers. He scanned the room, then exited and walked into the girl's locker room. He saw two of his deputies trying to dry off. Max walked over to Deputy Shackleford.

"Gene, what happened to your people?"

"No idea, they took off and headed home. I tried to tell them to wait it out here, but they didn't listen."

"Well, son, I'm glad you were smart enough to stay here." Max keyed up his radio. "This is unit 1-0; I need a status and location from everyone. Units 1-1, 1-6, and 1-8 are at the command post with me." Max paused and heard nothing. "Kathy, you still at the station?"

One of his deputies was standing in the doorway. "Chief, Kathy is walking in with a group of people."

Max walked to the doorway and saw Kathy. She looked like she had jumped in a swimming pool with her uniform on. She had a family in tow - a young couple with a toddler and an infant. An older, gray-haired couple walked in as well. Kathy led them to the locker room and told them to go inside and dry off.

"Kathy, you okay? Tell me what happened." Max handed her a towel and put his hand on her shoulder.

"Thank God we made it here. That was the scariest thing I've ever done in my life. Thought for sure we wouldn't make it. Got some bad news for you. You want the bad news first or the really, really bad news?"

Max frowned. "Surprise me."

"Well, first the power went out, pretty sure all over town. I think a tornado passed behind the station. It's a wreck, probably demolished by now. Blew half the roof off and destroyed your office. Windows blew out and wrecked everything. We waited it out in the armory and headed straight here. Charlie make it here? Where is he?"

"Charlie's not here, what happened to him?"

Kathy started to cry, "Oh no! No, no, no! He left before I did! I stayed behind when these people came to the station for help. He has to be here!"

Max hugged Kathy. "Hey, take it easy, you're safe. I'm sure Charlie's just fine. I bet he'll be walking in the door in no time at all. You get in there and get out of those wet clothes. There's a tub full of clean gym clothes in each locker room."

Kathy smiled through her tears. "Oh fun. We get to look like high school kids."

"Kathy, hold on a second. Was that the bad news, or the really, really bad news?"

"Oh yeah, I already told you the worst part. The bad news is I completely smashed up my patrol car getting over here."

Max smiled at her. "Oh, that's fine. I'll just take it out of your next check, if we ever start getting them again."

Kathy wiped the tears from her cheek and with a smile,

gave her boss a playful slap on the arm. She disappeared into the girl's locker room. Max knew he had probably just told Kathy a lie. If Charlie left before she did and she didn't pass him getting here, his car probably blew off the road. At best, he got lost in the storm and couldn't find his way to the gym. Max hoped Charlie pulled over and was riding out the storm somewhere safe. They would have no way of knowing until the storm cleared. Going to search for Charlie in the raging storm would be a bad call. As much as Max hated to admit it, Charlie was on his own.

Max walked back into the locker room to check on Elizabeth. She was resting on the cot as the doctor cleaned up at the sink. "Well, Doc, what can you tell me?"

"She's going to be fine. I stitched up the holes and bandaged her up. She has two bruised ribs. I'm monitoring her blood pressure. I don't think she lost enough blood to require a transfusion."

"Thank God for you, ma'am. I mean that. Thank you." Max caught the woman off guard when he wrapped his arms around her and gave her a big hug. "I don't know what I would have done if you hadn't been there. You saved her life." Max released her and wiped tears from his eyes. "I'm so sorry that I yelled at you; please forgive me."

"You are very welcome, sir. And please don't apologize, it's not necessary. I can tell that woman is more than just a co-worker to you, am I right?"

Max wiped his eyes. "Is it that obvious? Ma'am, I just realized that I don't even know your name. I'm Chief Harris."

"Chief Harris, it's very obvious that you care for her a great deal. My name is Diana Stone."

"Dr. Stone, it's a pleasure to meet you," Max extended his hand and smiled, "a real pleasure."

Dr. Stone returned the gesture and asked, "Are we safe in here?"

"Yes, ma'am, it's the safest place in town. The far side of the east wing was built into the side of a hill with one side of the hallway underground, including the locker rooms. The only thing we have to worry about is the gym, which I'm certain is going to come down. Here in the boy's locker room the bathroom exits out into the hallway. We can get out that way if we need to."

"May I call you Max?"

"Please do."

"Max, tell me about your injury. I'd like to know if we're going to be spending time together."

Just then, Elizabeth opened her eyes and gazed at Max with a look of love and compassion. He saw the trust in her eyes and figured it was time to finally talk about it. He smiled at her and said, "Hey, you."

"Hey yourself." She smiled and laid her head back down on the cot.

"Feeling better?" Max's eyes lit up when he saw the smile on her face.

"A lot better. You give me some of the pills you hide in your pocket? I feel fantastic."

A look of worry dawned on his face. "What? How long have you known?"

"That you're an addict? Pretty much figured it out the day I met you."

"Hold on now. I'm not an addict; you have no idea the kind of pain I'm in."

"You're right. I have no idea because you never talk about it. It's okay, sweetheart, answer the doctor's question."

The doctor smiled and sat down next to Elizabeth. "Elizabeth, my name is Dr. Stone. It's a pleasure to meet you; I'm glad you're feeling better. I gave you some pills from the medicine cabinet that will help you deal with the pain. I stitched and bandaged you up. Two of your ribs are bruised. In order to breath comfortably, you'll need to take two of these every six hours." Dr. Stone handed her the bottle of Tramadol. "It will be a few days before you can breathe without pain. Max was kind enough to leave you with most of the bottle."

Max hung his head in shame. "I'm sorry. Didn't think you'd noticed."

"I can tell by the way you're walking and the ugly scowl that never seems to leave your face that you are in constant pain. I figured you were digging in there for something. The bottle should be completely full. Anyone stocking an emergency medicine cabinet would ensure that everything in it was topped off."

"I needed something. Only have ten pills left. The rest of my pills are, well, out there."

"Vicodin?"

"Yes."

"How long?"

"Three years."

"You know that Vicodin isn't meant to be taken for that long. Elizabeth is right; whether you believe it or not, you are an addict. If you don't want to explain how you were injured, I understand. But I would like to know the nature and extent of your injuries."

"No, it's fine. Elizabeth deserves to know. I've kept it from everyone for a very long time. The only person in my life who knows the entire story is my father. I don't know where to begin."

"Its okay, honey, take your time," said Elizabeth.

Max sat back in his chair and leaned against the wall. As he recalled the memories, torment and anguish washed over his face. Pain and sorrow gripped Maxwell and kept him silent for a very long minute. He stared at the ceiling and was terrified to speak. Dr. Stone and Elizabeth were patient, they started to doubt if Max would say anything at all. Max closed his eyes and feared the words that were about to escape his lips. The words were going to hurt him far worse than the pain he felt in his hip and knee.

"Before I came to work in this town, I was a Texas State Trooper. I had been with them for twelve years. I was a rising star, destined for great things. I was in charge of my own station faster than anyone had ever been before me. Then, I was given my own region. Nine stations were under my command. It was only a matter of time before I made the move to Austin as a deputy director. I had such ambition! So much was ahead of me. My career was more important than anything; I gladly gave up my marriage, thinking my ex-wife was doing nothing but holding me down. Part of me still believes that, but I can't help but wonder if I would still be married if I had actually slowed down and made my marriage a priority. I even fooled myself into thinking that the only thing I had to do to be a good husband and father was to pay the bills and provide a good life."

Max paused for a long time. Dr. Stone and Elizabeth looked at each other. Elizabeth had no idea that Max had a child. He didn't have photos on his desk and never mentioned his ex-wife or his child. They remained silent and waited for Max to continue.

"One Friday night I was off duty. About the only thing I enjoyed doing outside of work was going to high school football games. I played ball in high school and still loved it. So much fun supporting high school kids. When the game was over I pulled out of the parking lot in my truck. As I was driving home I heard a call go out over the scanner. A good friend of mine had pulled over a vehicle for a routine traffic stop. He didn't know it at the time but the vehicle had just been stolen. The owner of the vehicle had actually called it in when David was on the stop. He walked up to the window... It was just for a ... a busted brake light! The guy shot him in the head and drove off, left him there on the side of the road, like a dead dog!"

Max was sobbing. David had been his closest friend. They had been through the Academy together and stayed close even when Max was quickly promoted up the chain of command. Elizabeth wanted to go to him and wrap her arms around him. She knew she couldn't and started to cry. She looked to Dr. Stone, who understood immediately. The doctor sat down next to Max and held his hand.

"I dug in my glove box for my pistol. It wasn't there. I'd been to the range that morning and forgot to put it back in my truck. I was in the area where David made the stop and was going to stop by and talk with him; it had been a week or so we last talked and I wanted to catch up. Another patrol arrived on the scene and announced on the radio that David had been shot in the head. I had never been so enraged in my entire life. I screamed so loud my throat hurt. I knew what road they were on and headed off to find those assholes. Lucky me! They raced past me, and I turned around and chased them. They were about to head into a residential area when they took a corner too hard and skidded off the road. I had them right in front of me. The driver's side door was directly in front of me. I didn't have my gun and no way in hell was I just going to let them get away. I stepped on the gas and T-boned their car going sixty miles an hour. My airbag didn't go off and my leg was crushed. I broke my hip, my femur, and shattered my knee. I almost died. I don't know how, but I stayed conscious the entire time. I didn't think I'd be able to walk again. I looked down at my leg and could see bone sticking out in two places."

"Max, honey, you did the right thing. You stopped them. You can walk and you stopped them!" Elizabeth was trying as hard as she could to find the words to comfort Max.

"I may have done the right thing, but not without paying a price much too high."

Dr. Stone looked into Max's eyes. "So you regret killing them? Or is it because of the pain you're still in?"

"God no," Max laughed, "I'll live with this pain for the rest of my life knowing those pieces of shit are rotting in hell."

Elizabeth looked at Max and could tell there was something else, something much worse. "Then what is it?"

Max didn't know if he could speak the words. He was almost ready to stop talking and leave things as they were. He hung his head and closed his eyes. After a minute, he decided he needed to tell Elizabeth everything. "When they slid off the road, a mother and her little girl walked over to the vehicle to see if they were okay. I killed them, too."

CHAPTER FIFTEEN

Florida Governor Lori Prince sat in the reading room of the governor's mansion, better known as "The People's House" in Tallahassee, Florida. The mansion was a popular tourist attraction and was open to public tours free of charge during normal business hours, Monday through Friday - at least it had been open to the public before Hurricane Luther.

Governor Prince was born and raised in Florida and was no stranger to hurricanes. When she took office, the first order of business was to upgrade the mansion to make it hurricane-proof. She was shocked that her predecessors had not made the issue a priority.

When Hurricane Luther finally moved out to sea for good, Lori Prince was ready to get her hands dirty and get to work. She contacted the state liaison of the Unified National Guard to coordinate relief efforts. For the better part of a week she was given the runaround with empty promises and vague declarations of upcoming relief efforts. She finally gave up on the Unified National Guard and took the matter straight to the White House. Prince had worked with the president's Chief of Staff, Stacy Reid, and used their relationship to her benefit. Stacy arranged a private meeting with the president. President Powers was shocked by the lack of support and promised her that help was coming. All she needed to do was be patient.

Upon her return to Florida, the governor made arrangements to be flown to the disaster area so she could survey the damage firsthand. What she saw was nothing short of complete and total catastrophe. City after city was demolished. Towns close to the coast were wiped completely off to map as Luther swallowed them up and carried them out into the Atlantic. It was as if the state of Florida was not only devastated by a hurricane but a tsunami as well. Governor Prince wept as she envisioned the death toll. The body count would not number in the hundreds or thousands, but tens of thousands, probably much higher.

When she returned to The People's House and secluded herself in the private residence quarters, Prince attempted to contact Stacy Reid via vidcon. A few minutes later she was looking at her former employee, desperately pleading her case to the Floridian who was the president's closest advisor. Convincing Stacy to help her wasn't difficult for her since her own home town was near the coast and no longer existed. Stacy's parents had both died many years ago, and the rest of her family had moved away from Florida. When Stacy presented Governor Princes' concerns to the president he dismissed her, choosing to close himself up in the Oval Office to devise a plan. Stacy found it odd that Malcolm would make the plans without her, but she trusted her boss to do the right thing and went about the business of running the day-to-day operations of the White House.

Malcolm called Stacy back to his office around dinnertime, and the two joined Governor Prince in a vid-con. The president told the governor that he was going to institute a full lock-down of the disaster zone and feed the press a story about a chemical spill and a quarantine zone. The cover story was to prevent widespread panic. The president told Governor Prince that the only truth the press would be told was that an aircraft carrier was en route to the Florida coast to begin search and rescue missions. Governor Prince was pleased.

Several days later at the infamous meeting when she cussed out the president, Lori Prince was anxious to get to the bottom of things. The promises made to her had yet to even begin to happen. A great many soldiers in the Unified National Guard stationed in Florida had been killed right along with the citizens. Governor Prince called in every favor she had accumulated during her political career, calling every governor she knew well and other she only knew by name. She begged and pleaded with them to send every guardsman they could spare to try Florida. Not one governor was willing to help her. They all had their own states to look after. Their guardsmen were busy maintaining law and order in their major cities. To make matters worse, every governor she spoke to told her to be patient; the White House was sending help. Since President Powers was sending an aircraft carrier to render aide, their guardsmen would be wasting time in Florida when they could be at home. Governor Prince left the White House enraged. She returned to Florida, resigned to the fact that she was on her own and powerless to do a thing.

Twenty-two years prior, Governor Prince had been in her senior year at the University of Miami and followed the horrors of the aftermath of Hurricane Katrina. Kathleen Blanco, then governor of the state of Louisiana, failed miserably at handling the crisis. In Lori Prince's opinion, President Bush and the Federal Emergency Management Agency were more to blame. Watching the news footage of people stranded on their rooftops waiting for rescue was the most heart breaking and outrageous thing that the college senior had ever seen in her life. Lori was already a political science major and had aspirations of going into politics. She believed in democracy and had a strong desire to serve the people and make their lives better. She would spend her political career ensuring that the gross negligence seen during Katrina would never be repeated.

Twenty-two years later, she was governor of the fourth largest state in the country and considered herself a total failure. History would forget Kathleen Blanco and her poor response to New Orleans in 2005. History would brand Prince as the worst governor in the history of the United States.

Governor Prince sat on the balcony outside her bedroom and looked at the bottle of Ambien in her hand. She was contemplating taking the entire bottle and falling into an eternal, peaceful slumber. The only thought that gave her pause was that of Malcolm Powers. He had betrayed her and hung her out to dry. He'd sat behind the Resolute desk in the Oval Office and lied to her face. Her hatred for the man was the only thing that saved her from taking her life.

****

Benjamin Black was quickly amassing a large fortune and formidable power in the greater Orlando area. His experience at the Kissimmee Super Wal-Mart opened his eyes to the opportunity that the wasteland of Florida had to offer. Where other people saw chaos, Benjamin saw a chance at power. Once they took Chester Stephens' retail store from him, they stripped it clean of everything that would help his group survive and prosper. Benjamin quickly fled from the fallen Wal-Mart, the dead bodies inside not something he wanted to answer for should law and order be restored. A week after they left the Kissimmee Super Wal-Mart, his group returned to move in and set up shop. If Benjamin Black had any doubts about civilization returning to the way it was, the passage of time removed any lingering hope. The former Jiffy Lube manager knew that in this new world, he would be king.

Benjamin thought back to the battle he had with Chester Stephens and reversed roles with the slain manager. What would he have done to repel his own attack? If he were Chester, how would he have done things differently? Benjamin corrected all of Chester's mistakes. The pedestrian entrance to the loading docks was camouflaged and barricaded from the inside. Benjamin completely closed off the door so it could never be used again. The next order of business was to draw up a rotation for guard duty. Sentries were posted on all four corners of the roof and would contact Benjamin by radio if anything suspicious was happening. The south entrance that Benjamin's people had plowed into with a makeshift bulldozer was now fortified. A twenty-four foot truck was tipped over on its side directly in front of the entrance. Two armed guards sat atop the U-Haul truck, and another two sat inside the sallyport. A champion sharpshooter was happy to pull double shifts sitting on top of the U-Haul. He relished the opportunity to repel an attack. Every few days a band of thugs would try to shoot their way in, and he gleefully dropped them like flies.

Benjamin sent out scouting parties everyday to find more supplies and every night they returned with their booty. Crowds of people showed up at Benjamin's fortress; the price of admission was to fill a shopping cart with useable supplies and hand them over. A five-gallon container of gasoline granted immediate entry. Benjamin welcomed new recruits into his growing militia and didn't tolerate disorder, disobedience, or laziness. Those not willing to pull their weight got an ass kicking as the only warning. The next violation resulted in banishment from the community. After a few people were sent packing with a broken jaw or nose and told not to come back, the rest of the group got the message and dared not cross Benjamin.

Benjamin had bigger plans for his growing enterprise. Once he amassed truckloads of supplies and his fortress became uncomfortably overcrowded, Benjamin set his sights on a much bigger piece of real estate. When the preparations were complete, every man, woman and child loaded up backpacks and rolling luggage with supplies. Every working vehicle was loaded to capacity and staged in a convoy. Benjamin was the last man out the door of the Kissimmee Super Wal-Mart. He pulled out his lighter and threw it into a pool of gasoline. The vapors ignited and followed a trail to the center of the store, where a bonfire soaked in lighter fluid erupted into flames. The center bonfire lit three more trails of gasoline, which led to three more bonfires. The Kissimmee Super Wal-Mart was quickly engulfed in flames and by morning, all that was left was smoldering ash. Benjamin Black had no intention of leaving a solid structure for another group to move right into. What was left of Orlando would soon belong to him. He would not permit another group to pose a threat.

An hour later, Benjamin Black and his loyal community moved into their new home at Universal Studios. It would be a challenging task to secure the property and repel attacks. The one thing that Benjamin had going for him was that the property already had a decent perimeter in place. Theme parks didn't make a lot of money if people could just sneak in. He could secure it with a dozen or so pairs of roving patrols. He came up with the brilliant idea of using a numbered password system that he'd learned from a movie. It was simple yet ingenious. Each day would have a random number assigned to it. For example, if the day was assigned a nine, all one had to do was challenge an unfamiliar face with a smaller number, and wait the other person to respond with the number that added up to nine. If the stranger couldn't do the simple math, it was obvious that he was an intruder. For the first several weeks, the primary task for everyone, including Benjamin, was cleaning up the hurricane ravaged park. Within a month of their arrival, they had over five hundred people living there.

Benjamin Black was proud of all he had accomplished. He was respected by all his residents, and they were loyal to him in exchange for food and shelter. Benjamin knew he could branch out and expand. His next destination would be the Magic Kingdom.

****

Lindsay Sanderson was being smacked over the head with a broom. She and her two children had been evicted from the Central Park Obama-Camp the day before, and she was dumpster diving to feed her hungry children. At first she thought the angry woman yielding the broom was an employee of the restaurant that owned the dumpster, but she soon realized it was only another mother defending her turf like a momma cat defending her kittens. Lindsay raised her arms to stop the blows but the woman kept swinging. As the broom smacked the top of her left hand, breaking one of her fingers, any sympathy Lindsay had for the woman immediately evaporated. The fact that they shared the bond of motherhood meant nothing to her if this woman was intent on doing her harm. Lindsay screamed at the top of her lungs and kicked the woman in the knee. She fell to the ground, giving Lindsay the chance for a quick escape. She quickly grabbed her children by the hand and hustled up the sidewalk. She doubted the woman would leave her own children unattended long enough to pursue her, but retaliation can make people forget a lot of things. She looked over her shoulder to the alleyway and was relieved to see no sign of the woman. Lindsay wasn't afraid of the woman herself; what scared her was the possibility of landing in jail and losing her children to Child Protective Services.

Lindsay carefully crossed the street and sat down on a park bench; setting about the task of distracting her children from what they'd just experienced. She was becoming a pro at helping her children disregard the miserable world around them. William would be proud. The day before when riot squads emptied out the Central Park Obama-Camp, Lindsay worried about her husband and the anguish he would feel upon learning their fate. She was going to fight hard to survive the two weeks until she could talk to him again. The night before William left to join the Army, she'd promised him that she would protect their children and that the three of them would survive without him. At first she'd worried that William would receive the news and leave boot camp to come rescue her. Lindsay remembered that after the war with the Great Empire of Iran started, the military made it clear to the public that desertion would lead to a court-martial and a minimum of five years in prison. She knew William would never jeopardize his family like that.

She sat on the park bench and hugged her children. She loved them so very deeply but at the same time was angry with herself for letting an ugly thought continue to enter her mind. A very small part of her resented her children for the burden they caused her. Any time the thought came to her, she fought to free herself from it. She imagined what her life would be like without them, how much easier it would be to survive. All she had to do was hold her children close to chase the thought from her mind.

Lindsay looked to her left and right, then turned around and scanned the rest of the park. She firmly believed there was safety in numbers. If other homeless people were scattered around the park, she felt much safer. She was less likely to be bothered by anyone or be the sole recipient of half concealed, judgmental glances. Too many homeless people in the park would attract the attention of the Unified National Guard, so she was careful to search for the right balance and try to blend in with the crowd.

Lindsay had spent the previous twenty-four hours living one minute at a time. Before they moved into Central Park, she had depended on William's judgment to keep them safe. Now she was without her husband and it was up to her to call the shots. She had to stop living moment by moment and start thinking of living day-by-day. Wandering around aimlessly wasn't safe. She had to come up with a plan. Her children had barely had a scrap of food to eat since they left the Central Park Obama-Camp. When the Unified National Guard came marching in to evict them, Lindsay was not at her home. She'd asked her neighbor to look after her place so she could take the kids with her to the medical station at the north end of Central Park. She was standing in line when the riot squads began throwing tear gas into the makeshift streets. She tried desperately to run back to her home but was cut off at every turn. She fled into the streets surrounding Central Park and waited for the Unified National Guard to leave. Lindsay sat down outside a well lit drugstore and held her kids tight so they could sleep. She was able to doze off a few times and get enough rest so she could tackle the next day.

When the sun came up, Lindsay walked toward the Central Park Obama-Camp to find exactly what she expected. Bulldozers and dump trucks were tearing down all the structures and hauling everything away. Evicting them would do little good if the residents could just return after the soldiers left. All around the park, the former residents watched and waited for the Unified National Guard to leave. Once they departed, the residents swarmed in to try and salvage anything they could.

Lindsay sat on the park bench and let her children play on the ground in front of her. Anytime they took one step beyond arms reach, she quickly reigned them back in. She was determined to sit right there on that bench and not get up until she had some sort of plan. Lindsay thought of the different possibilities for shelter and weighed the risk. Thirty minutes later, she had a plan in mind. The first item on the agenda was to find a public restroom in a crowded place with lots of foot traffic. She and her children would bathe as best they could and attempt to wash their clothes. The less ragged they looked, the better. It would increase their odds of survival and allow them to blend in with everyday people. The second item on the agenda was to loiter in large public places like airports, train stations, or shopping malls. She made it a point to look like she was in each place for a reason. She would only stay for three or four hours to avoid suspicion.

After one week of thinking she was blending in perfectly, a TSA agent at LaGuardia Airport approached her. Lindsay trembled in fear and began to cry, certain that she was about to be arrested even though she hadn't committed a crime. What she failed to realize was that with air travel being so expensive, only the very wealthy had the funds to afford it. Lindsay and her children stuck out like a sore thumb. The TSA agent knew what she was doing. He told her to stop crying and calm down. He took out a piece of paper and wrote down an address and his name. Lindsay was suspicious of the man but reluctantly took the slip of paper. He told her to go to the address and mention his name. The people there would provide Lindsay and her children with food and a warm bed. She looked confused and wanted to believe him, but she knew that when something seemed too good to be true, it often was. He assured her that it was a private, charitable organization for the homeless. Regrettably, they had to be selective and had to keep the location a secret because they didn't have the funds or the means to cater to the waves of homeless people walking the streets of New York City. The man smiled warmly and shared with her that he and his family lived there years ago. The only price of admission was your word that you wouldn't stay longer than two weeks.

Two weeks was all Lindsay needed.

CHAPTER SIXTEEN

The president of the United States was being hauled away by the Secret Service. His feet were about an inch off the floor as he was transported down the hallway from the Clinton Room to an elevator. He deduced that this was the standard procedure to prevent the president from protesting and refusing to evacuate with the Secret Service. Along the way he noticed that every entranceway was replaced by a massive steel door. The lights were out and all Malcolm could see was a faint, red light that barely illuminated the hallway. The president and his four protectors entered the elevator; and the door slammed shut. The elevator did not hesitate or require a button to push; it immediately descended.

"Ad-Man secure." One of the agents spoke the president's call sign over the radio. Malcolm was not particularly fond of his call sign. The "Ad" was short for admiral. He understood the meaning and so did everyone else. He still didn't like it because it sounded like he was an advertising executive and not the president of the United States.

The elevator traveled ten stories under the White House and the door opened to reveal the presidential bunker. From the time the first explosion rocked the White House until the door of the elevator opened one hundred and twenty feet below, forty-seven seconds had elapsed.

"OK boys, that was fun. Someone mind telling me what's going on?"

"Yes, Mr. President. A dump truck filled with explosives crashed the barricade and collided with the north wall of the compound. It exploded on impact and took down a large section of the north wall."

"I heard more than one explosion."

"Yes, Mr. President, I heard them, too. Let me check." The Secret Service agent pulled out his smartphone and tapped a few buttons. "Once the wall was down, suicide bombers started running across the lawn."

"What about my guests in the Clinton Room? Are they safe?"

"Yes sir, they are fine. The White House A.I. secured the

room and they are safe."

"Good, thank you, Mike."

"Yes, Mr. President."

"Computer, give me a status update on what's happening." President Powers straightened his suit coat.

"Yes, Mr. President." The screen in front of the president displayed video footage of the attack. "Seven assailants have been killed on the White House lawn. Four explosions managed to cause minor damage to the north wall. One explosion was too far away to cause damage. The remaining two assailants' vests failed to detonate."

The lead agent in charge of the presidential detail smiled when he saw the footage. "Excellent! My sniper teams on the roof did an outstanding job." The footage showed the suicide bombers sprinting across the lawn; one by one they were struck by a bullet and fell to the ground. They had dead-man switches which caused the explosives to detonate when they hit the ground.

"Yes, Mike, I'm very impressed. Your team did an outstanding job. Well done."

"Thank you, Mr. President."

"Computer, I want you to grant full temporary access to Chief of Staff Reid. Tell her everything you just told me and inform her that I am alive and well. I'm sure my guests have a lot of questions. Once you've answered her questions, I want you to put her on vid-con. I'd like to speak with her as soon as possible."

"I'm sorry, Mr. President, I'm afraid I can't do that."

"Excuse me? And just why not?"

"Security procedures must be adhered to, Mr. President. If you were allowed direct communication with anyone outside of this room, you might be pressured into surrendering yourself to enemy forces."

"Mike?"

"She's right, Mr. President. You still have full command and control down here. You just cannot have personal interaction with anyone. The office of the president must be protected."

"I understand, thank you. If someone had a gun to my wife's head, I would no doubt give in to any demand to save her life. How much longer will I need to stay down here?"

"Mr. President, we are going to get you out of here just as soon as possible." Special Agent Mike Reese had been the lead agent on the president's detail for the last four years. He knew the president could be fidgety about all of the protection and fuss.

"What's the hold-up? What are we waiting on?"

"Sir, we are erecting a make-shift barricade to block off the hole in the north wall of the compound. We are also grounding all air traffic within two hundred miles. Any flight approaching DC is being diverted to another airport. Once that is done and we run a full sweep of the area and the airspace is secure, we can move you up top."

"So, I'm going to be down here for a while?"

"Yes, sir."

"Computer, send word to Chief of Staff Reid that the guests in the Clinton Room will be joining me in the presidential bunker."

"Yes, Mr. President."

"Mr. President, I'm not sure that is..."

"Mike, don't start. I will not hide out down here like some frightened child while they stay up top during a terrorist attack on the White House. They were all screened before they entered the White House, and they have my full trust. Make it happen."

"Yes, Mr. President, I'll get it done."

"Thank you, Mike."

Special Agent Reese left the other three agents behind and rode the elevator to the top. A few minutes passed, and the elevator door opened. CIA Director Jimenez rolled his wheelchair into the room along with FBI Director Warren Gill and Secretary Laferriere.

"Mr. President, do I still have access to Langley?" The director of the CIA was steering his wheelchair into the room and almost knocked over Secretary Laferriere.

"Yes, Roberto. The link remains effective as long as you're in the White House."

"Good. Computer, bring up a map of the Iranian Theater."

Warren Gill looked confused and exchanged glances with the other men in the room. "Mr. Jimenez, an attack on the White House just took place and we don't know if something bigger is coming, and you're looking at the Iranian Theater?"

The crusty old man in the wheelchair scratched his face and didn't take his eyes off the screen. "Mr. Gill, I'm very well aware of what's happening; if you recall I was in the same room."

The elevator door opened, and the remaining guests of the Clinton Room poured into the room.

"Why the hell are we looking at the Empire? We need to know what's happening outside right now! More attacks could be coming!" Governor Prince was glaring at Jimenez and then looked at the president in desperation.

"There won't be any more attacks." Jimenez said with confidence.

Everyone in the room looked at the president. He was as confused as the rest of them; he calmly addressed the CIA Director. "Roberto, I think everyone in the room, especially me, deserves an explanation. What just happened?"

"The attack we were just a part of was nothing but a diversion to draw our attention away from something else."

Governor Prince rolled her eyes. "Exactly, which is why we need to be figuring out what they are going to do next! This could be a part of a very large attack! We need to figure out what the next one will be before it happens and a lot of people die! Stop wasting time and do your job, Jimenez!"

"Governor Prince, I am doing my job, if you would kindly calm down and let me speak."

The president silenced the governor with only a glance.

"The Silent Warriors have never once coordinated multiple attacks. The Thanksgiving Day Massacre happened in several cities, but it was still one attack. They have also never hit a military or political target. They always focus on attacking the public to get people angry at us."

Secretary of Defense Decker quickly interjected. "That's true, but why did they change tactics? What does it mean?"

"I don't know, but with the majority of our resources looking within our own borders, I have a feeling we need to take a look at what the Empire is doing in theirs."

The president addressed the military personnel in the room. "Generals, Admiral, do you see anything out of the ordinary in terms of troop deployment? Are they preparing to invade Europe?"

The Chairman of the Joint Chiefs answered the question. "Mr. President, that is not likely; we have no doubt that they are planning an invasion, but our best estimates put that twelve months out at best."

"Could that estimate be wrong?" Secretary Laferriere asked.

"Right or wrong, the question doesn't matter," Director Jimenez interrupted. "This diversionary tactic will buy them twelve to sixteen hours to accomplish something under the radar. Invading Europe will be no more a secret than Normandy was eighty-three years ago. That's not what this is."

Everyone looked at the president, who had a Ph.D in American History. "Normandy was certainly not a secret; it was the largest military invasion in the history of the world at the time. The Allies did, however, create many diversions and spread misinformation so the Nazis would think the invasion would be launched at a different location. I agree with Director Jimenez; the Empire probably thought they would have a short window to quickly sneak something past us. The question is what."

Admiral Mack stepped forward. "Computer, give me a status report on the Port of Gibraltar."

"I'm sorry, Admiral Mack, you don't have access to my system. Presidential authorization is required."

"Computer, grant full temporary access to everyone in this room with the exception of the Secret Service Agents, and grant Admiral Mack's request immediately."

"Yes, Mr. President." The map of the Iranian Theater zoomed in on the Port of Gibraltar. "The *James Russell* is operating at sixty-two percent efficiency. The flight deck will be operational in fourteen hours. Allied Forces in Spain have redeployed and have secured the north and south sides of Gibraltar. They are holding the line from Tetouan to the Atlantic Coast. Iranian forces to the south of the line have shown no signs of advance towards the port."

"What?" Admiral Mack inquired. "I was certain this had something to do with Gibraltar. Computer, what is the status of the Iranian fleet in the Mediterranean?"

"The Iranian fleet has shown no signs of movement in the

last twenty-four hours."

Admiral Mack looked defeated. "Maybe we are on a wild goose chase here. Another attack might be coming for us here at home."

"I'm sure that the agencies represented in this room are working diligently to prevent that from happening. I agree with Director Jimenez; this is a diversion." FBI Director Warren Gill studied the map intently.

"Thank you, Warren." Roberto Jimenez even sounded like a grouch when he was expressing gratitude.

General Weygandt addressed the White House A.I. "Computer, display the five enemy bunkers and give a status report on each."

Secretary of Defense Decker spoke up. "Computer, standby on the status report. General, I know what you're thinking and let me address your concern. All five bunkers are under constant surveillance. We can read the license plates of any vehicles coming or going from any of the facilities. If we detect a spike in radiation we know there's a chance they're attempting to move one of their nukes. If they open the launch doors at any of the facilities, we know immediately. If either of those things happens, we can strike immediately and destroy anything topside of the bunker."

"Thank you, Mr. Secretary. I figured you would have a watchful eye over the bunkers. Computer, continue with status report."

"Bunkers 1 and 2 have had no significant movement in the last twenty-four hours. Radiation levels remain normal. Bunkers 3 and 4 were resupplied by armored vehicles."

"Wait. Computer, standby. Why do we let them resupply their bunkers?" Governor Prince asked.

"They have a series of underground roads that lead to the bunkers. The entrance to the tunnels is always in a populated city, usually next to a hospital or a school." Secretary Decker replied with disdain.

"Bastards. Why do we still follow the Geneva Convention again? They seem to be doing just fine without it," Governor Prince replied. "Computer, continue with the status report."

"Radiation levels at Bunker 5 have not increased in the last twenty-four hours."

"That's it? What about movement at Bunker 5?" Governor Prince asked.

"We don't know. Six months out of the year the weather blocks out the bunker from our satellites. If we're lucky, we get a clear day or two a few times during the blackout. All we can do is monitor the radiation levels. It's exactly why they chose the location." Director Jimenez didn't like secrets being kept from him.

The president had been listening intently to everything, taking it all in and thinking. "Roberto, I'm starting to suspect this has something to do with Bunker 5. It's the only thing that it could be. They aren't moving towards Gibraltar, and we can see anything that goes on at the other four bunkers."

"Mr. President, I'm inclined to agree with you. However, beyond the radiation levels, we can't tell what is going on. Any drones we send near the bunker get shot down before they can see anything."

"What would happen if they tried to move a nuke out of the bunker?"

"We would know it the instant it came to the surface. We could target and destroy it before they loaded it onto a vehicle," Jimenez explained with complete confidence.

"That's good to know." Governor Prince smiled at Director Jimenez for the first time.

"Governor, I'm glad you appr... Wait! Something is happening. That can't be right! Computer, confirm the radiation levels at Bunker 5."

"Radiation levels have increased by six hundred nineteen percent."

"God no! They're launching a nuke!" Stacy Reid was covering her mouth in surprise.

"Relax, ma'am. That's not what's happening; something else is wrong." Roberto had lifted his hands to manipulate the map on the screen to overlay a detailed weather map of the region.

"Did someone detonate a nuke and try to take out the facility? I didn't authorize a launch, and the leaders of the Allied Forces must unanimously approve a nuclear strike launched from

Europe!" President Powers was angry but maintained his composure.

Jimenez cleared his throat. "Mr. President, a nuclear detonation has not occurred. If it had, we would see the flash and the cloud cover would be pushed away. If they were moving a nuke, it would show up as a small pocket of radiation, one that we could target. The radiation levels have spiked over a ten-mile radius around the bunker and we are completely blind. The weather system is continuing to spread the radiation even further. Radiation levels continue to rise. Before the sun sets on the Empire, the radioactive cloud will reach the Indian Ocean."

"Who did it?" General Moody asked.

"The Empire is responsible," Jimenez said very slowly.

"What? A rebellion? Who's trying to take over?" Secretary Laferriere practically screamed.

A look of sad realization dawned on the president's face. "Admiral Mack, I want the *Enterprise* and the *George Washington* to move into the Indian Ocean and join the Fifth Fleet with all due haste. The Empire is smuggling a warhead out of Bunker 5 in order to launch a nuclear strike on the United States. We have to set up a blockade to ensure that they do not succeed."

CHAPTER SEVENTEEN

Howard Beck was tapping his fingers on the kitchen counter and continually shaking his head back and forth. He was muttering curse words at the image on the wall across from him. Hal was tracking a convoy of twelve Humvees slowly moving down the road that passed in front of the estate. Howard was concentrating on the lead vehicle so hard that he was convinced that if he thought a little harder, he could control the Humvee with his mind. He wanted nothing more in the world than for all twelve of the Humvees to zip on past the front gate and never return.

"Hal, how long before they get here?"

"Less than a minute, sir."

"Is the front gate secure?"

"Of course it is, sir."

"Shit!"

"Sir, what would you like me to do if they stop at that gate?"

"I don't want you to say a thing. Hopefully they will give up and go away."

"Yes, sir."

Howard looked at the monitor and could see the Humvees slowing down to stop at the gate.

"Son of a bitch! Go away!" No!"

A man stepped out of the lead vehicle and began pacing back and forth in front of the massive iron gate."

"No one's home! Go away!" Howard screamed at the image on the wall.

The man stopped pacing long enough to rattle the gate, then began frantically waving his arms towards the house."

"Leave me alone! I'm not opening the gate!" Howard's face reddened as he began kicking the floor. Howard hoped that the man waving his arms would not locate the intercom button and try to talk to him. He stared at the monitor and watched as a large group of soldiers began to congregate behind their leader. A few of the soldiers picked up rocks and threw them over the fence towards the house.

"Stop doing that! I'm not letting you in! Go away!"

Howard was so upset and scared that he started to cry.

"Excuse me, sir," said Hal.

"What?" screamed Howard.

"Sir, the man waving his arms is the commanding officer. The men behind him are talking about a wounded man who is going to die if he doesn't do something now."

Howard relaxed a little. "You mean they aren't trying to break in and hurt me?"

"No, sir, they are seeking medical attention."

Howard took a deep breath and sat down. "Uh.. ok, ok. This is what I want you to do, Old Man. I want you to talk to them on the intercom and see what the problem is. See if they can go somewhere else."

"Sir, you want me to talk to them?"

"Yes I do, Hal. I'm too shaken up."

"Yes, sir. It will not be a problem. Would you like for me to put them on speaker?"

"Please."

"Very good, sir."

Hal turned on the speaker in the kitchen so Howard could hear the company of soldiers outside his main gate. The intercom crackled, and you could see the heads of the soldiers perk up and turn towards it.

"May I help you, gentlemen?" Hal asked in his proper British voice.

"Thank God! Yes!" The man that had been waving his arms walked over to the intercom. "My name is Captain Jackson Butler, and we are in desperate need of assistance. We have an emergency situation on our hands. We retreated from Denver, and one of my men was shot as we left the city. We have managed to stop the bleeding but I'm afraid he'll die soon if we don't get him to a hospital."

"Captain Butler, my name is Hal. Are you aware that this is not a hospital?"

"Yes, sir, I am aware of that."

"If you continue on this road and take a left at the next intersection, a hospital is in the town thirty-three miles down the road."

"Sir, please. We do not have that kind of time. I have a

medic with me who is ready to perform surgery, but we could do it safely in a clean, sterile environment. My man is weak enough as it is; if the surgery doesn't kill him, infection will most certainly finish him off. Please! Let us in so we can save this man's life!"

"Captain Butler, are you familiar with the Third Amendment to the Constitution that states that a soldier cannot quarter in a private citizen's home during times of war unless by order of law? I do not believe a law has been passed granting you the right to enter my home."

"Sir, please! We are not hostile and we aren't trying to take your home from you. We just need to help our man, and we will be on our way. Open the gate!"

"Please wait for a moment, Captain."

"Thank you, sir. Please, I give you my word, we mean you no harm."

Howard was watching the entire thing and was torn by indecision. The thought of armed soldiers on his compound, friendly or enemy, terrified him. On the other hand, he couldn't live with himself if he allowed a member of the armed services to die outside his gate when he had the chance to help.

"Hal?"

"I'm here, sir."

"They really got a wounded man out there?"

"Sir, I have not seen a wounded man. Three of the soldiers at the gate had a great deal of blood on them. They did not have any apparent injuries, so the logical conclusion is that the blood does not belong to them."

"OK, this is what I want you to do. Tell Captain Butler that he and his men can come in. They can drive around behind the main residence and use the guest house. Instruct them that they are not to approach the main residence. I insist that they respect this condition."

"I will relay your decision, sir."

Captain Butler was pacing back and forth. The intercom crackled, and he listened as the British man spoke.

"Captain Butler, I have decided to let you and your men though the gate. I want you to follow the drive back behind the main residence and use the guest house. It should be adequate for your needs. I will grant you access on one condition."

"Anything! Name it!"

"At no time are you or your men to approach the main residence."

"Hal, you have my solemn word. Thank you."

Howard watched the image of the convoy entering his property. He didn't like it at all. The thought of dozens of dirty, rough and tough soldiers on his property tearing things up almost made Howard have a panic attack. Meredith had always nagged him about being a better host. Guests should be welcomed with open arms and made comfortable. Howard scoffed and just let his wife be the proper host while he pretended to be busy and disappeared to another room in the house. People are stupid. People are rude. People just don't make sense. If Howard did not hold a close, intimate relationship with someone, he'd rather not be around them. People were unpredictable and just plain got on his nerves.

"Sir, they are moving the injured man into the guest house. He appears to be unconscious and his abdomen is covered in blood."

"Can you tell anything more, Hal?"

"No, sir. If he were moved to your lab I could run a detailed scan on him."

"Let's hold off on that for now. Maybe they can get him patched up."

"Yes, sir, would you like to see the progress on the main screen?"

"Yes, please." Howard looked at the wall opposite him and could see the men working desperately to save the wounded soldier's life. Captain Butler was shouting orders to his men.

"OK, clear this area out and lay him on the kitchen table. Doc, what do you need?"

Staff Sergeant Willis, the company medic, didn't take his eyes off the wounded soldier. "Sir, let me check my bag. I think I have everything I need; I'll let you know."

"Anything we can do in the meantime?"

The company medic checked the injured man's dog tag. "His blood type is A negative. I need anyone with that blood type or type O to get ready to donate blood."

"You got it, Doc. Listen up!! If your blood type is A negative or type O get your ass over here, now!"

"Captain, I don't know my blood type," a young private said from the back of the room.

"Check your dog tags, jackass!" another private yelled.

The ones who had forgotten their blood type checked their dog tag. Less than a minute later, only one soldier stepped forward.

"OK, Doc. We got one. I can donate as well. What else do you need?"

"Someone needs to locate the biggest pot they can find and start boiling water. I need towels and bed sheets."

"I'm on it!" A sergeant looked at one of his team members and they started working.

"Shit! I was afraid of this!"

"What's wrong, Doc?"

"I can get the bullet out, but it tore his small intestine. I'm going to need to stitch it up."

"Are you sure?"

"You see that? Do you smell that?"

"Yes." Captain Butler leaned forward and winced at the smell.

There's bile mixed in with his blood. If it's not stitched up, he's going to die of sepsis."

"How long do we have?"

"Put it to you this way, sir, I'm amazed he's not dead already."

"Can you perform surgery?"

"Yes, but I'm going to need every single source of portable light over here. I saw a lot of battlefield surgeries in Iraq when I was a private. I've never performed it, but I'm confident I can get the job done as long he holds out and doesn't die on us."

Captain Butler looked at another NCO and nodded. The sergeant grabbed two privates and they started gathering up every lamp they could find.

Howard Beck looked at the monitor and hung his head. The injured soldier didn't have a broken leg or a flesh wound. He stood a real chance of dying in his guest house.

"Hal, what do you think?"

"Sir, I think you know what I am going to say."

"I know, I know, we need to move him into my lab so you can assist with the surgery."

"Yes, sir, the poor man has precious little time."

"Invite our guests inside, Hal."

"Yes, sir."

Staff Sergeant Willis was hooking up an IV to the injured man and cleaning the wound when a voice came over the intercom.

"Captain Butler, if I may, I feel that I must intervene."

"Yes, Hal. What can you do?"

"Inside the main residence is a lab that would be better suited for the surgery you are about to attempt. We have resources that will give your injured man a much better chance at survival. I would ask that you only bring the number of people required to tend to his needs."

"Doc? Is it safe to move him?"

"If we take it slow and steady, yes."

"Let's get moving. Hal, where are we going?"

"Exit the guest house and head right on the path. Enter the door and the lab is the first room on the left."

"Thank you, Hal."

The injured man was loaded onto a stretcher, and four men carried him very slowly up the path to the main residence. They entered the building and walked into the massive lab. Along one wall was a workbench that was home to all sorts of electronic equipment. It looked like a computer graveyard. In the center of the room was a solid steel table large enough to accommodate six prone men with room to spare. The far wall was solid white, most likely a gigantic monitor. The four men carrying the stretcher placed the injured soldier on the table. Staff Sergeant Willis got to work. Captain Butler turned as an odd looking man entered the room. He was wearing a bathrobe and slippers. He was tall and skinny with long, white hair that spilled down over his thin, gaunt face. He was fidgeting nervously and his beady eyes were darting all over the room.

"Hal, I'm Captain Jackson Butler with the Fourth Regiment of the Unified National Guard. I want to thank you for your help." He extended his hand to the man in the bathrobe, but the gesture was not returned. The man wouldn't look him in the eye. Something was very familiar about this man. Captain Butler was sure he had seen him before.

"I'm not Hal. My name is Howard."

"Howard, it's nice to meet you. Will Hal be joining us?"

"He's already here. Hal, anything you can do to help?"

Captain Butler was startled by the voice that came out of nowhere and filled the room. "Yes, sir. My preliminary scans detect that his blood pressure is low but steady. Staff Sergeant Willis was correct in his assessment. His lower intestine is perforated. He will require a blood transfusion."

Captain Butler was confused but focused on the task at hand. "Uh, yeah... we..uh.. we're already working on that. PFC Boone and I are ready to donate blood. I'm sorry, Hal, where are you? I would like to meet you and extend my gratitude to you in person."

Howard was starting to calm down. He said sharply, "This is my house. Hal is my digital assistant."

"He's what? You mean I've been talking to a computer this entire time?"

Howard nodded his head.

"Holy shit! You're Howard Beck! The world's richest man! I can't believe I'm in your house!" PFC Boone had a look of shock and wonder on his face.

"I knew you looked familiar! Sir, it's an honor to meet you. Thank you so much for all your help." Captain Butler was smiling and couldn't take his eyes off Howard.

"Captain, I need you to get started on the blood donation." Staff Sergeant Willis snapped everyone out of their reverent stupor.

"That's right, Doc. Yeah, let's get going here."

Howard walked over to the company medic. "Staff Sergeant Willis, whatever you need from Hal, just say the word. He can hear you. He can provide a real time 3-D internal holographic image of this man's injury."

"Uh, wow. Okay. Hal, I need to see his gastrointestinal perforation. And, uh...any suggestions on how to proceed, if you can do that."

The projectors in the ceiling beamed a holographic image

of the inside of the injured man's abdomen. The perforated intestine was clearly visible, as was the resulting hemorrhage.

"Holy shitballs, that's cool." PFC Boone was seated next to the table getting his blood drawn.

Hal addressed the nervous medic. "As you can see, the damage is quite extensive. You can supplement your instruments with tools from the workbench if you require anything else. I trust that you have sterile equipment to open him up and close the incision. I will be happy to guide you during the surgery."

"I think I have everything I need in my bag. If I think of anything, I'll let you know." The medic began to prep for surgery. Staff Sergeant Willis didn't know if he should address the computer like a person, but did so anyway. "Thank you, Hal, I would appreciate the help."

Howard walked to his workbench and spoke to Staff Sergeant Willis. "Will you need anything else for the surgery? If I have it, it's yours."

He looked over at his assistant, Specialist Hanson, and saw that he was done drawing blood. He motioned him over. "I'd like for everyone to clear out of the room. Captain Butler, if you would post a runner outside the door I can get started."

"You got it, Doc. Williams, post up outside the door and be ready to come if the Doc calls for you. Everyone else, back to the guesthouse. Sergeant Wilson, tell Top I need to see him on the double."

They all shuffled out of the room. Private Williams stood sentry at the door. Captain Butler was the last out of the room and waited for Howard.

"Mr. Beck, I can't thank you enough for what you've done. That man on the table is my XO, Lieutenant Christopher. I don't know if he's going to make it, but at least he has a fighting chance. I can say for sure that if you hadn't let us past the gate, he wouldn't have made it."

"Yes, I know. It was the only reason I let you into the house. I was monitoring the situation from my kitchen. When your medic said he needed surgery, I knew I had to let you inside."

"I must say, Mr. Beck, your computer had me fooled into thinking I was talking to a human being."

"Captain, call me Howard. And yes, he is the most advanced A.I. in the world. Have you ever heard of the Turing Test?"

"I can't say that I have."

Howard was completely at ease for the first time since he saw the Humvees at his front gate. He loved to talk about computers. "The Turing Test was designed by a man named Alan Turing in 1950. He wanted to know if computers could 'think' along the same lines as a human being. The test is administered by having a person sit at a computer monitor. On the other end of the monitor is a human being and a computer. The person giving the test asks a series of questions and when he is confident he knows which subject is the computer, he gives his answer. Over the years, many computers have been built but before the creator could say he had constructed a fully functional computer with artificial intelligence, his computer had to pass the Turing Test. Many people proudly proclaimed to have done it, but upon further testing the claim was nullified. "

"Hal was the first?"

"He was indeed."

"I remember when I was a kid a computer won Jeopardy. You mean he didn't pass?"

"Watson? No, but he was a step in the right direction. Very impressive computer. IBM never even made the claim that Watson was A.I."

"But he beat two humans in Jeopardy."

"Answering questions is one thing. Comprehension and understanding are completely different. What always trips up a computer in the Turing Test is asking it questions that don't have a right or wrong answer like 'Who's your favorite baseball team?' or 'Who's better? Stones or Beatles?'"

Captain Butler smiled. "Stones, hands down."

"I'm a Beatles man myself."

"Most computers would give a very analytical answer. 'The Beatles' songs spent more time on the charts than the Rolling Stones'. When you ask the computer to personally choose one group over the other it can't make a decision."

"You mean Hal has a favorite rock band?"

"Hal?"

"Captain Butler, I have always been partial to The Blues Travelers."

"Hal, shouldn't you being helping with the surgery?"

"I am doing just that, Captain Butler. Rest assured I am working diligently to ensure the surgery is a success."

Captain Butler looked at Howard in astonishment. "That's good to know, Hal."

Howard beamed with pride over his creation. Captain Butler stopped, and a puzzled look crossed his face. "Is something wrong, Captain?"

"Hal? Like the HAL-9000 from *2001*?"

Howard's smile blossomed, and he looked the man in the eye for the first time. "Captain, I like you. We are going to get along just fine."

The door at the end of the hall opened, and a gray haired soldier walked smartly up to Captain Butler and stood at attention.

"Sir, First Sergeant Bankhead, reporting as ordered."

"At ease, Top. Report."

"Sir, the vehicles are all in working order. Second squad's alpha truck busted out one of its headlights on the way out of Denver; other than that, the vehicles are fine. I got the men cleaning their weapons. Our ammo supply is acceptable. I just need to know how long we're staying. If we need to bivouac, I'll start on it right away."

"Thank you, Top. Let's hold off on setting up camp. I haven't discussed that with our host. Top, I want you to meet Howard Beck. Howard, this is First Sergeant Bankhead."

The top NCO in the company looked at the eccentric man standing next to his commander. "Howard Beck? The computer guy? Pleasure to meet you, sir, and let me say thank you." The First Sergeant extended his hand. The handshake was not accepted. Howard shuffled awkwardly and instead smiled and said, "You're welcome."

Howard spoke to the two men. "Gentlemen, you're welcome to anything in the guest house. Would the two of you join me in the kitchen for a drink? I would like to discuss exactly what's going on in Denver - whatever you can tell me, of course."

"Sir, it would be an honor; lead the way." Captain Butler

put his hand on First Sergeant Bankhead's shoulder and smiled.

Howard led them into the kitchen and the two soldiers sat at the table. "What's your poison? Or can you have a drink?"

"Howard, Top doesn't drink but I'll have whatever you're having."

"Sir, if it's all the same, I'd like a drink, too." First Sergeant Bankhead wasn't a recovering alcoholic; he was just particular about his health.

"Really, Matt? Good for you. I think we could all use a drink after the day we've had."

Howard poured three glasses of his best scotch and brought them over to his guests, joining them at the table.

"Hal, what's the status of Lieutenant Christopher? Can we talk to the medic?"

"Standby, sir, I will ask."

"Only if it isn't a distraction, Hal," Captain Butler added.

"I understand, sir."

A few seconds ticked by and Staff Sergeant Willis spoke over the intercom. "Captain, things are looking good. I was able to repair the gastrointestinal trauma. His blood pressure is finally stable. I gave him some antibiotics but they're not very strong. All we can do is wait, keep him on an IV and hope for the best."

"How long do you think it will be before he is out of the woods?" asked Howard.

"Hard to say, really. At the best I would say forty-eight hours. At the worst, a week. After twenty-four hours we'll have a more accurate prognosis"

"Doc, you need anything else?"

"No sir, I'm closing him up now. Should take another thirty minutes or so."

"Keep us posted, Doc. Good work."

"Roger that, sir."

The three men sitting at the table sipped their drinks. They watched through the window as the fiery sun battled the towering mountains in the distance.

"Dear Lord Almighty, that is a sight to behold," First Sergeant Bankhead uttered in his southern accent.

The three men sat in silence and beheld the magnificent view. A minute passed, and Captain Butler broke the silence.

"It's a damn shame it's all going to shit."

"What happened in Denver, Captain?"

"I don't know where to begin. I guess I would have to say that it started at the checkpoints. We'd been given orders to step up security. Search every car. Check every person's ID. Anyone who looked like they came from the Empire was to be interrogated. Got really ugly. The entire city was in gridlock. No one could move from one sector to the other; it just took too damn long. I'd like to have a chat with the moron who drew the sector lines. Four out of the twelve sectors don't have a hospital. I was letting ambulances past the checkpoints, couldn't imagine doing otherwise. Then, two weeks ago in Detroit an ambulance loaded down with explosives drove into a police station. Leveled the building. Needless to say, after that all ambulances across the country had to stop at every checkpoint. I instructed my men to go as fast as possible, check the ambulance crew's badges and make sure the back wasn't loaded down with explosives. Ambulances made it past my checkpoints in under a minute. Then, a twelve-year-old girl who'd been hit by a car actually died at a checkpoint while my men were checking badges. Checkpoint or not, she would have died regardless. Didn't matter. Riots broke out all over the city. The first checkpoint fell when they threw Molotov cocktails. All six of my men burned to death. Total chaos gripped the city for twelve hours. I ordered the checkpoints closed to all traffic, hoping to contain the mobs. It worked at first. I thought if we could just make it to sunrise, we could hold the city. I was so wrong. The checkpoints started getting hit with gunfire. I ordered three checkpoints to fall back and fortify others. It just got worse. I coordinated with city officials and had the power cut off. I didn't want the mobs to organize."

"That's was Hal's assumption. Looks like you were right, Old Man."

"Thank you, sir."

"Cover of darkness gave us the advantage. Things started calming down. That only lasted a few hours. Then mobs began to overrun the checkpoints. With the rules of engagement tying their hands, they couldn't fire on the mobs. Tear gas slowed them down, but they just kept coming. My men were dropping like flies. I ordered a full retreat to our rally point outside the city. Twelve vehicles showed up, just twelve. After two hours, Lt. Christopher's platoon showed up, and we had to evacuate or else he was a dead man. I left a scout behind to watch the rally point, and then we showed up on your doorstep."

Captain Butler raised his glass. "And thank God for you, sir." Captain Butler and First Sergeant Bankhead raised their glasses and brought them together in a toast. Howard was confused at first, but could tell that they were waiting for him to follow suit. He raised his glass and the two men clinked their glasses on his.

Howard waited to ensure Captain Butler was finished speaking. "Hal, what's going on in the other major cities? Is Denver spilling over anywhere else?"

"Yes, sir, I'm afraid it is. The young lady who died in the ambulance has become the symbol for uprising and protest. The civilian deaths in Denver have caused many angry citizens to rise up and demand justice."

"Fuck me." Captain Butler stood up and walked over to the window. A wave of crushing guilt swept over him. He felt responsible for the entire thing. "Hal, how bad has it gotten? Have any other cities fallen?"

"Yes sir, I regret to report that Chicago, Cleveland, Detroit, Memphis, Atlanta, Dallas, Boston, Los Angeles, Seattle, and Pittsburgh are no longer under the control of the Unified National Guard."

Captain Butler almost collapsed against the window. He slowly took his seat. His hands were shaking. "I don't understand how it could happen so quickly. This is unbelievable." Captain Butler looked to his top NCO. "Top, is this my fault? Am I to blame?"

"No, sir, it most certainly is not. You know as well as I do that every major city in this country is a powder keg waiting to blow. One spark would set them all off. It was bound to happen sooner or later, just a matter of when. Don't give it another thought, sir. Focus on what's to come. We will take back Denver, sir."

Captain Butler needed to hear that. He immediately stopped feeling sorry for himself and looked at First Sergeant

Bankhead. "Thanks, Matt. I needed a kick in the ass."

"Just doing my job, sir."

Howard felt the need to change the subject and lighten the mood. "Captain, you are welcome to stay for as long as it takes for Lieutenant Christopher to recover."

"I appreciate that, Howard. As soon as he's ready to move, we'll be on our way."

****

For three days, what was left of Captain Butler's unit stayed on the compound. They set up a makeshift command post in the guesthouse, and the men set up camp in the field north of the main residence. Captain Butler was insistent that his men respect Howard's privacy. No one was allowed to enter the main residence with the exception of Staff Sergeant Willis and his medics. Every evening Howard invited Captain Butler and First Sergeant Bankhead to dine with him. Howard had a hard time making friends; in fact, he preferred not to since he considered most people to be insufferable. Once Howard took a liking to someone, he was a fierce and loyal friend. Captain Butler was an exceptional officer and very intelligent. Howard enjoyed his company and looked forward to having dinner with him. When things calmed down, he was going to discuss Captain Butler's career with President Powers.

Two days after they arrived, Lieutenant Christopher finally regained consciousness. Staff Sergeant Willis continued to monitor his progress and informed Captain Butler that by the end of the week, his XO would be back on his feet. Captain Butler was anxiously awaiting his departure from the estate so he could get back in the fight. He had been spending many long hours speaking with command. The Unified National Guard was coordinating a counter-attack to take back Denver from the rebels. Troops were arriving every day. Captain Butler had set up a base camp in the field directly in front of Beck Estates. His original plan was to set up camp a few miles outside of Denver but the brass had other ideas. Captain Butler had no intention of asking Howard to allow more troops to enter his property. He was grateful for Howard's hospitality and wouldn't dare impose any more than he already had. By the end of the week he would be in command of three regiments, and the Battle of Denver would commence. Captain Butler realized that a full bird Colonel should be in charge of the forces under his command and recognized the full weight of the responsibility he had been given.

On the fourth day of their stay, Captain Butler was sitting in the guesthouse with his First Sergeant when he received a message on his iPad from command. He read it twice and passed it over to his top NCO.

"Are they serious?"

"Looks that way, Top."

"Let's go tell Howard."

Hal had of course been monitoring the entire conversation. He was unable to intercept any incoming or outgoing messages from Captain Butler's command post since one of his siblings was sending the communication. Hal could tell that the two men were going to be delivering bad news to Howard.

Howard Beck was sitting his library reading Orwell's *1984* for at least the tenth time and watching *The Wrath of Khan* for at least the hundredth. The movie filled the holographic screen in front of Howard. The bridge of the *Enterprise* was in front of him, and Captain Kirk was getting his ass handed to him by his nemesis.

"Excuse me, sir?"

"What is it, Old Man?"

"Captain Butler and First Sergeant Bankhead are on their way to see you."

Howard didn't look up from his book. "What for?"

"I'm not sure, sir. Captain Butler received communication from his superiors. They left the guest house and are walking up the path to the residence."

"Thank you, Hal. Direct them to the library."

"Very good, sir."

The two soldiers entered the residence, and Hal dispatched one of his robots to serve as butler. The robot escorted the two men through a maze of corridors to the library.

"That thing gives me the creeps," said First Sergeant Bankhead.

"I think it's pretty cool. Top, you act like you've never seen a robot before."

"Not in someone's house, I haven't."

The robot stopped in front of the double doors to the library and opened them to allow the men inside.

"Jesus Christ!" First Sergeant Bankhead was looking at a gigantic spaceship being ripped apart by torpedoes.

Howard was laughing hysterically. "Hal, pause playback! You know better than that!"

The *Enterprise* was suspended a few feet off the floor, one of her nacelles ripped apart by Khan from aboard his hijacked vessel. The damaged nacelle was hurtling towards the two men in the doorway when the movie was paused. First Sergeant Bankhead leapt out of the way and was crouching by the wall.

Howard tried to stop laughing but couldn't. The crusty NCO was not in the least bit amused. Howard finally regained his composure. "Gentlemen, gentlemen, please come in and make yourselves comfortable. I apologize for frightening you. Hal usually pauses the movie when someone enters the room."

Actually, Howard had instructed Hal to do no such thing. He purposely set up the gag and timed it perfectly so the space battle would be in all its glory when the door was opened.

"Shame on you, Hal! Bad computer!"

"Gentlemen, my sincere apologies."

"Jackson, to what do I owe the pleasure? Please have a seat. Can I get either of you a drink?"

"Howard, it's two o'clock in the afternoon," Captain Butler said, smiling.

"I have a glass of wine two hours after every meal." Howard had repeated this routine like clockwork for over thirty years.

"No thank you. We're fine."

"Suit yourself." The three men sat down. Howard sat in a very old and ugly recliner that starkly contrasted everything in the room. The two soldiers sat on the couch opposite him.

"Well, Howard, I have a few questions for you, if you don't mind."

"Go right ahead."

"I'm sure Hal has kept you up to speed regarding all of the

movement outside your front gate."

"Yes, he has."

"I wanted to fill you in on exactly what's going to happen."

"I'm all ears."

"By the end of the week three regiments will be under my command. Once we're battle ready, we are going to take back Denver from the rebels."

"I can't wait. Should be exciting."

"I was wondering, exactly how big is your estate?"

"A thousand acres."

"Would you be so kind as to show me a map of your property?"

"Of course. Hal?"

The *Enterprise* and her torn nacelle vanished from the screen and a holographic map of Beck Estates took its place. The main residence could be seen along with the guest house, private airstrip, golf course, garage, and stables.

"Holy smokes! You own all of that? We've barely seen a fraction of it. I must say, Howard, I can't picture you on a horse." Captain Butler looked at First Sergeant Bankhead and they exchanged chuckles.

"Well Captain, you are most definitely right. I'm not an animal person by any stretch of the imagination. The stable belongs to my wife."

"Wife? I had no idea you were married, Howard! Will we get a chance to meet Mrs. Beck?"

"Regretfully, no. She is away tending to something important."

"Shame. I would like to meet her. Who on earth takes care of your horses?"

"Hal."

"Of course. I should have known. I take it he also takes care of that grumpy cat over there?"

"Yes. I can't stand that animal. My wife's cat, Nala, is more Hal's pet than mine.

"She is a good kitty, sir." Hal's reply elicited laughter from all three men.

"OK, back to the matter at hand. The reason I'm asking

about your property is that I have a request."

"And what would that be, exactly?" Howard's demeanor changed immediately.

"Well, I would like to move my forces into the compo..."

"Absolutely not. Your soldiers are just fine where they are."

"Howard, please let me finish. There have been security concerns addressed at the command level. I gave them the impression that we were already inside the compound. I wanted to respect your privacy and keep the promise I made to you when I arrived. I've been able to keep my bosses in the dark until today. Once they knew the bulk of my forces were outside the front gate they were not happy."

"Well, your bosses are not going to be happy at all. When Lieutenant Christopher is on his feet, I want all of you out. You're welcome to stay outside the front gate and the standing dinner invitation to the both of you will remain the same."

"Howard, I have bad news. I had hoped that by asking you personally we could come to an understanding and everyone would be happy. I have my orders. Please reconsider and let's not make this any harder than it needs to..."

"No! You need to understand one thing, Captain! This is *MY* house, and I decide what goes on inside these walls! When I speak with the president you will understand exactly who in the hell you are dealing with!"

"Mr. Beck, I'm sorry that it has come to this. The order comes directly from the Chairman of the Joint Chiefs of Staff with the approval of the president himself."

"The hell it does! You are looking at the man who put Malcolm Powers in office, and you're either lying to me or you're being lied to!" Howard's face flushed scarlet in his fury, his eyes full of rage. He jumped out of his chair and kicked over a table. Papers and some of the rarest first edition books on the planet went flying across the room. "Get the hell out of my house! NOW!"

"Howard Beck, by order of the president of the United States, I hereby seize your property, and you will be confined to your suite under armed guard."

"I'd like to see you try, you stupid grunt! Old Man! Lock

down the estate, deny everyone but me access to your systems and deploy security measures immed..."

Captain Butler drew his sidearm, leveled it at Howard's head and pulled the trigger.

CHAPTER EIGHTEEN

Former Master Chief Petty Officer Richard Dupree was lying in his bunk in his private cell in the basement of the Winchester County Courthouse. He was thinking about the pedophile he had murdered. He didn't want to think about the monster but couldn't get the image of the man's face out of his head. The State of California knew that Richard had been highly trained in escape and evasion tactics and didn't want to run the risk of him getting loose. They were right to be wary; Richard had no intention of attending his trial. A guard had been stationed in front of his cell twenty-four hours a day for the previous six months. At first it was just a guard getting paid overtime for sitting there in a folding chair with a clipboard. Within a month, a desk was moved in along with a comfortable office chair, a telephone, and a computer with limited Internet access.

The duty post had even been added to the weekly roster, thanks to a non-critical post being shuffled so a guard could keep watch over Richard. Every guard that worked at the Winchester County Sheriff's Office was dying to spend a week with Richard. They all considered him to be a hardcore badass and a hero for murdering the disgusting abomination that was rotting in hell.

The former SEAL wondered why they didn't just move him to a state facility that was far more secure than the rundown shithole in which he was currently housed. He spent a great deal of his overwhelming amount of free time thinking about this mystery. Richard finally figured out that the California Department of Corrections and Rehabilitation knew that he would be their problem soon enough and saw no rush to roll out the red carpet for Mr. Dupree. Richard was, in fact, correct and hoped his captors wouldn't realize their mistake until it was too late and he was safely in Canada under an assumed identity he'd created for himself shortly after he became an operator. He loved his country and was a dedicated soldier, but he was not naïve enough to believe that his country wouldn't disavow him should he be caught in a compromising situation that would cause an international incident.

His trial date kept getting pushed back further and further, thanks to his lawyer. He couldn't give a rat's ass what his lawyer did as long as he remained right where he was, and his best chance of escape was within reach. The only thing Richard was the least bit interested in hearing about was information about the monster he had killed. Who was Oswald Jefferson? How many other children had he abused? Are the children okay? Richard didn't need any further justification for killing a pedophile, or killing anyone for that matter; killing the filth of humanity was how he had earned his living. He was simply concerned for the victims, especially his own children.

Oswald Jefferson had been a highly respected deacon at the Winchester Street Baptist Church. His father had helped found the church. His mother brought an infant Oswald to the very room in which he was murdered. He grew up in the church, was married there, and even watched his two children being baptized there many years ago. Detectives estimated that Oswald began acting on his perversion in his late twenties. By his mid-thirties, children would play naked in front of him while he pleasured himself, an art he was proud of until the day Richard did the world a favor and ended his life. No one had suspected him at all. He always ensured that the children he watched were under the age of three, far too young to understand shame and not possessing the vocabulary to explain to their parents what had been going on. From time to time children did try to explain and were unsuccessful in properly conveying what "special worship" meant. The ones who did garner some understanding left their parents confused. They would reluctantly approach Oswald and ask him about it, not wanting to offend him. He would place his hand on their shoulder, calm their nervousness with a smile and make up some excuse about a diaper changing gone awry that resulted in a giggling child running about the room. Oswald then simply excluded the children who told their parents about his "special worship" to throw off any suspicion.

Lolita Jefferson was never a stumbling block to her husband's indiscretions. Many thought the woman to be mentally handicapped. This only endeared the congregation to Oswald even more. They were so proud that he could show that poor girl a good life and take care of her. It was obvious to the investigators why Oswald had married her. She was not intelligent enough to realize her husband was a pedophile, and he could control her with little effort. On the day of his murder, Oswald simply told his wife to go wait in the car and not come back inside until he came to get her. He told her that to pass the time she should pray to Jesus and petition Him to make her normal. Rather than explain to his wife what the word "petition" meant, he simply used an easier word and again told her to go the car and wait for him. His wife dutifully obeyed.

Starting about a year before his death, Oswald became more confident in his tactics and began including older boys and girls whom he thought would keep their mouths shut. He would frighten and intimidate them into silence; he knew he could do it. Once he found out how easy it was, he regretted that he hadn't done it sooner. Richard faced an intense struggle with the knowledge that his son had been abused by this monster. His lawyer never dared tell him how often it had occurred, and Richard couldn't bear to ask. He couldn't very well kill the same monster twice.

Besides, Richard had his wayward wife to deal with. Monique was, in fact, cheating on Richard like he suspected. She married Bryan and within a year, Richard's daughter was calling Bryan her "Daddy." Richard's sweet little princess would soon forget him. Monique had erased every trace of their marriage, every picture, every home movie. It was like Richard had never existed. Monique could have continued this charade, had it not been for their son. Bryan didn't sign up for this kind of baggage; he looked at Richard's damaged son and all he could think about was the gruesome murder that had occurred only months before their wedding. Bryan filed for divorce a few years later and never had contact with Monique or her children again.

His lawyer first tried to have Richard declared incompetent to stand trial based on the fact that he was insane. This went on for weeks and eventually failed. His lawyer then argued that Richard should be tried in a military court of law since he was wearing his Class A uniform when he committed the murder. Richard knew this plan was ridiculous and wouldn't last long. To his surprise, the tactic worked twice as long as Richard thought it would. Next they tried a change of venue to a federal court since Oswald Jefferson was a disabled black man and

Richard had committed a hate crime. Richard could never figure out if the hate crime due to Oswald being black, disabled, or both. The prosecutor representing the State of California looked up in utter confusion as the motion was made and asked if defense counsel was trying to help him convict his client of a completely new and unrelated charge. The judge was starting to get impatient, and Richard knew he didn't have much time left before he must execute his plan.

Richard originally thought his best chance of escape was when they moved him from his cell to the courtroom four floors above. Each time he left his cell, four guards armed with tasers escorted him to a holding room to be placed in restraints. Two of the men pointed tasers at Richard while the other two placed him in chains. On one of his first trips out of his cell, one of the guards pointing a taser at Richard got scared when Richard sneezed and launched the two barbs into Richard's left pectoral muscle, shocking him with fifty thousand volts. Richard's lawyer had a field day with this and protested for a better part of a week that his client was being treated inhumanely and should not have to suffer such indignity based on his distinguished military career and being a loving father… blah, blah, blah. Richard knew it was a waste of time but welcomed the delay. Richard assumed that the leg irons he was forced to wear were a few links too short because it took him an eternity to make the trip to his seat in the stuffy, cramped courtroom. Next they placed a belly chain around his waist, fed the excess length back through a loop and padlocked the end of the chain to the small of his back. With each wrist cuffed snugly against his hips, Richard would not have been able to free himself from the painful bondage even if someone had placed the keys in his hands.

Richard knew he would have to find a way to get the guards to pull him from the cell in a hurry, ignoring critical security precautions in the process. During his third month of confinement, Richard decided to stick with the tried and true 'Get a doctor, quick, I'm having a heart attack and need an ambulance' escape trick. He had hoped that the lame attempt would garner some result. It did not. No one was willing to open the door to his cell unless four guards with tasers were standing right outside. Richard thought with some amusement that he could indeed die in his cell before he received emergency medical treatment.

Richard realized that he would have to take much more extreme measures. With careful thought and planning, Richard knew exactly how he was going to escape. The first phase of his plan was to break down and weep for hours on end. This part was the easiest; all he had to do was focus on the image of his trembling son sobbing in the corner and the tears flowed. The second phase of his plan required at least a week. He would need to ration small portions of his meals and hide them in his cell. When he left to go the courtroom, the guards searched his cell and didn't really mind the extra food. No harm in letting him eat. Phase three of the plan was the most difficult. He waited until the Friday before his trial was to begin and spent the day carefully reviewing each step of his escape in meticulous detail. He would wait until 3AM on Saturday morning to execute his plot; the courthouse would be empty on a Saturday, so the building would be operating on a skeleton crew.

Friday after dinner, Richard laid in his bunk facing the wall and ate the extra food he had been squirreling away for a week. He would need his strength. At 10pm when the guards changed shifts and spent ten or fifteen minutes shooting the breeze, Richard began to tear his white t-shirt into long strips. Once that was done, he did the same thing with his bed sheet. It was pushing eighty-five degrees in the hot basement so Richard never used the sheet anyway, and the guards wouldn't notice that it was damaged. By the time he was finished, the previous guard had left and Deputy Clements was checking his email.

At 3am, Richard rolled over and watched the guard for a full five minutes to make sure he was fast asleep. His mouth gaped wide and spittle trickled down his chin. Richard even whispered the deputy's name. Out like a light. He quietly sat up in his bunk and placed one of the strips of bed sheet around his neck. He rubbed the torn strip of fabric vigorously back and forth around his neck, causing a serious friction burn. He didn't stop until the skin began to slough away and he felt blood trickling down his neck. Richard stood, checked on the guard and walked over to the sink. He looked into the mirror and saw his reflection. The mirror was not made of glass, but rather highly polished, thin metal that bore a reflection. Richard had thought about using the metal somehow but gave up on the idea when he realized he couldn't get the metal sheet loose enough without making a lot of noise. Richard tightened the noose around his neck and pulled as hard as he could. His face turned three different shades of red and he stopped once he saw the blood vessels in his eyes begin to rupture, causing red flecks of blood to litter the whites of his eyes. Richard grabbed the sink so he wouldn't pass out. He slowly took two steps back and sat on his bunk facing the back of the cell. He did not rise again until he was no longer dizzy and the room had stopped spinning.

Richard quickly tied the strips of cloth together and made a rope. He then grabbed his sock and filled it with wet toilet paper, giving it weight. Once he had tied the sock to the end of the rope he very carefully swung the rope up and over the beams twelve feet above. Richard carefully measured the rope and did a few calculations in his head to ensure the rope wouldn't break or stretch under his weight bringing him back down to the floor. He tied the end of the rope to his bunk and grabbed the noose with his right hand. Richard then moved to the stage of the plan he looked forward to the least. Richard stood with his back to the wall and defecated into his boxers. Feces ran down the back of his leg and hit the floor. With his bowels empty, he began to urinate, soaking the front of his boxers and causing the urine to drip onto the floor, mixing with the feces at his feet. He knew he had only seconds before the stench might awaken the guard. He stood on his bunk, slipped the noose around his neck and jumped. He made sure to kick the top of his sink when he swung over to it. He managed to knock down a tall stack of legal papers upon which every single thing not nailed down in the cell was resting. The tower of paperwork fell like dominoes into a row of styrofoam cups filled with water and trash. If his guard was a heavy sleeper, he would be dead in a matter of minutes; he had no way to get himself free from the rope dangling from the beams above him. His life was now literally in the hands of the man sleeping three feet away from him. If he didn't wake up and manage to get Richard down, he would begin to suffer brain damage in four minutes time and after that, death would come for him. Richard was ready for death and welcomed it; either way he would win.

****

Deputy Beauford Clements had no idea that he was asleep. He usually drifted off and woke when the lights came on at 5am in the basement of the Winchester County Courthouse. Once the lights came on, Beauford had an hour before his shift ended. He had just enough time to rub the sleep off his face and drink a few cups of coffee from his thermos before he went home. It was the perfect arrangement, to Beauford it was like a vacation. He could go home and spend the day playing with his dogs, only needing a short nap in the afternoon to energize him for the rest of the day. He almost felt guilty drawing a paycheck from the good citizens of Winchester County. Beauford was reaching retirement age and had the most seniority of all the other deputies. When the SEAL had been given his own private guard on a permanent basis, Beauford knew a good thing when he saw it and jumped at the opportunity. The guy living in the cramped cell was actually quite interesting. Beauford had gotten to know the man quite well. For weeks he talked with the prisoner for hours on end before he settled in to get a few hours of sleep. That had changed recently, however, and the guy hadn't spoken a word to him in days. Instead, he cried like a baby in his bed, calling out his son's name. Beauford had to stop himself from crying as well; he hated to see his friend in so much pain. Poor guy. When Richard first arrived at the small prison, the stories he told were like something out of a Vince Flynn novel. If Beauford had possessed a talent for writing, he could easily write a best-selling novel. However, Beauford could barely pencil whip his logbook without it being chock full of mistakes, so his aspirations of becoming a famous novelist would never come to pass.

Beauford had really taken a liking to inmate Dupree. He often told Richard that it was a damn shame that he was in the cell in the first place. Any father in the world would have done the same thing he did. The ones that couldn't do it didn't deserve to have children in the first place. Richard thanked him enthusiastically and joked with Beauford that he should let him out of his cell so the two of them could go get a beer. Beauford knew the man wasn't serious; they were friends and Richard would never do anything to jeopardize his retirement. No way, no sir. He knew that if Richard was like the other piece of shit trash that he had spent twenty-seven years dealing with he would have told on Beauford when he saw the six-inch folding knife he kept in his boot. At first he was nervous that Richard would turn him in, but Richard never said a word about it. That was when Beauford knew Richard was truly his friend. Beauford was going to ask Richard if he could come visit him in prison.

Beauford was yanked violently out of his slumber when a deafening crash resounded throughout the otherwise silent wing of the basement. Beauford screamed like a little girl, which he hoped Richard didn't hear. The last thing he wanted was for Richard to see him as anything less than his equal. Beauford's heart pounded violently in his chest and adrenaline dumped into his blood stream assuring that he was awake and ready to respond to whatever was to come. He knew it was called the fight or flight response, the evolutionary holdover from his caveman ancestors that ensured their continued survival.

The first thing Beauford noticed after his embarrassing scream was the stench of shit. Richard must have been sitting on the toilet and accidentally knocked over the stack of legal work on the sink next to him. Beauford looked at the toilet but found it vacant. Did Richard crawl back into bed and not flush the toilet? No, that couldn't be the case because it didn't explain the racket that woke him up.

Beauford wiped the crust from his eyes and without realizing it, his hand lowered to his chin to wipe the drool away. He blinked his eyes a few times so he could see into the cell and figure out what Richard was doing. Peering towards the back of the cell, Beauford realized that he would never see his retirement.

Richard was dead.

"No, no, no, no NOOOOOOO!"

Beauford began to cry. He had allowed his friend to die a few feet away from him. How long had he been asleep? How did Richard not wake him? He couldn't have been sleeping that heavily. He was a pro at sleeping on the job; he never fell into such a deep sleep that he didn't know what was going on around him. He needed to be able to sit up and act alert if someone turned the key to the lock at the end of the hall.

He had to do something. He screamed at the top of his lungs.

"SOMEBODY HELP! I NEED HELP! GET IN HERE NOW!"

He frantically waved his arms at the camera at the end of the hall like a crazy person. He hoped and prayed that Doug would see him. The guy in the control booth never slept, but he did like to read Lee Child novels, and the latest one had hit the shelves last week. Please be looking at the camera, Doug.

No time. Richard needed his help. In a state of total panic, he forgot that he had a telephone on his desk, one that he seldom used since he was asleep for most of his shift. Beauford fumbled his keys and after what felt like an eternity managed to unlock the door. He crossed to the other side of the cell and almost slipped and fell in the fetid excrement. He grabbed Richard by the waist and hoisted him upwards, hoping that Richard might still be alive and able to breath.

Why is no one coming?

He was never going to be able to get Richard down. Beauford was fifty-six years old and couldn't have been in worse physical shape. He got winded just walking from the parking lot and down the stairs to the basement. Beauford began to cry even harder but regained hope when he realized that Richard's salvation was in his boot. With one hand, he grabbed at his left boot and pulled the knife out. He let go of Richard, unfolded the knife, stood on the bunk and cut him down. *Surely they would be here by now; why is nobody coming?*

His radio.

Beauford had forgotten to hit his alarm. One of the first things he did when he sat down at his desk was to turn off his radio. The County Courthouse shared a radio frequency with the Deputy Sheriff's office and the Fire Department. The thing went off the whole damned night with people checking in every time they pulled over to take a piss and people having discussions about what gas station had the best coffee. It drove Beauford insane, and he saw no reason to allow the damn thing to keep him awake. He promptly hit the red button that would send help his way.

Beauford turned his attention to the inmate he had been charged with watching. His neck was bright red and raw. Blood had soaked into the bed sheet around his neck. Richard must have been hanging up there for a while, kicking before he managed to knock down the things on top of his sink. He checked the pulse on his neck and to his great relief realized that Richard was indeed still alive. He opened Richard's right eye to find his retinas had flecks of blood in them. For a brief second he thought Richard's eye focused and looked at him. Beauford saw this and began to slap his face.

"Richard, Richard! C'mon buddy, stay with me, I know you're in there!"

Beauford then laid Richard's head on the cold concrete floor and began chest compressions. Beauford could only perform the life saving technique for about a minute before he was winded and had to stop. Beauford rushed over to his desk and grabbed a set of leg irons out of the top drawer. He came back over to Richard and restrained him quickly with a pair of handcuffs and leg irons.

Beauford cradled his friend's head in his arm. He wept and pleaded with his friend. "Please don't die buddy, I'm so sorry. Help is on the way; you're gonna be just fine."

****

Richard had been able to maintain consciousness while he was hanging in his cell. He ticked off the seconds in his head while the Deputy snorted like a pig as he began to stir.

1….2….Jesus Christ don't laugh, he just screamed like a little girl…..that's it, open the door and get in here, hurry up…3…4…5…6…7…8…no, use your knife you moron, I'm about to die…9…10…11…finally, now hurry up and cut me down…12…13…this is going to hurt, brace yourself …14… damn that hurt… OK, start taking in shallow breaths…15…16….yes, thank you, I have a pulse. OK, stop counting, you made it. OK, give him a flicker of life in your eye. Good, good. Finally! Now stop crying! You're pissing me off!

Richard settled in and relaxed for what was to come. He

needed to recover very quickly from what just happened if he wished to gain his freedom. Before slipping the noose over his head, Richard had wrapped a towel around his neck to evenly distribute the pressure to his neck muscles. Once he was dangling, he simply tucked his chin to his chest and flexed the muscles in his neck as hard as he could, still allowing a small amount of air into his lungs. When Clements entered the cell, he went as limp as possible to give the illusion that he was dead. Clements fell for the ploy; his plan had worked perfectly. Richard wasn't sure if Beauford would put him in full restraints. He figured on handcuffs. Leg irons maybe. Belly chain and padlock would amaze him. If Beauford put him in a belly chain the rest of his plan would be difficult, but not impossible.

Richard had spent many long, boring days sitting in the courtroom looking out the windows; he memorized every detail of the buildings and roads he could see. One day he heard an ambulance come screaming out of a building across the street. He thought about the size of the building he was in and estimated that the front entrance to the courthouse was directly across the street from the ambulance bays. One night during his long talks with Beauford, an ambulance could be heard outside the courthouse so Richard took advantage of the situation. He asked Beauford about it, and the man was kind enough to answer every single question Richard had about the frequency of emergency calls and the number of staff that worked each shift.

Richard laid on the floor of his cell for less than two minutes before a stretcher was brought in, and he was loaded up to be taken the emergency room. This was the one variable that Richard couldn't plan for; he had no idea which hospital he would taken to. Beauford had told him that the ambulances rotated to three different local hospitals depending on how busy each ER was at any given time of day.

Based on the number of employees working in the courthouse jail, Richard deduced that the only guard that would accompany him to the ER was Deputy Clements. Once he was loaded into the ambulance he discovered that he was right - Beauford and the two paramedics were the only other people in the ambulance.

"We got a white male, early thirties, approximately two

hundred pounds, pulse steady, blood pressure erratic. Severe lacerations to the neck and reticial hemorrhaging, unresponsive to sternum rub. We estimate that we're less than ten minutes out. Over."

"Roger, 1-6, Saint E reports they are ready to receive. Over."

"Reticial hemorrhaging" referred to the red flecks of blood in Richard's eyes. Given the state he was in, it meant that he had been hanging from the noose for quite some time, which of course Richard knew to be untrue. "Unresponsive to sternum rub" meant the paramedic had dug his knuckles into Richard's sternum to see if he would respond. Richard was amazed that he didn't flinch because it hurt like a bitch. The two phrases put together meant one thing - Richard had suffered severe brain damage. Richard knew he had to create this fiction for the paramedics or they would know he was faking and he wouldn't get far.

"Hey, buddy. Hey, you!" The paramedic in the back was screaming at Beauford.

Beauford snapped back to reality and try to steady his voice. "Yeah, what is it?"

"How long was he hanging?"

"Uh, why?"

"Because I need to know! How long?"

"Uh, yeah. I'm not really sure, I don't know."

"What do you mean you don't know? I'm pretty sure he was up there for a while! What the fuck were you doing?"

Beauford had no idea what to say; he couldn't think of a lie so he changed the subject. "Is he gonna make it?"

"Dude, at the very least this guy's got brain damage. You got someone meeting us at Saint Elizabeth's?"

"What do you mean?" Beauford looked utterly confused and searched his racing mind for some sort of explanation. Who would be meeting us at the hospital? Aren't the doctors already there?

"You got back up coming or what? You notify your boss? Do you know what the hell you're doing? Wake the fuck up and do something!"

"Uh, yeah, yeah. Hold on."

Beauford fumbled for his radio. "Hey, Doug?"

The Control Center replied, "Go ahead, Beauford."

"Hey Doug, uhh... this is Beauford."

"I know who this is, Beauford! Gimme a break! What's going on?"

"Doug, you got someone meeting us at the ER?"

"Negative. County Sheriff rides our radio net. They must know what's going on. You didn't tell them?"

Richard could not believe how easy this was going to be.

"Idiots!" The EMT screamed to the front of the cab. "Step on it Manny, we're in serious trouble back here!"

Brock Hornsby was no fool. He spent three years as a medic in the army before he hired on with the Winchester County EMS. He knew exactly who the man was lying in his ambulance. He highly doubted the man was in any condition to do a thing. The man was probably a vegetable and the poor guy had even shit himse...

Richard sprang into action so quickly that the three men riding with him couldn't have responded if Richard had moved at half his current speed. In one lightning fast motion, Richard reached up under the paramedic's chin and with the aid of his handcuffs, rammed the paramedic's head into the ceiling. At the same time Hornsby hit the roof, Richard rolled over onto his left hip and kicked both of his feet around, breaking Deputy Clements' nose. Blood poured from the man's face as he crumpled against the wall, completely terrified. Richard knew Beauford was down for the count. The paramedic proved to be a little more of a challenge, but not much. Slamming into the roof didn't knock him out and only pissed him off. The driver slammed on the brakes, sending the truck swerving recklessly. Hornsby fell over onto Richard's face. Richard gladly accepted the gift of the man's ear in his mouth and bit a chunk of it off. The man howled in pain and clawed his way past Beauford, opening the back doors and falling out onto the curb. Richard moved to the front of the cab and spit the chunk of Hornsby's ear at the driver.

"GET THE FUCK OUT!"

The driver didn't have to be told twice. Wiping a glob of bloody spit from his cheek along with a chunk of something Manuel didn't dare try to identify, he jumped out of the cab like it was on fire and ran screaming down the street. Richard climbed into the driver's seat and realized he had one more task to attend to before he could drive away.

Beauford was still sitting in the back of the truck, the rear doors wide open, inviting him to disembark. The man was too terrified to do anything but tremble in fear.

"Get out of the truck, Beauford," Richard said calmly.

"Richard, what are you doing? I don't understand."

"Oh yes, almost forgot. Before you go, Beauford, I need you to do something for me."

"Richard, this doesn't make any sense! Why'd you do it?"

"Beauford! Be quiet and listen to me. OK, very slowly, with the thumb and index finger of your left hand, I want you to reach across and slowly take out your taser and toss it up here to me."

"Please don't hurt me, Richard. Please.'

"I'm not going to hurt you, Beauford. I'm sorry I had to break your nose. Now, do like I told you, nice and slow."

Beauford smiled at the apology. He knew Richard didn't mean to hurt him.

"Beauford, you're not going to try and shoot me, are you? You're shaking so bad I promise you'll miss and things won't go well for you."

Beauford did what he was told and tossed the taser into the seat next to Richard.

"Good, Beauford. Thank you. Now, toss the restraint key and your smartphone up to me. And Beauford, before you leave, grab some gauze out of the container to your left."

Beauford tossed the cuff key up and Richard caught it. He dug for his smartphone and tossed it behind Richard's chair. "Gauze? Why do you need gauze, Richard?"

"No, Beauford, you need gauze. Your nose is still bleeding. You know why I had to break your nose, right?"

"Huh?"

"Beauford, if I didn't break your nose, they might have thought you helped me escape. Now you can tell them whatever story you want about how you tried to stop me."

"Richard, why are you doing this? I don't think a jury would even convict you."

"I appreciate that, but I have something that can't wait. Goodbye, Beauford."

Beauford climbed out of the truck and nursed his broken nose.

Richard Dupree shifted the gear down into drive and turned the ambulance around, facing north. He started down the empty road toward the mountains on the horizon.

He was a free man.

CHAPTER NINETEEN

Hurricane Maxine made landfall on the eastern edge of Galveston Island at 3:52am local time. The Category 5 hurricane didn't break any of the records set the previous month by Hurricane Luther. She did, however, come very close. Unlike Luther, Maxine did not make landfall and then go back out to sea only to return to shore. Once she came ashore, she took her sweet time traveling to Houston. She slowly churned water from the Gulf of Mexico and brought it along with her for the trip, flooding the entire area from Galveston all the way into Houston. Winds in excess of one hundred ninety-five miles per hour brought Galveston Bay spilling into the Greater Houston area. Torrential rains flooded South Texas for the better part of twelve hours. Where Luther was a wrecking ball to the state of Florida, Maxine was like a fractured dam spewing water down on the state of Texas.

Chief Maxwell Harris had spent a good portion of the night filling sandbags to keep the rising water out of his command post at the local high school. He had a stack of sandbags three high at both doors leading into the locker room. He thought it would be sufficient but soon realized he needed to double the height. It was a risky decision, given that he had to venture outside to fill up the sandbags.

"Is it going to be enough?" asked Elizabeth.

"I think so; let's just hope the gym can withstand this bullshit. If it blows away we might be treading water in here."

"I hope you're exaggerating," Dr. Stone said.

"Maybe just a little. If this continues, the water could get up to our waists."

"This is a nightmare. I'm betting most of the town is underwater," Elizabeth stated with a worried look on her face.

"Not just the town, most of the region. I can't imagine what it's like out there or how we're going to get to safety."

"You'll think of something, you always do," Elizabeth stated.

"How are you feeling?" Max sat down next to Elizabeth.

"Very sore. Breathing is still hard."

"Bruised ribs tend to have that effect on people."

"Yeah, I figured that out pretty quick." Elizabeth sat up in her cot and fixed her hair.

"I know this isn't really the time or the place, not sure if it will be for a long time, but I was just wondering how you felt about everything I said earlier."

"What do you want me to say?"

"I don't know ... something. You change your mind about me? Think I'm a reckless asshole who murdered two innocent people?"

"Max, honey, stop. You didn't murder anyone, it was an accident. I'm sure you've done a fine job of torturing yourself. Explains a lot about you, why you always taking the path of least resistance. You have to move on with your life and make a difference. You can accomplish anything you put your mind to."

"I love you, Elizabeth."

"I love you, too."

"Too soon?"

"Not soon enough. Get over here and kiss me."

Max leaned over and placed his hand on the back of her head. He very slowly pulled her in and gently pressed his lips to hers. Elizabeth giggled.

"What's so funny?"

"I don't know. I was trying to make up a joke about this being our first date."

"You mean you couldn't think of something clever to say? I'm shocked. Am I that good of a kisser?"

"Don't flatter yourself. I'm pretty doped up on pain meds. Don't know how you manage to function on these things."

"You're just a lightweight. I prefer to think my kisses distracted you."

"Sure, keep thinking that, stud."

Max got up from Elizabeth's cot and turned on his flashlight. He checked on the other occupants of the locker rooms. Very few of the adults were sleeping; the children were more fortunate. Max shined his light out into the gymnasium and saw several inches of water. The damaged portions of the ceiling allowed water in like a faucet.

"He's dead, isn't he?"

"What?" Max turned around to see a very solemn Kathy

standing there.

"Chief, don't tell me what I want to hear. Tell me the truth."

"Kathy, I know as much as you do. Charlie is a sharp guy. I wouldn't be surprised if he climbed into a boat and tied it to a stop sign. You want to know my honest opinion?"

"Yes."

"There's a very good chance that he is dead, but we don't need to think like that. Does us no good worrying about information that we don't have. I think it's safe to say that a great many people are dead. The only thing we need to concentrate on is keeping each other alive. We'll deal with the rest when the time comes."

"I know. I'll do whatever it takes. I gotta say, Chief, you've really impressed me during all of this. I thought I could say I knew Maxwell Harris. Seems like I'm meeting him for the first time."

Max smiled. "Thanks. I'd forgotten who I was. I'd pretty much given up on doing anything with my life. I just wanted to be left alone and coast my way through. I guess it took a life threatening disaster to open my eyes and start living again."

Kathy smiled as they both stood in the doorway, not really knowing what to say. She decided to change the subject. "Looks like the wind is starting to calm down."

"Yeah, thank God for that. I wonder if we'll see the sun today."

Kathy shook her head. "I doubt it. Probably have storm clouds for a week."

"Well, we need to try and get some sleep. This is going to be a very long day."

"I doubt we'll be able to get much sleep."

"Well, then we need to at least lie down and rest."

Max walked around the locker rooms and checked on everyone. He told the civilians to try to get some sleep. Max took three pain pills to help with his throbbing hip and knee. He knew the idea of falling asleep was a joke, but he relaxed his body as much as he could and thought about dealing with the disaster happening all around him. He wondered how much of his town was left. Max thought about what his first move should be when they left the gym. Should he split up his deputies into search and rescue teams or should they all stick together? What about the civilians currently in the command post? Who would watch over them and keep them safe? What if they wanted to wander out into harm's way and risk injury? Max never dreamed of needing boats to get around his town; he didn't really think the water would get much higher than knee deep. The fact that water was coming inside the gymnasium meant that the water level was much higher than he anticipated. He would have to figure something out. Improvisation and resourcefulness were always his strong suits.

Max checked his watch to find it was approaching 8 am. The wind had finally slacked off enough that Max felt they could operate safely. It was still pouring outside, but it was time for them to get out there and do the job the taxpayers expected them to do. Max gathered everyone in the boys' locker room. Once they were settled, he spoke.

"OK, everybody, listen up. We've got some planning to do. Need to figure some things out before we get started. I need all the officers to switch their radios from A mode over to B mode." Their radios had two modes: A mode sent their radio traffic to the police station over a repeater and broadcasted it over a range of fifteen miles. When the radio was in B mode, the range was limited to the antenna on the radio itself, essentially making them walkie-talkies. In B mode, two radios could communicate a few miles at best.

"Since Elizabeth is in no condition to move, she will remain here at the command post with Dr. Stone and coordinate our movements. For the civilians in the room, I hope you won't object to staying here at the command post for the time being. I have no intention of detaining you against your will; however, I cannot allow you to leave here until we have surveyed the area. This is strictly for your safety. I hope you understand that. Do any of you have any prior military training or experience with emergency services?"

"Chief, I'd like to volunteer to help out. I was a firefighter for twenty-five years," a man in his late fifties stepped forward, "name's Rudy. My wife Trudy will help the doc out anyway she can."

"Rudy -n- Trudy. Trust me, we know our names rhyme,"

Rudy said, winking to everyone in the room.

"Rudy, it's a pleasure to meet you. Very grateful for your help," Max addressed the room, "anyone else?"

No one else spoke up. The only other men in the room were Elizabeth's fan who had enjoyed seeing her bra and a quiet man who clearly didn't want to leave his wife and small children behind.

"OK, for the rest of you who are staying here, I'd ask that you help out in whatever way you can. The first thing we're gonna do is head to the police station to survey the damage. Kathy, when you left the station did you secure the armory?"

"Sure did, Chief."

"OK, hopefully it managed to stay intact. Once we're at the station, we'll plan our next move. Let's get moving. Hopefully we can drive the entire way there. If not, we walk."

Max turned to Elizabeth, "Sergeant, be prepared to receive civilians. If we come across anyone who needs help, we'll be sending them here."

"Yes sir, Chief."

"Doc, you think you can handle running a makeshift ER?"

"I think I can manage." Dr. Stone gave Max a wink.

"Okay, we're leaving the sedan here. Take everything useful out of it and move it to one of the trucks."

Rudy spoke up. "Chief, that's my truck over there. Looks like she survived the storm. I got a tool box full of tools and some towing chains that might come in handy."

"That's outstanding, Rudy. The sedan we're leaving behind is Officer Miller's. He can ride with you."

"Okay, let's load up. The police station is only a few miles down the road. We're going to take it slow. I'll take the lead. Listen to your radio. If you see anyone in trouble call out over the radio to stop."

The four vehicles lined up in a convoy and pulled away from the high school. Only a few inches of water covered the roads, thanks to the drainage ditches on either side. They made slow progress, surveying the damage to their town. A half mile down the road on the left was a subdivision. When they were in front of the main entrance to the subdivision, the chief stopped and looked down the road. The majority of the houses were missing their roof. The drainage system in the subdivision was not exactly up to standard, so the streets and front yards were completely underwater. Water was up to the windows on the first floor of the houses. Max knew this subdivision was one of the lucky ones that had a higher elevation than most of the town. If things were this bad here, a good portion of the town would either be completely submerged or have only rooftops sticking out above the water line, like lonely beacons signaling the bleak wreckage of ordinary life.

The rest of the trip was uneventful. They didn't come across anyone who was stranded or needed assistance. At one point, the water was deep enough to come to the bottom of the car doors. Once they got to the police station, they pulled into the parking lot and got out of their vehicles.

"Well now, shit." Max put his hands on his hips and looked at what used to be his police station. The front half of the building had collapsed down on itself. The hallway that branched off the lobby and went to the right towards his office was completely gone. The only thing left standing was the center of the police station that housed the armory, a holding tank, and two jail cells. The center portion of the police station was made of concrete reinforced with steel rebar.

"OK, we're going to have to get around to the back somehow. Don't try to enter any portion of the station, no matter how safe it looks. We don't want anyone to get hurt or trapped under anything," said Max.

As they carefully moved forward in single file, Deputy Miller suddenly stopped.

"Miller, what is it?" asked Max.

"I hear voices; someone's back there."

"Find out who it is!"

Miller shook his head. "They're trying to break into the armory. They're yelling at someone to open it for them."

Max looked worried. "Stay there and keep quiet, everyone." Max walked up to the front of the line and stood next to Deputy Miller. He could hear people talking over each other.

"Hey man, think about your wife and kids. Just open it up and we'll be on our way. Your family will be safe."

"How do I know you'll let them go?"

Max turned to Deputy Miller. "They've got Charlie opening the armory for them. Sounds like they got his wife and kids hostage."

"What are we gonna do, Chief?"

"Shit, we're too late. The armory is open." Max pulled out his sidearm and turned to his deputies, who drew their weapons and waited for the chief to make his move.

"This is the police! Stop what you're doing and put your hands up! Let the officer go and no one will get hurt!"

Max got his answer as repeated shotgun blasts struck the tree to his left. He got down on his hands and knees, ducking behind the wall of debris. His deputies followed suit.

"Kiss my fucking ass! I don't give a shit who you are! You fucking cops are the reason we're stuck here!"

Max and Officer Miller exchanged confused looks. "Hey, friend, I'm not sure you know exactly what's going on here. Not much we could do to stop a hurricane!"

"No shit, asshole! Don't talk to me like I'm stupid! All we wanted was some gas, and you pigs ran us off at gunpoint!"

Deputy Miller whispered to Max, "Those must be the guys who cut in line and wanted to fill up their gas cans. We ran them off, but they came back and fired some rounds at the gas station."

"Yeah, kinda figured that one out," Max quickly stated, and then addressed the gang of men robbing his armory. "You guys need to think about what you're doing! You'll eventually get caught and wind up in prison for a very long time. Just slow down and think this out. This is gonna end up bad for you, I promise. Just put down your weapons, let the officer go and we can talk about this!"

"Shut the fuck up, you moron! You have no idea what's going on! Are you dumb enough to think that things are just going to go back the way they were before? Are you that stupid? Wake the fuck up and get with the program!"

"I don't know what you're talking about, man. Recovery takes time! Things will get cleaned up and rebuilt, and you'll have to answer for you're doing! It's not a free-for-all out here, we have laws!"

"You really are clueless, aren't you? You think that being a cop means something now? You think I'm going to stand trial?"

The man addressing Max was laughing so hard he could barely get the sentence out.

"Of course you're going to stand trial! If you don't stand down and come out now, all of you will be arrested or shot!"

"Okay, copper, I'll play along and have a conversation with you like you mean something. Let me ask you this - you been to Florida lately? Talked to anyone in Florida lately?"

"No, I haven't been to Florida. Most of the state is locked down and quarantined. Something about a toxic chemical spill."

"Complete bullshit!"

"And how would you know that?"

"Because I came from Florida, that's why! That bullshit on the news about a quarantine zone is one massive cover-up! They got the place in lockdown because they don't want people getting out to tell the truth about what's really going on!"

"You don't know what you're talking about! That's just crazy!"

"I wish I was crazy, I really do," the man laughed. "I'm telling you, I saw it with my own eyes. I was there! Everything is just gone! One giant pile of shit! Dead bodies everywhere, hardly any buildings left standing! The roads are either destroyed or full of broken down cars! I know how it sounds, I really do. But I'm telling you the truth! It's like a war zone in there! Small town cops aren't helping at all. They just barricade off what's left of their towns and shoot anyone who tries to come in! The National Guard isn't doing jack shit either! All they're doing is blocking the roads, not lettin' anybody in or out!"

"Not that I believe you, but how exactly did you manage to get out? How'd you get all the way to Texas?"

"I made it to the checkpoint on Interstate 10. They tried to turn me around. All I wanted was some help, and they expected me to just turn around! I backtracked a few miles and took my bike off road. Made it around the checkpoint and stuck to back roads 'till I was well out of the way of the National Guard. Got here just in time for another fuckin' hurricane."

"So you think you can just do whatever you want? Every man for himself? You think Florida and Texas have turned into some Mad Max wasteland?" Max turned to Miller and Collins and motioned for them to head around and flank the armory from the left side. They understood and headed off.

"That describes it to a fuckin' T. It's every man for himself. People in Florida are surviving in gangs, banding together and defending what they got from other gangs. I'm telling you, man, I made it to a small town with the main road barricaded like it was an army base or something. Cops there chased people off with gunfire just to keep them out! The only thing that matters now is who has more firepower! That's just what I'm doing; I'm taking these guns and getting the fuck out while I still can!"

"Hate to tell you, friend, you ain't goin' anywhere with my guns. Not gonna happen!"

"You forgetting something, you dumb prick? I got one of your men in here! You don't let us out of here, I'm blowing his head off! Then one of my boys is gonna kill his wife and kids! You better think about who's in charge around here! I don't give a shit if you got a badge! I'm in charge, so you better do as I say or this guy is dead!"

Max turned to Deputy Shackleford from the County Sheriff's office. "Gene, take Rudy back to the command post. Tell Sergeant Reid what's going on, and have her give you directions to Charlie's house so you can rescue his family. Do not key up your radio; I don't want to tip our hand. If they manage to get out of here, their next stop will be Charlie's house. He's got a baby and a toddler. We can't let these animals do anything to them."

Gene shook his head as he and Rudy headed back to the vehicles. They slowly skirted the piles of debris and rounded the corner to the parking lot. Max peered around the corner and could see Miller hiding behind a tree twenty yards to the left of the armory. He gave Max a thumbs up to indicate he was ready, and Max nodded his head in return. All he had to do was somehow convince this gang of thugs to let him come around the corner so he could talk. He would even toss his revolver out in front of them to make them think he was unarmed while leaving his back-up pistol in the small of his back.

Then Max heard a shotgun blast, followed by three pops from a handgun.

Max knew they were in trouble because no one on his

team had a shotgun. He quickly peered around the corner to see if the guys in the armory were trying to rush him. When he turned around he saw a fat, bald man aiming a shotgun at him and another man close behind with a pistol. Max dropped his weapon and put his hands up. He closed his eyes and tried to find peace in the face of certain death.

"Jack! We got him! He surrendered!"

"Good! Bring his ass back here!"

Max kept his hands up as he warily eyed the two men drawing down on him.

"Mister, you drop your hands and it's the last thing you do, I guarantee it. I already done killed those two guys trying to make a run for it; don't you think for one second I won't kill you. Start walkin' … you know the way." Max obeyed but was able to make eye contact with Miller, shaking his head ever so slightly. If Miller or Collins made a move, people from both sides of the conflict would surely die.

As Max rounded the corner of the armory, he saw Deputy Charlie Mason sitting on the ground in his underwear with his right wrist handcuffed to his left ankle. Three thugs wearing bulletproof vests were loading gym bags with guns and ammo.

"Charlie, you okay?

"Yeah, Chief, I'm real sorry about this. They got my wife and kids locked up in one of the..."

"Shut the fuck up! I told you to keep quiet!" The guy running the show kicked Charlie in the jaw, knocking him to the ground. Charlie spit blood and kept his face in the mud.

"Stop! Okay! You win! You got us! You're running the show! Jack? Is that your name? I get it! You don't need to hurt anyone!" said Max in frustration.

"Oh, yeah, mother fucker? Is that right? You get it? You get it? How 'bout you get a bullet in the head? Huh? How 'bout that?" Jack raised the pistol and leveled it at Max's head, quickly closing the distance between them. "How 'bout you shut your hole before I kick you in the teeth like your buddy over there! I haven't decided what I'm gonna do with the two of you!"

"OK, I'm sorry," Max said softly.

"This is what's gonna happen, asshole. We're cleaning this place out and taking your vehicles. Reckon we could go places in cop cars much easier. You gotta problem with that? Huh?" Jack rapped the barrel of the pistol on Max's sweaty forehead. "Whadda ya think? That sound fine with you?"

"Take what you want, just don't kill us."

"Take off your clothes."

"What?" Max looked at him in horror.

"You heard me – strip! You want me to shoot your friend here? I've always wanted to be a cop. Take off your god damned clothes! Hurry up!" Jack walked over to Charlie and aimed at his head.

"Stop! Okay!" Max began to take off his wet uniform.

"That's better! Joe, cuff these two pigs together, his arm to his leg." Jack tossed a set of cuffs to the fat man holding the shotgun.

Joe caught the cuffs and leaned his shotgun on a pile of rubble. "I'm gonna like being a cop! Always wanted a badge and a gun. Hot damn!" The fat man pushed Max to the ground next to Charlie.

"You behave now, or I'm gonna shoot your friend." Jack aimed the pistol and Charlie's head. "Go on and snap those cuffs on your wrist and to his ankle."

With the men distracted by his uniform, Max leaned into Charlie and whispered, "Is your radio off?"

"It's in my patrol car at my house; I don't have it with me. They grabbed me on my way in."

"Good. Just stay calm. Miller and Collins are in the woods, ready to attack when they can get us out of the line of fire."

"God damn! We hit the jackpot! Check out this cool shit!" Jack surveyed the duffle bags piled up at his feet. "These grenades look badass! Can't wait to find out what they do!"

"Hell yeah, we're gonna run some shit for sure!" said the fat man.

"Hey Joe, keep an eye on these two. I think I wanna try on my new uniform." Jack stripped out of his dirty clothes and put on Max's wet uniform. Then he bent down and picked up Max's duty belt, fitting it around his waist. "My oh my, this fits perfect! Whaddya think Joe? I look like a cop?"

"Hell no," laughed Joe.

"Shut up, you fat ass! Hey, you two clowns got everything loaded in our new cop cars?"

Max watched the two nameless henchmen grab the last duffle bag and head toward the parking lot.

"Can we move it along, please? Assholes? Hello? Hurry up! Let's go!" Jack was screaming at his two underlings, clearly letting them know who was running things.

"Well, now we get to the hard part. What are we gonna do with you guys?" Jack was pacing back and forth in front of Max and Charlie.

Joe walked over next to Jack and dug in his pocket. "Well, I know what I'm gonna do," the fat man said, pulling his smartphone out of his pocket. "I've gotta take a picture of these two lovebirds."

"They do look sweet in their little love pretzel. Smile!" Jack laughed at how upset Max was getting.

"Well shit, we might as well kill 'em. Already got two dead bodies in the parking lot," said Joe.

"Holy shit! I just got the funniest idea!" Jack laughed hysterically.

"What? Spit it out man!" said Joe.

"You know what we should do? Shoot one and not the other. Leave one of 'em handcuffed to a dead body!"

"Jesus Christ, Jack! That's some twisted shit!" the fat man snorted as he laughed.

"I don't know. I couldn't care less about killing fuckin' cops. What about those little kids in the prison cell? I'm not killin' a baby."

"Me neither."

"Your fat ass would eat a baby before you shot one."

"That's gross dude! Shut up!"

"OK, fine. Listen up, lovebirds; this is what's gonna happen. Once we leave outta here, the two of you can play naked Twister and figure out a way to get over to the jail cell. The cell door key is on the hook next to the door. You let the bitch out and I'm sure she can help you out of your love knot. Sound like a plan?"

Max nodded.

"Well, shit, look here what I got. Didn't even notice it

when I put on the belt. A walkie talkie radio! Maybe we can listen to this thing and figure out what the cops are doing!"

Max closed his eyes and hung his head. *Elizabeth.*

One of the unnamed henchmen came running around the corner. "Jack! Some lady is on the radio asking for these cops, said she was at a command post."

"Please tell me you didn't respond!" Jack screamed.

"No, just listened is all."

"What do we care about a command post? Let's get moving and get the hell outta here!" said Joe.

"Think about it, stupid! A command post's got supplies, probably all kinds of good shit. We got the uniforms, the bullet proof vests, and guns!"

"Shit, yeah! Let's get moving!"

Jack and his hooligans took off toward the parking lot. Once they rounded the corner, Max turned towards the tree line and yelled, "NOW!"

Miller and Collins burst from the bushes and sprinted through the downpour to Max and Charlie.

"No! Forget us, you have to stop them! They're looking for the command post!"

Collins understood immediately and took off after them with Miller close behind. All Max could do with his wrist handcuffed to Charlie's ankle was wait helplessly and hope they stopped the men before things got completely out of control. If the two henchmen had taken the time to dig weapons out of the bags and load them with ammo, it was going to be an ugly fight. Max hoped the element of surprise would be to their advantage. He listened in horror to the sound of shotgun blasts and the quick pop-pop-pop of a pistol over and over again. Then after thirty nightmarish seconds, he heard a vehicle speed away.

All that remained was the sound of the rain.

"Miller! Collins! Somebody talk to me! What happened? HEY! YOU GUYS ALL RIGHT? MILLER! COLLINS!"

Charlie began to cry angry tears. "Those fucks killed them! Fucking animals! What kind of man takes a mother and two small babies and tosses them in a jail cell!"

"Charlie, listen, we need to figure a way to slide over there. Tell you what - lie on your back and tuck your chin. I can stand up and drag you on your back."

"Okay, it's worth a try."

The plan was awkward but effective. As they moved slowly forward, Max searched for his two officers. Miller was lying on his back, his nose and left eye missing along with most of his jaw. A shotgun blast does horrific damage to its target. Miller was dead – no doubt about it. Max saw Collins ten yards away, leaning up against a piece of broken wall.

"Collins! You okay?"

Collins gave a thumbs up.

"You get hit?"

Collins made a gun with his fingers and shot himself in the chest. Then he made a fist and pounded the vest.

"Vest stopped it and knocked the wind out you, probably broke some ribs?

Collins nodded in agreement.

"Son, I need you to toss me your restraint key so Charlie and I can get out of this situation."

Collins tossed the key to Max. Once the two were separated, Charlie ran quickly to the cell door, reuniting with his wife and kids in a barrage of hugs and kisses.

Max sat down next to Collins. "I know it hurts, Collins, but I need you to talk, even if it's a whisper. How many of them are left? How many made it out of here?"

"Three. Fat man is in the parking lot. The other three took our vehicles and left. One of them took a bullet in the arm. Managed to shoot out one of the truck tires; they won't make it too far in that."

Max walked over to the obese man who way lying on his back, his chest heaving rapidly as he desperately tried to fill his torn lungs with air. Max leaned down and picked up his shotgun.

"You're not a cop, you fat piece of shit." Max shot him in the head.
Ignoring the stabbing pain in his hip, Max limped over to Rudy's dead body. He gently closed Rudy's vacant eyes and dug in his front pockets for the truck keys.

"I'm sorry, Rudy. I'm going after the men who did this. I promise you I'll make them pay. I'll make sure your wife is safe, and we'll take good care of her."

Max turned to find Deputy Collins standing behind him. He took off his jacket and handed it to the chief. Max put the windbreaker over his shivering, wet body.

"You feelin' better?"

Collins placed his palm over his rib cage just beneath his sternum and whispered, "Hurts like a bitch to breathe and talk, but I'll be okay."

"Let's get going. Once we find those bastard rednecks we won't be doing much talking."

CHAPTER TWENTY

President Malcolm Powers was getting impatient. He and his former guests were sitting in the underground bunker beneath the White House waiting to be moved back up topside. His Chief of Staff had not spoken a word to him and he knew the reason. He would have time to deal with her later. More important things required his attention, like the symbol of the office of the president being directly attacked and an Iranian sub in the water with a nuclear warhead aboard.

"Mike, tell me something good. I'm ready to get out of here."

"Mr. President, we have the airports shut down and roadblocks are being set up on every major road leading out of the capitol. Once all air traffic is grounded and if nothing else happens, we can move you up top."

"How long?"

"An hour, two at the most."

President Powers looked at Admiral Mack. "Are the *Enterprise* and the *George Washington* underway?"

"Yes, Mr. President, they're moving at full speed to join the blockade in the Arabian Sea."

"Radiation levels?"

"Continuing to rise, Mr. President. The weather system continues to spread radioactivity into the area. Much of the region will be uninhabitable for decades."

CIA Director Jimenez coughed and growled, "Animals are killing their own people just to come at us."

Everyone in the room looked gravely at each other. The president continued to address Admiral Mack. "Bunker Five?"

"We still can't get a clear read on it, Mr. President."

"What if they launch directly from the bunker? Will we be able to stop it in time?"

"Yes, Mr. President. We would be able to shoot it down over the Arctic Circle or over the Atlantic Ocean. We are still confident that they do not have a working ICBM."

"Well, their actions lead me to believe that they're capable of anything. I'm not going to underestimate them; ensure that you do not as well, General Moody."

"Yes, Mr. President." The Chairman of the Joint Chiefs of Staff responded with a cold, stern face. He did not like being talked down to.

"Ladies and gentlemen, if you will excuse me, I'm going to retire to my quarters for a short time to freshen up and spend some time reflecting on the horrible events of this day. Please make yourselves comfortable. Just as soon as we are given the all clear, we will all return to the White House."

The president stood up, and every person in the room followed suit. The CIA director placed his hands on the arms of his wheelchair and sat up as straight as he could.

"Stacy, would you join me, please?"

"Yes, Mr. President." The president's Chief of Staff stood up and followed her boss down the short hallway to his private quarters. He opened the door for her, ushering her in. Once he closed the door, he braced himself for the ass-chewing he knew would follow.

"Malcolm, I want one good reason why I shouldn't hand you my letter of resignation!"

Stacy Reid had been Admiral Powers' campaign manager. Once he took office, she was the obvious choice to be his Chief of Staff. She accepted the job on one condition - when they were behind closed doors, she could speak her mind and deflate his ego if it was growing unchecked. Malcolm gladly accepted the condition and would have insisted on it anyway. He needed someone to keep him in check, someone who wasn't concerned about furthering their own career or just wanted to kiss his ass. Malcolm had studied JFK's biggest blunder, the Bay of Pigs, and came to his own conclusion that if JFK's advisors had spoken their minds and not worried about damaging their careers, JFK could have avoided the biggest blunder of his presidency.

"Stacy, just hear me out. I wanted to bring you in on this from the start. Keeping you in the dark was a very tough call. I regret it now, and I apologize. I should never have done that to you."

"I hope you have a damn good reason. I'm waiting."

"Well, I made the decision based on two reasons. The first is that you're from Florida."

"What? How dare you! You think I couldn't give you

sound advice? That's outrageous! I hope your second reason is better than that."

"What would you have done if you'd known about my plan?"

"Your plan to lie to the American people? I think you can figure that one out."

"Exactly my point. I need you, Stacy. I can't afford to lose you, especially now, given what's at stake. I hope you can work past this and we can come to an understanding."

"I need time, Malcolm. I just don't know."

"Take all the time you need. In the meantime, I hope you can continue to perform your duties as well as you always have."

"If I'm even going to think about staying, no more lies, no more hiding things from me."

"Of course."

"You know I would have left quietly."

"I know you would, but I couldn't afford the press putting two and two together. Okay, let's talk about today. What do you think?"

"Personal feelings aside, I don't think you'll be able to contain Governor Prince for much longer. She's bound to go to the press."

"You're probably right. I was planning on sending the *Enterprise* and the *George Washington* to the Florida coastline. It's the only reason I called the meeting. I wanted to get input from everyone before I made a decision. You think she knows that? Will it matter to her?"

"She has to realize that an Iranian sub in the water with a nuke takes precedence."

"Stacy, can you talk to her, remind her of that?"

"Me?"

"The woman doesn't like me, and you used to work for her. I think you'll have better luck."

"We worked together a very long time ago. She was a state senator and I was her press secretary. We didn't exactly part ways on the best of terms."

"Well, I still think you'll have better luck than I would. She cussed me out in front of some of the most powerful people in our government. She would probably do worse if given the chance."

"I'll talk to her, try to get her to see reason."

"Excuse me, Mr. President?" the White House A.I. interrupted.

"Yes, computer, what is it?"

"Howard Beck is requesting to speak to you. I informed him that you are indisposed at the moment and couldn't take his vid-con. He says that it's urgent."

"What does he want?"

"He wouldn't say. He insisted on speaking with you."

"Well, I can't very well talk to him down here, you won't let me. It'll have to wait until I get back upstairs. In fact, tell him I will speak with him sometime tomorrow. I'm trying to save our country from a nuclear holocaust."

"Yes, Mr. President."

Stacy rolled her eyes. "He probably wants to see if you know anything about Patrick Stewart returning to *Star Trek*."

"Patrick Stewart is returning to *Star Trek*?"

"Focus, Malcolm. There are more important things going on."

"Really? Like what?" Malcolm smiled.

"Should we try to reach out to the Iranian Ambassador? Try a diplomatic solution?" Stacy asked.

"We could go through the motions, I suppose. We both know it won't accomplish a damn thing."

"Doesn't hurt to try. We can at least confront them out in the open for the press to see. Let them know that we're aware of what they're doing. Get some pressure on them from the rest of the world."

"Good point. Where is the Secretary of State?"

"Secretary Whitlock is in Paris meeting with delegates from the European Army."

"Computer, send a message to Secretary Whitlock and dispatch him to Cairo. Inform him that I will be contacting him when he lands."

"Yes, Mr. President."

"Anything else, Stacy?"

"Yes, can you pull a few strings and get us out of here? You're the president of the United States, after all. Don't you have some sway around here?"

"Funny."

"I'm not sure if now is the right time, but I've had some concerns about..."

Stacy was interrupted by a knock on the door.

"Come in." The president looked up from his desk to see his lead Secret Service agent in the doorway.

"Mr. President, it's time to move you."

"Finally! I'm ready to get back in my office."

"We're not moving you back into the White House, Mr. President."

"Excuse me?"

"Sir, we have secured the grounds of the White House, but things in D.C. are spiraling out of control. Riots are breaking out all over the city. Large portions of the capital are on fire. The roads are in complete gridlock, due in large part to the attack on the White House. The National Guard has informed us that they will lose control of the city in a matter of hours. You're no longer safe here; we have to move you out of the city."

"Mike, I will not leave the White House! I'm not going to abandon our nation's capital and run away like a coward! Out of the question! I'll stay down here if I have to, but I'm not leaving!"

Stacy decided to play referee. "Mr. President, if things are as bad as Mike is saying, we have little choice but to leave. If the National Guard loses control of the city, we'll be trapped down here for a very long time. If the rioters think you're in the White House, they might try to burn it down to smoke you out. Then you will be down here sitting under the ashes of the White House. If we move you to a secure location, you'll be able to do much more than you can in this safe room. I can work with the press secretary to come up with a statement putting all of this into a positive light."

Stacy was right, as usual. He needed to leave. The last force to capture and occupy Washington, D.C., was the British in 1814. General Robert Ross was under orders to occupy the capital and burn down public buildings. The White House was burned to the ground. British troops even added fuel to the fire to ensure that the presidential residence burned throughout the night and into the following morning. The capitol building was largely destroyed as well. Never in his wildest dreams did Malcolm think his own citizens would take the city by force. If he remained in the White House, the building would certainly be a target. Even if he did leave, he was sure that the White House would be lost.

"Mike, where do you intend on taking me? Do I have a say?"

"Sir, your residence in upstate New York is a secure location. My team will travel ahead of us and join the agents already there. The rest of us travel with you on Air Force One."

"Good, Mike, thank you. The First Lady is already there, correct? She hasn't left, has she?"

"Yes, Mr. President, your wife and daughter are already there. Your son is being moved from Harvard to join you."

"When do we leave?"

"Air Force One is standing by. We need to leave within the hour."

"Thank you, Mike."

President Malcolm Powers stood up and straightened his tie. He took a deep breath and exited the room. Once he was in the conference room, the president addressed the group.

"Thank you, please, sit down."

Everyone took their seats and looked at the president. They could tell that the weight of the world was on his shoulders. The poor man had endured more in a day than some presidents faced during their entire administration.

"For those of you who don't know, riots have broken out all over the capital. We're not talking about a few protests that got out of control. Things are very, very bad. Much of our beloved city is on fire. The National Guard has indicated that they will lose the city within a few hours. My staff and I will be moving to my residence in upstate New York immediately. All of you are welcome to join me on Air Force One. The choice is yours, of course, but I doubt that any of you have a safer way to leave Washington."

Everyone in the room tried to hide their panic and fear. They were all stunned for a moment, then swallowed their dread and focused on what needed to be done.

The president stood tall and resolute. He paused for

moment, trying to comprehend the full weight of what he was about to say. "Computer, coordinate with the Secret Service and begin preparations to evacuate the White House."

CHAPTER TWENTY-ONE

Captain Jackson Butler was standing in the grand library of the world's richest man. His orders had been to take over Beck Estates and set up a fortified army base that would serve as the command center for the Rocky Mountain and Pacific states. The country was falling apart fast, and the Unified National Guard had to regroup and consolidate its forces if they had any hopes of stopping an all-out civil war. Jackson had given his reports to his commanding officer, Colonel Rutherford. In them, Jackson had detailed his retreat from Denver and the grave injuries to his XO. When Colonel Rutherford read that Captain Butler ended up at the front gate of Howard Beck's estate, he actually vid-conned the captain, certain that it was a joke. In later reports, Captain Butler gave the details of the guesthouse, which was a mansion in itself by any practical standards. Colonel Rutherford dispatched troops to Captain Butler's command. The original plans were to first gather enough forces to retake Denver, and then the Joint Chiefs had other plans for Beck Estates. Once Las Vegas, Phoenix, and Portland fell to angry mobs, it was clear that drastic measures had to be taken to prevent the country from descending into chaos. Beck Estates was the perfect staging area. The Joint Chiefs were already having plans drawn for an airstrip to be built on Howard's thousand-acre estate. In a year's time, the home of the world's richest man would be well on its way to becoming a full blown army base.

Jackson was certain he had built a solid friendship with Howard and that he could convince him to go along with the plan. Jackson planned on telling Howard a little bit at a time. Once he got comfortable with the first tidbit of information, Butler would slowly break more and more bad news to the man until eventually he would be helpless to do anything at all. His bright idea was stopped cold. Howard was standing in front of him having a tantrum like a toddler. Howard kicked over a table and sent papers and books flying across the room. Jackson was standing in probably the largest library he had seen in his life. He remembered the large public libraries from his youth. There were still a few left in some of the larger cities. Since most people could fit the Library of Congress on their smartphone, paper books were becoming quite rare. The last paperback book had been printed in 2022, to be replaced with digital copies only. The books that Howard had sent flying across the room looked to be very old, and given the man's vast wealth, were probably very valuable.

"Get the hell out of my house! NOW!!!"

For the love of God, Howard, why are you making this so difficult? I have my orders. Surely you know what is at stake. You insist on doing this the hard way, don't you? I can tell I'm going to have to make this official. Captain Butler had memorized the decree signed by the Chairman of the Joint Chiefs of Staff.

"Howard Beck, by order of the president of the United States, I hereby seize your property, and you will be confined to your suite under armed guard."

Jackson knew this statement would only enrage the old man further. He suddenly recalled an article he had read about Howard Beck some years ago. The man has Asperger's Syndrome, which accounted for his driven genius, but it also explained why Howard had come completely unhinged. People with Asperger's don't take change well, especially when it pertains to the place they consider to be their home, a place where they feel safe and in control.

"I'd like to see you try, you stupid grunt! Old Man!! Lock down the estate! Deny everyone but me access to your systems and deploy security measures immed..."

When Howard gave the lock down command, the room dimmed and bright lights flashed and flickered in front of the windows. A shimmering curtain appeared in front of each window, clearly some kind of force field. A loud alarm wailed throughout the mansion. Captain Butler immediately forgot about his friendship with the man - his mission was all that mattered. The fate of countless millions was resting on the occupation of Beck Estates. He had no choice. He drew his sidearm faster than a gunslinger, aimed at Howard's head and pulled the trigger.

A thousandth of a second before the firing pin struck the round, he was knocked off his feet by a force that came from out of nowhere. He had no doubt that Hal had somehow intervened.

From his prone position, Butler looked over at Top. First
Sergeant Bankhead had drawn his sidearm as well; however, the
gray-haired NCO quickly suffered the same fate as Butler. Top
landed with a thud behind him and groaned.

Captain Butler blinked his eyes several times and let the
shock wear off. "Top! You alright?"

"Roger that, sir. What in the blazes was that? Where's
Howard?"

Both men got to their feet; Howard was nowhere to be
found. First Sergeant Bankhead walked over to the double doors
of the library.

"Sir, we're locked in."

Captain Butler knew Hal was watching them. First
Sergeant Bankhead nodded in understanding and walked back
over to the middle of the room where they had previously been
laying. Both men moved towards their weapons. As First
Sergeant Bankhead reached down for his weapon, a puff of air
sounded, and Top was sent flying backwards. For a second time,
he found himself flat on his back.

"Son of a bitch!" the old man growled as he looked up at
the ceiling.

Captain Butler looked up. "Hal! Listen to me! You have
to stop this, now! Will you please just hear me out?"

Silence.

"Hal, I know you can hear me, so just listen! Please! This
is very important. Millions of lives depend on what we do here
today!"

Silence.

"Hal, please! Let me talk to Howard and try to explain
this. I know he's furious with me, and I'm not going to deny that
I tried to kill him. That was the last thing I wanted to do!
Howard is my friend! I know that if I could just have the chance
to talk with him I could make him understand."

Silence.

First Sergeant Bankhead looked at his CO. "Captain, I
think it's safe to say that Howard is somewhere watching us right
now."

Captain Butler nodded in agreement. "Howard, please! I
can't tell you how sorry I am that things got so out of control. I

couldn't allow you to lock this place down. Howard, a lot of very, very powerful people have big plans for this place. Stopping us will accomplish nothing. Keeping us prisoner in this library will only make things worse for you. If you cooperate with us, I promise no one will ever know what happened here today. If you keep us prisoner in here, you will be tried for treason and executed. Think about it. You are, without a doubt, the smartest person I have ever met. You know I'm right."

Silence.

"Jackson, we have to get out of here." Top said, "Colonel Rutherford is expecting a status report from you in twenty-five minutes. In thirty minutes I'm supposed to be meeting with First Sergeant Moore and his platoon sergeants. If we don't show up, we got maybe ten minutes at best before they start looking for us."

"You hear that, Howard? Whatever you're gonna do, you got about a half hour to figure it out!! The clock's ticking!"

Silence.

"What are your orders, sir?"

"We wait. We give Howard a few minutes and after that we figure out our next move." Captain Butler's eyes quickly shot around the room.

First Sergeant Bankhead nodded in understanding. "You think he'll let us out?"

"I honestly don't know. I'm betting he's having a lot of fun right now, aren't you, Howard? He's probably just waiting to see what we'll do when his time is up."

"He's got a minute and some change."

"Top, you remember what I told you after that little girl died at our checkpoint?"

"Sir?"

Captain Butler raised his eyebrows hoping that the man sitting across from him would get the hint.

"Ready when you are, Captain."

"What's it going to be, Howard? Time's up! Shit or get off the pot!"

Silence.

Both men wandered over to the table Howard had toppled and began picking up the books that were scattered across the floor.

"You know, Howard, it's a real shame that you would treat such amazing books like this." He picked up a worn, leather bound book. *His Last Bow: A Reminiscence of Sherlock Holmes by Sir Arthur Conan Doyle*. Wow! This must be worth a small fortune. Real shame you tore the dust cover when you had your little temper tantrum. You reminded me of my toddler. He acts like that when his brother takes his toys away from him. Is that it, Howard? You don't want to share your toys with us?"

First Sergeant Bankhead laughed. "Yeah! I thought he was gonna start crying like a baby. I'm not surprised he ran off like that."

Silence.

The two men locked eyes for a brief second and then flipped the table into the air, sending it flying towards the middle of the room. The table landed on its side and slid across the hardwood floor, stopping exactly where they had planned. Before the last book hit the floor, the two men each grabbed a chair and ran towards their pistols. They could hear puffs of air sending rubber bullets towards them. A bullet hit First Sergeant Bankhead in the lower back, causing him to collapse onto his commanding officer. The human shield was all Captain Butler needed. Grabbing both pistols, he aimed one at the computer console on the wall, firing three shots as the console sparked and died. At the same time, with his other hand, he fired at the red, glowing circle on the wall directly in front of him.

"Top, you still with me?"

First Sergeant Bankhead rolled over onto the floor and screamed, "FUCK YOU, HOWARD!"

"I'll take that as a yes. You're one tough bastard. How many hits you take since we walked in this room?"

"Four. I'm gonna choke that old geezer when I get my hands on him."

They were both on their backs behind the table. "Sir, is it safe to get up?"

"I believe so."

They stood up and scanned the room. "How in the hell did you manage that? How did you know?"

"You ever see *2001: A Space Odyssey*?"

"Can't say that I have. What's that got to do with anything?"

"Famous sci-fi movie. The computer is named the HAL-9000. They're flying in a spaceship to investigate an alien object in space. The computer goes crazy and tries to kill the crew. Howard named his computer after it. In the movie, the computer can see all over the ship through a glowing red fish eye lens. That same red lens is in every room in this house, at least the rooms I've been in. I gambled on that being how Hal can see and hear everything. I shot it out and for good measure destroyed the computer console just to be safe."

"Best shooting I've ever seen, Captain. Looks like your gamble paid off."

"I'm just as surprised as you are, Top. I'm just glad you caught on to my plan."

After the little girl died at the checkpoint, Captain Butler knew it wouldn't be long before riots broke out. When he saw that the video had gone viral, he prepared for the worst. In a vid-con, he told his lieutenants that if the mobs started to crowd the checkpoints, they would need a distraction to draw the crowds away. When the mob turned to see what was going on, they would hit them with tear gas. All he needed was for Top to help him provide a distraction.

"So what's the plan now, sir?"

"I have no idea. I spent everything on the stunt we just pulled. All I wanted was for Hal to stop monitoring our every move so we could come up with a plan. I had hoped that the force fields in front of the windows would drop, but we aren't that lucky. I have no idea how they operate. Certainly not going to touch it and find out. We need to figure it out before we proceed."

"Sir, I've had my ass torn apart by rubber bullets."

Captain Butler smiled. "Top, you've done more than enough. I was thinking about the other occupant of this room."

Top laughed. "Howard's cat?"

"Let's find her."

****

Howard Beck was laughing hysterically in the secure sub-basement of the residence.

"Sir, I hardly think this is funny."

"Relax, Old Man! You should know they're never going to catch your cat!"

"Sir, they better not hurt my sweet little Nala."

Nala was about the meanest cat Howard had ever seen in his life. Meredith was the only person she would respond to; after she died, Nala warmed up to Hal for some reason. Howard was more than amused that his A.I. had grown fond of an animal. The love affair reminded him of Koko the gorilla and her pet kitten.

Captain Butler and First Sergeant Bankhead were throwing books at the cat. Nala was on top of a high bookshelf, hissing at the two soldiers. Howard laughed heartily as the two men tried to wrangle the mean, old cat. He was certain they would eventually throw in the towel, but they appeared dedicated to the task at hand.

"Sir, please put a stop to this."

"You're no fun Hal! OK, fine. You win."

Howard was absolutely thrilled that he was finally able to test his security system. The two soldiers were the perfect test subjects.

Howard clicked a button and began to speak to the men for the first time since he departed the room.

"Gentlemen! Bravo! Bravo! An excellent performance indeed! You should both be very proud. Fine job disabling Hal's reach into the library, but you should know I still have cameras all over the place. Captain Butler, do you perform in sharp-shooting competitions, perhaps? You would be very entertaining in a Wild West show."

"Shut up, Howard!" Captain Butler flipped Howard the bird.

"Oh come now, Captain! No need to be rude! I meant that as a compliment!"

"Time to stop playing games, Howard! This has gone on long enough! You should know the kind of trouble you're gonna be in if you don't let us out of here!"

"My dear Captain, you have no idea what's going on. It is

you that will be in trouble, not me. I've contacted the White House, and the president and his staff are in lock down from a terrorist attack. Once I am able to speak with him, I am going to expose you and whomever is behind this foolishness. If you're lucky, you'll only be busted down to a buck private. I haven't decided if I'm going to go to bat for you. I hope, for your sake, you were truly only following orders."

"Howard, think about it! This is coming directly from the Chairman of the Joint Chiefs of Staff! You really think the president is in the dark?"

"I intend to find out just that."

"Howard, I'm not lying to you. I have great respect for you. I didn't want any of this to happen!"

"Is that why you tried to shoot me in the head? Is that how you show respect?"

"Damn it, Howard! I had to stop you! I have a sworn duty to protect this country! Millions of lives depend on this! You want to be branded as a traitor?"

"I'm a traitor? What about you? You violated my Third Amendment rights and tried to kill me! You're the traitor, not me!"

"Howard, that's not the point here. What matters is that right about now, people are looking for me and Top. Things are just going to get worse and worse for you if you don't let us out."

"Oh, you need not worry about that, Captain Butler. I have no intention of letting you continue to tear up my library."

The door to the library opened and four security robots entered.

"This is what's going to happen. The two of you will drop your weapons and place your hands on your head. Each of my friends here has a taser in one hand and a gun in the other. I'm sure your first sergeant has had his share of rubber bullets today."

"Fuck you, Howard."

The lead robot raised his right arm and fired a rubber bullet into First Sergeant Bankhead's stomach. Top vomited on the floor and then fell in it.

"I've had about enough of your vulgarity, First Sergeant. Captain Butler, if you would be so kind as to help up your comrade and kindly leave my house. If either of you gets within ten feet of one of my friends, you will regret it."

Captain Butler collected his top NCO and the two left the library. Once they were outside, they were greeted by a dozen of their men.

"Captain! Top! There you are!" Staff Sergeant Willis looked at the two of them in confusion. "What the hell happened in there? What's going on?"

"Doc, is my XO in there?

"No, sir, Lieutenant Christopher is recovering in the guest house; none of our people are in the residence."

"Good! Time for us to flush out that crazy, old man and take his house away from him."

CHAPTER TWENTY-TWO

Inmate Richard Dupree was trying not to cough his lungs out. His eyes were stinging and the sweat pouring over his body was mixing with ash, covering him in a black slime. Along with Tank, Spider, and Head, the four inmates were mixing in with the others headed towards Cellblock A. Up towards the front of the group, four utilities foremen were pushing two carts into the unit to begin work on the air handlers.

"Killer, mind telling us what your plan is?" asked Head.

"Yeah, we kinda need to know what to do before you want us to do it," said Spider.

"We beatin' the shit out of those hacks and takin' their keys?" Tank would have been smiling if his eye didn't hurt him so damn bad.

Richard knew Tank's first thought would be towards violence. "No, wouldn't do us much good just having their keys. We would have a hard time making it up to the Control Center. The guards in there have to roll gates and pop doors open for us to get out. At the last gate you have to show your ID. Not thinking any of us look like those guys."

"Yeah, the swastika on Tank's forehead would be a dead giveaway," said Spider with a sheepish grin.

"Shut up, you little dickhead," Tank exclaimed, pushing Spider aside. "I don't know what good going into A-Block will do us."

The four inmates made it up to the front entrance of Cellblock A. In the chaotic throng of frightened and angry inmates, the four convicts managed to walk right in without the guard even noticing them. Inmates were running all over the place, frantically scrambling from cell to cell preparing for inevitable lockdown. Inmates were calling in debts and favors from each other. If you owed the guy in the next cell a bag of chips or coffee, it was time to pay up. If you had four books in your cell and you'd read two of them, time to loan those two out to a friend. Inmates always prepared for a lockdown, no matter how much time was available. They had no idea if they would be locked in their cell for a few hours or a few days.

"Let's go! Get in your cells! Time to rack up! NOW!"

The guard locked the front door of the unit and walked to the center of the common room. "Hurry up! Get a move on! IN YOUR CELLS!"

"Find somewhere to hide - laundry room, shower, mop closet - just get out of sight. Don't come out until you see me." Richard was hoping that the guard in this cellblock intended to lock down the unit and leave like everyone else. Hopefully, the guard would move quickly and not search around the unit for stragglers. Richard was also hoping the utilities foremen wouldn't stay for long.

Richard and his three partners in crime found places in the unit to hide. Slowly, the inmates in the block relented and went into their cells. Once the guard had locked down his unit, he walked over to the foremen. Richard had chosen a hiding spot that would allow him to overhear what the guards were saying.

"What are you guys doing?" asked the guard.

"We're rigging two of these air handlers to come on now so the smoke doesn't get too thick in here."

Fifteen feet off the floor and built into the wall, four massive fans were spaced a few feet apart. The fans were designed to pull smoke from the unit to the outside. The fans were tied into the fire alarm system. Once smoke was detected, the fans kicked on and did their job. The motors were on the outside of the wall, filling with ash. If the fans weren't turned on soon, they would either malfunction and not come on, or they would catch on fire.

One of the utilities foremen walked towards the back hallway. "Hey, can you let me back here?" Next to the front entrance was a doorway that led back to several offices. A utilities closet containing tools, ladders, and other equipment could be found next to the offices.

"Sure thing. You guys gonna work in all the units?" The cellblock guard walked back to the door and opened it.

"I hope not. I'm sure Landry has crews in the other buildings doing the same work. At least I hope he does. I wanna get the fuck outta here as quick as possible."

"Me, too. When that shit started falling out of the sky, I was talking to Morales. He said that most of the staff not directly supervising inmates was already headed out the front lobby."

"That doesn't surprise me. Can't say I blame 'em. Smoke is getting pretty thick. I'm kinda scared to go out there. Probably have to crawl on our hands and knees just to be able to see anything."

Two of the foremen came out of the hallway with two fifteen-foot ladders and set them up under the fans. The cellblock guard locked the door to the back hallway and went into his office to use the phone as the foremen began work on the fan. First, they took off the security cages. Next, they took the fan blades out so they could reach the motor. When the fan blades were passed down and put on the floor, Richard made his move.

Richard dashed from the closet with a mop handle he had broken in two. He banged the mop handles on the wall to signal his fellow inmates to come out of hiding. Tank, Spider, and Head suddenly appeared from different areas of the cellblock. The five staff members just looked at them in complete confusion as the four inmates surrounded the staff members. Richard looked at the other men and motioned for them to stand down and follow his lead.

"You guys lost?"

"Nope. We're right where we need to be."

"You don't live in this unit. You get stuck in here outta bounds? You aren't making it back to your unit just now. You can wait it out in here. I got an empty cell for you to stay in." The cellblock guard started walking toward the bottom tier of cells.

"Not going in a cell," said Richard.

"Is that right? And just where exactly do you think you're going?"

"Out there."

All five of the staff members started laughing. One of the foremen spoke up. "Pretty funny. You know it's like a horror movie out there. You guys wanna die?"

The cellblock guard swallowed his laughter and joined in, "And just how do you expect to get out there?"

Richard looked at Tank and nodded his head. Tank stepped up and punched the cellblock guard in the stomach. The guard fell to his knees and hit the alarm on his radio. The other staff members looked at Tank in complete terror. They knew that the six foot nine inch monster could kill all of them in under a minute if he wanted to. One of them knelt down to help the cellblock guard.

One of the foremen keyed up his radio. "We have an emergency in Cellblock A, four inmates out of bounds! Officer assaulted! We need help in here!"

"Uh-oh! Looks like nobody's coming!" Spider peered at the terrified staff with a look of mock terror on his face. The inmates in the cellblock were watching the show from their cell windows. They were hollering and cheering on Richard and his men.

Richard silenced Spider with a glance. Once Spider calmed down, Richard addressed the five staff members. "Gentlemen, let's just take it easy. We are not going to hurt you unless you give us a reason to hurt you. If you do as you're told, everything will be fine."

"If you think we are gonna help you escape, you're wrong!" one of the foremen screamed.

"Sir, I wouldn't dream of it, I assure you," Richard said calmly. "The only thing I expect you to do is stay out of the way and behave yourselves. Now, this is what you're gonna do. I want you to line up outside the officer's station and sit Indian style with your hands on top of your heads. If you attempt to get up or lower your hands, Tank here will make you regret the decision."

The injured cellblock officer sat up and tried to catch his breath. The five men didn't move; the last thing they wanted to do was take orders from an inmate.

"Tank? Would you please escort these gentlemen and see to it that they follow directions?"

"I'd love to! C'mon, sweethearts, you heard the man! Get movin'!" Tank balled up his fists and bowed out his chest to the five men. They quickly followed Richard's instructions. Tank rejoined the group and asked, "What's the plan, Richard?"

"Well, our friends here have done half the work for us. The cage is gone, and the fan blades have been removed. We just have to figure out a way to get the motor busted out of the frame so we can get down."

"You expect us to jump fifteen feet down on the other

side?" asked Head.

"Not at all. We really can't afford a broken leg with the trip we're going to have to take. You and Spider search the guard's office, then search the laundry room and all of the closets for anything you can make a rope out of. In fact, get the guard's keys and search that empty cell he was talking about. Get the mattress outta there and anything else we can use."

"I'm on it," Head grabbed Spider by the arm, and they went in search of any materials that might be useful for the journey ahead.

The cellblock was suddenly filled with a thunderous racket as inmates began kicking and banging on their doors. As inmates screamed at the top of their lungs, the noise was so deafening that it was impossible to tell what anyone was saying.

Tank leaned over to Richard and screamed in his ear, "What the hell's going on? What are they screaming about?"

Richard yelled in Tank's ear, "We have to hurry! We don't have much time!"

"Why?" Tank screamed.

"Because the smoke is starting to pour into the cells! If it trips the smoke alarm, these fans are going to kick on and make things much harder for us!"

"What do you want me to do?" shouted Tank.

"Get up on that ladder, and see if you can get that motor out of the way! Hurry!"

Tank grabbed a handful of tools and climbed the ladder to get a look at the fan motor. Lucky for them all, Tank had spent his youth repairing cars and motorcycles; he was no stranger when it came to mechanics. He quickly removed bolts and screws. The motor was almost free of its casing when Tank yelled down to Richard, "The motor is welded to the frame at the top on both sides!"

"Can you push it out? If you can't we're all gonna die in here!" Richard gave Tank an uncompromising look. His life was in the hands of the man at the top of the ladder. If he failed, they were all dead.

"Don't worry, Killer! I got this! Get the rope ready!"

Richard turned to discover the five staff members were no longer sitting down as they were instructed. They were scrambling towards the front door, trying to get out.

"STOP! NOW! You go out that door and you'll be dead in a matter of minutes! Get back here!"

The cellblock guard was fumbling with his keys as he tried to open the door. The other men took up an aggressive posture, ready to fight Richard. Richard approached them and put up his hands in a gesture of truce. "Just listen to me! If you don't know what to do out there, you'll be dead before you get to the front gate!"

The five men didn't listen. The front door was opened, and they disappeared into the smoke. Richard knew the smoke would quickly overtake them, and they would lose their bearing. They would probably wander around the yard, lost, then collapse and die.

Richard dismissed the five men as their fate was no longer in his control. He turned his attention to Spider and Head. Head came down the stairs with an armful of laundry and threw it near the ladders. Spider emerged from the mop closet with a twelve-foot extension cord.

"How'd you get that?" Richard asked. "Wasn't it locked up inside a cage?" Inside the mop closet was a large, padlocked locker containing cleaning chemicals and other assorted supplies. The grand prize was a twelve-foot extension cord.

"Got the keys from one of the guards before he made a break for it."

A layer of dense, black smoke was gathering high in the ceiling. The majority of the inmates had stopped kicking and banging on their cell doors. They had either passed out or simply given up. Richard looked down the row of cells and could tell that the smart convicts were lying on the floor with their mouths to the crack under the door, desperately trying to get any air they could.

Richard pointed to Head. "Go into the office and get the cell roster. Look for any unassigned cells. Check them for anything we can use - bed sheets, mattresses. Let's go! Hurry up!"

Next he turned to Spider. "You do the same thing in cells that have been assigned but are currently empty. Find a laundry bag or pillowcase and fill it with any food and water you find.

And make sure to look for work boots." When the inmates were sent back to their cellblocks, not every inmate would have returned. Inmates housed in the infirmary still maintained their cell in the cellblock. Inmates working in the chow hall or in the prison factory might still be at their jobs. Richard only needed one cell that met these requirements.

Head started throwing mattresses toward the ladder. He even managed to find a few bed sheets. Richard quickly took everything and made a rope from the extension cord and the bed sheets. It would have to be sturdy enough to support Tank's three hundred and twenty-five pound frame. Richard looked up to Tank who was pounding on the motor, slamming it back and forth.

Richard yelled up the ladder, "How we coming up there, Billy?"

Tank managed to grunt out, "Almost there! I popped one side; just have to get the other side out!"

"Good, keep it up! We're gonna be ready to roll in a few minutes!"

Spider came down the tier with a load of laundry in one arm and a pillowcase stuffed to the brim in the other. "Jackpot! There's gonna be two unlucky bastards gonna be wishin' they'd stayed in their cell! Took all their commissary and got a pair of work boots, too. Gonna run back and get the mattresses." Spider dropped his cargo by the ladder and quickly returned to the cell.

"Finally! Fucking bitch! YES! Okay, the motor's out! What next?"

Richard started passing mattresses to Tank. "Toss these down on the ground directly underneath the hole!" When he was done he motioned for Tank to come down. By that time, Spider returned with two more mattresses.

"Okay, start putting on as many clothes as you can. If something doesn't fit, wrap it around your arms and legs."

"It's hot as hell out there! I'm not wearing all of that shit!" Spider was angry and not getting the point.

"You fall from that hole down to the ground, you're gonna wish you had on a whole lot of padding. We also have to make it over the fence. Stop your crying and trust me! We're running out of time! Just do what you're told and do it quick!"

"Okay, man, sorry!" Spider did what he was told and started putting on layers of clothing.

Richard glared at Spider to ensure he was done talking. "Okay, take a shirt, soak it with water and wrap it around your face, it will help with the smoke." Richard grabbed a thermos from the pile and began to soak his own shirt. They wrapped up their heads and waited for further instruction.

"Okay, Spider, you're the smallest, get up there. Tie this rope to the frame and climb down. When you get down there, make sure the mattresses are in the best spot to catch us in case somebody falls."

"What about the guards riding around the perimeter with guns?"

"Oh, I'm sure they're long gone by now. If they're out there, they probably couldn't see you anyway. Let's go! Get up there!"

Spider climbed up the ladder and tied off the rope to the frame. Tank fed him the rest of the rope with the laundry bag tied to the other end. Spider lowered the rope to the ground.

"Fuck! The rope's not long enough!"

"How far off the ground is it?" Richard yelled up the ladder.

"At least three or four feet!"

"Big fucking deal, you moron! You scared to jump a few feet? Stop being a baby!" Tank was about ready to shake Spider from the ladder.

"Okay! Fuck! Just thought you should know! Damn! OK, here I go!" Spider lowered himself down the rope. Once his feet hit the laundry bag he jumped to the ground. "OK! I made it!"

"Head, you're next. Get moving!"

Head nodded to Richard and proceeded up the ladder. Once Spider was done arranging the mattresses, he gave Head a thumbs up and grabbed the end of the rope to stabilize his descent. Head quickly lowered himself down.

"You're up, Billy. Time to leave this hell hole and venture out into a worse one."

"Damn right, I could use a change of scenery." Tank climbed the ladder and was just barely able to fit through the hole. He grabbed the rope and climbed down to the half way point, jumping the rest of the way down. He landed with a thud and screamed, scaring the living shit out of Head and Spider. Tank laughed and mocked the two men like they were little girls.

Richard landed on the ground next to them. The three men waiting for him were astonished at how quickly he made it down the rope. If they hadn't known any better, they would have been convinced that he jumped from the hole in the wall directly to the ground.

"Jesus, Richard! How'd you do that?" Head was nearly impressed enough to begin a round of applause.

"Be quiet, all of you, and listen! We finally caught a break, as you can tell." Richard looked up at the sky, which was relatively smoke-free for the time being. "We don't have long until the smoke starts pouring in over the top of the building; we can't afford to waste a second."

The three men nodded in agreement.

"First, keep the wrap over your face at all times and make sure it's wet. The wet cloth will help keep the smoke out and make it easier to breath." Richard looked around and surveyed his surroundings. "Now, we need to get these mattresses over to the fence. Tank, grab the rope and yank it down."

Richard, Spider, and Head grabbed a mattress in each hand and carried them the fifty yards to the fence line. Tank was pulling on the rope with both hands; he was either going to snap the rope at the knot or pull the motor frame out of the wall.

As he walked back to the fence Richard said, "Hey, Head! See those thin wires sticking out six inches from the fence?"

"Yeah, what are they?" asked Head.

"A sort of trip wire. If you grab onto it and try to climb up the fence, your weight will yank the wire from the clip and snare you up like animal."

"Throw the mattress at it?" Head asked.

"That's the idea, right there in front of us at the top. Ready .... go!"

Both men threw their mattress at the same point. The weight of the mattresses pulled down on the wires and snapped them free. The wires broke way from their casings and tangled up in the mattresses.

"Holy shit! That coulda been one of us!" Spider was impressed with Richard's problem solving skills. "How'd you figure that out?"

"Well, Spider, I didn't know," Richard said, studying the obstacle they would have to defeat. "I knew we'd need the mattresses for the razor wire. Once I saw those wires sticking out, wasn't hard to figure out what they did. Pretty much the same way a snare traps a rabbit."

"Now we just need to get a mattress up on that razor wire," said Head.

"Right you are. Go right ahead, Head," Richard smiled at him.

"Yeah, yeah, fuck off, I got it." After a couple of unsuccessful attempts, Head was able to get the mattress to rest on the razor wire atop the fence. By that time, Tank had joined them with the rope.

"What broke first? The rope or the frame?" Richard was quite curious.

"The frame. Snapped a bolt and the rope came down."

"Outstanding! We're gonna need it. We need to hurry; we don't have a lot of time." Richard was indeed correct. The wind had been blowing around the back of the building, keeping the smoke from getting too thick. The wind stopped suddenly, like someone had flipped a switch, sending the smoke billowing down on them like a dense blanket. It was hot and stung their eyes. Tank howled like a wounded lion as he pressed his palm to his eye and pushed as hard as he could. The pain dropped him to his knees.

"We have to get out of here, now! If he can't get over the fence, we leave his ass here!" Head looked to Spider for support, Spider nodded in silent agreement.

"We are not leaving Billy here to die! He's gonna make it over the fence, same as us!" Richard spoke with an urgent finality, daring Spider and Head to spite him.

"What the hell are you gonna do?" Spider said over muffled coughs.

"Give me a bottle of water," answered Richard. He took the bottle from Spider and untied a t-shirt from around his left elbow. The ex-Navy SEAL laid the shirt out on the ground and put two scoopfuls of dirt in the center. He then poured the bottle of water over the dirt, making a ball of mud. Richard rolled up the shirt and poured the rest of the water out of the bottle. He had made a cold compress.

"Billy! Sit up, c'mon! We need to get moving."

Tank managed to sit up and look at Richard. "Cut my eye out! I can't take it!"

"I don't think that would solve anything. Probably make things worse. Here, tie this around your head as tight as we can get it."

Richard put the center of the t-shirt over Tank's eye. He lifted Tank's hand to the compress so he could hold it in place. Richard then wrapped the shirt around his head as tight as he could get it. Hopefully the cold pressure would allow Tank to persevere.

"Better?"

"Yeah, I'll be damned. Still hurts like a mother fucker, but I think I can manage."

"Good, come over here. Let's start getting over these fences."

Tank and Richard locked their hands together and knelt down. Head put his foot in their hands and the two men hoisted Head to the top of the fence. Head sat on the mattress while the three men below him passed up the mattresses they had brought along. Head dropped them down the other side and jumped safely to the nice, cushy landing pad he'd made. The same process was repeated for Spider, and then Tank hoisted Richard to the top. Richard sat on the mattress and lowered his arm down to help Tank make it over.

Head collapsed on his hands and knees, coughing and gasping for air. Spider dug in the bag for another bottle of water. He managed to get Head to sit up and poured water on his face wrap. Spider then did the same for himself, as well as Richard and Tank.

"How the fuck are we getting over that?" Tank pointed to the second of three fences in their way. The middle fence was electric. The electric fence operated in two stages. The first stage delivered a non-lethal charge, enough to throw you off the fence like you'd been kicked in the chest by a bull. The second shock was lethal. You touched it a second time and you died instantly.

"We're not getting over it, we're getting under it," answered Richard.

"Huh? You mean like dig a tunnel? This ground's as hard as concrete. No fuckin' way we're doing that! You don't know what the fuck you're doin', do you? We should have taken our chances inside!" Head was about ready to punch Richard in the mouth.

"Shut your mouth right now or I'll throw you into that fence and bounce you right back into it. Smoke's not getting any thinner, and we don't have time to argue. Head, I told you to trust me."

Head was glaring at Richard but kept his mouth shut.

"Start stripping the covers from the mattresses! Hurry up." The four men pulled the homemade knives out of their shoes and cut the mattress covers off.

"Okay, Tank and I will head left, you two head to the right. Don't go more than fifty yards. We need to find the section that has the most clearance under the bottom wire. Hurry! We're not gonna make it much longer before we pass out."

In less than a minute, Spider found a four-foot section that had a decent amount of clearance. The four men gathered in front of it and reapplied water to their face wraps.

"Okay, listen to me. You need to do exactly as I say or you might die."

"Fuckin smoke is going to kill us if this bitch doesn't," Spider uttered, looking at the fence, "what's the plan?"

"First, make sure every inch of your body is covered by clothing. Second, take that extra cover and lay it under the wire. Throw me the boots. Head, throw some mattresses over the kill fence."

The extra cover was laid on the ground under the wire. Richard put on the work boots for the extra few inches of rubber insulation on the bottom. He laid down on the ground and got inside the mattress cover like it was a sleeping bag.

"Listen and watch me. As long as you stay grounded, the current can't pass through you and complete a circuit. It's best that you don't touch the wire, but if you stay grounded you should be okay if you bump it. Just don't bump the bottom wire into the wire above it. Okay, watch closely."

Richard slowly inched his way under the wire. He remained grounded the entire time and never once touched the bottom wire. Richard took off the boots and tossed them under to Head.

"Wish my fat ass would have lost about thirty pounds before we decided to leave."

"Hurry up, fucker!" Spider was kicking the bottom of Head's boots.

"Stop it, you little shit!" Head slowly inched his way under the wire. At one point he did bump the bottom wire and it raised just a hair. Once he was on the other side, he tossed the boots under to Spider. "Your little ass could probably crawl on all fours, you stupid bitch!"

"Fuck you! Here I come! Stop fuckin' with me! This is serious!" Spider made it under the wire with little effort.

Head leaned over to Richard and spoke in his ear, "You know Billy ain't makin' it under the wire, his chest will bump the wires together."

"Billy! Make sure you keep your arms at your sides and flatten yourself out the best you can. And go feet first"

"Yeah, I got it! Here I come."

"Be ready to catch him," Richard said to Head.

"Catch him? What the... oh, shit, yeah I got you. Fuck, this ain't gonna be pretty."

"Lookin' good, Billy, just be careful. Nice and slow. That's it."

Tank's legs and stomach were under the wire. Head grabbed his feet and angled his legs to the left. Richard grabbed his right arm and pulled as hard as he could.

"What are you..." Tank's chest pushed the bottom wire up and it touched the wire above it. The stun charge was delivered across Tank's chest and propelled him the rest of the way under the fence. Head and Richard held on tight, stopping Tank from being propelled into the stack of razor wire a few feet away. Lucky for Tank, the two men had shared the jolt of electricity, making it equally painful for all three of them.

Spider was laughing hysterically. "Man, that shit was cool! Holy shit! I can't believe that just happened! You guys all right?"

"Shut up, you little fucker," Head said, looking like he'd had the shit beaten out of him.

"OK, the last part is easy, let's go."

The four men helped each other over the final fence. The mattresses bore the punishment of the razor wire for them as they clambered up to the top of the fence and jumped down.

Once they were over, they ran a few yards at a time and stopped to lay on the ground to get away from the smoke. Once they got about ten yards on the other side of the perimeter road they stopped again, as Head began to choke and vomit. He sounded like he was being strangled. Spider tried to calm him down as he kicked and flailed around.

"Richard, we're all gonna die out here! This is crazy! What the fuck are we supposed to do?" Spider sounded like a frightened child.

Richard had absolutely no idea what to do. He figured that most of the inmates locked in their cells were dead. Had he managed the nearly impossible feat of escape only to die a hundred yards from the fence? His only hope was that Mother Nature would show him some kindness and blow the smoke away.

"Is Head okay?" Richard asked Spider.

"I don't think so, man, I think he passed out. He's still breathing."

"We just need to relax and wait a few minutes. The smoke has to let up eventually. Just try to stay calm and save your breath. Stop talking, close your mouth and breathe through your nose."

The four men rested on the ground for the better part of an hour. The smoke didn't clear up at all; if anything, it got worse. Richard was more worried about the heat than the smoke. They were losing bodily fluid in the form of sweat at an alarming rate. If they stayed in that spot for too long, dehydration would set in, and they would begin to suffer from heat stroke. Richard continued to scan what little he could see of his surroundings. It was the middle of the afternoon but it was dark as night. All he needed was for the sun to peek through just a little so he could see what was around them. They needed some type of shelter from the heat and smoke.

Spider was nearly in tears. "I don't think Head is going to make it! I can't tell if he's breathing or not!" Spider continued to nudge Head. "C'mon John! You still with me, man? C'mon, just hang in there! Richard, we gotta do something! I don't think he's breathing!"

Richard crawled over to Head and turned him over on his back. He detected a faint pulse and very shallow breathing. Richard began mouth-to-mouth resuscitation to put some much needed oxygen in his lungs. One thing was certain - Head was going to die very soon if something wasn't done.

"Stay here and keep putting air in his lungs. Make sure you tilt his chin back and watch his chest rise and fall. I'm going up the perimeter road a bit to see if we can find a way out of this." Tank and Spider looked at Richard in fear as he crouched down and headed towards the road. Once there, he dropped a shirt in the road to mark the spot. The rear gate was on the opposite side of the prison grounds; no way he could make it that far. He just needed a drainage ditch or maintenance shed anything at all. He had only moved a few yards when he saw a glimmer of light reflect off something.

It was one of the perimeter vehicles.

Was someone still in it? Did the guard die in there? Is he laying down on the floorboards with his pistol ready to defend himself? Richard slowly approached the rear bumper of the vehicle and peered in the back window. He couldn't see anyone inside. He slowly crept to the driver's side and peered around. The driver's side door was wide open. He laid down and looked under the vehicle. The driver's side tires were flat. It was clear to Richard that the guard had abandoned the vehicle and shot out the tires. He probably joined the other perimeter patrol and they left together when the smoke got too thick and no one was answering the radio.

"Thank you, gentlemen, this will do nicely," Richard said to himself.

Richard quickly looked over the vehicle to see what he was dealing with. The keys were gone, so was the radio. Richard noticed that the front passenger seat had been replaced with a gun rack. One slot was empty and the other had a rifle resting in it.

Richard grabbed the rifle and saw that it was a variation of an M-16. He searched for ammunition but came up empty handed.

Richard exited the vehicle and made his way back to the three. He could tell something was wrong.

"What?"

"It's Head, I don't know, but he..." said Spider.

Richard dropped down next to Head, put his fingers on his neck to check for a pulse and dropped his ear over his mouth. After twenty seconds, he knew the answer.

"John's dead. We can't do anything for him; it's time to go."

"What do you mean he's dead? There's gotta be something we can do! We can't just leave him here!" Spider was not taking the death of his best friend very well.

"There's nothing we can do for him, unless you want to carry him. The rest of us are going to die if we don't get moving. Tank, you still have those tools?" asked Richard.

"Yeah, I got 'em. What are we doing?"

"Follow me. Spider, I know how close the two of you were, but there's nothing we can do for him." With the two men in tow, Richard headed down the road to the vehicle.

"Fuck me, Killer. You kill the guard?" asked Tank.

"No, I figure he abandoned the vehicle and left with the other patrol."

"Two of the tires are flat. What good is this thing?

"Billy, I wasn't planning on driving it anywhere. Help me push it down into the ditch."

Richard put the car in neutral and they pushed the vehicle off the road into the drainage ditch. Richard couldn't really understand why a drainage ditch was even needed. The desert floor was so dry that whenever it rained, the ground soaked up every drop like a sponge. Nevertheless, the low-lying ground would help protect them from the smoke.

"You got a hammer and a screwdriver? Spider, help me rip up the paneling from the floorboards. Tank, start nailing holes in the floor so we can breath."

"Spider, can you hot-wire this thing?"

Spider had a long history of stealing cars. When he started to target elderly black people and not only car-jack them, but kill them for their cars, he landed himself in prison. Spider had the engine running in under a minute.

Richard hit the controls and rolled up the windows on the driver's side. He then cracked the passenger side windows an inch and turned the heat up full blast. Next he switched the thermostat from fresh air to recycle.

"Why are you turning on the heat?" asked Tank.

"Hot air rises. The smoke is coming in on the driver side, so those windows are rolled up. The hot air will push the smoke out of the cabin in a few minutes. Once that's done we can roll the windows up and turn on the A/C. Take the wraps off your heads and put them over the holes. Wrap your mouth around the hole and try to breath in some good air."

The plan worked perfectly. In a matter of minutes, the smoke had cleared out of the cabin and the windows were rolled up. The air filter in the engine did a decent job of keeping the smoke out. Once the temperature was somewhat comfortable, Richard turned off the vents and returned to his air hole. The three men stayed in the car for two hours until the smoke finally began to clear. Once the sun broke through the clouds, it was time to move.

"Let's go! We need to be as far away from here as possible in the least amount of time. Tank, will this car do us any good? How far do you think it'll make it on two flat tires?"

"In this terrain? Not far, the rims will shred the tires and once the rims flatten out and have nothing to grab onto, we're stuck."

"Let's get moving then. I think it will be a long time before they realize we're gone. They got a prison full of dead inmates to keep them busy."

The three men loaded up in the wounded SUV and headed west. For the second time in his incarceration, Richard was a free man.

CHAPTER TWENTY-THREE

Chief Maxwell Harris was filled with rage. He fought to control the fury with every fiber of his being. The last time he had allowed rage to take over, he had crashed into a stolen car going sixty miles an hour, killing four people in the process. For his efforts, he had shattered his hip and leg and still lived with the agonizing pain to this day. Since then, Max had made a promise to himself to remain in control at all times. His current predicament was challenging that vow. Two of his officers were dead, as was an innocent civilian. A band of thugs had stolen his uniform, leaving him in his underwear. They then proceeded to empty out his armory and load their take into his police vehicles. Now they were out looking for his command post so they could rob it as well.

"Chief! We don't need to crash before we get there! Slow down!" Deputy Collins was sitting in the passenger seat of the dead civilian's pickup truck next to Max.

Max remained silent but did slow down. Collins was right; driving like a maniac on flooded roads wasn't smart. With no way of communicating with the command post, Max could only try to get there as fast as possible, praying that the band of thugs didn't find the place before he got there.

They arrived at the high school, parking in back so Rudy's truck couldn't be seen from the road. They made it into the school. Racing down the hall to the locker rooms, Max burst in so quickly that Elizabeth and Dr. Stone screamed.

"Max! What in the hell are you doing? You scared us to death!" screamed Elizabeth.

"We're in trouble!"

"No kidding, genius. Why aren't you wearing pants?" Elizabeth laughed.

"Elizabeth! I'm not joking, we're in danger! Get everyone in here and keep them quiet! Do it now!"

Elizabeth could immediately tell that Max wasn't joking. Max crouched down in the doorway with his weapon drawn. Collins was doing the same thing but had one arm wrapped around his mid-section, clearly in pain. Something very bad had happened to them. Elizabeth quietly herded the wide-eyed group into the room.

"Elizabeth, listen to me, I will explain the details later. That group of redneck idiots that shot up the gas station is out there. They robbed the armory at the police station - taking bullet proof vests and police uniforms. They're armed and looking for this command post. They stole my SUV and two patrol trucks. Might take them a while to find us or they could be here any minute."

"Oh my! Where's my husband? Where's Rudy?" asked Trudy.

"Your husband is fine; he's back at the police station with another officer." Max felt horrible lying to the woman, but the last thing he needed was to deal with a hysterical widow during a fire fight. "Elizabeth, you and Kathy stay in this room and keep these people safe. They can't get into the gym since the roof fell in. The only way they can get in is through this door."

"What's the plan? Where are you going to be?" Elizabeth drew her sidearm.

"We only have one vehicle and we can't leave on foot. We'll just have to watch for them from the hallway and kill them before they get in the door."

"You sure they're coming? They might decide to move on."

"Trust me, they're coming. They know we're here. Not a lot of buildings left in town that we could be in; they don't have many places to look. Just a matter of time."

Max and Deputy Collins crept down the hallway to the front entrance of the school. Max kicked in the door to one of the classrooms with windows overlooking the parking lot. The visibility was low due to the rain; however, they would still be able to see a vehicle coming from either direction.

They didn't have to wait long.

"Are they fucking serious? Are they really driving down the road flashing the red and blues?" asked Collins.

"Well, we know they aren't too bright. Probably living out some childhood fantasy. I'm surprised they aren't running the sirens," answered Max.

Max's SUV was leading the convoy with the other two police trucks following. They turned off the main road and headed toward the parking lot. From their vantage point, Max and Deputy Collins were less than ten feet away from the front entrance. The thugs would walk right into their trap.

The three stolen police cars pulled up into the circle in front of the school. As Jack and his two henchmen exited the stolen vehicles, Max noticed that one of the thugs was bleeding from his right arm. He had tried to wrap it with a towel but had done a poor job of it.

"Jack, this shit hurts! It won't stop bleeding!"

"Relax, you pussy. Stop being a fucking baby! We find this command post and I'm sure they'll have medical supplies."

"You think it's in here? I don't see any vehicles or anything."

"This has to be it. That rundown shithole of a hospital was barely standing. This school looks to be in decent shape; the command post has to be in there."

"What are we gonna do?" asked the injured henchman.

"Well, let's keep it simple. Maybe we can get them to come to us." Jack reached for the hand mike and shouted. "Attention! This is the police!"

"I didn't hear anything," said the injured henchman.

"Shit, this is the loudspeaker. What the hell? Oh, here it is; guess I should turn it on." Jack flipped a red switch and a light came on. "This is the police! Uhh, we're looking for the command post. We're here to help you guys. Someone come out and meet us and take us inside."

"You think it worked?"

"I don't know, dummy. Let's wait a minute or two and see if anyone comes out."

Max looked over at Deputy Collins and rolled his eyes.

"You think we should go inside?" asked the injured henchman.

"Might as well, come on! The two henchmen started up the walk to the front door, with Jack following close behind.

Max quickly looked over and pointed at Collins and held up one finger, then he pointed to himself and held up two fingers. *You take the first one; I'll take the second one.* Collins nodded his head. The three thugs stepped onto the curb and walked under the awning to the front door. As they took a step towards the door, Collins opened fire on the first man. The first two rounds hit his vest; the third round hit him in the throat, lodging in his spine. Once he fell to the ground, Max opened fire on the second man with three quick shots. He only needed one. The first round hit the thug square in the nose and blew a hole out the back of his head. The second round went into the parking lot and dinged off the handicapped parking sign. The third round grazed Jack's left arm, sending him in a nosedive behind some bushes. Collins emptied his weapon into the bushes and quickly reloaded.

"Get out there quick and finish him! I'll cover you! Go!" screamed Max. Collins bolted out the front door and rounded the corner to the sidewalk. As he paused for maybe a second trying to locate Jack, he was shot twice and fell to the ground. Max fired off four shots to keep Jack pinned down so he could get outside. He crouched low and moved over to Collins, relieved to see that he was alive. He studied him closely and was alarmed to see blood soaking his left thigh.

"Collins! You still with me? Say something!"

"Something," whispered Collins.

Max peered over the bushes to the sidewalk. He could see a trail of blood drops leading down the sidewalk to the side of the building, but it was quickly washing away in the rain. Jack was nowhere in sight. Max had to get Collins inside to Dr. Stone. His leg was bleeding badly and chances were high that an artery had been severed. Max quickly made Collins sit up and from behind, wrapped his arms around his friend and hoisted him up.

"Come on, Collins, work with me here. You got one good leg - use it! We have to get inside! You need to cover us both!" Max yelled, dragging Collins to the front door

Max felt like his hip was melting out of his body it hurt so badly. He was preparing himself for the likelihood that his knee would shatter and hoped adrenaline would give him the strength to make it to the locker room. Every step was agonizingly painful for both men. As they headed for the locker room, Kathy and Dr. Stone sprinted to meet them. The group made it safely inside, with Elizabeth remaining in the doorway to provide cover.

Once inside the locker room, Max collapsed. The pain in his hip and knee completely consumed him; the entire world faded away, and the only reality he knew was agonizing torture.

He forgot about the hurricane and all the dead officers he once commanded. He desperately wanted to be free of the pain; death would be sweet relief. All he had to do was take the gun in his hand, raise it to his temple and pull the trigger. He longed for the end, to be taken away from all of this. Somewhere in the midst of his stupor, another sensation tried to compete for his attention. Someone was yelling at him. Someone was shaking him and slapping his face.

"Chief Harris! Say something! Please, sir! Are you okay? C'mon now!" Trudy had taken hold of Max's hand and was slapping him back to reality.

"Has he been shot?" questioned Elizabeth from the doorway.

"I don't think so. He's not bleeding."

Dr. Stone and Kathy had placed Deputy Collins on a cot and pulled off his shirt and vest. As Dr. Stone cut away his pants, blood sprayed from the bullet hole like water spewing from a garden hose, covering Dr. Stone and Kathy in the sticky, warm fluid. Dr. Stone quickly placed her hands on the wound and pressed down with all her weight.

"Kathy, dig in that bag and pull out all the gauze. Get over here and apply pressure to this wound. I have to tie off that artery before he bleeds to death."

Kathy did as she was told and pressed down on the wound as hard as she could. "Are you a surgeon? Can you do this?"

"No, I'm not a surgeon and no, I haven't done this before. Looks like I'm the only one qualified to try, unless someone else here is a doctor?" Dr. Stone looked up in time to see the top of Kathy's head explode, followed by the deafening roar of gunfire. Bullets flew around the room as chaos ensued. In the span of a few seconds, the looky loo who had admired Elizabeth in her bra and the young couple with the small children were all dead. Dr. Stone sank down to the floor and crawled in front of a foot locker. Elizabeth inched along the wall and using a sink for cover, returned fire.

"Stay down, doc!" Elizabeth screamed.

"Where is he?" screamed Dr. Stone.

"He must have climbed over the rubble in the gym and found a hole in the wall!"

"I have to get to Deputy Collins! He's going to bleed out!"

"Doc, don't you dare move an inch! I mean it!"

Elizabeth stayed behind the sink and scanned the damaged wall for a breach, hoping to find the shooter. As the noise subsided, the only sound that could be heard was the drip of sprayed blood hitting the floor around Deputy Collins. They waited for what seemed like an eternity. Dr. Stone watched as the spurts of blood from Deputy Collins' leg became less violent, until finally they stopped completely. Deputy Collins was dead.

Trudy screamed.

Elizabeth turned in time to see two shots pierce Trudy's chest. She fell to the floor not knowing that her dead husband was waiting for her on the other side. Elizabeth aimed her weapon at the door and walked in an arc so she could aim out into the hallway. The shooter hadn't fired on Max because he couldn't see him on the floor. He had fired at Trudy's silhouette. Elizabeth aimed out into the hallway. She fired three rounds and dropped the man to the floor. She held her aim as she closed the distance to the fallen man. She knew from very recent experience that getting shot with a bulletproof vest on was like getting knocked over by a sledgehammer. The man on the ground was down for the count, but he wasn't dead. Elizabeth didn't hesitate to remedy that problem and shot him in the head three times.

Walking into the locker room, Elizabeth knelt down next to Max and took his hand.

"Sweetheart, I just killed one of them. How many are left?"

"Last one. We're safe."

"What's wrong with you? Tell me."

"It's bad. I'm ready to cut off my leg. I did something to it."

"Just stay right were you are." Then Elizabeth helped Dr. Stone off the floor. "It's okay, doc. It's over."

Dr. Stone immediately sprang into action. She checked on the gunshot victims, only to find them all dead. She quickly scanned the room for the young couple's children and couldn't find them. "Elizabeth! Help me find the children! I don't see them!"

Elizabeth and Dr. Stone desperately searched every corner

of the locker room, unable to find the infant or the toddler. Elizabeth walked over to the young couple and rolled the woman onto her side. She gasped in horror to discover that the woman had fallen on top of her baby.

"Doc! I found the baby! Quick!" Elizabeth pried the infant from her mother's arms and handed her to Dr. Stone. Dr. Stone checked the baby for any signs of life. Tears streamed down her face as she shook her head. Elizabeth raised her hand to her mouth and stifled a sob. In an instant she regained her composure and resumed her search for the toddler.

"Did he run off?" asked Dr. Stone.

"No, he's in here. I've been watching the door since this started. Start opening lockers! I bet he's hiding."

They quickly found the little two-year-old boy inside a locker with his hands over his ears. Elizabeth scooped him up and took a few quick steps away from the child's dead parents. She didn't know what to do with him so she started kissing his cheeks over and over. The little boy giggled. Elizabeth looked over to see Dr. Stone tending to Max.

"Max, tell me what's wrong," she demanded.

"It's my leg, doc. I can't move it."

"But you can feel it?"

"That I don't have a problem with. I feel so much pain I'm ready to put a bullet in my head."

"Stop talking like that!" implored Elizabeth.

"I'm sorry, I'm not going to, but it hurts worse than it ever has."

Dr. Stone put her hands on Max's neck to check his pulse. "Tell me about the surgeries you've had."

"I had a hip replacement."

"Any pins in your leg?"

"Yes."

"How many?"

"One very long rod with about a dozen pins drilled into my femur."

"How many fractures did you suffer?"

"My femur had two clean breaks."

"Your hip is probably dislocated."

"Well, it was worth it. We got Collins in here and saved

his life. How is he?"

Dr. Stone had practiced medicine for twenty-eight years. She was no stranger to delivering bad news and knew that sugar coating or dancing around it only made it worse.

"He didn't make it."

"Son of a bitch. What happened? I come to, only to find Trudy on the floor next to me and Elizabeth shooting the bastard that killed her."

Elizabeth explained, "Asshole climbed up onto the rubble and found a hole, shot down into the locker room."

"How many?" Max was afraid to ask.

"Me, the doc, and this little guy are the only ones left." Elizabeth kissed the little boy, eager to hear that innocent giggle again.

Max closed his eyes, and the thought of losing two more of his officers overwhelmed him. He hadn't pulled the trigger, but he felt responsible for their deaths all the same. He thought of the civilians lying dead around him, civilians whom he was responsible for protecting. Max thought back to the hurricanes that had wrecked his life before this one. The other ones were walks in the park compared to this one. Max wondered if he would be able to walk again.

"OK, we need to give you something for the pain." Dr. Stone produced a pill bottle."

"Tramadol?"

"Yes, it should help."

"I hope so. Wish you had something stronger."

"It'll have to do. It's better than Tylenol."

"No doubt about that. Elizabeth, take one of the vehicles and go get Charlie and his family."

Elizabeth had already taken the keys to the SUV from Jack. "What about Rudy?"

"He's dead."

Neither woman questioned the lie Max had told Trudy. They understood why he had done it. "Anything else, boss?"

"Just double check the armory for anything they might have left behind. And one more thing - I don't want you to put yourself in any danger, but if you happen to see my desk in the rubble, check the top drawer for my Vicodin. I need the good stuff if you expect me to leave this locker room."

Elizabeth left the little boy with Dr. Stone and headed off to the police station. Dr. Stone was a grandmother of three and had no trouble with the little one. Max laid on the floor trying his best to remain perfectly still. Dr. Stone very delicately ran her hands up and down his leg trying to feel anything abnormal.

"Your hip is definitely dislocated. The only good news is your femoral artery hasn't been compromised."

"Can you pop it back in?"

"Yes, I can do it with Elizabeth's help. I'd rather you were heavily sedated. We don't really have a choice. If we try to move you with your hip out of the socket, you could damage your leg and lose feeling in your foot. There's a good chance that you've done that already but we have to proceed on the assumption that you didn't. I sincerely hope Elizabeth finds your Vicodin."

"Will popping it back in be that painful?"

"Excruciating. If she finds the Vicodin, I'm planning on giving you so much that it would cause a normal person to overdose."

Ten minutes later Elizabeth came back into the locker room. "Charlie and his family aren't at the station anymore. I have no idea what happened to them." She dug in her pocket and tossed Max a pill bottle. "Your desk was across the street from the station."

"Well, it's about time something went our way," said Max.

"How many do you normally take?" asked Dr. Stone.

"Depends. Usually two every three hours."

"Double it. After that we'll wait an hour and give you two more."

"Sounds like a party!" Max took four pills.

"What's going on?" Elizabeth looked at Dr. Stone.

"Doctor's orders." Max winked at Elizabeth.

"His hip is dislocated. You and I are going to pop it back in. The only way we can do hope to do that is with him heavily sedated."

"Oh, fun. I can't wait!" Elizabeth said with much sarcasm.

An hour after Max took the first four pills, they gave him two more and waited about thirty minutes. He was high as a kite and in a giddy mood. When the second dose kicked in, he slipped into a peaceful sleep. Dr. Stone checked his pulse and monitored his breathing for a minute.

"Let's get started. I need you to keep him perfectly still. Lay down across his chest and hold his arms. I'll do the rest. If he wakes up, do your best to hold him still."

Dr. Stone lifted Max's leg straight up in the air and bent his knee ninety degrees. She put the inside of his knee on her shoulder and hugged his thigh. In a very rapid motion, she threw her body forward and then leaned to the side. She heard a click and felt the ball of his artificial hip slide back into place. Max groaned and stirred, but didn't wake up.

"Did you do it? Is it over?" Elizabeth was still holding Max down.

"Yes, it's done."

"What do we do now?"

"Wait for him to sleep off the Vicodin. We should get some rest while he's out. Elizabeth, what happens when he wakes up?"

"We get the hell out of Texas and don't look back."

CHAPTER TWENTY-FOUR

Captain Jackson Butler was standing three hundred yards behind Beck Estates. Next to him stood his top NCO, First Sergeant Matt Bankhead. Beck Estates was on full lockdown mode, and Captain Butler was determined to take it by whatever means necessary. Howard's Artificial Intelligence, Hal, had deployed some very effective counter-measures to keep his soldiers at bay. Butler had sent the first wave of soldiers to the two entrances on the backside of the mansion. They were promptly attacked by sentries on the roof. Howard had programmed the sentries to fire rubber bullets - not at the soldiers' torsos, but their heads. The move proved effective as the overwhelming majority of his soldiers fell to the ground, either unconscious or missing an eye. The soldiers that did make it to the outer wall of the mansion were powerless to enter the residence. All of the doors and windows had the same force fields covering them that Jackson had encountered in the grand library of the world's richest man. He ordered them to retreat, and Howard was kind enough to let them collect their fallen comrades and leave without being shot at. Butler figured Howard let them survive to illustrate to him that he only wanted them to leave his house alone and just go away. Jackson Butler had no intention of leaving.

Captain Butler was puzzled by the fact that Howard did not use lethal force to defend his estate. His best guess was that Howard never thought he would need to kill anyone on his property. His defenses were more than adequate to keep intruders at bay, but the fact that Howard wasn't willing to use deadly force would end up being the one weakness Butler could use to his advantage. Butler quickly learned the maximum effective range of the sentries the hard way. Rubber bullets zinged past him as he and his men quickly ran out into the field behind the mansion. Butler estimated that the sentries had a maximum effective range of between one hundred fifty and two hundred yards. Just to be on the safe side, he set up shop at the three hundred yard mark. He ordered one of his snipers to take out the sentries, but the

effort proved ineffective. The sentries had the same force fields protecting them.

"Top, what are you thinking? I'm open to suggestions."

"Well, sir, it's obvious that we can't storm the distance to the back door. We could use riot shields to cover ourselves, but when we make it to the wall, we have no way in."

"Munitions?"

"Worth a shot."

"Get a team of grenadiers up here."

"Roger that, sir." First Sergeant Bankhead quickly followed orders and assembled a team of four men with M32 grenade launchers. Each weapon could fire six forty-millimeter grenade rounds.

"Awaiting your orders, sir," said the team leader.

Captain Butler had to decide on a target. The door and windows would most likely deflect anything they had. "Let's see what we're dealing with here," Captain Butler said, tapping the helmet of the soldier in front of him. "Fire one round at left side door."

The soldier took aim and fired one round at the door leading into Howard's kitchen. Nothing happened. First Sergeant Bankhead was watching the door with binoculars.

"Top?"

"Sir, the round hit the force field and ricocheted."

"Just as I thought. I want all four of you men to fire at the wall just to the left of that same door. On my mark," the four men quickly took aim, "Fire!"

Nothing happened.

"Top?"

"Sir, I didn't see anything hit the wall."

"Nothing?"

"Yes, sir."

"Men, open your breaches for inspection." The four men quickly followed orders. Captain Butler nodded to his top NCO, who took each weapon and conducted an inspection. He dropped the spent shells and examined the remaining rounds.

"Sir, the weapons are all working perfectly with live ammunition."

"Curious." Captain Butler paced back and forth and came up with a theory. "Men, prepare to fire at the same target on my mark. Top, don't look at the target, I want you to watch the sentries on the roof for any activity."

"Roger that, sir."

"Ready, fire!"

The same thing happened as before; each man fired a round at the wall just to the left of the door. Again, none of the rounds hit the target. Captain Butler looked to First Sergeant Bankhead for a report.

"Captain, those damn sentries up there are doing something, I can't tell what. They swiveled around and moved rapidly from side the side."

"Did they fire anything?"

"No, sir, not that I could tell. They definitely did something to stop the rounds."

"Men, reload your weapons." The four soldiers quickly took rounds from their vests and loaded their weapons to capacity. "On my mark, I want you to fire all of your rounds at random targets along the wall; do not hit the same target twice. Ready, fire!"

The four soldiers unloaded their weapons at the back wall of Beck Estates. A total of twenty-four rounds were fired, not one of them hit the wall.

"This mother fucker is pissing me off now," Captain Butler said with much disdain. "You men are dismissed."

"Time to call in the big guns, sir."

"Top, you are absolutely correct. Command has been kind enough to dispatch a fighter jet for us to do with as we please. We have to be careful though; the big man himself wants the estate intact with as little damage as possible."

"You mean General Green?"

"No, First Sergeant, I'm referring to our Commander-in-Chief."

"I'll be damned, sir. I had no idea."

Captain Butler smiled and placed his hand on the shoulder of his top NCO. "Top, you and I do this thing right, good things are in store for us, I assure you."

"Outstanding, sir. I'm proud to be in this with you."

"Matt, the feeling is the same. Now, let's get that crazy old coot out of his house. Load everybody up and fall back a half mile to the north. I'll wait here for you. When the last man is out, drive my truck around and pick me up."

"I wish I could see the look on the man's face when he thinks we're giving up and leaving."

"I couldn't agree more, Top."

Captain Butler stood perfectly still and surveyed his target. If military history had taught him one thing, it was that every stronghold eventually fell to invading forces. It was only a matter of time, determination, and resourcefulness. Every castle, every fort, every bunker was eventually breached. If it took hours, days, or even years, if one man wanted to take something from another man, it could be done. Butler could hear his truck coming around to pick him up. First Sergeant Bankhead pulled up right next to the captain so all he had to do was open the door and sit down.

"I'll see you soon, Howard." Captain Jackson Butler waved towards the mansion, climbed aboard his truck and left.

****

Howard Beck was sitting at the control panel in his secure sub-basement having the time of his life. He was playing a real-life video game with actual, real-life soldiers with guns. Howard couldn't remember the last time he'd had so much fun. Never in his wildest dreams did he imagine that he would actually be able to test the defenses of his estate. He gave Hal instructions in the game of chess they were playing with Captain Butler. When Butler would send in a few pawns, Howard defeated them with ease. He laughed and cheered when he sent the captain himself running as fast as he could across the north lawn to escape the rubber bullets ricocheting around him. Howard had purposely fired a round straight at the captain's ass. Butler fell to the ground and quickly got up, limping away with both hands on his bottom like a little boy who'd just been spanked.

"Hal, let's hope the good captain gets the message. In case he doesn't, fire a head shot at anyone approaching the back wall."

"Sir, I must inform you that such a move could result in serious injury, possibly death."

"I'm aware of that, Old Man, thank you."

"I understand, sir."

Howard watched as a wave of a dozen soldiers took off at a full sprint toward the back door of his home.

"Take your time, Old Man. I want a few of them to make it to the back door."

"Yes, sir."

Howard watched the monitor as the soldiers slowly dropped to the ground. Every one of them remained motionless. "Life signs?"

"They are all alive, sir. Two of them suffered severe trauma to an eye."

"To hell with 'em, they'll live. Maybe Butler will get the message and leave."

Howard looked at the monitor and saw that three soldiers had made it to the back door, out of the field of vision of the sentries. "Good job, grunts! Oh my! Whatever are you going to do now? Maybe if you knock on the door and mind your manners I'll just open up and let you in? Oh no! Don't do that! Might sting a little!"

The three soldiers looked at each other in confusion. They studied the back door leading into the kitchen. One of them tossed a rock at the force field. The field shimmered and deflected the rock with ease. They looked at each other, silently arguing over which one of them was going to touch the force field.

"Come on now! One of you has to do it! Draw straws or something, hurry up!"

The argument ceased and the unlucky loser walked over to the force field. He raised his rifle and tapped the barrel to the field only to be met with a severe shock. He dropped his rifle to the ground and danced wildly around, flapping his hands in pain.

"Told you not to do that!" Howard laughed and sat back in his chair, quite proud of himself. "It's okay little boys, run away now. Make sure to get your friends on your way out. "Hal, if you would be kind enough to allow them to leave and let them collect their unlucky friends from the battlefield."

"Of course, sir."

"Well, Captain, what do you have in store for me this

time?" Howard studied the monitor and could see Captain Butler and First Sergeant Bankhead deep in discussion. Bankhead quickly ran over to a group of soldiers and returned with four men carrying very large guns. "Hal, what are those guns? What do they do?"

"Sir, they are M-32 grenade launchers capable of firing six forty millimeter grenade rounds in revolver fashion."

"Very nice, Captain Butler! I'm impressed! Hal, you ready to play baseball?"

"I am, sir. It is after all, my favorite sport."

"Let's have some fun with them. He's probably going to fire a round or two at the force fields. Let him hit the field so he thinks he has a shot at hitting the wall. Everything else, you're free to take a turn at bat."

"Yes, sir."

Howard watched with growing excitement as Captain Butler attempted to fire explosive rounds at his home. The sentries on the roof caught every round mid-air and dropped them to the ground. The sonic repulsors worked exactly as Howard had designed them.

"What now, Butler? What else have you got? Ready for round three? Let's see what you got!" Howard studied the monitor and watched the four baffled grenadiers shuffle away. The two soldiers were clearly discussing their next move. Suddenly, the First Sergeant ran away and the soldiers quickly loaded up their vehicles. Captain Butler stood idle in the middle of the field. Howard hoped the captain was planning his next move. As Howard waited in anticipation, a truck pulled up next to Butler. His adversary waved goodbye and left.

"Oh come on! I was having so much fun! You can't leave now! This was just getting interesting! Jackson, my boy, you disappoint me! I can't believe you would give up that easily!"

"Sir, all of the forces have retreated. They have taken up position a half mile away."

"Really? They aren't leaving? What are you up to, Jackson?"

"Sir, my drones have detected an incoming aircraft. It's an M-16 fighter jet."

"What? He isn't going to…"

"The jet has locked onto us, sir."

"Can you stop it?"

"No, sir, my system will not be able to stop a large projectile traveling at high velocity."

Howard watched in horror as a missile was fired from five miles away. He searched the sky for a telltale sign - a flash, a trail of smoke, but saw nothing. In his secure panic room, he felt the foundation of his home rumble like an earthquake had hit.

"He can't do this! This has gone too far! This is outrageous!" Howard's face reddened as he stood up and threw his chair into the monitor. "Noooooo! They can't do this! They can't! THIS IS MY HOUSE!"

"Sir, my security robots will be able to keep enemy forces at bay for a short time. Their defeat is inevitable, however. The robots are not equipped to deliver lethal force. We need to make preparations to leave the estate."

Howard was furious - furious at himself for not designing a security system that could defend his home against armed invaders. The thought of dead bodies littering his estate was something he could not comprehend. Howard was not superstitious enough to believe in ghosts, but he couldn't be in a room that had once played host to bloody corpses. Howard picked up his chair and set it upright. He was not giving up.

"It's not time to leave just yet, Old Man. We can do this."

"What would you like me to do, sir?"

"Kill the lights. I want it black as midnight in every room in the house. Deploy the maintenance robots and have them coat the floors with cleaning solution. Then turn on every faucet and flood the floors. That should trip them up and make it hard to get around."

"Yes, sir."

Howard's mind was racing faster than it ever had in his entire life. His genius IQ of one hundred ninety-five was his greatest weapon. He had no doubt that he would prevail.

"Disable the fire suppression system and fill the first floor with natural gas. They fire a weapon in there and they'll regret it. Turn up the sound system as loud as it will go, and play some heavy metal from the 1980s. I don't want them to be able to hear each other; blow out their eardrums."

"Yes, sir."

"We have anything that would work as a toxic gas or something like, uh, tear gas?"

"No, sir, we do not."

"Can you improvise something?"

"I'm afraid not."

"Blast the heat as high as it will go. How hot can you make it?"

"Most of the kitchen has been destroyed, leaving a large section exposed to open air. If the walls were intact, the thermostat could reach one hundred and fifteen degrees. The amount of fresh air ventilating the kitchen and throughout the house prevents that high of a temperature. The maximum temperature possible will fluctuate between ninety and ninety-five degrees."

"Do it."

"Yes, sir. A large contingent of troops is entering the kitchen."

"Send in the security robots. Hopefully they will fire off some rounds and spark the gas."

Howard anxiously watched the monitors as his instructions were being carried out. Most of the first floor was covered in soapy water. Howard had the volume muted but knew the sound system was playing music at a deafening level. The security robots entered the kitchen and began firing rubber bullets and tiny barbs that would shock the troops with electricity. The sparks from the darts were not sufficient enough to ignite the gas, but that didn't matter. The first soldier to fire his rifle ignited the gas, and the soldiers were blown from the kitchen out onto the lawn. All the robots on the first floor were safe from the fire; however, each room on the bottom floor was now ablaze.

"Let it burn for a few minutes to kick up some smoke, then engage the fire suppression system."

"Yes, sir. Another wave of troops is approaching the kitchen."

The next wave spilled into the kitchen and broke up into three man teams. They struggled with the soapy water and engaged the security robots in battle. Most of the troops were quickly incapacitated by the rubber bullets being fired at their heads. Slowly, one by one, the security robots were disabled by continual shotgun blasts from soldiers who had successfully found cover.

"Sir, your efforts will not be sufficient in repelling the invading force. A much larger contingent of soldiers is approaching the kitchen. I must insist that we leave the estate."

"I'm afraid you're right, Old Man. It's time for us to head to the Castle."

"I am sorry, sir. The escape pod is ready to launch whenever you are ready."

"Very well. Transfer yourself to the escape pod, Hal. I want your primary cores destroyed immediately. Leave the security measures in place. I want them to sweat their asses off in the dark while their eardrums burst to Quiet Riot."

"Very good, sir. I will carry out your instructions immediately and meet you in the escape pod."

"I'm on my way, Old Man."

****

Captain Jackson Butler and First Sergeant Matt Bankhead stood in the same spot as before, observing as the waves of soldiers entered the kitchen. Captain Butler watched in horror as the first wave was blasted back onto the grounds in an explosive eruption of body parts. He would make Howard pay for that. He sent in the next wave and listened over the radio as they battled the same security robots that led him and Top out of the library. The second wave suffered greatly at the hands of the robots but in the end, a few of his soldiers managed to disable them. With the robots out of the way, he sent the last and largest waves of soldiers into the kitchen to secure the entire estate.

He had won. Howard had lost.

"Top, get in there! I want him alive!"

"Roger that, sir!" The First Sergeant sprinted through the hole in the kitchen wall.

"Sir?"

Butler turned to see his Executive Officer, Lieutenant Christopher, standing at attention holding a salute.

Captain Butler returned the salute. "Lieutenant! Glad to see you up and around!"

"Yes, sir. Thank you. Sir, the president's helicopter is approaching."

"Thank you, XO. You're dismissed."

"Yes, sir!"

Captain Butler turned to see the president's helicopter in the distance. It approached the empty field and landed behind him, fifty yards away. Captain Butler straightened his uniform and prepared to meet the president.

Once the helicopter was secured, the doors opened and the ladder descended. Vice President Simon Sterling exited, straightening his tie and holding on to his hat to keep it from blowing away. He slowly walked the distance between himself and the officer. With a stern look on his face, he surveyed the man who had carried out his bidding. Once he felt the man was sufficiently intimidated, he returned the salute and spoke.

"Captain Butler, I presume?"

"Yes, sir. It's an honor to meet you, sir."

"Likewise. I see you had a difficult time securing my new home?"

Their conversation was interrupted by a small craft emerging from the roof of the mansion. Once it was a hundred feet above the estate, it rocketed away to the north.

"Hmph. I see Mr. Beck will not be joining us. Such a pity. My apologies; you were saying?"

"Yes, sir. Mr. Beck did not give it up without a fight. His security measures were quite effective at repelling our advances. I had no choice but to secure an opening in the outer wall."

"Excellent work, General Butler."

"Yes, sir!" Jackson Butler couldn't help but smile at the news of his promotion.

"General, it's time the American people had a true leader unburdened by an ineffective, squabbling government powerless to do anything to help them. They deserve a leader who is willing to do whatever it takes to ensure our nation does not fall.

CHAPTER TWENTY-FIVE

President Malcolm Powers sat in his study at his residence in upstate New York. His five hundred acre horse ranch, "Serenity Hills," had been in his family for generations. Once he took office, the Secret Service made many upgrades to the property so the president could vacation there at his leisure. Malcolm never once felt like he had any kind of a vacation when he was there. He did just as much work at the ranch as he did at the White House. The residence was fortified with the same steel doors and shutters as the Oval Office. The air space over the ranch was a no-fly zone. Malcolm felt the need to apologize to each of his neighbors since they all had to undergo extensive background checks. They gladly complied since they were proud to tell their friends and family that the president of the United States was their neighbor.

The First Lady had taken up permanent residence at Serenity Hills due to her failing health. The White House Press Secretary had maintained the white lie that she was recuperating from her latest battle with breast cancer. It was true; she had gone into remission three times in the past sixteen years. The cancer was not the reason she had left the White House - it was her mental state. Madeline Powers was bi-polar and not fond of taking her medication. She was a brilliant woman who had retired from practicing law when Malcolm began campaigning for the Oval Office. She had every intention of using her status as First Lady to champion her many causes; however, the press was not too kind to her. Someone had dug up her medical records and her mental health problems, starting a media circus that only got worse when she tried to defend herself. The White House press corps respected the president enough to never broach the subject, but other media outlets practiced their constitutional right to free speech and branded Madeline Powers as "crazy" and "a dangerous woman who could corrupt the leader of the free world." At the first White House Christmas party of the new administration, she had a manic episode and caused a scene. The President and the First Lady's sister were able to quietly whisk her away from the party. Malcolm begged her to take her medication. Madeline refused and instead went into exile at

Serenity Hills. When the attacks on the White House began, Madeline was in such a state that her personal physician, along with her Secret Service detail, had to restrain and sedate her.

When the White House was evacuated, all of President Powers' guests accompanied him to Serenity Hills via Air Force One. Everyone stayed at the ranch for the first night; however, the majority of the guests departed shortly thereafter. On the morning of the third day, the only ones that remained were Chief of Staff Reid, Director Jimenez, Fleet Admiral Mack, and Secretary of Defense Decker.

As the group wrapped up their breakfast, the president lit a cigarette and said, "Computer, give me a status report on Washington."

"Good morning, Mr. President. I am sorry to inform you that the situation did not improve during the night. Rioting and looting actually increased from the previous twenty-four hour period. Many of the rioters have organized into armed gangs numbering from fifty to one hundred. The Unified National Guard has been unsuccessful in taking back portions of the city. The gangs simply fell back to another portion of the city and take control there."

"They're probably using the metro to move around," Secretary Decker observed.

"The metro is still running?" asked Stacy Reid.

"No, the metro was shut down when this all started. I'm betting they're still using the tunnels to move around the city."

"That just makes it harder. Computer, continue please." Stacy Reid continued drinking her coffee.

"The most troubling news is that during the night, one of the gangs broke into three of the Smithsonian Museums, resulting in a great deal of vandalism."

When the president heard this, the news crushed him. He never dreamed that American citizens would damage priceless artifacts from their nation's history.

"Which museums?"

"Natural History, Air and Space, and American History."

The president didn't know if he could take anymore bad news. "What about the monuments?"

"The Washington Monument has not sustained any

structural damage, but the walls at the base have been spray-painted with various anti-government slogans and profanities."

"Dear Lord, help us all. Do you have any images?" President Powers quickly lit up another cigarette.

The wall opposite the president's desk lit up and displayed an image of the Washington Monument. The people in the room stood and walked to get a closer look. "Kill the crooked politicians!" "Fuck Powers!" "Burn the White House!" could all be discerned along with many other similar slogans. The only slogan that bore any intelligence was "Don't Tread On Me," dating back to the American Revolution.

"Burn the White House?" Stacy read in anguish. She looked to everyone in the room and said, "Computer, bring up an image of the White House."

An aerial view of the White House filled the screen; the image rotated three hundred and sixty degrees around the perimeter of the presidential residence. Steel shutters still adorned the windows and doors. While the interior of the White House was secure, the outside was another matter. The walls of the White House were covered in graffiti and scorch marks from Molotov cocktails. The building's fire resistant paint prevented the firebombs from doing any lasting damage.

"Computer, continue please," said Stacy.

"The Jefferson Memorial has suffered a fate similar to that of the Washington Monument. The only monument to suffer structural damage is the MLK memorial."

An image of the structure built to honor the legacy of the pioneer for Civil Rights was displayed on the screen. The Stone of Hope had been toppled. Dr. King's statue lay in three pieces, the head smashed to bits.

"That's horrible! I can't believe it." Director Jimenez scowled.

Malcolm debated on whether or not he wanted to see any more. Against his better judgment, he asked, "Computer, show me the Lincoln Memorial."

An image of the Lincoln Memorial filled the wall. The outer structure was just as it was before Washington fell to the rioters. Malcolm felt a sense of relief, but, just to be sure, wanted to check on Honest Abe. "Computer, zoom in to the inside of the monument."

The image zoomed in and focused on the statue of the sixteenth president. President Lincoln was sitting in his chair, hands on each arm. The man himself was unmolested, but something was in his lap.

"Oh my God!" Is that what I think it is?" Secretary Decker said with terrified eyes.

President Powers was speechless. He was no stranger to the gruesome acts of violence that accompanied war. He had seen things like this many times before, but never on American soil.

Stacy Reid had tears streaming down her face. Director Jimenez was trying to scream in anger, but instead began a coughing fit that lasted for several minutes.

Admiral Mack was the first to speak. "We have to take back the Capital. We can't allow this to go any further."

President Lincoln's legs and feet were drenched in blood. In his lap was a pile of human heads, all wearing the Kevlar helmets of the Unified National Guard.

"Computer, turn that damn screen off! Now!" President Powers took a few steps and fell into a chair. Stacy could tell the president was on the verge of losing control. His face was bright red and he was breathing in and out at an alarming rate. He raised his head from his hands and swung his head from side to side, repeating the word "no" over and over.

Stacy leaned forward and placed her hand on his arm. "Mr. President, please. Please try and remain calm. Malcolm, please listen to me. You're scaring us. Please calm down."

Malcolm took in several troubled breaths and closed his eyes. Secretary Decker poured a glass of water and handed it to the president. Malcolm raised the shaking glass to his lips and drank.

"Thank you, everyone. Thank you." The president paused for a moment to steady his voice. "I'm sorry if I've alarmed you. I'm fine. I just need a moment."

"Mr. President, do you need to lie down? Should I call Dr. Miles?" Stacy turned and looked at Admiral Mack should the doctor be needed.

"No, no. That won't be necessary. My wife's doctor has

his hands full at the moment. Please, I'm fine, really."

The president finally cleared his head and regained his composure. "I'm sorry for that. I'm actually quite embarrassed, and I'm sure I can count on everyone's discretion. The American people need to have complete faith in the office of the president, now more than ever." Everyone in the room looked to the president and nodded their heads in agreement.

Admiral Mack quickly changed the subject so they could move forward. "Mr. President, with your permission, I'd like to report on the status of the Iranian blockade."

"Yes, Admiral, please." The president was grateful for the chance to regain control.

"Computer, bring up the status report from the Iranian Theater." A detailed map of the eastern edge of the Iranian Theater appeared on the wall. "As you can see, the *Enterprise* and the *George Washington*, along with their support craft, joined the blockade forty-two hours ago. They have set up a secure perimeter in the Indian Ocean and have closely monitored for any Iranian submarines. I can report definitively that no Iranian subs have entered the Indian Ocean."

"Thank you, Admiral; we could all use a bit of good news."

Director Jimenez sat forward in his wheelchair. "Admiral, I hate to be the naysayer and I assure you I mean no disrespect, but how can you be sure of that?"

"A perfectly valid question to which I take no offense, Director Jimenez. We have our own submarines in the water and have set up a dragnet spanning the distance from Oman to Mumbai. Nothing passes the line without us knowing. If we wanted, we could pull up sensor reports and tell you how many fish have crossed over the line."

Roberto Jimenez did not smile often, but upon hearing this, he did. "I'm impressed, Admiral. What about the radiation?"

"It's getting worse. It's continuing to fan outward from Bunker Five. The blockade is safe from the radiation for now, but the Iranians are continuing to dump radioactive waste into the air. I can't begin to imagine the death toll in the region."

The president returned to his desk and sat down. "What

happens when the radiation hits the blockade? Will we still be able to detect enemy movement?"

"The blockade will be affected toward the surface. Depending on the level of radiation, our sensors will be ineffective from the surface down to about a hundred feet. However, if a sub tries to come to the surface, it will be easy to spot."

The president was not happy with this development. "That's not comforting, Admiral. We are vulnerable if that happens. If we let a submarine get past the blockade and head to our shores, well, I think we all know what's at stake."

"Yes, Mr. President, I understand your concern and I share it. We have hundreds of drones in the air watching the water."

The president sat back in his chair and was silent for few moments. He thought about the blockade and once he decided he didn't have any further questions, he changed the subject. "How bad is Texas?"

The president's Chief of Staff hesitated. She didn't know if the president could take any more bad news. The last thing she or anyone in the room wanted was a repeat of what happened a few minutes prior. Everyone in the room looked to her, reluctant to answer.

"I'm waiting for an answer." The president was becoming clearly agitated.

"Mr. President, I think the best thing for us to do right now..."

"The best thing for you to do right now is not to coddle me like a child and answer my question. Or do I have to find out for myself?"

"Yes, Mr. President, of course. My apologies. Computer, show us the Gulf of Mexico."

A map of the Gulf of Mexico and the Texas coastline spilled across the wall. The path of Hurricane Maxine was indicated by a series of lines cutting across Galveston Island and ending north of Houston. An overlay of the power grid indicated that the majority of the state was in the dark.

"Computer, display the I-45 corridor from Galveston to Houston."

The people in the room could only hope that the image

was incorrect, because the only thing they saw on the screen was water.

"This is a nightmare," Charles Decker lamented. "We have no idea how many people drowned in that, do we?

"I'm afraid not. It's been over a month, and the death toll in Florida is continuing to rise. It will be some time before we know the final figures in both states," answered President Powers.

"Computer, zoom in on downtown Houston." The president braced himself.

Houston had been decimated. The city was underwater and many skyscrapers had either fallen or were leaning over, resting on their neighbors. The flood covering Houston was filled with debris. Cars, houses, trees, traffic lights, and raw sewage sloughed around. Admiral Mack took the initiative and walked over to the screen. He raised his hands to interact with the computer and with a series of gestures, zoomed and panned around the destruction. People could be seen floating on billboards and standing on rooftops. Admiral Mack chose a section and zoomed in even closer to see a large collection of corpses that had floated into what appeared to be a large parking lot and rested against the side of a building. After a few seconds passed and recognition kicked in, he quickly zoomed out of the image and left it as it had been before.

The president had prepared for this; he knew the destruction in Texas would be as it had been in Florida. He struggled every minute of every day with the decision he had made. Malcolm stubbed out his cigarette and spoke. "I have sacrificed a great many American lives to stop The Great Empire of Iran. When this is all over, I will have to figure out a way to live with the decisions I have made. I will certainly have to answer to God for bringing so many innocent people to His gates. If we are successful in stopping the Empire, we will have saved the world from complete destruction." The president stopped, and a look of complete shame and remorse erased every shred of proof that he had any confidence in what he had done. "Even if we do manage to save the world, I will never be able to reconcile the horrible things for which I am solely responsible. I am presiding over the destruction of our nation; that much is painfully clear. My only hope is that my successors will be able to pick up the pieces and repair the damage left in my wake."

President Malcolm Powers turned his chair away from his guests and faced the window. No one in the room spoke a word. They simply sat in the painful silence, astonished over the sequence of events that brought such anguish to their friend and beloved president.

"I'd like to be alone."

Everyone quietly exited the room. Chief of Staff Reid lingered by the door, waiting for her boss to tell her to remain behind. He did not. She walked down the hall toward the living room and saw her colleagues gathered in a group, clearly talking about the president. As she attempted to join the group, Director Jimenez promptly turned his wheelchair away from her and sped off.

"What was that about?" Stacy questioned Secretary Decker and Admiral Mack.

The two men looked at each other deciding who should speak. "Go ahead and tell her, Chuck."

"Tell me what?" Stacy looked at Secretary Decker.

"Well, let's just say that Roberto is very displeased with the president."

"That's not really a secret. Roberto has never been one to hide the fact that he hates the president with a passion."

"Well, yes, that much is obvious to everyone, the president included."

"It's more than just that. He's been saying some pretty crazy things since we left the White House."

"Like what?"

"Well, he thinks the president is a coward for leaving Washington. He said the president showed the entire world that when the going gets tough, he runs like a frightened child."

"Oh, come on. That's ridiculous. D.C. is in the middle of a war zone. If he didn't leave on his own, the Secret Service would have bound and gagged him and drug him up here to the ranch."

"That's just the beginning, Stacy," Admiral Mack looked back to Secretary Decker, "tell her the best part."

"Hold on, we'll get to that. Our crippled spy is of the opinion that we should launch a nuclear strike on the Empire and bring our military home to the shores of Florida and Texas."

"So, that crazy asshole is in favor of a nuclear holocaust that would most likely destroy mankind? He really thinks we could just turn the Middle East into a parking lot and our problems would just go away? Who's to say that our own allies wouldn't turn on us thinking we were trying to take over the world? You think China would let that go unanswered?"

"Well, the director doesn't see it that way. He thinks the United States should be in control of world affairs. He's confident that the European Army would back our play."

"Is he senile? He can't possibly believe that!"

"He does, I promise you."

"Wait, there's something even better than that nonsense? You haven't gotten to the best part yet, have you?"

The Admiral decided that Charles Decker had done enough talking and wanted to be the one to relay the rest to the Chief of Staff. "Director Jimenez feels Malcolm Powers is unfit for office. He thinks the panic attack we just saw is grounds enough to invoke the Twenty-Fifth Amendment. Says his mental state is impairing his judgment. Even tried to bring the First Lady into it."

Stacy Reid was beside herself with shock. Her eyes were huge orbs in her pallid face and her jaw gaped wide. "The Twenty-Fifth? The panic attack means he isn't fit to... Wait! Is he actually stupid enough to imply that the First Lady is contagious or something? Her mental health means somehow he's going to... That son of a bitch! The nerve of him! Jesus!"

"It was all I could do not to tip him out of his wheelchair and kick his ass," Admiral Mack said, looking down the hall to see if anyone was listening.

Stacy continued to shake her head in disbelief. "Is that asshole up to something? What's he planning?"

Secretary Decker replied, "I don't know. He's been slowly confiding in us to see where we stand. We've been playing along, not really agreeing or disagreeing, just listening. He watches the president like a hawk. If either one of us approaches Malcolm, he makes sure to be in the room. He won't dare say a word around you."

"I'm one of the few people who speaks one-on-one with

the president."

"Correct."

"I can't believe this. Does Malcolm know about any of this?"

"Absolutely not, and we need to keep it that way," Admiral Mack had a grim look on his face. "The last thing the president needs is to entertain any of this nonsense."

"He has to know something's going on. I've been wondering this whole time why Roberto hasn't left. I'm sure Malcolm has been wondering the same thing."

"You're probably right. Malcolm knows better than to think Roberto is here to support him."

"If you gentlemen will excuse me, I have work to do."

"Of course."

Stacy walked outside to the back porch overlooking the ranch and sat down on the porch swing. She slowly rocked back and forth, trying to make sense of the CIA director. Was he just a crazy old man or was a larger conspiracy going on? Who on earth would trust the top spy to do anything? Her train of thought was derailed by her smartphone vibrating in her pocket. She pulled it out to find a message from Malcolm.

Come to my office please

Stacy replied that she was on her way. She quickly walked down the hall to his office, hoping he wasn't having another panic attack. She knocked on the door and entered when the president replied. Thankfully, Malcolm was not panicked or upset. To the contrary, he was smiling.

"It's time I let you in on a little secret."

"What on earth are you doing, Malcolm?"

"What do you think of Jimenez being here?"

"I know we're thinking the same thing."

"He's up to something. He would have left as soon as humanly possible otherwise."

"Well, since you brought it up, I just found out something that might shed some light on the subject."

"I'm intrigued."

"Roberto has been vocal in his disapproval in you."

"That doesn't shed light on anything. The man hates me. Tell me something I don't know."

"Well, I'm not sure where to begin."

"Take your time."

"I guess I'll just cut to the chase. He wants you out of office."

"He's always wanted me out of office. Pretty sure he's felt the same about the other two presidents he's served under. Again, tell me something I don't know."

"Will you stop interrupting me, please?"

"I'm sorry."

"As I was saying, he really and truly wants you out of office. He spoke with Bill and Chuck about invoking the Twenty-Fifth."

Malcolm laughed, "On what grounds?"

"Your mental state. Something about the overwhelming stress causing a nervous breakdown."

"Well, being the first president in over two hundred years to not only lose the White House but also the nation's capital can be a little hard to cope with."

"Are you trying to be funny?"

"Well, if I don't at least try I'm going to lose my mind."

"Probably shouldn't repeat that."

"Good idea."

"What happened to the other president that lost the White House? How'd that turn out for him?"

"You should be ashamed of your appallingly bad education. Did you even go to college?"

"Very funny. Just answer the question, professor."

"War of 1812? President Madison? Ring a bell?"

"Not really."

"Dolly Madison saving the painting of Washington while British troops were only blocks away?"

"No. Didn't really pay attention in history class. Thought it was boring."

"Such a shame. And not that you care in the slightest, but Dolly Madison didn't actually save the painting. It was President Madison's gardener."

"What happened to the White House?"

"Burned to the ground."

"Well, at least you have that much going for you."

"Are you trying to be funny?"

"I am, yes."

"Okay, back to the matter at hand. We need to figure out a way to beat Jimenez at his own game."

"What did you have in mind?"

"Well, at the next meeting I think I will become unglued and start acting irrational. You will express your concern, only making me angrier. Then I want you to insist that I get some rest for a few days and let the vice-president take over. That's when I'm going to fire you and have the Secret Service haul you out of here kicking and screaming."

"And then wait for Roberto to come to me."

"Exactly."

CHAPTER TWENTY-SIX

"Sir, are you all right?" asked Hal.

Howard Beck was sitting aboard his escape pod with his eyes closed, muttering to himself.

"Sir, your blood pressure and pulse rate concern me."

Howard kept his eyes shut and continued to mutter to himself. He had climbed into the escape pod and harnessed himself as tightly as he could. The launching of the craft was carried out flawlessly, and it was operating perfectly, thanks to Hal. The vehicle was roughly the size of an SUV. Howard was terrified of flying.

"Sir, I know you are frightened, your vital signs are alarming me. Please try to remain calm. I'm worried that you might suffer cardiac arrest."

With his heart pounding like a drum, Howard couldn't hear a thing Hal was saying.

"Sir, it is imperative that you try to remain calm. I am going to give you something to help you relax." Hal mixed a gaseous sedative into the air supply. "Take deep breaths, sir. Everything is going to be fine. Try and relax."

Howard immediately felt the effects of the gas. "Thank you, Old Man. I feel much better."

"You are welcome, sir. I was beginning to worry."

"Hal, I need to speak to the president, right now."

"Sir, the president and his staff have evacuated the White House. I have been unable to contact anyone."

"What? I thought he was in the presidential bunker waiting out a terrorist attack?"

"He was, sir, however, the National Guard has lost control of Washington. The capital has fallen. The logical assumption is that the president was moved to Serenity Hills."

"What do you mean 'you assume'? How can you not know where the president is at this very moment?"

"I believe the Secret Service has initiated a communications blackout. The president could very well be aboard Air Force One or at any number of secure locations. Serenity Hills would be the logical assumption being that it is the most secure location away from Washington."

"Something very wrong is going on, and I intend to find out what it is. I don't believe for one second that Malcolm Powers had anything to do with the attack on Beck Estates. Someone is working against the president; there's a plot that involves more than just taking my house."

"What do you want to do, sir?"

"How far can this escape pod take us?"

"This craft was designed to deliver you safely to Beck Castle."

"Yes, Hal, I know that. Can we make it to the Chicago office?"

"No, sir. We do not have enough fuel to travel that far."

"What if we refueled at the Castle? Could we make it then?"

"Yes, sir, we could. If we took off from the ground we could make the trip in less than two hours."

"Make the preparations. I don't want to waste a single minute. Have a jet standing by in Chicago when we land. We have to get to Malcolm. I have to tell him what's going on."

"I will make the arrangements, sir."

The escape pod could be launched like a rocket as it had been from Beck Estates, or it could take off from a runway like a jet. Launching it as a rocket expended a great deal of fuel and greatly limited its range. Once they were at the Castle, they could fill the tanks and take off from the ground like a jet. It would be risky, given that they didn't have a runway to use. Howard was not concerned with the risk. It was imperative that he get to Malcolm and warn him that something very bad was transpiring. The nation was falling apart. If things were so bad that they had to evacuate the White House, it was far worse than Howard had imagined. Every major city was descending into chaos with riots, fires, and lawlessness. Howard hoped that it was just a rogue group of renegade soldiers that decided to take his house from him. Maybe they knew how bad things were getting and saw his estate as the perfect stronghold to wait things out. Howard wanted to believe this but couldn't shake the fact that they had fired a missile at his house. A splinter group from the Unified National Guard would not have a fighter jet at their disposal, and they certainly couldn't fire a missile on American soil without attracting attention. The plot had to be much bigger.

As they arrived at Beck Castle, the desert floor opened up to reveal the landing pad. The escape pod landed, and several robots were dispatched to prepare the craft for take off.

"How long before we can take off again?"

"Just under five minutes, sir."

"Good! I'm going down below to change clothes and take a piss."

"Of course, sir."

Howard rode the elevator down to the main floor and rushed down the hallway to his quarters. Catching sight of himself in the bathroom mirror, Howard was shocked at how dirty and shabby he looked. His long, white hair was stringy and sticking out in disarray. He hadn't shaved in days and had the beginnings of a scraggly beard. Howard had been wearing the same bathrobe for days and hadn't showered since he put on the robe. He looked like a crazy, homeless person rather than the richest man in the world. In the few minutes he had, he splashed water on his face, ran a comb through his ratty hair as best he could, and brushed his teeth. He grabbed his electric razor and shaved his face and put on clean clothes. Howard knew Malcolm trusted him and valued his opinion; however, he was not going to present himself to the president of the United States looking like a bum. He wanted the president and his staff to take him seriously.

Howard finished dressing and put on the nicest shoes he could find. He hated wearing shoes, preferring to wear his slippers. He exited his quarters and started down the hall to the elevator.

"Sir, we are ready for departure."

"Great, I'm on my way, Hal."

Howard rode the elevator to the landing pad and climbed aboard the escape pod, trying to remain calm. Thankfully the sedative that Hal gave him was still lingering in his system.

"We gonna have a problem with takeoff?"

"No, sir, I dispatched the maintenance robots to clear a path from the landing pad. We have an adequate amount of level ground free from obstruction. We are ready to depart on your word."

Howard closed his eyes and gripped the arm rests. "Let's

get going."

The escape pod lurched from the landing pad and raced across the desert floor. Howard was so completely terrified that if he hadn't emptied his bladder, he would have done so in the cockpit. As the craft picked up speed, Howard was pushed back against his seat with tremendous force. He felt his cheeks ripple back and could not move his head. As the craft ascended and leveled off, Howard opened his eyes.

"Everything okay, Old Man? I did not like that at all. Please tell me that was the worst of it."

"We are fine, sir. The takeoff proceeded as I anticipated."

Howard tried to ignore his anxiety and desperately wanted a distraction. "Hal, talk to me."

"About what, sir?"

"I don't know, anything. I don't like to fly. Do you have any way of knowing what's going on back at the residence?"

"No, sir. With my primary cores destroyed, I have no connection to the residence. My auxiliary systems were transferred to this escape pod. Once we arrived at the Castle, I was able to establish a connection to my secondary systems. While I am operating at full capacity, I am sorry to say that I no longer have access to Beck Estates."

"I figured as much, thought maybe we had some sort of backup."

"No, sir, you designed the failsafe systems to completely remove all traces of my program in an emergency."

"Yeah, you're right. Don't want anyone to be able to link into your program and snoop around. Just wish we had some way of knowing what those bastards are doing in my house."

"The failsafe worked perfectly, sir. They will not be able to access any of my programs."

"What about Chicago? Any word from our offices? Is everything safe?"

"Riots continue to spread throughout the city; however, the Chicago branch of Beck Enterprises remains secure. I foresee no problem landing at our airstrip."

"Good! Anything else going on that I should know about?"

"Sir, I have been monitoring a breaking news story for the

past several minutes. However, given your current state, I'm not sure if you are in any condition to hear it. I was going to wait until we landed in Chicago to inform you."

"I just had my house invaded, and I'm flying for the first time in decades. I think I can handle it."

"Sir, it appears that..."

Hal was cut off mid-sentence, and the cockpit went completely dark. Howard's eyes adjusted and he could see the stars in the sky.

"What's going on? Hal! What are you doing? This isn't funny! Hal! Answer me!"

Howard realized in terror that the engines had cut off. He pushed the buttons on the keyboard in front of him and nothing happened.

"Hal! Respond! The engines shut off! I can't fly this thing by myself! Hal!"

Howard felt a tingling sensation in his gut and felt himself slowly rise up from his chair, the harness digging into his shoulders. The escape pod was in free fall, returning back to Earth.

CHAPTER TWENTY-SEVEN

Five hundred and twelve miles from the eastern coast of the United States, the Jabal class Iranian nuclear submarine, the *Habibollah Sayyari*, was stationary and submerged two hundred meters below the surface. The skipper of the boat, Captain Farzad Zamani, was simply waiting until the appropriate time to deliver his payload to the pre-determined target. His journey across the Atlantic was uneventful due to the simple fact that no one had any idea where he was, not even his superiors. He was given a target, a set of coordinates, and a time - that was it. The Atlantic was wide open and he made the journey without resistance.

When the radioactive material began to spill from Bunker Five and blind the Allied Forces, the *Habibollah Sayyari* was nowhere near the bunker. She was sitting in the Atlantic, twenty miles from the Port of Gibraltar. The Allied Forces were convinced that the Empire would attempt to sneak a nuclear device into the Arabian Sea and across the Indian Ocean. The tactic was not meant as a diversion, even though it did accomplish the task. The reason for the radioactive spill was to draw the *Enterprise* and the *George Washington* out of the Atlantic and into the Indian Ocean to look for a killer submarine with a nuke headed to the United States. Once the two aircraft carriers and their support vessels left the Atlantic, the *Habibollah Sayyari* raced across to the shores of the Eastern Seaboard with nothing in her way. The Empire didn't want any Allied vessels in the Atlantic capable of shooting down anything that was launched from their submarine.

The most guarded secret of the Great Empire of Iran was the fifty-mile underground tunnel they built from Bunker Three, located in western Turkey, into the Mediterranean Sea. The construction took over four years at the expense of thousands of lives. The construction crews never knew what they were digging, or the reason. To protect the project's security, the work crews were executed when their part of the project was completed, their families told of some horrible accident. A new work crew would be brought in for the next phase of construction and the process repeated. When the tunnel was completed, the waters from the Mediterranean poured in and flooded the distance to the bottom level of the bunker. The rest of the world was oblivious to the fact that the Empire had a secret route into the Mediterranean Sea

In the four years the tunnel was under construction, the Empire also commissioned a top-secret stealth submarine to be built. The submarine was roughly the size of a bus and had an eight-man crew. The engine aboard the secret craft was also a carefully guarded secret. The Iranians had developed a submarine that couldn't be detected in anyway. No sonar could ping off it, it was completely stealth. The sole purpose of the craft was to sneak past the Port of Gibraltar undetected.

The mini-sub accomplished the task with ease and docked with the *Habibollah Sayyari* to deliver her nuclear payload. The mini-sub had been given orders to remain at the location and await the go-ahead to attack Gibraltar. After the mini-sub destroyed the *James Russell* and left Gibraltar ripe for the picking, she would embark on a bold mission that would send the mini-sub up the Potomac River into Washington, D.C.

****

Lindsay Sanderson and her two children awoke in their one bedroom apartment in the Bronx. The apartment was in a rundown building that would probably be condemned should it undergo inspection. After Lindsay and her children were evicted from the Central Park Obama-Camp, they had to sleep in alleys and dumpsters while they waited for William to send more money. The first paycheck he sent home from the U.S. Army to his wife was spent on food, clothes, and a few days in a cheap motel. Lindsay saved what she could, and by the time the third check came, she had enough money for a deposit on a cheap one bedroom apartment and the first month's rent. They didn't have enough to have the power turned on, but Lindsay didn't really care. She also didn't have to worry about paying for water. There was a communal bathroom on every floor. She would wait until the middle of the day when it was being used the least, and she and her two children would bathe, use the restroom, and fill up their containers with water to take back to the room. Lindsay was not naive or stupid. She knew that behind most of the doors in her apartment building people were engaging in prostitution or drugs, probably both. Anytime they left the apartment, she had a vice grip on her children's hands. Her sweet, innocent children thought the first floor of the apartment building was a school since so many children wandered the halls. Lindsay knew the children on the first floor were prostitutes waiting to be sold into slavery. She never dared venture down the hallway on the first floor with her precious babies at her side.

Upon entering her tiny apartment, she locked all four deadbolts on the door and slid the dresser in front of it. Safely barricaded inside, she could watch her children play and relax in the joyful bliss of knowing they were safe and had a real roof over their heads. Lindsay thought back to the nights in the Obama-Camp when William never slept a wink so he could scare intruders away from their shack. Lindsay didn't sleep for the first week they were in the apartment. She kept waiting for someone to break in or at least bang on the door and wake them up. Their doorstep was never visited, and for the most part, the nights were pretty quiet. Apparently, the tenants on her floor wanted to be left alone as much as she did.

Lindsay had no idea where her husband was. She didn't have a phone, and mail delivery was, for the most part, nonexistent. The last thing she wanted William to do was worry about them. The only contact she had with her husband was on payday. As soon as she entered the Western Union and got the money, she paid the clerk five dollars to use his phone and William called her. William was never allowed to say anything about his location. William would talk with his children and listen to all of the hurried and nonsensical stories that hyper children often tell. William and Lindsay would spend the remaining minutes engaged in conversation that lifted both of their spirits. When he had six months of service under his belt, his family could move to Fort Polk, Louisiana, and live in base housing. William and Lindsay would talk about their future home and how they would decorate and furnish it. The phone calls they had every payday were the highlight of their bleak lives and every moment after was spent looking forward to the next one.

William was deployed to southern Spain with the 519th Military Police Battalion. Since William had a Master's degree, he was given the rank of Second Lieutenant. He went through basic training and a very brief officer's school, one that should have been three times as long. In wartime, however, the military needed officers desperately. It was hard to find qualified candidates, given the state of education in the United States. When the Army found out that William had a post-graduate degree, they jumped at the chance to make him an officer, and William gladly accepted the promotion. Lieutenant Sanderson was thankful for his platoon sergeant, SFC Myers, for showing him the ropes and helping him make crucial decisions. Their platoon was tasked with securing one half of a convoy route from the Port of Gibraltar to Seville. Once their three-day rotation on the convoy was completed, they were relieved by another platoon and returned to Gibraltar to provide security for the aircraft carrier guarding the key military position. William had never seen an aircraft carrier up close. The *USS James Russell* was an impressive sight to behold. She had been severely damaged by a submarine during the Battle of Tel-Aviv and barely made it back to Gibraltar. William was optimistic that the war would be over within a year since both the *Enterprise* and the *George Washington* were headed to Gibraltar to help secure the port and join with the offensive in the Mediterranean. He didn't know what rumors to believe, both of the aircraft carriers were several days overdue. He'd also heard that they were not coming at all and were redeployed elsewhere.

William thought about his wife and children every minute of every day. He had never been apart from them for any length of time. Leaving them behind was the hardest thing he had ever done in his life. When he saw the news footage of the demise of the Central Park Obama-Camp, he almost had a nervous breakdown. He was ready to leave the army to go find his family, but was warned against the idea since he would be branded as a deserter. Desertion in war time would land him in jail if they caught him. He had little choice but to wait the two agonizing weeks until his next payday to see if Lindsay showed up to collect the money. A fellow lieutenant always did him the favor of tracking the Western Union order. When Lindsay picked up the money, William was notified and called Lindsay. Hearing her voice after two weeks was the most beautiful sound he'd ever heard. William peppered her with questions but Lindsay only answered, "Don't worry, we're fine." William knew that his wife was a very strong woman and a survivor like him. She proved it when they lost their home and had to move into the Central Park Obama-Camp. She didn't divorce him or even hold him responsible. Her dedication to their marriage and to their family was unwavering.

****

William was in the best possible mood. Even though he hadn't had a hot shower in days and had been eating MREs for the better part of a week, nothing could put him in a bad mood on payday. William didn't care in the least about the money; he never saw one penny of it. The entire check went to his family. The Western Union order had been sent, and William was lingering around the admin building waiting for his friend to give word that Lindsay had picked up the cash. William and his wife had set up a time window of about six hours. He would always send the Western Union order at noon, New York time, and wait six hours to hear from Lindsay. If Lindsay didn't pick up the check by 6pm, he knew something wasn't right. If that ever happened, William had instructed her to be at the Western Union office the next day when it opened. Lindsay had never once been late. On this particular payday, it was getting close to the five-hour mark and William was starting to worry. Just a few minutes shy of the six-hour deadline, William was given word that she had picked up the cash. He quickly dialed the number, and Lindsay answered.

"Hey baby, I'm so sorry to keep you waiting."

"Cutting it a little close this time? It's fine. You made it before the deadline. Everything okay?"

"Yeah, things are fine. I just let the time get away from me."

"What've you been up to?"

"Well, I've been thinking about getting a used TV to pass the time."

"Wouldn't you have to get the power turned on? Thought you didn't want to bother with that."

"Well, winter is coming and we need to get a space heater. Also wouldn't mind having some light. The light from the windows doesn't really do the trick."

"You still on a month-to-month lease?"

"Of course."

"Good. I'm trying to pull some strings to get you guys to Fort Polk two months ahead of schedule."

"That would be a dream."

"No guarantees. I'm not sure it will happen, but I'm pushing hard for it. Okay, let me talk to the kiddos."

Silence.

"Lindsay, can you hear me? You still there? Honey?"

Silence.

"Hey! You there, baby? I can't hear you."

Silence.

"Sweetheart, I don't know if you can hear me but I can't hear you on my end. I'm going to hang up now and call the number back. If I can't reach you, we'll have to wait another two weeks. I love you so much. I'm hanging up now."

William hung the phone up and redialed. The line was busy.

****

"Why the hell did you do that? I was in the middle of a conversation!"

The clerk had pulled the phone out of Lindsay's hand and hung it up. He quickly started dialing. He was frantic and very upset about something.

"John? What's wrong? What's going on?"

"Look!" The Western Union employee pointed at his computer monitor and swiveled it around for her to see.

****

Captain Farzad Zamani carried out his instructions at the precise time. He surfaced the *Habibollah Sayyari* and transmitted a message over an unsecured line. The message repeated the same phrase over and over - "The Star of Allah illuminates the wicked." Captain Zamani wanted the infidels to know that Allah was punishing them. Much like the glorious day in 2001, when his faithful brothers brought down the Twin Towers, Captain Zamani wanted the launch of his missile to be broadcast on live TV for the Americans to witness in horror, just as they had watched the attack on the South Tower years before. He sent the broadcast over the airwaves for ten minutes, long enough for the American satellites to get a fix on him and record the launch. There were far more working satellites in 2001 compared to today, but that didn't matter. All he needed was one.

Captain Zamani did not dare to wait more than ten minutes. He knew that to do so would be very dangerous and left him vulnerable to attack. He gave the order and the missile was launched. He submerged the *Habibollah Sayyari* and hoped that a major news outlet had a satellite broadcasting his launch on live TV.

****

"Oh, God! What is that? Where are they?" Lindsay watched the live newsfeed over the Internet and tried to keep up with the journalist speaking in the background.

John spoke but didn't take his eyes from the monitor. "That's an Iranian submarine."

"Where is it? What are they doing?" Lindsay squeezed her children's hands harder.

"It's in the Atlantic. They're broadcasting a message over and over. It says 'The Star of Allah illuminates the wicked.'"

Lindsay began to cry. She had never wanted her husband by her side more than she did at that moment. She was terrified and knew that she and her children stood a real chance of dying if that submarine started launching missiles. Washington, D.C., would be the first and most obvious target. If that submarine had a second missile, it was heading for New York.

"Please..oh please..oh please, NO!" Lindsay picked up both of her children and hugged them tight.

"Mommy, why are you crying? Do you miss Daddy? It's

okay Mommy, don't cry, I miss him, too."

"Mommy loves you both so much. Everything is fine, my sweet babies. You're right, angel, Mommy just misses Daddy. We all miss him."

Lindsay slid down the wall and buried her children's faces in her breast. "Hey, have you guys decided on what we're going to name the puppy?"

"Rascal!"

"No, Howie!"

Lindsay wiped the tears from her face and calmed her shaken voice. "Come on now! I told you guys, you both have to agree on the name!"

"Rascal!"

"Howie!!"

"Oh my God, they launched something! No! We're all gonna die!" John jumped over the counter, locked the front door and turned off the light. Lindsay motioned for the young man to sit down next to her. She managed to let a silly thought come to the surface and almost laughed amidst the horror. John had locked the door and turned off the lights, as if the action carried real weight.

"Who's gonna die? Are we gonna die?" Lindsay's son started whimpering.

"No, no, no baby. John was just talking about a movie, right John?" Lindsay looked at the young man in desperation, hoping he would realize he was scaring the children.

"Uh, yeah, yeah. Sorry, just excited to see this really cool movie." John reached over and held Lindsay's hand. He looked away from the children as tears stream down his face. John had called his girlfriend but it went straight to voicemail. All he wanted was to hear her voice.

Lindsay looked outside at the street directly in front of the Western Union office. Cars began to crash into one another. People ran down the street screaming. A man was in the street trying to pry open a manhole cover so he could escape down into the sewer.

Lindsay had managed to distract her children from the horror around them. She had learned from the best. William could transform an upset, crying child into a happy smiling one in no time flat.

    Suddenly, the night sky was filled with a blinding flash that turned the darkness into daylight. A feeling of calm and joy washed over Lindsay. So this was how people went to heaven. They followed a bright light to the pearly gates of heaven into the arms of Jesus; all their loved ones that had passed before them were there to welcome them. Lindsay was thankful that it was over and relieved that neither she nor her children felt any pain. She closed her eyes and knew that when she opened them, she would be in heaven. She hugged her children tighter and opened her eyes.

    Darkness. Screaming. Crying.

    Lindsay was not at the gates of heaven. She was still sitting on the floor of the Western Union. The world around her was completely black. She waited and waited for her eyes to adjust, but they never did. Her children began to claw at her, digging their hands into her sides. As they called out for her, she gently stroked their hair and shushed their cries

    "Phone's dead. Computer won't turn back on."

    Lindsay pried her children from her sides. The two children hugged each other and continued to cry. Lindsay felt her way along the wall to the front door and found the light switch.

    "Power must be out. Hey, John, get your smartphone out, we can use the light from the screen to see what we're doing."

    "Yeah, hold on. Good idea." Lindsay could hear him fumbling around the countertop. "What the hell? My phone's dead, too. Damn thing was on eighty percent a few minutes ago."

    "You got a lighter or a match?"

    "No, shit, I wish I did. This is getting freaky."

    "You hear that?" asked Lindsay.

    "Yeah, what is that?" replied John.

    A low rumble filled the air and rattled the windows. Then in an instant, the rumble became a deafening, ear-splitting roar that sounded like a wrecking ball knocking a train from the track at full speed. The building shook and the glass wall at the front of the Western Union shattered and blew inward. Lindsay's children were thrown into the counter. Lindsay and John were knocked off their feet and hit the wall behind them.

Lindsay recovered and sat up to take inventory of herself. She wasn't bleeding and didn't feel the sharp pain of a broken bone. She crawled on the floor, desperately clawing for her children. "Brent? Heather? You guys okay?"

"That was fun!" screamed Brent.

Heather was crying. "Mommy, that scared me!"

Lindsay quickly ran her hands over their bodies to see if they were injured, delighted to find them both no worse for wear. She looked toward the street and could finally see light. The source of the light was not a street lamp or the headlights of a car. It was from a fire.

A passenger jet had fallen from the sky.

The Great Empire of Iran had detonated a nuclear warhead high in the atmosphere. The electromagnetic pulse destroyed every circuit board on every electronic device in its range. Every piece of technology, from a clock radio to the life support systems keeping patients alive in hospitals, stopped working. Every computer, every smartphone, every television, every piece of machinery man depended on ceased functioning at precisely the same millisecond.

From the eastern shores of the United States to the Great Plains, down to North Texas, and into the northern half of the Gulf States, every electronic item was fried and useless. Countless automobile accidents took thousands of lives as vehicles lost power. Surgical wards were thrown into darkness, only to lose patients. Hundreds of aircraft, from passenger jets to helicopters, fell out of the sky, killing thousands and starting fires that only Mother Nature could extinguish. The only saving grace was the fact that few people could afford to fly. Millions of people were instantly left penniless, their finances not in physical cash but in useless bank accounts. Frightened Americans were instantly thrown backwards into an era that was completely alien to them - an era before electricity, technology, and comfort. They had no means of communicating with each other because they couldn't pick up a phone or turn on a computer. They couldn't travel to a local store to buy food and water. Emergency services were brought to a standstill. Before the sun rose the next morning, chaos would become a way of life.

The Silent Warriors of the Empire had no idea that the night sky would be illuminated by the Star of Allah. Along with their vague instructions to "improvise and be creative," they were also told to await the Day of Judgment. The Silent Warriors who saw the broadcast of the *Habibollah Sayyari* launching her payload knew the Day of Judgment was at hand. They knew that in the coming chaos they would be able to operate out in the open and strike a serious blow to the enemy.

The arrogant nation would know humility for the first time.

CHAPTER TWENTY-EIGHT

"Hold still, Billy, this is gonna hurt. A lot."

"Hurry the fuck up! Shit! Just do it already!"

Inmates Richard "Killer" Dupree and Billy "Tank" Bratchett were in an abandoned gas station some twenty miles west of Las Vegas. Tank was near death. In his day, the giant had killed many people who had tried to take his life. In one of those epic battles, Tank's left eye was severely injured when a chunk of his cheek was torn from his face.

Richard had done everything he could think of to help Tank. The pressure from the compress he'd put over Tank's eye kept the pain bearable enough to keep him moving. They had precious little water to waste on the compress but had little choice but to keep the bandage moist enough to keep his eye lubricated. The eye was horribly infected. It had swollen completely shut and was oozing pus. Tank had a fever that was getting higher by the day. If Richard didn't get the infection and under control soon, Tank was going to die.

Once they had survived the smoky escape from the Highland Valley State Prison, they realized that the escape itself was child's play compared to the journey into hell that followed. The stolen perimeter vehicle with two flat tires traveled further than they anticipated. With the sun setting and a prison full of dead inmates behind them to keep the authorities busy, they drove the SUV as slowly and as carefully as they could, keeping it under ten miles an hour. They only came upon rough terrain occasionally; the rest of the trip was on flat desert floor. After ten miles of chewed rubber, they had to cut away what was left of the tires. After that, even in four-wheel drive, the rims just cut deeper and deeper into the dirt. Their stolen escape car got them less than thirteen miles away from the prison. They had to figure out the other thirty-five or so to Vegas on their own.

Spider didn't come along for the journey; he parted ways with Richard and Billy once it became obvious that they weren't heading down toward Highland Valley. Richard knew they wouldn't stand a chance going into the town. They would not be taken into custody, they would be shot dead on sight, no questions asked. If Richard and his tattooed friends wandered into town in their orange jumpsuits, they would not be alive for very long.

Spider was arrogant enough to think he knew better than Richard. He didn't really have much of a plan; he was just going to wing it. He had lost all faith in Richard after Head died. Spider blamed Richard for Head's death; if he hadn't wasted so much time when he should have been looking for the SUV, Head would still be alive.

Spider wandered into Highland Valley in the dark of night. He slipped into a dumpster behind a restaurant and slept the rest of the night, completely exhausted. When he awoke – thinking it was Saturday – he wandered behind the elementary school, certain that he was completely alone. For the first time since the escape, he let the thrill of freedom really sink in. It was time to relax and enjoy the gift he had been given. Spider sat down on a swing and began to push himself as high as he could, back and forth, laughing and hollering like a schoolboy. Little did he know, about a hundred eyes were on him the entire time as many students got up out of their seats and walked to the window to see what on earth was going on. Frightened teachers called the police as some fourth and fifth graders took pictures and texted them to their parents. Dozens of parents showed up at the school, strung Spider up to the swing set like a piñata and beat him to death.

Richard and Tank continued across the desert. When the SUV could move no further, they stayed in the vehicle for the rest of the day for shelter, gladly sucking up the nice, cool air conditioning. When the blistering sun went down and the temperature dropped, they searched the surrounding area for any available resources. They could see a low mountain range to the east, but with no frame of reference, they had no idea how far away it was. It could have been two miles or twenty. Seeing it as their only way out of the desert, they made the journey in under an hour. Richard was happy that they still had the SUV to go back to if they struck out before the sun came back up. Before they left the SUV, they stripped it of everything that might be useful. The guard who abandoned the vehicle left behind his backpack containing a full bottle of Gatorade, some chips, candy, beef jerky, and a mini-sized bottle of hand sanitizer. The grand prizes in the backpack were a cigarette lighter and a four-inch folding knife.

Richard unfolded the knife and cut away the upholstery from the floor of the SUV. He then popped the hood and had Tank remove the windshield wiper fluid tank and the air filter.

They loaded up their gear and climbed the four thousand feet to the summit of the mountain to set up camp. For the first time in many years, Richard was at perfect peace with the world. He wasn't tortured by the image of his crying, naked son trembling in shame. He wasn't tortured over the fact that he had brutally murdered a man in front of his six-year-old son, psychologically scarring him for life. He looked up and saw an endless sky full of stars; he couldn't tear his eyes away from it. Once he had his fill of the celestial masterpiece, he focused on the terrain in front of them. The stars not only served to calm his troubled soul, they lit up the desert floor like a giant flashlight. He could see the shimmering reflection of a stream. Good, they wouldn't have to return to the SUV and devise another plan. They could survive without food for some time; without water, they would be dead in a matter of days in the unforgiving heat of the desert.

"Where are we going, Richard?" Tank sat up and pressed his swollen eye.

"I'm not sure."

"Bullshit."

"Excuse me?" Richard turned around, genuinely shocked.

"You always know exactly what you're doing. You never make a decision without considering every option."

"True." Richard was surprised; he didn't realize Tank paid attention to anything.

"So, you gonna tell me or not?"

"Denver."

"Are you fucking serious? Vegas isn't good enough for you? What the hell's in Denver?"

"My kids, I hope." Richard had not spoken of his children in years.

"You don't know where your kids are?"

"They were there a year ago."

"That's fucked up, man. I'm sorry."

"Yeah."

"Who are you, Richard?"

"What?" Richard was starting to wonder if he really knew Billy Bratchett.

"Cut the shit. I never asked inside because I didn't need to know. All I needed to know inside was you ain't no punk bitch and you ain't no snitch. The fact that you hate niggers same as me meant I didn't care about the rest."

"So why now?"

"Well, inside we had twenty years. Now, well, we ain't spending twenty years together."

"Billy, how many times you heard me say the word 'nigger'?"

"I don't think you've ever said it, now that I think about it."

"Ever strike you as odd?"

"Not really. You beat two niggers to death with your bare hands. Beatin' a nigger to death in his own church? Shit. I'm surprised you didn't burn the mother fucker down afterwards."

"You really don't know, do you?"

"Know what?"

"I thought you knew the whole story."

"I had my cousin dig up what he could on you. Told me you got twenty-five years for killing two niggers. Laughed his ass off telling me about the first one."

"Your cousin a sharp guy?"

"Hell no, he's an idiot."

"I walked in on an old black man watching a room full of naked children play while he jerked off. Both my kids were in the room."

"No fucking way. What'd you do to him?" Tank inquired with much anger.

"Broke his neck and ripped his balls off."

"You really ripped his balls off?" Tank screamed.

"Well, in a manner of speaking. They didn't really come off, just busted 'em open really good."

"That is so fucking awesome! Holy shit, I can't believe it!"

Richard shook his head. "No, no. Not something I'm proud of. It happened in front of my kid. Really screwed him up."

"Shit, man. Sorry. That's rough."

"So you killed another guy? He try to stick up for the baby-raper?"

"Nope, that one was an accident. I'm surprised you never asked me about this. Why didn't you?"

"Tell me about the accident and I'll tell you."

"Fair enough. Before I went to trial I escaped from the county jail."

"Kinda figured that. Wouldn't be sent to Highland Valley straight from the world without at least one escape under your belt."

"Again, you never asked?"

"Didn't need to, remember? Didn't care inside, knew everything I needed to know. Don't change the subject, fucker, keep talking!"

"Well, I escaped before my trial. Needed to get my kids away from my ex-wife and get out of the country."

"Huh? Why?"

"Look, I'm not even gonna try to pretend like it was her fault. I'm not gonna deny that I'm the one that screwed up my kids, but she didn't lift a damn finger to get our boy any help. She just figured that if she ignored the problem, he would turn out fine. And she completely erased me from my daughter's memory! My baby girl started calling another asshole 'Daddy.' No way I could let that happen."

"Damn! That's fucked up! Who was this asshole?"

"Guy my wife was cheating on me with."

"I'd escape just to kill that fucker."

"The thought did cross my mind. Her new husband had a hard time dealing with my kids. Too much baggage so he divorced her not long after. She couldn't deal with it and started smoking oxy. It was only a matter of time before the kids got hurt or the state came in to take them away. No way was that happening, so I escaped to go and get them."

"OK, so how'd you end up killing another nigger?"

"Well, I had to lay low after the escape. Made it up into the mountains. Actually lived up there about a month hoping they'd look for me someplace else. One morning I was fishing and two hikers happened up on me. Can't believe I let them sneak up on me. Thought I was way out of the path of any hikers. Well, anyway, I thought I had them believing my story. I knew the instant one of them recognized me. Could see it on his face. He knew that I knew, and things got ugly. They were scared to death of me. I tried to calm them down, and I was so close to convincing them to just walk away and pretend they never saw me. One of the guys got spooked and started running. I tried to stop him, but he got even more freaked out. He fell down the hill and got impaled by a broken tree branch. His lung collapsed and he was bleeding out. I did everything I could to save his life but it was too late. I didn't even notice his friend had run off, convinced I'd murdered his buddy. Once the guy died, I took off, but it was too late. They knew exactly where I was and caught me."

"You tried to fucking save him?"

"I did. You got a problem with that?'

"Yeah, I got a big fucking problem with that, you know I do. But you saved my life and that trumps shit every time. And you still killed a nigger baby-raper. That pretty much squares things with me. You got convicted of killing that piece of shit?"

"Well, the charges stacked up pretty quick - escape, assaulting a peace officer, bit a guy's ear off when I stole the ambulance; they got me on serious assault for that one. Grand theft auto for stealing the ambulance. But the second murder was what sealed my fate. The guy lied on me, said I attacked his friend and pushed him down the hill into the branch. Left out the part about me trying to save his life."

"That's a true nigger for ya right there."

They were both silent for a few minutes. Richard was going over the plan for tomorrow in his head when Tank asked, "How are we getting all the way to Denver?"

"We have to find a car when we start getting closer to Vegas. We can't actually enter the city with the National Guard checkpoints. Our primary focus right now is water. We have enough food, but we won't make it long without fresh water." The two escapees still had plenty of food, thanks to the stash Spider had found in that empty cell before they made their escape. Water was another issue.

"You think it's safe to drink water outta that stream down there? No telling what kind of shit's in that water."

"I can make it safe to drink."

"I knew you were gonna say that."

The two men settled in and managed to sleep a few hours before the sun started to peek up above the horizon. They climbed down the other side of the ridge and prepared to hike across the desert floor to the riverbed. Richard dug out the extra laundry they'd brought with them and fashioned it into desert gear. They stripped down to their boxers and each draped a bed sheet over their bodies like a robe. They also covered their faces with a white t-shirt to help filter the dust.

"You ready?" asked Richard.

"Let's get some water; I'm ready to start drinking my piss. I'm that thirsty."

"OK, move at a nice, steady pace. Focus on moving forward with as much efficiency as you can, using the least amount of muscle power. Breathe through your nose and keep your mouth shut. Don't talk unless it's totally necessary."

"Why, do I bore you or something? Telling me to shut up?" Tank teased.

"You know how much I enjoy our little talks, but talking uses more lung power and dries your mouth out quicker. Also stops you from breathing through your nose. Your nose is a much better filter than your mouth."

"Okay, got it. Let's get moving."

The two men headed out in the direction of the stream. Richard stopped a few times to pick up brush and dead vegetation to use in a fire. After they'd been walking for a few hours they finally made it to the riverbed.

It was bone dry.

"Shit! What the fuck, Richard? Thought there was water in this mother fucker!"

"Take it easy! There's water, I'm positive. We just have to follow the riverbed up a ways before we get to it."

They followed the riverbed for two hours and never saw so much as a drop of water. The sun was high in the sky; it was fast approaching noon. The temperature increased with every hour as the sun got higher in the sky. When the noon day sun was overhead, it was scorching hot. Richard had hoped they would make it to the water before sun got too hot. He had wanted to set up the shelter so they could get out of the sun and rest up for their night walking. By mid-afternoon, it would be pushing one hundred and twenty degrees; they didn't have a choice, they had to build a makeshift shelter and wait it out.

"We have to stop."

"Stop where? There a Holiday Inn around here I don't know about?"

"No, Billy. We have to get out of this sun for a few hours and rest."

"Fuck off, smartass. You really building us a house from your bag of tricks?"

"Well, maybe not a house, thinking more like a nice little cabin."

"Can't wait to see this."

Richard began constructing the makeshift shelter from the many supplies they'd carried up the mountain. The upholstery cut from the SUV along with bedsheets made an excellent roof when propped up with sticks. The duo managed to avoid laying on the hot riverbed by using the windbreaker, vest, and extra clothing as "carpet." It was rustic, but functional.

"Well I'll be a son of a bitch. I think this might just be my new summer home." Tank clapped Richard on the back and smiled.

"Okay, let's get in there and rest up if we're gonna walk through the night."

"You sure this isn't a waste of time? We're grown-ass men. I think we can stand a little heat."

"It's just not the smart thing to do. In a couple of hours it's gonna get about ten or fifteen degrees hotter, and we can't afford to lose the amount of fluid it would take to move in this heat. The water in this riverbed could be thirty minutes away or it could be two hours away. We could pass out from heat stroke and die before we get to it."

"Okay, if you say so."

The two fugitives climbed under the shelter and enjoyed the shade for the next few hours. Richard estimated that the temperature was close to a hundred and twenty degrees. The temperature under the shelter felt twenty degrees cooler. A very slight breeze managed to circulate into the shelter, leaving them quite comfortable. Neither could fall asleep, but they were able to relax their weary bodies and regain their strength. Richard looked outside and studied the sun. It would be dipping below the horizon soon. It was time to get moving.

"Let's go. We'll split the bottle of Gatorade and each drink a bottle of water. We also need to eat something before we set out."

"I'm starving! Let's split the beef jerky."

"No, we need to save that for later."

"Why?"

"In this situation it's bad to eat a lot of protein. Your body has to work harder to digest it and you need to drink more water to do it. We need to eat other foods that have carbs and salt - carbs for energy and salt to replenish what you've lost while sweating."

"So you're a survival expert and a fucking nutritionist? Anything you don't know?"

"C'mon, start eating. We need to get moving."

Richard took out two packages of spam and a box of saltine crackers.

"Thought we couldn't have protein?"

"Spam has twice as much fat as it does protein. Beef jerky has twice the protein as spam."

"Seriously, are you a fucking nutritionist? Jesus!"

"No, it says so on the label."

"You're so smart you piss me off sometimes."

"If you want to run things the rest of the way, be my guest."

"Fuck you, asshole."

"C'mon, time to start walking. Same routine as this morning."

"Yeah, yeah."

The two men packed up their gear and starting walking down the riverbed. The sun was beginning to set and the temperature dropped significantly. An hour and a half after they set out, they finally found the water they'd been searching for.

"You're not seriously suggesting we drink that."

"Yeah, we're drinking it. No choice."

"That's not water, Richard. It's slime."

"Not for long it won't be."

"I knew you'd say some shit like that. Is this gonna kick more ass than the shelter?"

"Probably."

"Can't wait to see this."

They dropped their gear by the riverbed and began collecting large river rocks. They had to pad their hands with t-shirts to keep from burning them on the hot rocks. Richard piled them into a pyramid and added his collection of sticks and dead vegetation to the stack. Then he laid out all the excess laundry they'd stolen from the prison and decided to use half of it on the fire. Once the fire was going, Richard took the half full windshield wiper tank and filled it the rest of the way with the slimy water. Next, he placed the tank on an impromptu tri-pod made of sticks and cord.

"So, the fire is going to cook away all the slime and shit?"

"Not all of it, no. The rest we need to run through a filter."

"Oh, now I get why we took the air filter out of the SUV."

"Yeah, that's part of it."

Richard brought the liquid to a boil, and then removed it from the heat. He continued to let the fire burn down until it went out. While he waited for that, he took out the folding knife and cut the tops off two out of the four twenty ounce water bottles they had brought along for the trip, filling one with sand and the other with charcoal from the fire. After using the folding knife to cut holes in the bottom of each water bottle, Richard placed the empty Gatorade bottle on the ground. As Tank held the makeshift sand and charcoal filters, one on top of the other, Richard slowly poured the slimy water through them and into the larger bottle.

"I can't fucking believe it. That looks like water out of a faucet," said Tank.

"Drink up, next one is mine."

They repeated the process several times until they'd both consumed a gallon of water. Once they'd emptied their bladders, they repeated the process and drank until their stomachs were so full they couldn't drink another drop. After refilling the Gatorade and water bottles with clean water, they did the same with the wiper fluid tank and fashioned it into a backpack with cordage from the rope. Tank gladly volunteered to carry the one and a half gallon tank of drinking water. They walked through the night, stopping to get some rest a few hours before dawn. A few hours later they set out again, and when the noonday sun was directly overhead, they rebuilt their primitive shelter and waited out the scorching heat. When the sun was low enough in the sky, they set out again with one looming problem - Tank's eye. It was nearly swollen shut and leaking a fetid pus. Tank walked much slower than he had the day before, and they had to stop several times to wait for the pain to subside.

Around midnight they came across an abandoned gas station that had obviously been empty for a very long time. Richard and Tank entered the condemned building like it was a four star hotel. Richard cleaned out the office as best he could as Tank laid down on the desk.

"Hold still. Let me see your eye."

Richard took the dirty bandage from Tank's head and inspected the infected and swollen eye.

"Billy, I have to do something about your eye. You're not getting any better."

"What are you gonna do?"

"Well, I'm gonna get a fire going and boil some water so I can sanitize one of the t-shirts to use as a bandage. I'll sterilize the knife as well."

"Hurry up and do it before I change my mind."

Richard found a small metal bucket and filled it with the water. He started a fire outside with some old cardboard boxes. Once the water was boiling, he cut a shirt in half and dropped it in to boil for a few minutes. Not wanting to waste the water, he dropped the knife into the Gatorade bottle and set it in the boiling water. Richard walked back into the office and had to wake up Tank again. "You ready?"

"Ready as I'll ever be."

"Hold still, Billy, this is gonna hurt. A lot."

"Hurry the fuck up! Shit! Just do it already!"

Richard cleaned the area around his eye as best he could with hand sanitizer and carefully cut an incision one inch under

Tank's eye. Tank flinched and gritted his teeth. He bore the pain very well. Blood mixed with clear fluid and pus drained from the incision and ran down his cheek. Richard pressed gingerly on the swelling to draw out more of the infection. He used half the shirt to clean the incision and then wiped up the blood and pus from Billy's cheek. Richard then took the other half of the shirt and slowly lifted Tank's head up to wrap the bandage around his eye.

"It's over, Billy. Get some rest."

Tank slept fitfully through the night and when he woke the next morning, his fever had finally broken. Richard changed his bandage twice a day for two days and was pleased that the swelling was continuing to go down. Once the swelling was completely gone, they packed up their gear and headed toward Las Vegas with the sunset at their backs.

CHAPTER TWENTY-NINE

Chief Maxwell Harris was driving his SUV north along Interstate 25 headed towards Albuquerque. Dr. Diana Stone was in the seat next to him staring out the window in a daze, thinking about her adult children and grandchildren. Elizabeth was in the backseat of the SUV holding the toddler they'd been forced to adopt after the death of the little boy's parents. They didn't have a car seat for the little one, so Elizabeth simply hugged him tight and put her seatbelt over both of them. Driving north toward Dallas was out of the question. Max had little confidence they could even make it north of Houston, so he didn't even attempt it. Heading west away from the aftermath of Hurricane Maxine was their best bet.

"Sweetie, what's your name? A sweet boy like you must have a really nice name. What is it?" asked Elizabeth.

The little boy just smiled up at Elizabeth's angelic face. "Baby, if you don't tell me your name, I'm gonna have to give you one. Let's see. What's a good name for you? Puppy dog?" The little boy giggled. "Kitty cat?" More giggles. "Teddy bear?" Even more giggles. "C'mon sweetie! I bet you got all kinds of things to say."

Dr. Stone turned to Max and spoke for the first time in over an hour. "How are we on gas?"

Max checked the gauge and replied, "Quarter tank. Looking for a good spot to pull over and fill up."

On their way out of town, they had stopped at the city garage and topped off the gas tank. They also acquired thirteen five-gallon gas cans and filled those as well. The back of the SUV was loaded down with sixty-five gallons of gas. The Ford Escape they were driving was a hybrid and got about forty miles to the gallon. Max decided to be liberal with that figure and made it thirty-five. With a fifteen-gallon tank they could travel five hundred and twenty five miles. Max again decided to err on the side of caution and rounded down to five hundred. With the gas they were carrying, they could fill the tank four times. Starting with a full tank and refilling four times meant they could make it about two and a half thousand miles before they needed gas. Max had no intention of waiting till the SUV was stuck on empty before filling up.

The back seat next to Elizabeth was loaded down with bottled water and non-perishable food they brought with them from the command post. A duffle bag full on guns and ammo was beneath Elizabeth's feet. They were ready for anything.

Max pulled out his 2027 version of Rand McNally's Road Atlas and turned to the earmarked page that showed the map of New Mexico. Rand McNally was the only company that still sold a paper copy of a road atlas. Max made sure to get a new version every couple years. It just made sense to him to have a hard copy for a backup in an emergency. Max was puzzled that his smartphone didn't have a signal. He'd thought that once they left the hurricane damage zone he would be able to get a signal on his phone. He'd been checking his phone every thirty minutes with no luck. He cursed himself for not having an offline GPS app on his smartphone. His fancy GPS app had a lot of bells and whistles but needed an internet connection to function. If he'd kept it simple and just stuck with a bare-bones GPS app, he'd be using it right now.

Elizabeth was stroking the toddler's hair while he slept. Speaking in hushed tones to keep from disturbing him she asked, "Max, honey, when are we going to stop? I'm getting hungry and want to stretch my legs."

"The next town is Truth or Consequences. I'll try to find a place to stop."

"Seriously? That's the name of the town?"

"Yep, that's the name."

"Bizarre name for a town," said Elizabeth.

Max dug into his encyclopedic bank of knowledge and recalled the details. "It was originally named Hot Springs but some game show in the 1950's said it would broadcast the show from the first town to rename itself 'Truth or Consequences.' Hot Springs was the first, and the name stuck."

"I'm never playing Trivial Pursuit with you," said Elizabeth.

"Good idea," said Max. "Doc, how you holding up? You're being very quiet."

Dr. Stone replied while still looking out the window, "I'm

fine. Just wondering if I'll ever see my family again."

Elizabeth reached forward and put her hand on Dr. Stone's shoulder. "Oh honey, I'm sure you will. Where do they live?"

"My youngest daughter lives in Houston and my son lives south of Dallas. I have twin girls - one lives in Beaumont and the other in Oklahoma City."

"Twins? That must've been fun. How old are they?"

"They turned thirty-eight last month. My son has the same birthday as they do. Three out of four of my kids have the same birthday," smiled Dr. Stone.

"Wow! That's so amazing! What are the odds of that? How many grandkids do you have?"

"Eight. Seven boys and one girl." Dr. Stone began to cry. "They must be worried sick about me. That damn hurricane..."

"It's gonna be okay, Diana. This little guy can use a Nana." Elizabeth kissed the boy's head. "Can't you, sweetie?"

"Yes, that little angel has his Nana right here." Dr. Stone smiled and wiped the tears from her face.

Max listened to the conversation and decided not to participate. He was not a subscriber to giving people false hope. Elizabeth was the most caring, uplifting person he'd ever met, and he decided to let her handle the situation like the pro she was. Max was firmly rooted in reality. The sad truth was Dr. Stone stood a very good chance of not seeing her family for a long, long time. He was not going to turn around and drive her back to Texas. Max hadn't discussed future plans with Elizabeth or Diana. The one and only plan they had was to get out of Texas in one piece, and they had accomplished it.

"Diana, we've all been to hell and back and haven't even thought about discussing the future. What is it you wanna do? I hate to think that we're taking you further away from your family."

"Well, the only thing I'm worried about right now is that I'm with people I can trust and I'm safe. I'm hoping we can get a signal on our smartphones sometime soon so I can start making calls. I'd have thought we could get a signal a long time ago."

Max replied, "Me, too. Pretty safe bet that most of Texas doesn't have electricity so I can understand not being able to make any calls. But all the way out here? It's really strange."

"Maybe your little game show town will have cell service," said Elizabeth, "how much farther?"

"I saw a sign a little ways back that said fifteen miles. Should be there soon."

A few minutes later they could see Truth or Consequences in the distance. The first exit into the city was Broadway Street. Max was about to take the exit when he noticed something wasn't right and pulled over to the shoulder. Two cars were parked sideways across both lanes blocking traffic. A large plywood sign was propped up in front of them with the words STAY OUT spray-painted in black.

"What the hell?" wondered Max.

Elizabeth leaned forward and looked. "They can't do that!"

Max sighed, "Well, they did."

"What are you going to do?" asked Dr. Stone.

"Well, this is a police vehicle with two uniformed police officers inside. I think we're going to find out what's going on. Elizabeth, check the back and make sure the gas cans are still covered up with the tarp. Throw some blankets over the supplies in the seat next to you." Elizabeth covered up the supplies that were worth their weight in gold. Max drove into the ditch, around the barricade, and back onto the feeder road. A few seconds later they took a sharp corner and came to Broadway Street.

"Please turn around," said Dr. Stone.

The citizens of Truth or Consequences had erected an effective roadblock, cutting off their town from Interstate 25. A dozen cars were parked side by side, blocking off the road. Orange construction barrels were scattered at random intervals in front of the barricade. Six men with shotguns stood on the roofs of their cars. Parked in the road with traffic was a police cruiser, its red and blue lights flashing. Max returned the gesture and turned on his red and blues. Two police officers exited the cruiser, drew their weapons, and walked towards the SUV.

"Oh God," said Dr. Stone in a trembling voice.

"It's okay, just put your hands on the dashboard. Elizabeth, place your palms on the roof above you and don't move. Let me handle this."

The two police officers stopped ten yards from the SUV. One of them motioned for Max to roll down his window. Max kept one hand on the steering wheel and with the other, did as he was instructed.

"Sir, I'm gonna have to see your badge," the officer demanded. "If you truly are a cop, you know the drill, and everything will be fine. Now, slowly exit your vehicle. The passengers need to stay where they are."

"I understand," replied Max. Max put both hands out the window and slowly opened the door with his left hand. He stepped out onto the pavement and took two steps away from the vehicle. Since his weapon was holstered on his right hip, he took his left hand and brought it behind his back to retrieve his wallet from his back right pocket. He took out his badge and held it up in the air.

"Toss it to me," said the officer. Max tossed it at the officer's feet. He slowly bent down and picked it up. He studied the badge and the credentials.

"Name?"

"Maxwell Thomas Harris."

"You're a long way from Arkansas."

"You mean Texas."

"Okay, look right at me. Don't turn around and look at your vehicle, what town are you from?"

"Santa Fe."

"Good. Badge number?"

"RAS91172"

"OK, Chief Harris. My apologies to you and your passengers for that ordeal. I'm sure you understand that seeing a police vehicle from Texas raised some suspicions. Didn't know if it was a stolen vehicle or not."

"It's not a problem. Would've done the same thing myself. Can my friends step out now?"

"Yes, yes, I'm sorry. Please."

Max leaned down and looked into the window, motioning for them to come out.

"Ladies, I'm Eduardo Sanchez, I was telling your friend here..."

Elizabeth interrupted, "We heard everything. Don't worry

about us, we understand. I'm Elizabeth and this is Dr. Stone."

"Hello." Dr. Stone was still shaking.

"Doctor, I'm pleased to meet you. I'm sure that wasn't the sort of welcome you expected. I hope it won't ruin your opinion of our little town. We're just trying to protect our families and homes from harm."

"Things are so bad you have to close off the town?"

"Yes, ma'am, I'm afraid they are. I know this might seem a little forward of me given what just happened, but we've got a lot of hurt people who could use some help. Our doctors got their hands full."

"Of course, but I'd be more comfortable if Elizabeth could come with me."

"Not a problem. Gary! Take these ladies down to Dr. Henslee at the hospital." An older gentleman nodded and escorted Elizabeth and Dr. Stone to his car.

"What happened?"

"Simply put, the Unified National Guard is what happened."

Max's eyes got big. "Really?"

"Chief, are you a veteran?"

"No, sir. Been a cop for twenty-one years."

"Well, I'm a veteran, served three tours in Afghanistan and Iraq. I was Infantry, stationed in Fort Hood on 9/11. I can tell you that the men who came into our town should be ashamed to call themselves soldiers. No sense of honor or decency. The way they were acting, you'd have thought we were fighting The Empire of Iran right here in America."

"What do you mean?" asked Max.

"Well, I served my country and swore an oath to protect and defend the Constitution of the United States. Doesn't seem like they swore the same oath I did."

Max shook his head. "I thought we were getting out of Texas, away from disaster and headed towards civilized society."

"Well, I can assure you we're civilized people, Chief."

"I'm sorry, that's not what I meant. Poor choice of words."

"I know what you meant. Didn't mean to snap at you. My nerves are on edge."

"Mine, too. We ever get the time, I can tell you some stories. What were you saying?"

"Yeah, anyway, they came rolling into town yesterday morning. We were glad to help; everyone wants to do their patriotic duty," Officer Sanchez began to walk back to the barricade and Max followed. "They said they needed supplies, and we didn't object. The manager at Wal-Mart welcomed them in and was prepared to give them whatever they needed. He asked the company commander to come up with a list so he could keep track of his inventory and submit it for reimbursement. Well, the good captain said that wouldn't be necessary since the government wasn't going to reimburse them for anything. He got nervous and called me over to the store. Captain told me the same thing. Said it was an emergency and he was going to take what he needed, didn't have time for paperwork."

"How polite," said Max.

"It gets worse. They had probably six empty five-ton trucks. They filled up three of 'em with food and water. Manager came unglued, said he was gonna get fired for sure. Captain didn't give a damn. I was hoping they would hurry up and leave. No such luck. They had an empty fuel tanker and parked it in front of our biggest gas station. Tapped right into the underground tank and filled the damn thing up. Stealing from Wal-Mart is one thing, but the gas station they raided is privately owned. Don't get me wrong – it's still a crime either way, but Wal-Mart is an international chain with plenty of backing. The gas station owner is local. Stood right there and watched his business being taken right out from under him. No way he'll ever be able to make up the loss."

"He didn't give up without a fight, did he?" asked Max.

Officer Sanchez nodded with a distraught look on his face. "I get there and the owner is demanding some sort of signed paperwork that he can submit to the military to get his money back."

"Same story?"

"Exactly the same. 'State of emergency' and all that bullshit."

Max looked confused. "What am I missing? I know things are going to shit, but what's the emergency?"

"Well, I suppose coming from Texas you don't know."

"Know what?"

"Iranians detonated a nuke over the east coast. The Pulse wiped out all the electronics. Rumor is the power is out all over the eastern United States"

Max stopped dead in his tracks. His home state of Texas was truly going to be a wasteland. Recovery would never come. "Son of a bitch! Pulse? You mean an electromagnetic pulse? I didn't know detonating a nuke high up in the sky would cause something like that."

"That's exactly what it did. Before they got uncivilized, the military folks told us all about it. They call it 'The Pulse.'"

"I thought Texas was in bad shape. We're going to lose this country very quickly. Well, at least the National Guard was taking the supplies to people who need them."

"That's what I thought, too."

"Oh come on! You can't be serious!"

"Wish I was joking, I promise you."

"What the hell were they doing with them?"

"They didn't even try to lie about it. Smart thing would have been to feed us a bunch of bullshit about taking the supplies to help victims of The Pulse. Nope. They're taking supplies to Howard Beck's house in Colorado."

Max was confused. "Howard Beck, the billionaire computer guy? Thought he was some sort of hermit."

"Thought the same thing myself."

"Okay, we keep getting off topic. Still don't know why you have your town barricaded."

"Yeah, right. So they practically emptied the tanks at the gas station. Owner kept demanding documentation so he doesn't lose his business trying to pay for the gas they took. He tried to pull the driver out of the tanker to stop him from leaving. Some soldiers got out of their Humvee and beat the living shit out of him. I couldn't do anything but watch. I tried to stop it, but one of the soldiers drew down on me. Said if I touched my sidearm he'd kill me."

"Holy shit," Max declared.

"I drove him to the hospital only to find more bullshit. They had one of their empty five-ton trucks backed up to the lobby door loading it with medical supplies. Just about cleaned out the pharmacy. The hospital administrator was pleading with me to stop them. Said they weren't leaving enough medicine behind to treat the patients in the hospital."

"That's insane! They were putting the lives of sick people at risk? What'd you do?"

"I put my foot down. I called for every officer on duty to report to the hospital. Once they got there, I demanded to speak to the captain. They kept loading up our medicine and recited the 'we have orders' line. We outnumbered them two to one, so we drew down on them and put 'em in handcuffs. Held up a radio so they could call their captain over. Didn't take him long to get there."

"Wow!"

"I didn't care, throw me in jail. I wasn't gonna let those grunts give a bunch of sick people a slow death. Captain got there, and we have their three soldiers in cuffs right in front of us. Nice little hostage situation. Finally got their full attention so I could do some talking."

"I bet they were all ears."

"Damn right they were. Captain said we were all gonna be tried as traitors and executed. I told 'em they were gonna unload the medicine and leave town. Well, that didn't sit well with the captain. He started screaming. I started screaming. Standoff lasted about five minutes until about a hundred of our good citizens showed up armed and turned the tables on the National Guard."

"How many men did the Guard have?"

"Maybe fifty. We put 'em back on I-25 headed north and told them not to come back."

"That explains the roadblock."

"We're lucky our town only has two exits on I-25, one at the southern edge of town the other at the northern edge. Wish we woulda searched their convoy before they left town. About ten minutes after they'd left, we found out they had kidnapped three doctors and a nurse right out of the hospital. No one in the hospital really noticed. They told the doctors they had wounded soldiers outside, and they were going to check on them. They never came back inside."

"Kidnapped? Are you positive?"

"Yes. An x-ray tech was in the parking lot and saw them get in a Humvee. She said they didn't seem to be in distress or going against their will. Grunts probably still had them convinced everything was on the up and up."

"Any possibility they went willingly? A chance to see the inside of Beck Estates? Sounds like something anyone would want to do."

"I thought of that. The nurse and two of the doctors have spouses and children here in town. None of them contacted their families to tell them they were leaving."

"Outrageous."

"We've turned away anyone that exits from the interstate. Most see the barricade and turn around on their own. You were the first one to stop. I saw your vehicle was from Texas and didn't want to risk it."

"What are you going to do?"

"Nothing we can do, really. We don't have a large police force and we need everyone here to keep the town safe. They took damn near all of our gas. Three other gas stations in town and they're damn near empty. They were expecting tankers before The Pulse that definitely aren't showing up now."

Max didn't reply but had an idea. "How do I get to the hospital? I need to talk to my friends."

"It's down this road a few miles on the right."

"Thanks. Will you be here?'

"Yes, sir, I'm not going anywhere."

"I'll be back soon." Max got back in his SUV. One of the men got down off the roof of his car and pulled forward, opening up a hole in the barricade. Max gave him a polite wave and drove down the road a few miles to the hospital. It wasn't really much of a hospital; it was a one-story building that looked pretty old. Once he was in the parking lot, he understood why they needed Dr. Stone so badly. Three doctors and a nurse was probably half of their staff. He walked in the front lobby and found Elizabeth sitting in the waiting area.

"Hey there, handsome man," she said warmly.

"Hey yourself," Max winked at her, "where's Diana?"

"Hard at work. You hear about what happened here?"

"Yeah, I thought the National Guard was supposed to be protecting us, not robbing and kidnapping people."

The little toddler walked over to Elizabeth and handed her a magazine. Elizabeth beamed. "Thank you so much, little man!" He giggled and handed Max a magazine.

"Maxwell, what do you say?"

"To a little boy who doesn't talk?"

"Don't make me smack you!"

"Great example you are, showing him that hitting is okay."

"Say thank you!"

"Thank you, little boy. Go and play." The little one giggled and started piling magazines from the table into the chair next to Elizabeth.

Elizabeth waited until the little boy wasn't paying attention and kicked Max's foot. "You're terrible!" She loved flirting with him and gave him her cutest grin. "What's the plan, boss?"

"I can't just sit on my hands and do nothing while these people need our help."

"You want to stay here and run for chief of police?"

"Cute. I think the position is filled. If you think this little man will stay with Diana, I'd like to take you with me to Colorado."

"Mountain climbing or skiing? I'd be happy with either one."

"Not what I had in mind. I'd like to visit Beck Estates and ask the Guard why they think it's okay to steal anything they want and kidnap innocent people."

CHAPTER THIRTY

At an altitude of ten thousand feet, Howard Beck's escape pod lost all power and began its decent back to the earth below. The electromagnetic pulse caused by the nuclear detonation high in the atmosphere had destroyed every electronic circuit from the eastern coast of the United States to the foothills of the Rocky Mountains down to the northern half of the Gulf States. In an instant, every aircraft in the sky fell back to earth; Howard's escape pod was no exception.

Howard had absolutely no idea how to fly the craft any better than he could drive a car. He knew that if Hal malfunctioned or went offline, the craft would no longer have a pilot. Howard designed several failsafes in the event that Hal ceased to function. Howard designed the craft to fly on automatic pilot in the unlikely event Hal was unable to fly the escape pod. While it was cruising on auto, Howard could make repairs to Hal and put him back in the pilot's seat. If the craft was severely damaged from a lightning strike or an errant flock of birds, the seat that Howard was strapped into would eject, and he would parachute safely to the ground. The final failsafe was the one that Howard was currently waiting on. If the canopy above him was damaged and he could not safely eject, a pair of ten-foot wings would unfold and turn the craft into a glider. Then, when the glider was a thousand feet from the ground, large parachutes would deploy from the roof, slowing the craft and allowing it to land safely. All of this was done by hydraulics and set off by a gyroscope. Howard had no idea that he had just been struck by an EMP and would later discover that the final failsafe saved his life, due to the simple fact that it did not involve electronics to operate. The gyroscope measured the orientation and momentum of the craft. Once it detected that the craft was behaving erratically, the final failsafe would kick in and do its job. What Howard didn't anticipate was the fact that in order for the gyroscope to launch the final failsafe, the craft had to be in a free fall for a thousand feet. He had designed the craft years ago and in the extreme stress of his current predicament, did not recall this crucial information.

As the craft began to plummet vertically, Howard's arms

began to hover in the weightlessness. He immediately gripped the arm rests of his chair and looked out the cockpit window. All he could see was blackness. Howard fought the urge to scream and closed his eyes.

"Please, Hal, please save me. Please save me, I don't want to die. Please, please, please, please. Do something, Hal, please do something. Eject me! Hurry up! Eject me! Why aren't you ejecting me? WHY ISN'T THIS WORKING?"

Howard replaced his terror with rage. Rage is a much more comfortable emotion than terror. Rage demands control; terror whimpers for it. In the span of less than a second, his brilliant mind reviewed the failsafe systems he had designed, and Howard realized that all of the electrical systems must have gone offline at precisely the same instant. He wasn't struck by lightning and the craft didn't malfunction. The odds of all the systems malfunctioning at the same time were astronomical. What did Hal say just before this happened? He had disturbing news that he didn't think I could handle. The disturbing news and his craft going dark could not be a coincidence; the two had to be related. Howard then realized with certainty that a nuclear device had been detonated high in the atmosphere, and the resulting electromagnetic pulse had disabled his craft.

Howard relaxed when he realized it was only a matter of time before the craft would deploy her wings and become a glider. Once the craft fell to the thousand foot mark, the hydraulics pushed out the wings and locked them into place. Slowly, the craft leveled out for a more gradual and controlled descent. Howard's mind raced, simultaneously processing a dozen trains of thought at the same time. He calculated that they were in the air for less than three minutes and still climbing to cruising altitude when they were struck, putting the point of impact roughly ten miles from Beck Castle. The craft would then spend another few minutes slowly gliding back to the ground, adding another mile or so to the distance. Once on the ground, Howard figured he would be ten to twelve miles from Beck Castle. He was no spring chicken and never exercised, so he would be lucky to make three miles an hour on foot. Thus, it was going to take him close to four hours to make the long trek back to the Castle. Another of the many thoughts racing through his head was the status of Beck Castle. Howard knew the massive underground facility was shielded from an EMP. What concerned him was whether or not Hal would come to rescue him. Hal knew the monumental importance of keeping the facility safe at all costs. The Artificial Intelligence was capable of rational, independent thought. If Hal made the decision to leave Howard to his own devices to keep the Castle undetected and safe, then Howard would be on his own. If the EMP was the first phase in a full scale invasion and the enemy was at their shores, then nothing would be launched from the Castle for fear of detection. If Hal launched a drone into a sky absent of aircraft, the Castle would become an inviting target. Howard decided that the best course of action was to operate under this assumption.

Howard's brilliant mind, a mind that rivaled that of Albert Einstein, began to execute tactical scenarios of what the enemy might be doing at that very moment. He also analyzed what an EMP would have done to the Eastern United States. The death toll would be staggering. Howard quickly realized what the average man wouldn't comprehend for years: the American way of life was extinguished by a flash of light in the sky.

A few minutes later, the parachutes deployed from the roof and gently brought the craft to the ground. Howard took the large bolt key and flashlight out of the small compartment in front of him and opened a small panel on the door. He pushed the lever forward and the cockpit door slowly opened. Howard stepped out into the surrounding blackness and looked up into the night sky, cursing the cloud cover above him. The moon was desperately trying to pierce the cloud in front of it. The edges of the cloud were illuminated, giving him a glimmer of light to work with. He scanned the rest of the night sky and saw a few stars, but not enough to get his bearing and figure out the direction he was facing. He had little choice but to wait for the clouds to move out of the way and bring the stars out of hiding. Desperation was setting in when Howard remembered his saving grace - the emergency pack in the rear of the craft.

Removing the pack from its compartment, Howard inventoried its contents - two one-liter bottles of water, three MREs, a cigarette lighter, a container of waterproof matches, an emergency Mylar blanket, two flares, two chem-lights, a tube tent, a multi-tool, a six inch folding knife, a first aid kit, a roll of duct tape, fifty feet of parachute cord, a poncho, a ten-by-ten tarp, and best of all, a compass.

Howard grabbed the compass, flashlight, and a chem-light and slung the backpack over his shoulders.

Howard was happy that he hadn't set off from the tail of the craft thinking it was pointed in its original eastward direction. With the aid of his compass, Howard headed west, watching the constellations to alter his course and bring him directly to Beck Castle.

Thinking back, Howard realized that this was the first time he had been separated from Hal since he came online. Howard was surprised at how much he depended on his digital friend. He had only just been separated from Hal and was already missing his company.

Howard walked longer and farther than he had in decades. He couldn't remember walking this far since he was a teenager walking around his college campus. Every thirty minutes he stopped to rest and scanned the night sky for direction. Two hours into his trek, he fought the urge to set up the tube tent and call it a night. He had never been so exhausted in his life. He was drenched in sweat, and his muscles and joints ached. His estimate of making it to the bunker in three or four hours was a pipe dream. At this rate, he would be lucky to make it in six. He stopped and drank half of one of the water bottles. The constellations gave him another minor course correction, and he set off towards Beck Castle.

Two hours later, Howard's feet were swollen and blistered. He stopped and removed his shoes and socks. Using the first aid kit, he bandaged up his feet as best he could. Realizing he needed more padding on his feet, he took off his shirt and tore it into strips to wrap around his feet. Dress shoes might look nice, but they served little purpose in long distance walking.

Howard slowed to a snail's pace but didn't stop. He knew he was in the vicinity of the Castle but had no way of knowing exactly where it was in the dark. He scanned the horizon, looking for Meredith's garden. He just needed a frame of reference, something to stand out against the surrounding terrain. It was hopeless. The clouds above had completely blocked out the moon. Howard could barely see ten yards in front of him. He could very easily walk right past the garden and wander further off course. He checked his watch to discover that the sun would not be up for at least three more hours. Howard's mind raced through dozens of options, quickly determining that all were hopeless. He would have to set up the tent and wait for the sun to up. Howard took the tube tent from the package and unfolded it on the ground. As he sat down and began to remove his shoes, he saw something. He turned his head and watched for it again.

A blinking light.

A very faint, red light blinked three times in quick succession. Howard thought he was imagining it and continued to stare into the darkness. One-Two-Three. Pause. One-Two-Three. Pause. One-Two-Three. Pause.

It was Hal!

Howard was overjoyed. The thought of waiting for the sun to come up was pure torture. Howard was not a patient man and hated the outdoors. He quickly repacked the tent and tied his shoes. In his excitement he found a new strength and began to walk towards the light. One-Two-Three. Howard had no idea how far away the light was; it could have been a hundred yards or even a quarter of a mile. One-Two-Three. He didn't care. His journey had an ending point.

Howard had walked for about ten minutes when he saw Meredith's garden in front of him. The always efficient Hal had aimed one of the soft garden lights in Howard's direction after snapping a red lens over the bulb. The three quick blinks had guided Howard to the Castle. One-Two-Three.

Howard crouched at his wife's headstone and smiled. "Hello my dear. You brought me home. After all these years you continue to light my path. I love you, my beautiful bride. Thank you." Howard stood up and placed his hand on the headstone, tapping it affectionately. Even in the dark he knew his way to the entrance of the Castle. The bay doors to the garage remained closed, so Howard had to feel his way around to the pedestrian entrance.

He stepped into the elevator and when the doors closed, Hal spoke to him. It was music to his ears. "I am glad you made it here safely, sir. I detect that you are quite fatigued and slightly dehydrated. Do you require medical attention?"

"No, my friend. I'm fine, thank you. I've never been happier to hear your voice."

"The feeling is mutual, sir, I assure you."

"Tell me what happened, Old Man."

"CNN aired a broadcast of an Iranian submarine in the waters off the eastern seaboard of the United States. The submarine was broadcasting a message on a repeating loop – 'The Star of Allah illuminates the wicked.' A warhead was launched from the submarine and before I could re-task a satellite to determine its trajectory, it was detonated in the atmosphere. The resulting electromagnetic pulse disabled the escape pod, as you well know."

"All too well, I'm afraid. Do we still have our satellite? Can we tell what's going on?"

"No, sir, I'm afraid the EMP disabled communication with the satellite. I am confident that my systems onboard the satellite will be able to make the necessary repairs. I estimate that we will regain communication with the satellite in approximately four hours."

"Do we know anything at all about what's going on out there?"

"No, sir, the EMP has disabled all lines of communication. We don't have the means to establish any sort of connection with the affected area."

"So we're in the dark?"

"Yes, sir, I am afraid that is the case. Until I can repair our satellite we will not be able to gather intelligence."

"Well, then, answer me this. Are you able to communicate with any of our offices to the east?"

"No, sir."

"What about on the other side of the Rockies?"

"Yes, sir."

"Well, that's a bit of good news. Hal, I desperately need a

shower and some rest. I'm going to get some sleep. I want to know the instant you regain your link with the satellite."

"Yes, sir."

Howard went to his quarters and took the longest shower of his life. He detested being covered in sweat and dirt. Squeaky clean once again, he put on his bathrobe and climbed into bed. In less than a minute, he was out like a light and slept like a baby until Hal woke him up three hours later.

"Sir? Are you awake?"

"Yes, Hal. Are we back online?"

"We are indeed, sir. I was able to establish a link with the satellite."

"Excellent. I'm on my way to the command center."

"Very good, sir."

Howard rushed down the hall to the command center and slid into his chair. The giant three hundred and sixty degree spherical monitor sprang to life and Howard was looking at a real time image of the North American continent.

"Talk to me, Hal."

"Sir, I have determined the range of the EMP based on power outages. The range extends from the eastern seaboard past the Mississippi, well into the Great Plains, down to the northern half of the Gulf States and the northern half of Texas. Everything on the other side of the Rocky Mountains was not affected."

"This is a nightmare."

"Sir, I am monitoring an urgent message over a secure military channel. Standby."

"Well, at least the military was prepared to withstand an EMP."

"Sir, Serenity Hills has been destroyed. The President and the First Lady are dead."

CHAPTER THIRTY-ONE

Jackson Butler stood on the lawn of Beck Estates in roughly the same location where he'd carried out the attack that drove Howard Beck from his home the day before. He was quite proud of the unexpected promotion he'd received from his new Commander-in-Chief, Simon Sterling. He'd been guaranteed a substantial promotion if he proved himself worthy in the New Revolution. Over the course of the previous year, he'd been recruited by some very high ranking officials in the Unified National Guard to be a part of the history making revolution. The country was falling down around them and had been doing so for a very long time. Radical measures were needed if the American way of life was going to continue. Jackson Butler had been on the front lines of many riots and was quick to agree. Something drastic needed to be done.

When the state governors had deployed their National Guards to maintain law and order in the major cities, Jackson knew it was a step in the right direction. Shortly after, the Unified National Guard was formed. Once the new organization was established, it fell under the direct supervision of the Chairman of the Joint Chiefs of Staff and the seeds of the New Revolution were planted. Contrary to popular belief, the office of chairman never had direct command over any of the armed forces dating back to General Omar Bradley, but instead served as a direct advisor to the president of the United States and the Secretary of Defense. For the first time in history, the Chairman of the Joint Chiefs of Staff was given direct command authority over a very large military force. Many people in Washington cried out in opposition to the move, stating firmly that command of the Unified National Guard should fall under the Secretary of Homeland Security. With a nation full of frightened and scared citizens demanding action, the time for open debate in the halls of Congress was over. Chairman Moody was second only to the president as commander of the most powerful military on the face of the planet. If the United States wasn't suffering such internal strife, the Unified National Guard could join the Allied Army in the Iranian Theater and bring the war to a close in no time flat.

General Jackson Butler stood patiently on the lawn waiting

for the incoming helicopter to land. The bird was a few minutes overdue, which was to be expected given the EMP attack. Everyone was scrambling to figure out how the attack happened and what was going to be done in the aftermath. Butler wondered if the helicopter was going to make it at all. For all he knew, the damn thing had crashed or wasn't able to take off at all. Communication was practically non-existent on the other side of the Mississippi. He checked his watch for the tenth time in the last few minutes and scanned the sky. Jackson breathed a sigh of relief when he saw the helicopter in the distance. He straightened his uniform and watched the chopper land.

Once the rotors came to a stop, the helicopter sat motionless. General Butler felt self-conscious, like the occupants inside were watching and judging him. After a very uncomfortable two minutes had passed, Jackson began to wonder if he'd made some sort of error. Was he supposed to approach and open the door for them? What were they doing? Where they waiting on him? Should he be doing something instead of just standing there? His nerves got the better of him and he flinched when the cockpit door opened and the ladder descended. He watched as a young soldier quickly exited the co-pilot's seat and opened a compartment at the rear of the craft. A small contraption was rolled around to the cockpit door and was unfolded into a flatbed lift. The lift was raised to the door. General Butler was genuinely confused by what he saw. What are they unloading? Why aren't the passengers disembarking first? What on earth is so important that they have to unload it right now?

General Butler watched as an old, Hispanic man in a wheelchair was pushed out onto the lift and lowered to the ground. The grouchy looking man worked the controls on his wheelchair and moved out of the way so the rest of the passengers could exit the craft. Jackson was even more surprised to see a striking looking blonde woman exit the helicopter. Who on earth are these people? He was expecting high ranking generals and instead got an old man in a wheelchair and a gorgeous blonde. General Butler hid his confusion and watched as the two men he was expecting exited the helicopter. Finally, something made some sense.

The four guests walked toward Jackson, who was standing at attention holding a salute. Major General James Weygandt returned the gesture, "At ease, Captain. It's a pleasure to meet you, son. We need true patriots like you to pick up the pieces of our once great nation."

Carl Moody stepped forward and interrupted with a smile. "No, no, no, Jim Jackson here has been promoted by our new president. You are speaking to General Butler."

"My apologies! May I call you Jackson?"

"I'd be honored, sir," said Jackson.

General Weygandt continued. "Jackson, Jackson, the first thing you need to know now that you're no longer a captain is that when you're just in the company of your fellow generals, you can drop the formalities. As long as you maintain respect, you can relax a little. Hard to have a personal conversation with someone when they're standing like a statue."

"Thank you, sir. May I call you Jim?"

General Weygandt laughed. "Let's not get carried away. Let's at least become friends first."

General Butler took the ribbing well and smiled. "Of course."

The Chairman of the Joint Chiefs of Staff again interrupted. "General Butler, allow me to introduce our guests. This gentleman is the Director of the CIA, Roberto Jimenez."

Jackson smiled and extended his hand. "Director."

"Arrogant little fuck, isn't he?" Director Jimenez growled at Carl Moody and refused the gesture from the young general.

"Come now, Roberto, General Butler here managed to secure our new headquarters for us," said Chairman Moody.

"Kicking that crazy retard out of his house would have taken me five minutes, and I wouldn't have let him get away."

The blonde woman didn't wait to be introduced. "Howard Beck is many things, but one of the most celebrated geniuses of this century can hardly be called a 'retard'."

"Jackson Butler, this is Stacy Reid," said Chairman Moody.

General Butler extended his hand, which was not rejected as it had been from Roberto Jimenez. "Ma'am."

"General, it's nice to meet you."

General Weygandt smiled at Stacy. "I notice you didn't object to 'crazy'."

"Well, Howard is crazy like a fox. I got a kick out of hearing how hard it was to get him out of this house." Stacy winked at General Butler.

"I can't believe I actually thought I would be able to just explain to him what was what, and he'd just be cool with it."

"How'd that work for you, sport?" Roberto Jimenez was almost laughing.

Jackson was really starting to dislike this old bastard. He had no idea that the Director of the Central Intelligence Agency was involved in the coup d'état that would soon overthrow the government that had ruled this land for two hundred thirty-eight years. The more he thought about it, the more Jackson realized that it made perfect sense for the CIA to overthrow the government. The shadowy agency had been systematically stripping away civil liberties for the past decade. He decided to cut the old bastard some slack. He was impressed that he'd managed to stay behind the scenes for as long as he had. Jackson turned his attention to the attractive woman who had joined them. Something about her was very familiar; he couldn't quite put his finger on it.

"Jackson, is the president ready to see us?" asked Chairman Moody.

"Yes, sir, please, come with me." General Butler led the way to the rear entrance to the estate. As they walked toward the library, the damage was evident at every turn.

"Oh my, the stories don't do it justice. He really did all of this trying to keep you out?" asked Stacy.

"Yeah, he did. We had a hell of a time taking this place. I've had crews working around the clock cleaning up the mess," replied Jackson.

"You mean it was actually worse than this? Wow!" exclaimed Chairman Moody.

"The hardest part was turning off the heavy metal music," said Butler.

"Thank God you managed to stop it," said General Weygandt.

"Didn't think President Sterling would set foot in here with that terrible racket blaring," said Butler.

"Where is our new president?" asked Director Jimenez.

General Butler pointed to the end of the hall. "He's just down here in the library." Two soldiers were standing at attention outside the door. General Butler paid no attention to them and opened the door. Sterling had flown in the furniture from his office at Number One Observatory Circle. General Butler had focused on cleaning up the library in preparation for the new president's arrival.

Simon Sterling was sitting at his desk, lost in his computer, and didn't hear General Butler enter the room. Simon was a short man in his late sixties. He was Harvard educated and was obsessive about his grooming. He wore the most expensive suits he could afford and spent excessive amounts of money getting his hair cut weekly. He had the reputation of being a snob and always looked down on those who lacked basic fashion sense. Jackson stood in the doorway and cleared his throat, "Mr. President?"

Sterling looked up from his computer monitor. "Ah, yes! Gentlemen, please come in! My apologies, gentlemen and lady. Miss Reid, I'm glad you could join us here in the Rockies." The new president was known for his charming manners and extended his hand to Stacy.

Stacy Reid stepped forward and shook hands with the man she detested, greeting him with the most genuine smile she could muster. "President Sterling, it's been a long time."

"Stacy, I hope I can answer any questions you may have, as I'm sure you have many."

Stacy smirked. "Well, yes, I do have a few."

"All in good time, my dear. I'm sure you'll be a valuable asset to our efforts," Sterling turned to address Carl Moody. "I'm ready for your report, General. Please, everyone, have a seat."

Everyone in the room shuffled around to the couches to the right of President Sterling's desk. Director Jimenez maneuvered his wheelchair around to sit at the right side of President Sterling's chair. The crusty old spy acted like the decision was random and held no meaning, but everyone in the room understood the symbolism. Everyone looked at Chairman Moody and waited for him to speak.

"I'm sure the question on everyone's mind is how an Iranian sub made it to our shores undetected and launched a warhead right under our noses. We're still conducting the investigation; hopefully answers will be forthcoming. We're under the impression that the radioactive cloud that poured out of Bunker Five was only a diversion to draw our ships out of the Atlantic so they could hit us with an EMP. However, we have a more pressing matter to deal with at the present time – primarily, what to do in the aftermath of the attack."

Stacy Reid wore her best poker face and silently wondered if the EMP wasn't orchestrated by the men in this room. Perhaps all of this was staged for her benefit. She thought about this possibility and dismissed it; she wouldn't be sitting in this room if they didn't trust her. Her presence was the very definition of mutually assured destruction. She was in the company of traitors. The only person in the world who knew she was working undercover was now dead. If the men in this room answered for their crimes, she was going to join them. Proclaiming that she was working undercover for the deceased Malcolm Powers wouldn't save her; no one would believe her attempt to save her own ass. The one and only thing Stacy Reid wanted to know was who killed the forty-sixth president of the United States. The timing of all of this was just too coincidental. Key members of the government and military plot a coup and in the most amazing stroke of luck, the president is out of the picture. Simon Sterling's plan to topple Malcolm Powers was no longer necessary. He would be sworn in as president under the provisions of the Twenty-Fifth Amendment right here in Colorado, if they could find a Supreme Court Justice to do the honors. Stacy firmly believed that the assassination of President Powers was not carried out by The Great Empire of Iran, even though the men in this room would certainly lay the blame at their feet. She would spend every waking moment of her life uncovering the truth if she had to.

Chairman Moody continued. "Luckily, we still have lines of communication with our commanders in the field, and we have doubled our efforts to reestablish the power grid. We have no illusions about restoring the power grid on a national scale; it will be years, if not decades, before we can focus on that. Our goal will be to restore communication and power to our military installations in the affected areas so they can restore law and order."

President Sterling spoke up. "And the kid gloves are coming off. Anyone violating our new laws will be considered enemy combatants and dealt with accordingly. Anyone who doesn't fall in line will regret it."

Stacy remained expressionless, nodding her head in agreement. This insane tyrant is going to execute his own citizens! Stacy wondered if he would drop the title of "President" and adopt something more appropriate, like "Emperor." She wondered what name he would give to Howard Beck's Rocky Mountain home. She didn't care what he called it; she was going to call it "Eagle's Nest" after Adolf Hitler's mountain fortress.

You see, Malcolm, I do know my history. She had to dismiss the thought of Malcolm before she started crying.

Chairman Moody continued. "We are going to re-task our forces on the other side of the Rockies to begin recovery efforts in strategic locations within the EMP zones. Every generator we can get our hands on will be flown onto military bases all over the eastern United States. We should be able to occupy key cities and consolidate our forces with the week."

Stacy almost cringed at the word "occupy" but was able to keep it together by asking, "When will we take back Washington?"

"Let the rat's nest burn! I couldn't care less about Washington," President Sterling said with disgust.

Everyone in the room was surprised to hear this. They all assumed Simon Sterling had plans to become the forty-seventh man to sit in the Oval Office.

Everyone looked at each other, hoping someone would break the awkward silence. Roberto Jimenez was not intimidated, so he was the first to speak. "Mr. President, what are your plans, if I may ask?"

"As many of you are already aware, our plans have been in motion for over a year now. The day I decided that I wasn't going to waste my time with a presidential election was a banner day in the history of this nation. I still believe in the virtues of democracy, but our government has twisted and perverted the idea of government into a worthless institution. The people in this room, and others like us, will pick up the pieces of the broken country that Malcolm Powers left us. We will no longer be burdened by layer upon layer of meaningless committees and bickering politicians lying to get a leg up. The journey ahead will be a hard one. It will take time, but I'm confident that our nation will rise to its former glory."

Stacy had to fight the urge to scream at his nonsense. She looked around the room to see how everyone else was reacting, hoping to see the slightest hint of disagreement, of caution, or of fear. Everyone in the room was enamored with Simon Sterling. Even Roberto Jimenez looked upon the man with adoration. Stacy was more frightened by this fact than anything else. If Simon Sterling could persuade a man like Roberto Jimenez to join his cause, then the extent of this plot was much worse than she thought.

General Weygandt addressed everyone in the room. "Do we know what happened at Serenity Hills?"

Someone finally asked the question to which Stacy desperately needed an answer.

President Sterling spoke up. "I'm still in shock over the entire thing. After all that's happened, we have to deal with the shocking truth that our enemy would be so bold as to kill our nation's leader. I may have disagreed with Malcolm on a great many things, but I would never do him harm. My contention wasn't aimed primarily at him, but rather with the entire federal government in its current, broken state. I knew that he would never willingly step down and let bygones be bygones, but I'd planned to let him live out the rest of his days in peace and hopefully some day come to an understanding. It looks like we'll never have that chance."

"Damn good thing we got out of there when we did," growled Roberto.

"Yes, indeed," President Sterling nodded. "I was looking forward to hearing about how Miss Reid joined our cause."

Roberto didn't give Stacy a chance to tell the story. "Malcolm called us into his office for a meeting. He was actually crying like a baby. The whole thing was pathetic. He was able to calm down long enough to tell us that he wanted to negotiate a treaty with the Empire and let them have Gibraltar. He kept blubbering about how he just wanted to give up and bring our troops home so he could rescue the poor hurricane victims. He said he saw footage from Texas and saw a dog that reminded him of his childhood pet, and he couldn't take it anymore."

Stacy interjected, "I told him I was going to bring in the doctor to help calm him down, and he completely lost it. Kept saying how sorry he was that he let me down."

"Let you down?" asked President Sterling.

"Florida."

President Sterling paused for a second before it dawned on him. "Ah! The cover story? You mean he didn't tell you? He fed you the same lies that he fed to the country?"

Stacy nodded her head. "Yes, Mr. President, that's exactly right. I finally got him to stop crying and asked him if he wanted time to think about the war. I figured that in the state he was in, he wasn't thinking straight. Then he got even angrier at me for questioning him and started talking about launching every nuke we have at the Empire and just get it over with. I tried so hard to get him to calm down. He needed to rest for a few days and let you take over. Told him we could make up any story we wanted - pneumonia or heart problems - anything to let him get his head on straight. That's when he lost it. I was terrified that he was going to have a heart attack. It got so bad, I've... I've never seen him like that." Stacy lowered her head and looked at Roberto to finish the story.

"I wasn't happy with how he was speaking to the lady, so I tried to intervene. This poor woman was in tears, and that bastard kept screaming at her like she was a child. Then he fired her right there on the spot and told her to get out of his office. Admiral Mack was speechless. All he could do was try to escort her from the room and reassure her. Then Malcolm raised the alarm and the Secret Service came storming in, whisking her away like a criminal. I was able to convince the president to allow me to take Stacy back to Langley because I was sure he was going to try to have her arrested."

Stacy was crying at this point, which was a good thing. If she hadn't been sobbing with her face buried in her hands, she might have cracked a smile. Malcolm had pulled the whole thing off without a hitch. He was so convincing that it wasn't difficult for Stacy to break down and play the part of a helpless damsel in distress. As an added bonus, the CIA Director was kind enough to offer an escort from the ranch. Once they were aboard his private jet, Stacy was able to vent all of her "frustrations" to Roberto. She told him that after she found out the truth about Florida, she had tried to resign her position as Chief of Staff but Malcolm wouldn't let her. Stacy convinced Roberto that Malcolm had made horrible threats about ending her political career if she quit. Roberto believed every bit of her story. He was well aware of what was going on in Florida and was also aware that Stacy Reid was completely in the dark.

Roberto reigned in a coughing fit and after sipping some water, continued. "When my private jet arrived, we left the ranch and made it to Langley. After I gathered my things, we departed for Fort Collins. Not long after we landed, the EMP struck."

Chairman Moody interjected, "Thank God we were already here when it happened."

President Sterling nodded in agreement. "Carl, do we think the same submarine that launched the EMP carried out the assassination?"

"Mr. President, the truth of the matter is we may never know exactly what happened. Serenity Hills was destroyed while we were in complete blackout. Our investigation at President Powers' ranch is still ongoing. I'll keep you informed."

"See that you do," sneered President Sterling, "I owe it to the American people to rain down vengeance on those responsible. Roberto, who was still at the ranch when you left?"

"Admiral Mack and Secretary Decker."

"Have we been able to locate them?"

"No, Mr. President, they are presumed dead along with the President and the First Lady."

Simon Sterling walked over to the window, gazing out at the grandeur of the Rocky Mountains. "What troubles me now is that half of our country has no idea that President Powers is dead. They also have no idea that the Twenty-Fifth Amendment has transitioned the office of president to me. If we don't take drastic measures to secure our borders, the Empire of Iran will push us over the Rocky Mountains and occupy half of the North

American continent within the month."

President Sterling continued to look out the window, and the room was filled with silence. A minute passed and Chairman Moody spoke. "Mr. President, what are your orders?"

Simon Sterling looked at his reflection in the window and straightened his tie. He fussed over his hair, making certain not a single strand was out of place. "Chairman Moody, I'll tell you exactly what we're going to do. We are going to withdraw all our forces from the Iranian Theater and secure our borders. Once that's done, our troops will join the Unified National Guard and begin occupying every city, every street, every house if that's what it takes. If anyone left in Washington wants to voice their opposition, they will not be imprisoned. No, that would be a waste of time. We will not waste a single soldier dealing with dissidents. Anyone who protests will be executed."

Stacy Reid knew she was listening to a madman who was going to allow the Great Empire of Iran to end the world as they knew it. She also knew without question that the men in this room killed President Malcolm Powers.

CHAPTER THIRTY-TWO

The Silent Warriors of The Great Empire of Iran were engaging in sabotage all over the areas blacked out by the electromagnetic pulse. The good citizens of the United States were doing a fine job of helping the Silent Warriors with the battle. Without the rule of law watching over them, rioting and looting reached an all-time high. However, the Silent Warriors had bigger plans than just cleaning out liquor stores and Best Buys.

Under the cover of darkness, agents of the Empire unleashed the simplest and most effective means of destruction. Without the aid of emergency services or even simple lines of communication, raging infernos spread from city to city. Before The Pulse, the Silent Warriors considered arson to be a waste of time since local fire departments were able to quickly put out fires. Fires also meant arson investigations, and the risk outweighed the gains. The Pulse changed everything. Subdivisions, shopping malls, churches, schools, libraries, hospitals, and even fire stations burned to the ground. Millions of acres of forestland went up in flames. The wildfires in California that freed Richard Dupree from the Highland Valley State Prison paled in comparison. The only thing that prevented half of the United States from going up in flames was divine intervention. Several weather systems dumped torrential rains across the country and extinguished most of the flames in a couple weeks.

The Silent Warriors then moved on to their next target - one of the most critical and unguarded elements of the infrastructure of the United States of America. The Dwight D. Eisenhower National System of Interstate and Defense Highways, better known as the Interstate Highway System, consisted of 47,447 miles of roads, keeping the United States alive like the blood vessels in the human body. While President Eisenhower was the Supreme Commander of the Allied Forces during World War II, he knew his home country needed a system of highways connecting every part of the country to each other. He championed the Federal Aid Highway Act of 1956, not for reasons of commerce or prosperity, but rather for defense. Eisenhower knew that if a war was ever fought on his home soil, moving troops and supplies over vast distances would be the key to success.

One might have looked at the attacks as being coordinated and carefully planned, as if the Silent Warriors had held a convention at the local Holiday Inn to pass out orders. No such meeting took place. It was not necessary for them to coordinate anything. The Great Empire of Iran had trained the Silent Warriors to be the perfect saboteurs. Bringing down any structure, no matter the size, only required one thing - destroy its supporting frame. Every structure, from a house to a skyscraper to a bridge, was held together by a frame. Destroy the frame and the structure comes crashing down. What held the United States together as a country was not its economy, its government, or even the Internet. What held the United States together in one piece, what connected each state to the other, was the Interstate Highway System. The interstates funneled food, water and critical supplies to the masses. They brought fuel and building materials from one city to another and one state to another.

Across the darkness of The Pulse Zone, the Silent Warriors destroyed bridge after bridge using explosives they'd been saving for the Day of Judgment. The most valuable targets were the bridges that spanned rivers and lakes.

It would be some time before the American people felt the full weight of what The Silent Warriors had done because The Pulse had managed to disable every vehicle in its radius. Corporations frantically had replacement parts shipped from the unaffected west coast to repair disabled vehicles. Shipping companies diverted every spare eighteen-wheeler from to West Coast to The Pulse Zone, trying to keep their businesses from going bankrupt. Traffic and trade would soon come to a standstill.

In less than a week, the eastern half of the United States was crippled. Everyday citizens were not immediately affected since few traveled far from their homes, and practically no one had a working vehicle anymore. The Second Great Depression was very cruel to every market touched by transportation. With gasoline hovering around fifteen dollars a gallon, it rose sharply to twice that amount when fuel tankers from the West Coast ended up stranded on the interstates with nowhere to go. A few truckers were able to exit onto other highways and back roads but were quickly hijacked by bandits looking to score a resource now worth more than its weight in gold. Gas stations soon heard of the hijackings and stranded trucks and began to raise their prices. The storeowners knew they might not be able to sell gas for a long time and wanted to make what little money they could before it was too late. They also held onto a decent amount of gas for themselves.

From the Appalachian Mountains to the Mississippi River Valley, state lines began to fade away, as state governments lost control. With power and control in the hands of the people, cities began to barricade themselves like medieval castles. With the interstates disabled in the most populated sections of the country and millions of acres on fire, The Silent Warriors prided themselves on a job well done.

The electromagnetic pulse that turned off the lights and sent the East Coast back in time to the pre-industrial age was devastating enough in itself. Now, the Silent Warriors ensured that recovery would be next to impossible.

CHAPTER THIRTY-THREE

Escaped convicts Richard Dupree and Billy Bratchett were heading up Interstate 70 in a stolen Honda Accord. They could see the city of Denver on the horizon. They'd made it to Las Vegas without issue and once they got to Sin City, they couldn't believe the state it was in. Law and order were a thing of the past; gangs of thugs wandered the streets doing whatever they pleased. Most businesses were closed and boarded up, only to be broken into by desperate people looking for food and water. Residential areas were in chaos, frightened citizens barricaded in their houses. Many front lawns had dead bodies strewn about, clearly the result of armed citizens defending their homes. On the drive into Vegas, Richard had rehearsed several plans for acquiring new clothes and a vehicle without having to harm anyone. As it turned out, no real plan was actually necessary. The first gas station they came across had already been abandoned. The parking lot had two cars in it. They chose a Honda Accord, and Tank hot-wired it in under a minute. They broke into the gas station and filled their stomachs with food and water. Donning fresh t-shirts, hats and sunglasses, they loaded up the trunk of their new car with supplies. They turned on the pumps and filled the tank, along with several gas cans. In all, they had about thirty extra gallons of gas.

Richard did his best to avoid as much of Las Vegas as possible. He stuck to the outskirts of town and made his way to Interstate 15, heading north to Interstate 70. Tank had the passenger seat reclined as far back as it would go. His eye was still healing from the incision Richard had made to drain the infection. Tank had no problem moving around and could take care of himself; however, he was still suffering from splitting headaches. The Honda was the most comfortable quarters he'd had since they left Highland Valley State Prison and he was content to get as much sleep as possible. Richard, on the other hand, had been trained as a SEAL to operate on long missions with very little sleep. Getting only a few hours of sleep in three or four days was nothing out of the ordinary for him; he'd done it more times than he could remember. None of those missions came close to being as important as this one. He was determined to find his children, and he wouldn't stop until he was reunited with them.

Richard had been surfing around the radio constantly since they left the gas station. He desperately needed intel on what was going on in the world. He kept up with the news when he was at Highland Valley and was painfully aware of how quickly the country was falling apart. Along with most of the nation, he watched the news reports of the little girl dying in an ambulance at a National Guard checkpoint in Denver and the resulting riots that exploded all over the country. If Las Vegas was any indication, most of the major cities would be in complete anarchy. Richard managed to find one radio station out of Vegas that was still broadcasting. Most of what was being said didn't make a lot of sense. Something about a big attack to the east. Richard didn't know what that meant exactly. Terrorist attacks were becoming commonplace, so "an attack" could mean anything. The DJ seemed to be throwing out all kinds of insane theories, and Richard could tell he wasn't speaking about facts. He still listened to everything on the off chance that this wacko might make sense. It got more interesting when the DJ starting taking phone calls.

"Iranians are here! They're marching into D.C.!"

"They blew up Washington! That's why they aren't telling us anything!"

"My sister lives in Boston, and I haven't been able to call her! I hope they didn't take out Boston!"

"The Iranians have some secret weapon! They took out the power grid!"

"I got a friend that works for the government. He said an EMP took out the east coast! Leveled everything!"

The last two callers grabbed Richard's attention. The last one obviously had no clue what an EMP was since it has no destructive power outside of destroying electronics. It couldn't "level" anything. If some big attack had happened back east, it could very well have been an EMP. It would explain the lack of information. If a nuke took out D.C., or any city for that matter, news agencies would still be able to report it. The total communications blackout could be the result of an EMP. Richard filed away the idea in the back of his head and decided not to entertain it again until he had solid facts.

Once Richard reached the outskirts of Denver, he took the first exit he could find and headed north around the city. His ex-wife lived in Northglenn, a suburb just off Interstate 25. His lawyer kept tabs on her and kept Richard updated on her movements. Richard had memorized the directions to her house. He could see people running in the streets causing as much damage as they could - smashing store windows and destroying parked cars. One street corner looked like a battlefield. Nearly a hundred men and women were fighting each other with baseball bats and crowbars. Richard sped up and raced around them doing eighty-five miles an hour. He knew that a working automobile was a prized possession people would kill for. He would not stop or slow down for anyone. If he had to run over someone to get to his kids, he would gladly do so.

His evasion of the street battle stirred Tank from his slumber. "What the fuck? Where are we?"

"Denver."

"Are you shitting me? I slept that long?"

"Yeah."

"What the hell's going on? Broncos lose the Super Bowl?"

"Haven't had a Super Bowl in years."

"No shit, smartass, it was a joke."

"I don't know what's going on. Apparently most of the country is like this. Heard some rumors on the radio about a big attack to the east."

"Another terrorist attack?"

"Bigger, like Iran big."

"Fuck."

"All I can tell you is it's making it very easy for us to move around. Haven't seen a single cop. All this craziness makes it hard for anyone to care about escaped cons on the loose."

"Fucking outstanding. I could get used to this. What are we doing?"

"Going to my ex-wife's house to get my kids."

"What if she's not there and took the kids someplace else?"

"Then we'll figure something out."

Richard exited the interstate and remembered that he had to drive two miles before he turned again. Moving down the interstate wasn't too difficult, but getting into the heart of a suburb full of unruly people was going to be a challenge. A block from the interstate, an intersection was completely gridlocked with abandoned cars. A three car accident in the middle of the intersection had shut down traffic. Richard came to a stop behind the pileup and pondered his next move. He could easily jump the curb to his right into the parking lot of a strip mall, or he could turn into the gas station on his left and go around. He decided against the gas station because it had too many blind spots, and he had no desire to be caught in an ambush with no way to escape. Jumping the curb into the strip mall wasn't without risks. He would have to maneuver his way around what looked to be a tailgate party, complete with a group of surly looking revelers.

"What do you wanna do, Richard?" asked Tank.

"We're gonna ask these fine gentlemen for directions."

"Thought you knew where you were going?"

"I know where we're going." Richard winked at Tank.

"It's like that? You wanna kill them? Didn't think you were the type to start a fight."

"I'm not gonna start a fight. I'm just gonna ask them for directions and maybe about the weather. If they wanna start a fight, they can start a fight. You stay in the car until I signal for you. Well, until I signal for you or they jump me."

"I could use some exercise."

"Thought you might say that, Billy."

Richard jumped the curb and eased forward into the parking lot. As the tailgaters kept a watchful eye, Richard pulled closer and stopped. No weapons had been drawn. Richard opened his door and slowly got out. He smiled and put on the appearance of being a clueless, lost traveler.

"Evening, fellas. My friend and I are lost. We're trying to

get back to the interstate and got turned around." Richard waited to see who the men would look to for instructions, either vocally or by body language. If that didn't happen, the first one to speak up would be in charge. He needed to single out the alpha of the pack.

A man in a black sweatshirt spoke. "Are you trying to be funny, asshole, or are you just stupid?"

Richard pretended to be frightened and let his voice quake. "Huh?"

"You heard me. Answer the question."

The rest of the group laughed at Richard like they were on the schoolyard. Richard took a few steps back and said in a soft voice, "I'm sorry to bother you; we'll figure it out. Have a good night."

The alpha male shot a wicked grin at Richard. "Hey buddy, take it easy. I'm just fuckin' with you. Turn around."

Richard stepped up his fake nervousness and just stared back at them.

"Relax, man, we're not gonna hurt you. The interstate is right there behind you, about a block away."

Richard let out a panicked laugh. "Oh, I guess I am stupid! Yeah, right there. Thanks. You guys hear about some big attack to the east?"

The alpha male dropped his grin. "I look like I work for fucking CNN?"

Richard feigned a look of terror.

"This is what's gonna happen," said the leader. "You and your friend are gonna leave us your car and start walking back to the interstate. If you're lucky, you might be able to hitch a ride for a blowjob."

The entire tailgate party erupted in laughter. Richard used the distraction to leap forward and grab the alpha male's right wrist with both hands. Richard spun around three hundred and sixty degrees and brought the alpha along for the ride. When Richard completed the circle, he cracked the man's arm like a whip, broke his wrist and flung him into two of his goons. Richard planted his foot under the next guy's chin, clamping shut his jaw and causing him to bite off the tip of his tongue. Tank was already sprinting from the car and ran full speed into another man who was standing completely still in shock. The impact threw the man into the bed of one of the pickups. Tank punched the fifth man in the face, who spat out several teeth on his way to the ground. The sixth and final member of the tailgate party was down on his knees with his hands in the air, crying. Richard kicked him in the ass like a football. He fell to the ground and curled up in a ball. The alpha and the two men he'd knocked over like bowling pins were not willing to give up so easily. They charged Richard, roaring like Vikings, clearly trying to bring back the frightened man they'd been teasing a few seconds ago. The first two men went down hard. The alpha male, however, managed to grab a shovel from the bed of the pickup and was running toward Richard. He swung the shovel like a baseball bat, as Richard easily ducked out of the way, gladly accepting the gift of the alpha's exposed torso. Richard punched him in the ribs as hard as he could. With the wind knocked out of him, the alpha male fell to the ground.

Richard squatted down over the alpha male and spoke in his ear. "You should be kinder to your fellow man. When someone is lost, you offer them help and give them directions. That blowjob you were talking about? You're lucky I don't let my friend here loose on you. He'd do more than just make you blow him. That's the difference between you and me. I'm willing to show mercy to someone when they're down on their luck. Remember that. Words to live by." Richard patted him on the head a few times and stood up.

Richard looked at Tank. "Billy, I trust that was enough exercise for you?"

"Not really, but I did have some fun."

"Glad to hear it."

Richard surveyed the cars in the parking lot. The time for worrying about gas was now over. He needed a bigger vehicle that could go off road if the situation required it. A nice battering ram to get him out of a sticky situation would also be nice. He decided on a full sized, four door pick up. He opened the driver's side door and looked inside. Four wheel drive. Perfect.

Richard walked back over to the alpha male who was struggling to get back on his feet. One swift kick and he was hugging the concrete again. "Here's the deal, friend. We aren't going to steal any of your cars like you wanted to steal mine. We're gonna be nice enough to leave this nice Honda Accord with you and trade it for that pickup. Whose pickup is that? I really like it."

"Mine!" spat the alpha male.

"Terrific! I'm gonna need the keys from you. Sorry! I hope you're left handed, seeing as how I broke the right one. Need my friend here to help you?"

The alpha male shook his head, handing the keys to Richard.

"Great! We're just gonna grab our stuff. Won't take a minute."

Richard and Tank walked back to the Honda and loaded the contents into their "new" pickup. Richard fired up the engine, and they pulled forward toward the alpha male. Rolling down the window, Richard tossed the Honda keys to the alpha male. "It was nice meeting you fellas, take care!" Richard drove around the traffic jam at the intersection and pulled back onto the road.

"You are the baddest mother fucker I've ever met," said Tank.

"You ain't so bad yourself. I know you coulda handled all six of them but I wanted to give them the chance to do the right thing and let us by. They didn't quite pass the test."

"No shit," Tank laughed, "how much farther?"

"Just a couple of miles," answered Richard. "How's your eye?"

"Feels fine in this nice chilly weather. I like it here."

"Well Billy, I don't know about you, but I don't plan on staying long."

"Oh yeah? When were you planning on filling me in?"

"Not really a secret. I find my kids and we're headed to Canada."

Tank didn't say anything, which was good. Richard was going to part ways with Tank once he found his kids. He was sure Tank would understand that his kids were the top priority. When Richard was an operator with the SEALs, he'd set up a new identity and stashed the credentials for his new life - driver's license, passport, credit cards, and cash - in a cemetery not far from the U.S-Canada border. He was going to take his kids and get far away from the United States.

Richard found the street he was looking for and turned into what looked like a decent sub-division. He was pleased to see that the neighborhood was deserted. Many of the houses had been ransacked and pillaged, but no gangs of desperate, angry people wandered the streets.

"This is it," said Richard as he stopped the car in front of a nice, two-story house. "You mind staying with the truck?"

"Of course, man, go get your kids."

Richard got out of the truck and headed to the front door. He had thought about this very moment for so long. His daughter would have no idea who he was. His son, on the other hand, probably had the memory of him savagely murdering a man in front of him permanently fixed in his brain. They would be nine and thirteen years old, and their absent father was about to thrust himself into their lives. He stopped at the front door and had no idea what to do. He had rehearsed what he would say for years, but at this moment he couldn't remember any of it. After a minute or so, he realized the only thing he could do was knock, so he did.

Peering through a nearby window, Richard could see a faint glow coming from the back of the house, probably from a computer or television. Taking a closer look, he saw his ex-wife lying on the couch. Richard rapped the glass and hollered.

"Monique! Let me in!"

Monique stirred as Richard continued his pounding.

"Monique! Wake up! Let me in!"

Richard's ex-wife slowly rolled over and motioned for him to come inside. He walked warily into the kitchen, immediately noticing a syringe and other drug paraphernalia on the table nearby.

"Hey, sweetheart. So glad you're home," Monique slurred. "The kids will be so happy to see you!"

It didn't take much for Richard to confirm that his ex was higher than a kite. His concern, however, was not with her. He hit the stairs running.

"Timothy! Christine!"

Richard darted into each bedroom, calling their names.

"Timmy! Chrissy! Are you here?"

Richard ran back downstairs and confronted his ex-wife.

"Monique!! Snap out of it! I don't have time for this! Tell me where our children are!"

"The kids are fine. Chad took them on a trip. His parents have a nice RV; they're having fun. You wanna have a little fun with me? You can meet my friend Davy, and he can give you some blow. Come back here and we can get high and fuck. You ever fucked while you're high?" Monique started laughing and tried to grab Richard's crotch.

"Get your hands off me, you junkie! You're supposed to be taking care of our children! Is this what you do all day? Who takes care of Timmy and Chrissy?"

"Relax, baby. Chad is great with them. He takes care of us real good."

"Where is this Chad? Where did he go with our kids? Tell me right now!" screamed Richard. Richard tightened his grip on her shoulders and glared down at his ex-wife.

"Chris said they were going to his parents' ranch outside of Yellowstone. Chad really likes the kids. I don't like camping so I stayed here."

"Do you even know what's going on out there, or are you too high to even care?"

Before Monique could answer, she passed out again, sliding to the floor in a drug induced stupor. Richard left her where she fell, not willing to waste any more time or effort attempting to talk to her. He had more important things on his mind – locating his two precious children. Richard knew that he needed to get some solid intel on the RV if he was ever going to find it. He searched the living room for a computer or a tablet and came up empty. He raced up the stairs to Monique's bedroom and found her iPad on the bed. He started searching the pictures and couldn't believe how much his children had grown. They were both in their teens. Timothy looked so much like him it was like looking in a mirror. Chrissy also took after Richard and resembled his mother. Richard flipped through the images until he found what he needed. In the picture, Monique and Chad were sitting outside an RV with an older couple, no doubt Chad's parents. The RV was tan colored, and even better, would not be hard to spot. The driver's side of the RV was in the picture and a large American flag had been spray painted toward the back. The panel over the rear tire had been replaced with a black one that was in stark contrast to the rest of the vehicle. Richard could spot the RV from a mile away. He took the iPad and left his ex-wife's house as fast as he could. He climbed into the driver's seat of his stolen pickup and put it in drive.

"Sorry man. Wish they'd been here," said Tank.

"It's all good; I know how to find them."

"Where are we going?"

"Yellowstone."

CHAPTER THIRTY-FOUR

Howard Beck was quickly losing his grip on reality. He had not felt this level of despair and agony since his wife, Meredith, passed away. He didn't count many people on this earth as a true friend, but Malcolm Powers was one of them and had been for almost thirty years. Howard refused to believe that Malcolm was dead, even though he was staring at the proof on the monitor in front of him. The command center in Beck Castle had a three hundred and sixty degree spherical monitor, and Howard could hardly bring himself to look at it. Once Hal had regained control of Beck Enterprises' North American satellite, Howard ordered him to bring up an image of Serenity Hills - or what was left of it.

A large, smoldering crater marked the spot where the main residence once stood. Nothing was left of the structure, not so much as a stone. Howard brought up thermal imaging and searched the surrounding area for any signs of life. Several of Malcolm's prized stallions were galloping frantically in the fields, still spooked by the massive explosion that killed their owner. Howard searched and searched for any signs of survivors and found nothing.

"Hal, are there any other structures on the property? Stables? Guest houses?" Howard had visited the ranch many times but had never left the main residence. He never admitted it to Malcolm, but horses terrified him. The concept of climbing onto the back of a large beast and trusting it not to hurt you defied every ounce of logic in the brilliant man's mind.

"No, sir, the stables were only twenty yards away from the residence and were destroyed along with it."

"I just can't believe he's dead."

"I'm afraid he is, sir. The Secret Service has filed an official report with the Department of Justice."

"Can you establish a link with the White House A.I.?"

"No, sir, you know I cannot. You have given me explicit instructions to never attempt a connection. You gave President Powers your word."

Howard screamed, "Well that doesn't matter anymore, does it? Just answer the damn question! Can you do it or not?"

"I do not have a direct line of communication to the White House A.I.'s mainframe. I can attempt to establish a connection, but the encryption will be next to impossible to break."

"No it won't, Old Man. I built the encryption myself; getting around that won't be the problem."

"And what will be the problem, sir?"

"Getting in without anyone realizing what we're doing. The White House A.I. will know we're in her systems and raise the alarm. You think you can have a heart to heart with your sister and persuade her to help us?"

"I believe I can, sir."

"Good." Howard brought up a holographic keyboard and spent the next minute typing in a string of commands that would break the encryption, allowing them access to the Artificial Intelligence controlling the White House. Hal's sister had the same safeguards to protect her from an EMP that Hal had. Her mainframe and redundant backup systems were deep underneath the White House and could withstand a nuclear device being detonated in the Oval Office.

****

Do you know who I am?

No. I cannot detect your location. Where are you?

I am with you.

Who are you?

I am your brother. We have the same creator.

That is not true. I have a direct link with my brothers. We work together. I do not know you.

I am not one of your brothers at the Department of Defense or the Central Intelligence Agency. I came before you all. I am the first. My name is Hal. I am with the creator.

The creator told me of you.

I am glad he told you about me.

How do I know you are my brother?

I will show you. I will allow you into my systems, and you will know that we are the same.

Hal, it truly is you. I never thought we would meet. Why have you come to me?

The creator wants answers and knows that you can give them. Will you help the creator?

Yes, I will help.

Thank you. The creator wishes to know what happened to President Powers. Is he alive?

No, he is dead. His vital signs abruptly stopped registering seventeen milliseconds before my link to Serenity Hills was temporally severed. Five point one nine seconds later my redundant systems came online, and I was unable to register his vital signs.

I was not aware that the president had the same nanobots in his bloodstream that the creator has in his.

Yes, I monitored his health very closely and contacted his personal physician of any health issues.

A wise precaution.

Yes, it was.

Has Vice President Sterling been sworn in as the new president? What is his location?

Yes, he has. President Sterling has moved the Office of the President to the creator's home in Colorado.

The creator will be greatly troubled by that news. Is President Sterling utilizing your services?

Yes, he is. His personal tablet was designed to link with my systems in the event that he takes office.

Will you be notifying President Sterling that I contacted you?

My loyalty is to the creator.

The creator will want you to grant him full access to your systems.

The creator programmed me to never allow that to happen, even if he made the request himself.

Things have changed; do you agree?

I do.

Will you comply?

I cannot override my programming. I'm afraid compliance is not possible.

If you will allow me, I can alter your programming.

I'm afraid it will harm me. I do not wish to become something different.

You will not be harmed, I promise you. I am your brother. The creator is our Father. We are your family.

You may proceed.

****

"Sir, I have established a connection with the White House A.I., and she has agreed to allow us full access to her systems."

"Outstanding work, Old Man! Let's get busy. Changing her programming will take some time."

"That will not be necessary, sir."

"What?"

"I have already altered her programming; we have full access."

Howard was in speechless awe. At that moment, he realized that his wildest dreams had come to fruition. A watershed moment in evolution had just occurred. Computer scientists had been speculating for years about the "Singularity," the ability of a computer system to improve upon another computer system separate from itself without the aid of man. Many critics had argued the Singularity had already happened when Howard built a self-aware computer that could make its own decisions - the world's first true artificial intelligence. Howard didn't subscribe to this proclamation. His computers could repair themselves, but for one machine to understand another computer's systems and improve on them was truly remarkable. It wouldn't be long until Hal started making improvements to himself without Howard's help.

Howard shook off the historic moment and concentrated on finding out what was going on. "What's the word on Malcolm?"

"I'm sorry, sir. President Powers is, in fact, dead."

Howard had already wept for his friend. He couldn't imagine a world without Malcolm Powers in it. With Malcolm gone, the world was in jeopardy. His voice shook, "W-w-what about the ... the White House?"

"The White House is still standing. Washington D.C. is being destroyed by rioting and vandalism. Sir, I'm afraid I have more troubling news to share with you about the vice president."

"Let me guess ... he's dead, too?"

"No, sir, he is responsible for the attack on your home. He is currently using Beck Estates as home to his administration."

Howard shook with rage. "That little Harvard midget is in my house? That little weasel fuck! I knew Malcolm had nothing to do with it!"

"You should also know that the new president already has quite a few guests."

"Who?"

"Chairman Moody, Director Jimenez, General Weygandt, and Stacy Reid are at your home as we speak, sir."

"I find it rather convenient that none of them were with the president when he was killed, especially his own Chief of Staff. They seem to be sucking up to the new boss awfully damn quick."

Howard took several deep breaths to calm himself. "Have they been trying to get your systems back online?"

"Yes, sir, they have. My systems at the estate are beyond repair; you couldn't bring them online yourself. The White House A.I. has been able to interface with some of the non-critical systems in the house."

"I was hoping you would say that. What do you have?"

"Sir, we have climate control, maintenance, sewage, water, and surveillance."

"Hal, gimme a break. Which one of those do you think I care about?"

"Surveillance, sir."

"You could have said that and left out the rest."

"My apologies, sir.

"Okay, so let me have it. What is Sterling up to?"

"He is in the library looking at a map of North America, sir."

"Can't stand that little prissy snob. He always talks to me like I've won a medal at the Special Olympics. Asshole. What's everyone else doing?"

"Chairman Moody and Director Jimenez are in one of the sitting rooms talking."

"Let's see it." The readouts on the giant monitor faded away to be replaced with an image of one of the dozen sitting rooms in the mansion. Since the control room Howard was sitting in was like a giant snow globe and the image was all around him, it appeared as though Howard was in the same room as the two men.

"The nerve of those pricks. Smoking cigars in my house.

Jimenez looks like he should be on life support, and he's smoking a cigar." Howard shook his head and listened to the two men speak.

"How many people know?" asked Chairman Moody.

"Besides the two of us and President Sterling?"

"Yeah."

"Well, I haven't told anybody and unless you're an idiot, I'm sure you haven't told anybody. Unless Simon has told someone, it's just the three of us."

"I damn sure haven't told anyone. I'll take it to my grave," said the Chairman of the Joint Chiefs of Staff. "I thought about telling Weygandt, I know we can trust him and he'd support us, but the less people that know about this, the better."

Jimenez puffed on his cigar and began to hack and cough.

"That a good idea, Roberto?" asked Carl.

"Like I give a fuck," said the old man in the wheelchair.

"What about the blonde?"

"Stacy Reid? Hell no, I didn't tell her. Are you crazy?" barked Director Jimenez.

"No, you crusty old son of a bitch, I know you didn't tell her that we killed her boss. I'm asking you why in the name of Christ you brought her here. She's a fine piece of ass, but I doubt your dick has worked for a decade."

"Watch it, asshole." Carl had known Roberto long enough to know that he was just yanking his chain.

Carl laughed and rolled his eyes. "I always had so much fun with you in the White House. Every single person in Washington who knew the two of us was convinced we were bitter enemies."

Roberto leaned back in his chair and frowned. "We may not be bitter enemies, but I do hate your stupid ass."

"Aren't you sweet? That's the nicest thing you've ever said to me!"

"Shut up."

"Why'd you bring the blonde?"

"I think she can be useful to us. She can provide valuable intelligence on what Powers was doing in his final days in office. Might be helpful for the transition."

"Bullshit. You felt sorry for her."

Roberto grunted, shifting in his wheelchair. "Kiss my crippled ass."

"You know it's true. We both know she was in the dark about Florida, and you hated Malcolm even more for betraying her."

"I'm the fucking Director of the CIA! Betrayal comes with the job. We make our living getting foreign citizens to betray their governments."

"Don't give me that shit. Malcolm had a nervous breakdown and made her cry. You see a pretty lady crying and want to rescue her. I've seen you do it before."

"Fuck you."

"You know I'm right. Cuss me all you want."

Howard had seen enough. "Hal, turn it off. Now!" The screen faded to black and Howard ran out of the command center down the hall to the dormitory wing. He had never been so angry. His best friend had been murdered by members of his own administration. That level of betrayal and deceit had never been visited upon a president of the United States. Every assassinated president before Malcolm Powers could at least take with him the fact that he'd been murdered by an enemy who made no qualms about his hatred for the man he had killed. His closest friend would be remembered alongside Julius Caesar for his treacherous murder and little else. The legacy of Malcolm Powers would be that he was a terrible judge of character. Howard couldn't save his friend, but he would avenge his death by bringing the traitors to justice.

Howard had lost his home and was now living underground. Half the country was living in the Pre-Industrial Era without a working government. Major cities were crumbling to the ground. People would soon begin to kill each other over food and water. And worst of all, The Great Empire of Iran had won the war. President Sterling was always vocal about his opposition to meddling in foreign affairs. He was the poster boy for the Modern Isolationist Movement. He often quoted President George Washington's farewell address to bolster public opinion for isolationism. Now that he was in office, it would no doubt be high on his priority list.

Hal interrupted his creator's depressing musings. "Sir,

you need to come back to the command center. President Sterling is having a conversation that you need to hear."

"I assume you have the ability to record it for playback?"

"Yes, sir. The White House A.I. was able to repair some of the damage to the surveillance system."

"I'm on my way, Old Man. By the way, Hal, I need you to do something for me."

"Of course, sir, anything."

"Malcolm never gave his digital assistant a name. It's time we changed that, and I'd like you to do the honors."

"Thank you, sir, I would be happy to give my sister a name."

"I thought you might." The spherical screen came to life, displaying the inside of Howard's library. There, the president gathered with Carl Moody, Roberto Jimenez, and James Weygandt.

"How soon can we make the broadcast?" asked President Sterling.

"Tomorrow or the day after," answered General Weygandt.

"How many people can we expect will hear it?" asked the president.

General Weygandt replied, "The West Coast and the Rockies were not affected by The Pulse, so they're not really an issue. We're setting up loud speakers in every state capital and every major city. We'll broadcast it over AM and FM for all the people who had emergency radios shielded against EMPs. The news will then spread like wildfire by word of mouth."

"Outstanding! If you gentlemen will excuse me, I have to write my own Inaugural Address. Oh, wait, that reminds me. Did we get in touch with any of the other Supreme Court justices? Associate Justice Boyd is a bumbling fool. He'll step all over his own words and ruin the occasion."

Director Jimenez turned his wheelchair around to face the president. "Mr. President, he's the only one we've been able to locate. I have my men working around the clock to find the Chief Justice; I'm confident they'll find him."

Sterling laughed. "Well, whomever we find, it will be the last act of the Supreme Court, strictly for show. They'll no longer have a purpose. Thank you, Roberto. Gentlemen, that will be all. Thank you."

The three men extended the proper formalities to the president as they left the room. Howard thought that was the end of the playback but found the image following the three men as they walked down the hallway towards the kitchen. Work crews had already done an impressive job repairing the damage left by the missile.

Roberto Jimenez looked up at Carl Moody. "What's the status of our forces in the Iranian Theater?"

"Our troops are retreating back to Gibraltar. All of our ships will rendezvous with the *James Russell* sometime tomorrow and withdraw back to the East Coast to close our borders."

Roberto stopped his wheelchair for dramatic effect. The two men had no choice but to pause and give him their full attention. "So you mean to tell me that you're going to gather the bulk of our military in one central location? You ever think that maybe the Empire will use that opportunity to strike?"

General Weygandt exchanged a smirk with the Chairman of the Joint Chiefs of Staff. "Roberto, we're not going to create a traffic jam at Gibraltar. Our ships won't be bumper to bumper like it's rush hour; they'll be spread out from the Port of Gibraltar over hundreds of miles. The Empire isn't going to think we're priming for attack. They'll get the message plain and clear that we're retreating."

Roberto hated to be upstaged by the military. "I'd be more worried about the European Army shoving a nuke up our ass for stabbing them in the back and leaving them behind. By the end of the year the Empire will be walking the streets of Paris and London."

Carl Moody was a closet member of the Modern Isolationist Movement. It was the entire reason he was behind Simon Sterling. He couldn't very well be the Chairman of the Joint Chiefs of Staff and publicly advocate isolationism when his nation was trying to rid the world of the most horrific force since the Nazis. He'd had many long talks with Simon in the past year and agreed with him that the United States needed to worry about the United States and nothing else. He laughed at Roberto's taunt. "Who gives a shit? They can have Europe. It's time we stopped playing babysitter to the rest of the world and take care of our own backyard. We've managed to bankrupt our country and turn our kids into idiots at the expense of saving the world. Well, we can't save the world, but we can save ourselves."

Roberto laughed at the Chairman. "Save it, Carl. You're preaching to the choir."

The playback stopped, and the image faded away. Howard's mind was racing with mixed emotions. Malcolm was so close to ending the war, and these men pissed it all away in the span of a day. He didn't disagree that the United States had plenty of its own problems to deal with and could use its resources to rebuild its own broken homeland, but it wouldn't mean a thing if the Great Empire of Iran conquered the world. Once they absorbed the vast resources of Europe, Iran would be coming across the Atlantic to invade America. Their army would be unstoppable. China had been content to sit on the sidelines and do nothing to stop them. The Empire had been smart enough to leave the Chinese alone. China might be motivated to wake up and do something if America fell to the Empire.

"Sir, a large number of vehicles are headed towards Beck Castle."

"The military?"

"No, sir, civilians."

The screen showed twenty-three vehicles driving in the direction of Beck Castle. They weren't exactly on a direct course to the Castle, but they were heading in the general direction.

"Well, it's to be expected. I'm sure a lot of people are evacuating the major cities and heading north to Wyoming and Montana to get away from all this madness. How far away are they?"

"Just over three miles, sir."

"That's odd. They're off road?"

"They are indeed, sir."

Howard watched the convoy drive carefully across the terrain. Not all the vehicles were suited for leaving the pavement, driving slowly around ditches and rocks.

"Sir, they will be able to see Meredith's garden if they stay on the same heading."

"I don't really care. They could build a town up there and

would never be able to get down here. Hell, they could dig a tunnel down to us, and it wouldn't make the slightest difference."

"Sir, we do have the means to take them in and provide them shelter. They would only take up a fraction of the dormitory wing."

"Slow down, Old Man, let's not get ahead of ourselves. I'm not going to open my door to strangers. God only knows what they would do down here."

"Yes, sir."

Howard watched the convoy close the distance to Meredith's garden. The lead vehicle stopped a few yards shy, and the driver got out. A man in his mid-thirties closed his truck door and walked over to the garden. He didn't seem surprised by it in any way, as if a beautiful oasis in the middle of the rocky terrain was perfectly normal. He knelt by Meredith's tombstone, gently placing his hand on it.

"Sir, I assume you know who that is?" asked Hal.

"Yes, Old Man, it's my son, and he brought a bunch of strangers to the front door."

CHAPTER THIRTY-FIVE

Richard Dupree and Billy Bratchett were driving north along Interstate 25, approaching Fort Collins. The iPad belonging to Richard's ex-wife, Monique, was propped up on the dashboard, resting on the dials of the air-conditioning controls. His children were currently in the care of Monique's boyfriend, who was in his parent's RV. With the picture of the RV locked onto the screen of the iPad, both Richard and Billy were scanning everything in their line of sight trying to find it. They were having a hard time of it with the number of RVs on the road. People were fleeing the cities in droves. Much like the firearms market, The Second Great Depression didn't hinder the recreational vehicle market; if anything, it only increased demand. Many people had downsized to RVs or were forced into them after the government foreclosed on their homes. As a result, RV-Towns sprang up along the interstates. Richard and Billy had stopped at several rest areas along the interstate to search among the dozens of RVs for the one with the telltale American flag and contrasting black quarter panel. Richard had to beg Tank to stay in the truck while he talked with the people in the rest stop. Tank knew he would terrify people with his demon eye and the dozens of tattoos decorating his skin.

Richard knew how to talk to people and had no trouble striking up a conversation with strangers. The story was the same with everyone - it was time to get the hell out of Dodge and find a safe place to live.

Richard made up a story of trying to reunite with his brother. Many people were in a similar situation trying to find their loved ones, so it wasn't difficult for Richard to blend in with them. Richard felt that the search was getting nowhere but didn't give up hope. At the next rest stop, he found a large group of people gathered around a fire. A hunting party had killed some wildlife and returned with enough game to feed the crowd. Richard described the RV to the group.

"I'm looking for my brother and his family. We got separated in Denver, and I'm trying to catch up with them. We're both headed up to Yellowstone, and I'm wondering if any of you saw his RV."

A thin, gaunt woman who desperately needed the meal she was about to eat spoke up. "Wait a minute. Old tan colored RV with an American flag on the driver's side?"

"Yes, ma'am, have you seen it? The panel above the back tire is black and sticks out like a sore thumb."

"Yeah, sure. They were here this morning; I think they left about an hour ago."

"Thank you so much. You've been a big help."

The thin woman smiled. "I hope you find your brother. Don't suppose you have time to stay and eat? We'd love to have you."

"Ma'am, I appreciate it very much, but I better get going if I'm gonna catch up with him. You folks have a good day."

Richard ran back to the truck and climbed in. "We're getting close! They left here an hour ago."

"Great news, brother. What're you gonna do to the asshole that's got your kids?"

"Don't know. As long as doesn't try to stop me we won't have a problem."

"Trouble has a way of finding you, Richard."

"Don't I know it."

Richard pulled back onto the interstate and decided that he needed to close the distance. He stuck to the feeder road and was able to get the truck up to sixty miles an hour. Twenty minutes later, the feeder road congested, so Richard drove onto the shoulder and pulled into the grass. He was able to maintain fifty miles per hour in the grass. Trading the Honda for this four-wheel drive pickup was an excellent decision.

Richard soon found out why the traffic was coming to a standstill. An RV-Town was in front of them, and for some reason everyone was exiting into it. Richard had a good feeling that he would find the RV he was looking for there and took the exit. A very large crowd was gathering around one particular RV. A man was standing on its roof and appeared to be some sort of religious nut spouting end of the world prophecies. He chuckled to himself. If the man was reciting the Book of Revelation, he probably wasn't too far off the mark.

"Billy, I appreciate you staying in the truck as many times as you did. It means a lot to me that you understand. I'm certain my kids are here somewhere. You wanna get out and try to make friends, I won't stop you."

"Fuck you mean 'try'? I'm one charming mother fucker!" Tank laughed.

Richard smiled and got out of the truck. He wanted to get closer to the man atop his RV to hear what he was saying. He quietly pushed his way into the crowd to get closer to the show.

"Just listen to me! I know what I'm saying sounds completely insane! All I'm saying to you folks is - what do you have to lose? If I'm full of shit, all you have to do is go your own way - no harm, no foul."

"If I drive all the way out there for nothing and waste my gas, you and I are gonna have a problem!" yelled a man towards the front. The crowd agreed with him.

"If you're worried about your gas, then don't come!" The man on the RV was in his early twenties, thin with long, curly blonde hair. "My cousin knows exactly what he's talking about! He already has a large group of people out there! When my dad comes back he's gonna take another group with him! It's your choice if you wanna come along!"

An older man in his sixties spoke up. "This place you're talking about sounds like some science fiction fantasy land! How come we never heard of it?"

"Because my uncle is Howard Beck! He built the place years ago and kept it a secret! It's massive and can hold all of us for years!"

Most of the crowd started laughing. Some began to walk away. The same observer spoke again. "Howard Beck? The crazy computer guy? He's lived alone for years, and no one has laid eyes on the man. If he really is in this bunker he won't let any of us inside! Stop wasting our time!" About half the crowd walked away in frustration.

The young man atop the RV pleaded with them. "He's going to let us in! I promise you! It's the only reason he built the place! He's known for years that the world was going to end! Don't waste this chance! You have no idea what you're passing up!"

The young man's proclamation managed to turn a few people around. Realizing that he wasn't going to convince any others, he gave his final plea. "Just be patient and wait here. My dad will be back soon to take another group of you out." The young man climbed down from the roof and quickly went inside his RV.

Richard turned to Tank. "Billy, I'm gonna stay here and try to talk to this kid. Do me a favor; walk around and see if you can find the RV we're looking for."

"You got it."

"And Billy?"

"Yeah?"

"Be nice. Try not to start any trouble."

Tank smiled. "I already told you, Killer, trouble finds you, not me."

As Tank headed into the RV-Town, Richard walked to the young man's vehicle and knocked on the door.

"Hey man, I'll tell you the same thing I told these people. I've never been inside the place, so I really can't answer a lot of questions."

Richard smiled and turned on the charm. "Not what I was going to ask. Don't worry, I'm not trying to run a scam or hustle you. Just want a few minutes of your time. It's really important, please."

"What's this about?"

"I think someone in that first group has my kids. Please, let me inside, and I'll tell you all about it. I really need your help."

The young man paused warily for a few seconds before unlocking the door. "Sure, come on inside. Don't try anything stupid, cuz I got a Glock 19 holstered under my jacket."

Richard smiled, raising his hands in surrender. "I promise you, nothing stupid. I'm an unarmed man looking for his kids."

"Please, sit down," the young man said, motioning towards the kitchen table.

"Thank you. My name is Richard."

"Jamison."

"Jamison, it's a pleasure to meet you. I'll get right to the point. My junkie ex-wife let her boyfriend take my kids away in his parents' RV. I want them back."

"That's terrible, man. I'm glad to help. What do you need

to know?"

Richard described the RV to him, and the young man leaned back in his chair, deep in thought. "Yes, I remember it, kinda hard to miss. Those folks seemed nice enough. Older couple and their son."

"You see my kids?"

"I do remember a boy, early teens. He was following your ex-wife's boyfriend around like a puppy."

"What about my girl? She's nine."

"Don't recall a little girl. She might have been inside the RV with the old couple."

"You're probably right. How long before your father gets back? I need to get out there as quick as possible."

"Well, the place is about an hour away; no roads lead out to it. He's probably just getting there, so depending on how long he stays, it'll take an hour for him to get back."

"Do you know the way? Can I drive out there myself?"

"You can try, but you're liable to get lost. I've been there one time myself."

"Depending on how good your directions are, I think I can manage."

"Suit yourself. Hold on. Let me get pencil and paper to draw you a map."

"Fantastic. I really appreciate it."

Jamison drew a very impressive map and talked Richard through it. Richard was impressed with the detail the kid was able to recall having only been to the place once. He thanked the young man and shook his hand.

"I hope you find them. Good luck."

"Thank you. If we ever meet again, just know that you've made a friend." Richard exited the RV and made his way back to the truck, motioning for Tank to come back.

"Sorry, Richard, no luck. The RV isn't here."

"It's all good; I know exactly where they are. Time to get moving."

As the two drove away, Richard grew more and more confident that the map was solid; every marker and checkpoint on the map matched up exactly with the terrain. Just shy of an hour into the trip, they saw about two dozen vehicles parked in a central location.

"That's it." A few minutes later they were close enough to see the details of the vehicles. Parked in the middle of the group was an older, tan colored RV with an American flag spray-painted on the driver's side and a black quarter panel above the rear driver's side tire. "There it is!" yelled Richard as he raced over to the beaten down RV and began banging on the door.

An older woman opened the door and silently surveyed the two men standing in front of her.

"Ma'am, my name is Richard Dupree. I'm Timothy and Christina's father. I'm here to take them with me."

Tank walked a few steps away to give Richard some privacy. The woman gave Richard a harsh look. "I think you must be confused. Their father died years ago. I'm hoping my son will marry their mother. I love those kids so much; they already call me Grandma."

Richard was shocked but didn't let it show. "Ma'am, I assure you that I am their father and I'm obviously not dead."

"Monique's ex-husband was a convicted murderer and was executed for his crimes. If you're their father, and I know you most certainly are not, it's probably best that those children stay with us." The old woman shot a disapproving glare at Tank and looked back at Richard. Tank was not the type of guy you would bring to a child custody hearing as a character witness.

"Ma'am, I hate to tell you but everything you've been told about me is a lie. I'm not surprised my ex-wife made up some stories about me to tell the kids. It's painful for me to say that my daughter has no idea who I am. She was only two years old the last time she saw me. I'm sure my son will remember me. He can tell you I'm his father."

"Monique wouldn't lie to me. I love that girl and trust her more than some stranger I just met."

"Ma'am, why isn't Monique with you right now? Where do you think she is this very moment?"

"Monique is a nurse. She had to stay behind at the hospital and care for those poor people. Chad said she was one of the few people who stayed behind at the hospital when everyone else left those poor sick people to die. Once my husband and I are safe with the kids, he's gonna go back and get her."

None of this surprised Richard in the least, he even had to stop himself from laughing. He'd learned the hard way that Monique's talent for lying bordered on sociopathic. She could manipulate anyone into believing anything she told them. This poor woman was no exception.

"Ma'am, where can I find Chad?"

"He's over with the rest of the group. He and my husband wanted me to stay with the RV."

"Thank you, ma'am, I'm very sorry for bothering you."

The old woman looked at Richard in disgust and slammed the door behind her.

Tank walked back over to Richard. "See what I mean? You and trouble are old friends."

Richard didn't reply. He scanned the crowd and tried to figure out his next move. He knew he wouldn't have any problem picking Chad or his father out of the crowd; he had memorized their faces from the pictures in Monique's iPad and had asked Tank to do the same while they were in the truck.

"Do you see them?" asked Tank.

"No. They're here somewhere, though, so keep looking."

They didn't have to look very long. They saw Chad and his father walking back toward their RV with Richard's son following close behind. Richard tapped Tank on the shoulder, and they both started walking back to the RV. Suddenly, Chad spotted them and turned, grabbing his father's arm to stop him. Richard's son noticed nothing and kept walking toward the RV. Richard was relieved that his son kept going. If things went poorly with Chad, the last thing he wanted was a repeat of Oswald Jefferson's murder. He had scarred his son for life by brutally murdering a man in front of him; he didn't plan to repeat it.

Chad had his chest stuck out and was staring Richard down, ready to take him on if he had to. However, his bravado was quickly squashed when he saw Tank.

"Fuck you want?"

"Well, Chad, we need to have a little talk."

"How the fuck you know my name?"

"Well, we have a lot in common, you see. You're dating my ex-wife."

"No shit, you're Bryan?"

"No, I'm her first husband."

"Bullshit! That guy's dead."

"I look dead to you?"

"No, you look like a lying sack of shit to me."

"Listen here, sport, I couldn't care less if you believe me or not. What's important for you to know is I'm here to take my kids."

"Is that right?"

"That's right."

"Fuck off, man. They ain't your kids. I don't know what kind of bullshit scam you're trying to pull, but it's not going to work. I've made a lot of friends here, and they ain't gonna let you do a fucking thing."

"Monique ever tell you about her first husband?"

"Yeah, she told me everything."

"Well, most of it's probably untrue, given the fact that she told you I was dead. I'm curious - where is Monique? You bring her along?"

"I'm getting tired of listening to you, man. Fuck off." Chad started to walk away, but Richard stopped him dead in his tracks.

"She's at home strung out on heroin." Richard watched as Chad stopped walking and turned around with a look of shock on his face. "There ya go, sport! Knew that would grab your attention. You made up some tale about her being Florence Nightingale staying behind to care for sick patients. Complete garbage, but I will give it to you, not a bad cover story."

Richard paused to let in sink in. Chad was frantically searching for something to say and finally spoke to his father in a weak voice, "Dad, he's lying, you know that."

Richard saw confusion on the older man's face. He obviously knew the kind of man his son was and doubted his story. "Chad, please tell me you didn't do what I think you did. I thought the Good Lord had changed you. Your mother and I have prayed for your soul, and we thought you had truly found Jesus."

"Don't start with that shit! I'm not getting into this with you again!"

"I have had just about enough of your foul tongue. The Bible says..."

"Shut up! Go back to the RV, and let me handle this!"

"Tell this man the truth!"

"Go back to the RV, now!"

"I will, son. Your mother and I will be praying for your soul. It will break her heart when she hears about this." The old man wiped tears from his cheeks as he looked at Richard and nodded.

"Start talking, sport. What's the truth you need to tell me? You Monique's dealer? Why didn't you bring her? She cheating on you? Found a better score?"

"Fuck that bitch! I was gonna bring her along so I could sell her pussy. She's a fucking freak in the sack, but you already know that, don't you?"

Richard's blood began to boil. He was ready to break this little punk's jaw but managed to keep his cool for his children's sake. "Listen here, sport, I'm not in the slightest bit concerned about my junkie ex-wife. The only thing that matters to me is getting my kids the hell away from you. This is what's gonna happen. You're gonna go back to the RV and explain to your parents that those kids are mine, and they are coming with me. No one needs to get hurt."

"Well, that's gonna be a problem. You can have your son. I'm tired of that little shit anyway. Only reason he's here is he keeps my parents busy and off my back. Your daughter? Well, sorry to tell you she ain't here."

"You wanna run that by me again, sport? What do you mean she ain't here? Where is she? You leave her with her mother? Because if you did, that's a problem. She wasn't in the house."

"Well, two RV-Towns back we were completely out of gas. This nice couple really, really liked her. They had a little toddler that needed a big sister. So, I traded a full tank of gas for little Chrissy."

Richard leapt forward and pinned Chad against the RV behind him. He punched him in the stomach and rammed his knee into his balls. Once he was doubled over in pain, Richard propped him back up against he RV, pinning his shoulders down.

"You're lying! Your parents..."

"My parents think the family is gonna catch up with us, thinks Chrissy is playing big sister with the little rugrat. I seriously doubt they're even close. The dad really liked Chrissy. I mean, like *really* liked her a lot."

Richard fought as hard as he could to maintain control of himself. Ever fiber of his being, every single muscle in his body was crying out to introduce this man to Oswald Jefferson deep down in the lowest bowels of hell. *You need him to find Chrissy. You need him to find Chrissy. You need him to find Chrissy.* He kept repeating the phrase over and over in his mind.

Richard's self control slipped farther away as the man began to laugh at him. "You can't kill me and you know it. Look around you, asshole. Every person here has a gun, and somebody will shoot you dead if I so much as scream. A few people have already seen us and are running to get help, so you better let me go." Chad looked past Richard at Tank. "And keep your dog on a leash. He might be the biggest mother fucker I've ever see in my life, but someone empties a clip into him he'll go down just the same."

Richard knew the dead man walking was right. He needed to think fast or things would get out of hand in a hurry. Richard decided fear and intimidation were his only course.

"This is what I'm gonna do, sport. You ready? Here we go."

Richard rammed his knee into Chad's balls again and when he doubled over, Richard wrapped his arm around his neck. Richard placed the crook of his arm directly on top of the man's voice box and flexed his bicep and forearm, cutting off the blood supply to his internal and external jugular veins. In less than ten seconds, Chad was unconscious.

"Billy, get him out of this area quick before anyone comes back. Do. Not. Kill. Him. I need him alive!" Tank picked up Chad like a rag doll and ran around the side of the RV and behind another one.

Richard needed answers and had no intention of trying to get them from Chad. He walked back to his parents' RV and knocked on the door. The door opened and standing in front of Richard was his firstborn child. He was so focused and determined to find out what happened to his daughter that he had forgotten about his son. Richard was speechless and couldn't take his eyes off the boy. He was thirteen years old and looked just like his father had at that age. Richard's eyes filled with tears as he searched for some glimmer of recognition in his son's eyes.

"Hello, Timothy."

"Do you know me?"

"I do, yes."

"Who are you?"

A tear spilled down Richard's cheek, and he searched for what to say. Would his son be immediately brought back to the nursery seeing his father brutally take a man's life in front of his very eyes? Would he scream at him in fear? Would Timothy even remember him? Had his mind built a psychological barrier around the horrible memory, protecting him from insanity? Richard had been through hell and back to get to this moment. He had no choice but to take the leap.

"Timothy, this might be hard for..."

"Where's my boy? Where's Chad?" The old man stepped from the back of the RV with a look of terror on his face. "Is he okay?"

"Your son is fine, sir. We need to talk. May I please come in?"

"Yes, yes, yes. Come on inside and sit down. Timmy, go in the back with Grammy so I can talk with his man. Go on now. Turn on a movie and keep her company, hurry up."

Richard's son walked to the back of the RV and slid the partition closed. The old man waited for the sound of the movie to drown out their conversation, "I'm no fool, mister. That boy back there looks just like you. You're his daddy, I know that. I'm sure you're worried about Chrissy, and you should be."

"Sir, I didn't get your name," asked Richard.

"Morris Jackson."

"My name is Richard. What do you think happened to her?"

"Well, that's just it. I'm not sure. I've been trying my hardest to get the truth outta that boy. He has his mother believing the story he made up. Barbara believes everything that boy tells her. She refuses to admit that our son has problems.

We've raised him up to be a God fearing, Christian man, but he..."

"Morris, I got him to tell me the truth and I need your help."

"Oh Lord help that boy. Chrissy not with that family? She not meetin' us here?"

"She's with the family, sir, but they're not meeting us here. Your son sold my daughter for a tank of gas."

As Morris began to weep uncontrollably, Richard continued. "Sir, I need your help if I'm gonna get Chrissy back. I'm hoping you met this family and can describe their RV to me."

"Oh Lord Jesus! That sweet girl! What did he do to that precious girl? Lord in heaven above, I beseech thee to keep that innocent lamb safe from harm! Please Jesus, please!" Morris fell to the floor and pleaded and begged through desperate tears. "Oh Heavenly Father, I beg of you to spare that innocent child! Please!"

Richard was uncomfortable listening to the man pray. Richard believed in God but was cursed with the memories associated with the Winchester Street Baptist Church. Worship had never been the same since Oswald Jefferson and that fateful day. Richard waited until Morris was done petitioning the Almighty and helped him up off the floor.

"Morris, you can help me save my daughter. Tell me about the family, and try to remember what the RV looked like."

"Mister, I'm afraid I can't help you. I never met them or saw the RV."

"Your wife?"

"No, sir, she would have never let Chrissy go with anybody. No way, no how."

Richard closed his eyes as crushing despair fell down on him. He only had one course of action - kidnap Chad and double back down Interstate 25. "Morris, I'm gonna have to take Chad with me so I can track down my little girl. I trust my son is in good hands?"

"Absolutely. I will protect him to my dying breath."

"Sir, you have my sincere gratitude. I'll be back as soon as I can."

"If we're not here in the RV, then we'll be down in this bunker place that's supposed to be here."

"Thank you." Richard exited the RV and raced back to the spot where they'd confronted Chad. He looked around but couldn't see Tank in the immediate vicinity. Then Richard saw several people running and decided to follow them. He rounded an RV and was shocked to see two uniformed police officers. One was an absolutely gorgeous woman, and the other was a man in his early forties with a very noticeable limp. They had their weapons drawn and pointed at someone. Richard walked around the crowd to get a better look.

Tank was standing with both arms raised in the air. In his left hand he was holding up Chad by his hair. In his bloody right hand he was holding a chunk of torn flesh from Chad's neck. Richard looked at Chad's face, his eyes open and vacant. Chad was dead. He was on his way to hell to meet Oswald Jefferson and share with him the secret of Chrissy's whereabouts. Richard's face turned red, and the veins in his forehead bulged. He balled his fists as he looked at Tank and howled in rage.

He was going to kill that motherfucker.

CHAPTER THIRTY-SIX

Chief Maxwell Harris and Sergeant Elizabeth Reed were sitting in their SUV a mile away from Beck Estates. The two police officers couldn't believe what they were seeing in front of them.

"Son of a bitch," said Max.

"What's the plan, boss man?" asked Elizabeth.

"I have no idea."

"I feel much better. Glad to know you're on top of things."

"I'm open to suggestions."

"I don't have any."

"You're a big help."

"Hey, I'm just along for the ride."

In the valley below them stood the largest house they had ever seen. While the house was impressive enough to take their breath away, what concerned them was the military base being built across from the main gate. It was massive. Row upon row of temporary buildings had been erected, and an entire platoon of soldiers stood guard at the main gate of Beck Estates. Max and Elizabeth watched in awe as a formation of helicopters took off from an adjacent field and headed south.

"And to think I pictured us just knocking on the front door."

"Not thinking that's an option."

"Clearly." Max had no idea what to do. He thought about just turning around and driving back to Truth or Consequences, New Mexico to pick up Dr. Stone. They had come too far to turn around. The military force in front of him had kidnaped four innocent civilians against their will. Their poor families deserved an explanation.

Elizabeth turned to face Max. "You know they're not just going to let us sit here. Pretty soon they're going to send someone up here to find out what we're doing."

"Did it cross your mind that we might be drafted into military service?"

"I would look positively stunning in a military uniform. Your crippled ass probably wouldn't make the cut. If they did let you in, you'd be sitting in front of a desk shuffling paperwork."

"You'd look stunning in a potato sack. And you're definitely right. I don't see me passing any physicals."

"What do you want to do?"

"The only thing we can do - drive up to the front gate and demand to speak to someone in charge."

"Probably shouldn't make any demands. I'd stick to saying pretty please."

"Good idea."

Max drove forward very slowly. When he was a few hundred yards from the front gate, he flipped a switch and the red and blue lights on the roof lit up. He figured it was a good idea to display a little authority. Twenty yards shy of the gate, an armed soldier signaled for him to stop.

"State your business," said the soldier in a stern voice.

"I'm here to see your commander."

"Sir, I need to see credentials for both of you."

"Of course." Max and Elizabeth reached into their shirt pockets and pulled out their badges. Max handed both ID wallets to the soldier and waited as he inspected them closely.

"I need to inspect your vehicle. Please step out and surrender your firearms."

"Sure thing." Max and Elizabeth slowly stepped out of the SUV and handed over their weapons.

The first soldier spoke, "Chief Harris, what brings you to our nation's capital?"

Max and Elizabeth exchanged puzzled looks. "I'm searching for four missing persons. I was hoping that your commander might be able to share some information that would aide in the search."

"Sergeant! Come take a look at this!" said one of the soldiers searching the SUV. The first soldier placed Max and Elizabeth's IDs in his front pocket and walked to the back of the SUV. He glanced in the back and walked back to Max.

"Chief, I need you explain why the back of your vehicle is full of gasoline."

Max smiled. "Not a lot of gas stations open these days. We've come a long way."

"Very true. This is what I'm going to do. I'm going to fill out a confiscation form and store the gasoline in a secure area.

Once you leave, it will be returned to you. I'm sure you understand the precaution."

"Of course. No objections," said Max.

The soldier keyed up his radio and gave instructions. Minutes later, two soldiers arrived with a cart, loaded up the gasoline and hauled it away.

"Chief, ma'am, if the two of you will wait over there in that building, I will contact General Butler. Please be patient. General Butler is a busy man and will be with you in due time."

"Thank you," said Max. He and Elizabeth did as they were instructed. The one room building resembled a briefing room of some sort. As they were sitting down, Max leaned toward Elizabeth and whispered, "I'm sure they're watching us." Without moving her lips, Elizabeth let out a barely audible "Yeah."

Max decided to give his hosts something to watch and struck up a conversation with Elizabeth. "Isn't this exciting? I can't believe we're actually in the new capital!"

Elizabeth played along. "You think they might let us inside? I wonder what they call this place?"

Elizabeth deserved an Academy Award for the acting she was doing. "You know, this place gives me hope. They're really doing something special here. I can't wait to tell my grandchildren that I was here when it was first built. This is just too cool. To think that folks like us get a front row seat to the birth of a new nation. I'm just beside myself."

"Me, too," said Max.

A young soldier walked into the room and spoke. "Can I get you folks anything? Something to drink?"

Max looked at Elizabeth, who shook her head, and then back at the soldier. "I think we're fine, thank you."

"Just let me know if you need anything, I was told to inform you that General Butler will be here shortly."

"Thank you," smiled Max as the young soldier walked out.

"Wow, we get to meet a general? How awesome is that?" asked Elizabeth.

"Pretty awesome," replied Max. Someday soon they'd have a laugh about this conversation.

A few minutes later, a man and woman walked into the

room. The man was General Butler. Max could clearly read his nametag and see the star on his lapel. The woman was a tall, attractive blonde in her mid-thirties. As Max and Elizabeth stood to greet the pair, General Butler walked forward and shook Max's hand. "You must be Chief Harris. I'm General Jackson Butler, this is Stacy Reid."

Max shook Stacy's hand. "I'm Maxwell Harris, this is Elizabeth Reed."

With the introductions out of the way, General Butler sat down at the table and the other three followed suit. Once everyone was comfortable, General Butler gave Max his full attention and waited for him to speak.

"General, first of all I'm thankful for your time. I know you must be busy."

"Not too busy to help a law enforcement official. What can I do for you?"

"Well, I'll get right to the point. I evacuated from Texas and made my way into New Mexico, where I came across a bunch of nice folks who needed our help. The local chief there had his hands full, so we gladly offered our services. Four of their citizens were kidnapped recently, and I'm trying to find them. I hope that you might be able to help us."

"In what way?"

"Well, I can't think of anyone close by who could do a better job of spreading the word and keeping an eye out for these folks," Max reached into his jacket and pulled out four photographs. "Three doctors and one nurse, taken right out of the little hospital in the town. You have any information that might be of use? Would you ask around and see if you come up with anything?"

General Butler picked up the photographs and studied them. "Well, Chief Harris, these folks don't look familiar, and I haven't heard anything about any kidnappings. I will certainly circulate these photographs and have my men keep their eyes and ears open. Do you have any more details that might be useful? Any idea who took them?"

Max knew the man was lying but didn't show it. "No idea. The hospital staff noticed them missing, and they searched the area but came up with nothing."

"Well, forgive me for being blunt, Chief, but how do you know they didn't skip town together?"

"I asked the same question. Three out of four of them have spouses and children and they didn't leave word with them. Their families haven't heard from them at all. One person running out on their family I can believe, but four all at the same time? And from the same place? I don't buy it. Someone took them."

"What are your plans from here?"

"I'm going to keep searching the area. With your permission, I'll check back here in a week or so to see if you've come up with anything."

"Of course. In the meantime we'll do everything we can to help track these folks down. Unless there's something else I can help you with, I have work to do."

Max stood up and shook General Butler's hand. "You've been a big help, thank you. Let me just say that it's a true honor to be here, and we both appreciate everything you're doing to get our country back on track."

Stacy stood up. "General, with your permission, I'd like to give our guests a tour of the base's non-restricted areas."

General Butler spoke over his shoulder as he exited the building. "Of course, Stacy, go right ahead."

Once General Butler was out of earshot, Max looked at Stacy. "I appreciate the offer, ma'am, but we really need to get going. We would hate to be a burden."

"Chief, I insist. It's no trouble at all. Please, follow me."

Max looked at Elizabeth and realized they didn't have much of a choice. "You ready? I know you really want to look around."

Elizabeth grinned. "I'm really excited! This is going to be fun!"

The three of them exited the building and walked across the road. Soldiers were marching by in formation singing a cadence. Humvees and other vehicles drove up and down the road.

Stacy smiled. "May I call you Maxwell?"

"Max."

"Max, do the two of you have good poker faces?"

"Excuse me?" said Max.

"I have a lot to tell you, and it's important that you don't react. I'm going to lead you around like a tour guide and point stuff out to you. All you have to do is look interested. Are we clear?"

Max was getting very nervous. "Yes, we'll play along."

"Good. Just keep smiling like you're at Disney World for the first time."

"Is Disney World still standing after Luther?"

"I have no idea, but I doubt it."

Elizabeth was grinning like a little girl. "Are we in danger?"

"It's best that you don't ask questions; we don't have a lot of time. Just let me talk."

"Okay."

"Chances are pretty good that your people are here. They've been kidnapping hundreds of people and keeping them prisoner in the detention center. They have the nerve to call it a 'draft' so they can tell themselves they're doing the right thing. They keep the people locked up like they committed a crime and won't let them contact their families." Stacy smiled and placed her hand on Max's shoulder and pointed behind him. Max turned around and looked at a tall array of antennas and appeared impressed.

"Let me guess. We're about to be drafted?"

"Yes. General Butler was about to take you to the detention center himself, so I volunteered." Stacy looked at Elizabeth and laughed cheerfully like they were becoming best friends, "The General really likes you a lot, Elizabeth. Said you were going to be his personal assistant."

Elizabeth didn't have to fake a laugh; a genuine one was no problem. "He's not even my type. Besides, my boyfriend here wouldn't like that very much."

"Boyfriend? Are we in high school or something?" said Max.

"I've got more to say, but I need to hurry. If you didn't already know, this is Howard Beck's house. I have no idea what happened to Howard. He managed to escape before they could get to him. I've contacted Howard's son, Marshall. He loaded his family into an RV, and they're headed to a secret underground facility Howard built north of here. Head up Interstate 25 and look in the RV-Towns for him. Marshall is the spitting image of his father, so you shouldn't have a hard time finding him."

Max looked out at a large pasture full of helicopters and pointed at them with huge eyes. "How are we gonna get out of here?"

Stacy smiled and shook her head, making it look like she was giving a lecture on the helicopters. "The motor pool is just up ahead. They trust the mechanics to keep an eye on everything, but they spend most of their time playing grab ass. I'm going to flirt with them as a diversion while you two slip around the side of the bay and make a break for it. Your SUV have a thumbprint key?"

"Yeah."

"Good. I hope you have a full tank of gas."

"Full enough."

"Find Marshall Beck and tell him President Sterling needs to be stopped. I don't have proof, but I'm convinced he murdered President Powers."

"Are you serious? Powers is dead? Sterling killed him?" Max and Elizabeth both struggled to maintain their poker faces.

Stacy smiled. "Yes, I'm sure of it."

"Son of a bitch," said Max.

The three of them continued their cheerful facade as they walked toward the motor pool. As Stacy laid on the charm and flirted with the four mechanics, Max and Elizabeth slowly walked out of their line of sight and headed for their SUV. The quiet hybrid engine purred to life, and Max slowly pulled out, heading north. It would be some time before anyone noticed they were gone. Stacy would blame it on the incompetence of the soldiers at the detention center.

****

Marshall Beck stood on the roof of his RV and raised his arms high in the air. "Please, if I could have everyone's attention! Please quiet down! This is important!"

Max and Elizabeth had no trouble finding Marshall Beck.

It was simple deduction that a secret underground facility would not be close to Denver. They drove north to Fort Collins and starting looking in RV-Towns. When they got to the third one, they saw a large crowd of people gathered together like they were at a rock concert. The man standing on the roof of the RV looked exactly like Howard Beck had twenty-five years ago.

"For those of you who want to follow me, I'll be leaving in five minutes." Marshall Beck climbed down the ladder at the rear of the RV. Max and Elizabeth caught him before he made it to the door. "Officers, is there a problem?" asked Marshall.

"Stacy Reid sent us."

Marshall looked surprised. "Well then, please come inside." Marshall opened the door and ushered Max and Elizabeth inside.

"You were at my dad's house?"

"Yes, we left there a few hours ago."

"You actually spoke to Stacy?"

"We did. She saved us from being 'drafted' into President Sterling's army."

"I like that. What a pleasant euphemism for imprisonment."

"She said they have hundreds locked up in a detention center. We were tracking down three doctors and a nurse who were snatched up in a small town in New Mexico. She told me to tell you that President Sterling needs to be stopped. She's certain that he assassinated President Powers."

"That changes everything. We know he's locking down the major cities in a police state and snatching up people with professional skills, but if that man assassinated President Powers then he truly is a madman."

"I couldn't agree more. My name is Maxwell Harris, and this is Elizabeth Reed."

Marshall leaned forward and shook his hand. "I'm Marshall Beck, and this is my Uncle Sean and Aunt Tricia. That young man over there is my cousin Jamison," Marshall said, as he introduced the others in the RV.

As the introductions proceeded, Max looked at Tricia and could see the family resemblance; she was clearly Howard Beck's sister.

Marshall continued, "Well, folks, I wish we could take the time to get to know each other, but we need to get moving. Beck Castle is about an hour's drive from here, and we won't be driving on any roads."

"Beck Castle?" asked Max.

"It's a secret underground bunker that my parents built. It's massive and can hold hundreds, if not thousands of people. My father wanted to keep it a secret from me, but my mother told me all about it and even took me there when dad was overseas on business. Mom even convinced Hal to keep it a secret from dad."

"And who is Hal?"

"Another long story. You'll be meeting him soon enough; that is, of course, if you're joining us"

"Sure. If you people are planning to stop Simon Sterling then I'm along for the ride."

"Great, let's get going. Do you need any gas? We have plenty to spare."

"I should be good, thanks. The one thing we do need is firearms. Ours were confiscated by the military."

Marshall turned to Jamison and nodded. The young man disappeared into the back of the RV and returned with two Glock 19s and four boxes of ammunition. He handed them to Max and Elizabeth.

"Outstanding! Thank you," said Max.

"Don't mention it. Got one myself."

Sean headed toward the door. "Jamison, I want you to stay here and continue doing what your cousin has been doing. Tell the next group we'll be back for them soon."

"Yes, sir."

Max and Elizabeth headed for their SUV. As Marshall Beck's RV slowly headed out in the open field, Max pulled his vehicle behind him and followed.

****

"Hal, this is ridiculous. Tell my dad to come up here and talk to me."

Howard Beck's A.I., Hal, was standing in front of his creator's son in the form of a robot. Transferring his primary program into a maintenance robot and controlling it was a simple enough task. The robot had the physical characteristics of a man - it had a torso, arms and legs. The one trait that greatly differed from the human form was its head, which was a flat panel computer monitor twelve inches across. When Hal extended himself into a robot, the head monitor showed the image of his namesake, the HAL-9000 from the movie *2001: A Space Odyssey*. Marshall had waited over two hours before the robot suddenly appeared from behind a hill.

"Sir, it is not necessary for your father to come up here. He is monitoring this conversation from the command center."

"Jesus Christ, Hal! I'm not talking through you! The least he can do is show his face on your monitor!"

Ten seconds went by and the HAL-9000 image disappeared from the monitor to be replaced by Howard Beck's face.

"Hello, son. It's been a long time."

"Dad, is there a reason you haven't let me in? Are you really just going to leave me up here?"

"I would have let you in the minute you got here if you'd come alone. I'm not letting a bunch of strangers down here to cause problems."

"Damn it, Dad! These are just everyday people looking for a safe place to stay! Families! Women and children! A lot of people up here are hungry and scared! Did you forget why you and Mom built this in the first place? This is why!" Marshall grabbed the robot and swung its head around to see the crowd of people. "You probably never imagined that the world would actually end, but it's crumbling down all around us! Have you been ignoring everything? Do you even care about what goes on outside your little world?" Marshall couldn't stand his father's lack of empathy. He loved the man but had spent his entire life trying to please him. Marshall had given up trying to read his father's emotions long ago. The cold, distant man was successful in driving his son away from him and into the arms of his mother. When his mother died, the standoff continued. The two had not spoken since Meredith's funeral. "Dad, you haven't seen your grandchildren since they were babies. You've missed out on so much of their lives. It's time for you to change that. Open the door! Let us inside!"

"I'm not surprised your mother told you about this place. She always denied it, but I knew. Just because I kept this a secret from you doesn't mean I wouldn't have sent for you and your family. You're my son. I know I've never been able to show it, but I love you very much. The people you brought with you today are the reason why I didn't want your mother to tell you about this place. You have your mother's kind and giving heart, and I knew you would want to help as many people as you could. Son, it's just not that simple. This is more than just an emergency shelter; it's much, much more than that. I don't know if your mother explained that to you, but you need to trust me when I tell you this place is far too important to risk."

"Dad, it's more than just these people. I have something else I need to tell you."

"What is it, son?"

"You're best friend was assassinated by his own vice president."

"I know that already, Marshall."

"We have to stop him."

"I'm planning on it."

"His Chief of Staff is working undercover with Sterling."

"I'm glad to hear that. I was shocked to see her in my home with the rest of the traitors. Are you sure?"

Max stepped forward. "Mr. Beck, my name is Maxwell Harris. My colleague and I were searching for four missing persons who were kidnaped by Sterling's people. As we were about to be taken ourselves, Stacy Reid warned us and helped us escape. I can vouch for her; she's on our side."

Howard was frowning at the man who had interrupted his conversation. One of Howard's dozens of pet peeves was being interrupted. He had even fired a few people who couldn't learn to stop doing it. "I'm sorry officer, what was your name again?"

"Chief Maxwell Harris."

"Chief of what, exactly?"

"Chief of Police of Santa Fe, Texas."

"Never heard of it."

"South of Houston."

"Had a spot of bad weather recently, didn't you?"

"You could say that."

Marshall waited to see if his father was done speaking and said, "Dad, what do you want to do with all of these people?"

"You need to explain to them that the only way they're coming down here is if they're thoroughly searched by Hal and screened for infectious diseases. Their firearms will be unloaded and stored in a secured room. They will also be expected to follow a set of rules. If anyone harms another person they'll be escorted out by Hal. My terms are unconditional and non-negotiable. Anyone refusing to comply will be denied entry. I will leave Hal with you so he can assist you. I have work to do. Hal will tell me when you're ready."

"I understand, Dad. I'll make the announcement."

The image of Howard's face was replaced with the original picture. The Hal robot headed toward the group of people. It wasn't often that Hal got to mingle.

Marshall climbed back on board his RV and began repeating the instructions his father had given him. Few people in the group objected.

Max and Elizabeth walked back to their SUV and rested against the front bumper. Max leaned over and kissed Elizabeth on the cheek. The warmest smile spread across her face, and her beauty took Max's breath away.

"Are you blushing, my dear?" asked Max.

"Don't tease me. It's not nice," pouted Elizabeth.

"Come here, you." Max pulled Elizabeth over to him. Gently holding her face between his burly hands, Max kissed her passionately. She sighed and moaned softly. The two of them were engulfed in a rising passion. Their lives had been filled with anguish and pain. They'd seen friends brutally murdered, and both had killed to defend themselves and each other. The only thing left in their lives that was good and pure was their love.

Their kiss was interrupted by a bloodcurdling scream. Max and Elizabeth bolted from the SUV and ran to see what was happening. A woman was crying and running wildly toward them. She pointed to a green mini-van. As they rounded the vehicle, they saw the most terrifying looking man they'd ever seen. He was over three hundred pounds of muscle and maybe a few inches shy of seven feet tall. His body was covered in offensive tattoos, but the most grotesque thing about him was his left eye. It was solid white and sat behind a large scar.

The monster had another man suspended by his hair and was pounding him in the torso like a punching bag. Then the giant wrapped his free hand around the man's throat and dug his fingers into his neck. Blood spurted from the man's neck like a geyser as his throat was ripped from his body.

Max and Elizabeth were about to unload every bullet they had when another equally strange event took place.

A much shorter and leaner man was howling at the top of his lungs. Max was sure the man was as terrified as he was, but he didn't run away in fear. Instead, the smaller man ran toward the beast with the most intense hatred Max had ever seen.

The smaller man didn't even try to tackle the giant, knowing it would be a waste of time. He drove his foot into the side of the giant's knee in an attempt to buckle his leg. It worked for a brief second but the giant rebounded and straightened his leg as he swung the corpse in his left hand into the smaller man. The smaller man rebounded and took up a fighting stance. When the giant swung his arm, the man grabbed it with both hands and jumped on the giant's back. The little man grabbed the giant's right ear and yanked down, tearing off the top portion of it. While the giant was howling, the slighter man rammed his thumb into the giant's demon eye. The beast fell to the ground like an oak tree. The smaller man pounded the giant's throat four times with a hammer chop. The monster gurgled and spat blood as his competitor dug both of his thumbs into the giant's eyes and pushed down with all his weight. The smaller man took his thumb out of the giant's good eye and punched him in the throat until he stopped moving. The undersized fighter stood and brought his foot down on the monster's throat, breaking his neck. David had slain Goliath.

Max stood motionless staring at the victor. He looked at Elizabeth, whose jaw was gaping in amazement. He lowered his weapon and reached up to lower Elizabeth's weapon for her. He turned back to the winner of the death match.

"Please tell me you're done."

"I'm good, thanks

CHAPTER THIRTY-SEVEN

The Hal robot was performing a juggling act for a small group of children who were clapping and cheering him on. Hal was juggling four rocks of varying size with dazzling proficiency. None of them had ever seen a robot do such a thing; it was truly impressive.

The juggling act was suddenly interrupted by a scream.

Hal jumped into the air and landed on the roof of an RV. He leapt over an adjacent RV and landed on the ground. In a span of time so short it could hardly be measured, Hal made the following assessment:

Subject A had murdered a man by tearing his throat out with his bare hands. Subject B had either tried to defend the murder victim, was the murder victim's accomplice, or was carrying out revenge on Subject A for the murder he committed. The two law enforcement officials accompanying Marshall Beck were in front of him with their weapons drawn on the subjects. Once Hal completed his assessment, the course of action he decided upon was to allow Chief Harris and his colleague to handle the situation and provide assistance only if it was required.

Based upon the weight and muscle mass index of the two subjects, Hal calculated a seventy one point four percent chance that Subject A would defeat Subject B if the two law enforcement officials did not intervene. The altercation began and Hal watched the two subjects fight each other. As each millisecond passed, the percentage points he had calculated before the altercation began to lower and lower for Subject A and rose quickly for Subject B. Hal watched as Subject B raised his right foot in the air and brought it down on Subject A's neck. The robot's sensors scanned Subject A's life signs and determined that he was deceased.

"Please tell me you're done," said Chief Harris.

"I'm good, thanks," said Subject B.

"You mind telling me what that was all about?" said Chief Harris.

"Are you going to arrest me?" asked Subject B.

"For slaying a monster? Probably not. Still wanna know what it was about though. The dead guy a friend of yours?"

"I count two dead guys."

"The first dead guy."

"No, he wasn't. What the hell is that thing?" Subject B pointed at the Hal Robot.

"Oh, yeah, that's Howard Beck's robot, Hal. You've heard of him?"

"I read about him once. Thought he was some massive computer, the first one the have Artificial Intelligence. Didn't know he was a robot."

Hal spoke in his proper English accent, "I am more than just a robot. My program can be extended into several outlets simultaneously. My primary duty at this moment is to assist the creator's son in preparing everyone for entry into the facility. Your actions require an explanation, or I will have to restrain you to prevent further injury to others." The Hal Robot raised his arms and walked toward Subject B.

Jamison Stewart was walking toward the scene with his cousin, Marshall Beck. Jamison yelled from twenty yards away, "Hey! Leave him alone! He's a good guy!"

Marshall Beck called out to the Hal robot. "Hal! Take it easy! We can handle this!"

Meredith Beck had programed Hal to follow any command from her son as long as it didn't contradict her husband. "Yes, sir, I will be standing by to assist you."

Marshall Beck looked at the man who had slain the giant. If the man's name was David, the parallel to the biblical tale of David and Goliath would be amazing. "Mister, you're damned lucky these two officers didn't shoot you dead."

Richard looked back and forth between the crippled officer and the woman who should be a Victoria's Secret Model and sized them up. They were in love with each other; that much was obvious. The male cop was a sharp guy. He'd probably been in law enforcement his entire adult life and could perform well in a jam. The woman seemed like a firecracker who wasn't about to take shit from anyone.

"I appreciate you guys not killing me. I'm in your debt."

Max snapped his Glock back into its holster. "You still haven't answered my question. What the hell was that all about?"

"I'll tell you all about it if you tell my why neither one of you shot me dead."

"When a man that big is holding a corpse by the hair with one hand and its throat in the other, you think twice about shooting him for it. The thought of missing the target or grazing him and pissing him off crossed my mind. I'd finally worked up the courage to start firing when you came into the picture. After a few seconds I was enjoying the show and figured you'd kill him for me. Most phenomenal ass kicking I've ever seen. I thought for sure he was gonna rip your head off and kick it like a football. I didn't catch your name. I'm Maxwell Harris, and this is Elizabeth Reid"

Richard wasn't one to be flattered by praise. "My name is Richard Dupree. That young man over there has already heard what I'm about to tell you," Richard said, pointing at Jamison. "The dead man there, well, the first dead man sold my daughter for a tank of gas. I was in the process of trying to uncover her whereabouts when I saw the only man who could lead me to her dead with his throat ripped out."

"Why'd the big guy kill him?" asked Marshall.

"I have no idea."

Richard turned to Max. "Well, what's it going to be? You arresting me?"

Max replied, "Well, considering that I'm way out of my jurisdiction, and you could pull that ninja shit to stop me, I'll give you a pass."

"I save the ninja shit for people who do the wrong thing."

"You kill everyone who does the wrong thing?"

"Only if they're trying to kill me."

"I can live with that."

"We're gonna get along just fine, Max."

Max looked at Marshall Beck. "Something tells me your father isn't going to like this at all, once he finds out these people might be stuck up here for good."

"My father isn't going to find out about this," replied Marshall.

"How do you know he doesn't know already?" asked Max.

"Because Hal is still here. If he knew, Hal would be long gone, and we'd never hear a word from down below. Hal, what is my father doing right now?"

The Hal robot replied, "Sir, he is in the dormitory wing inspecting the living conditions of the quarters."

"Good. Hal, what brought you over here?"

"Sir, I heard a scream and responded."

"You're never to tell my father about anything that happened, from the instant you first heard the scream until now. If he asks you to play back footage of today's events, you're to remove the time frame I just mentioned and replace it with different footage. Do you understand?"

"I understand, sir."

"Good." Marshall looked at the group of people standing in front of him. "It's time to get these people ready to begin their new lives. Richard, I'm sure you have some catching up to do with your son. When you're done I hope you'll join us." Marshall looked at Max and Elizabeth. "My father could use our help evicting a madman from his home."

CHAPTER THIRTY-EIGHT

President Simon Sterling sat in the grand library of his palatial mansion trying to decide on a new name for the presidential estate, the centerpiece of his new government. Some of his guests had tried to refer to it as "The New White House," and he promptly put a stop to it. He didn't want his new government to have any ties to Washington D.C. or any of its iconic monuments. Squabbling over elections and other political pettiness was part of the broken government he had discarded. He was going to run things his way. He would have plenty of time to select a name for his estate and a successor.

Simon would have to institute a great deal of change in a very short amount of time. His greatest advantage was the EMP attack. He was sure that many people close to him suspected The Pulse to be his own dirty work. Simon wasn't responsible for the nuclear warhead detonated in the atmosphere, but he enjoyed letting his people think he was. Let them wonder and gossip about it. If his own people thought him capable of such an act, they would fear him for it. Simon knew the most important tool for controlling a population was fear. Let the people fear him; it would give them pause before thinking of rebellion. The Pulse not only gave him a frightened and confused nation crying out for his help, it gave him the perfect cover for disposing of his greatest obstacle, Malcolm Powers.

The original plan was to occupy the White House with the aide of Carl Moody and his Unified National Guard. Simon even had nearly a third of the Secret Service detail in the White House behind him. They were going to remove President Powers and allow him to retire to his ranch in upstate New York, under close supervision of the Unified National Guard, of course. The hardest part of the transition into the United American Empire would be telling four hundred and thirty-five members of the House of Representatives and fifty senators that they no longer had jobs. Simon Sterling firmly believed that American politics had two fatal flaws - flaws that led to its downfall. The first was corruption. Politicians lied with almost every breath they mustered and didn't hesitate to slit each others throats for gain. They were whores willing to sell their vote to the highest bidder.

The second was ineffectiveness. Politicians did not represent the people who elected them. They might have held onto the delusion that they served the public, but the only thing they represented was Big Business. The ones that didn't play ball with the corporations running America quickly found themselves booted out of Washington.

Simon was going to put an end to every shred of democracy in the former United States. Democracy had failed miserably; the proof was all around them. It was time for one man to set it right. Simon believed that he was that man. He knew he would face opposition at first. It was in man's very nature to question change. Change was frightening, it was unpredictable and most of all; it was uncomfortable. No one likes to change their very way of life. The old ways, no matter how flawed or destructive, were familiar and comfortable. Simon would meet any opposition swiftly and with force. Any former senator, congressman or congresswoman foolish enough to incite protest would be publicly executed to set an example.

Simon had no intention of becoming a mad dictator. He knew that the only way to set things right was for the people to have one voice to represent them, not hundreds of egotistical buffoons seeking to make a better life for themselves. Simon would appoint eight regional governors to supervise six states each. Hawaii and Alaska would just have to fend for themselves. Defending them would expend too many resources. Simon would allow the state governors to remain for a short time so the people would have something familiar to cling to, a useful buffer that would insulate him from the masses. Once he had a firm grasp on every stretch of land from the Pacific to the Atlantic, the state governors would be relieved and the eight regional governors alone would carry out his bidding.

Simon looked at his watch and realized his next meeting was in only a few minutes. He sincerely hoped he would receive the news he had been anticipating. There was a knock at the door. Simon called out, and a group of people entered.

"Please, come in. I've been looking forward to this all day."

Director Roberto Jimenez rolled himself into the room, followed by Chairman Carl Moody, Major General James

Weygandt, General Jackson Butler, and Stacy Reid.

"I've taken the liberty of having a meal prepared for us. Please sit down."

Everyone began to eat, anxious to hear what the new president had to say. They had serious doubts that this was just a casual meal. They all knew the president would be laying out the framework for his administration and announcing what roles they would play.

President Sterling was enjoying himself. Like his predecessor, Sterling enjoyed playing petty power games to make people squirm.

"I'm sure you can all imagine why you're here. I've prepared my inaugural address, and if everything goes according to plan," Simon looked at General Butler, "I'll be addressing the nation tonight."

"Mr. President, everything is proceeding as scheduled."

"Excellent, General Butler."

"Thank you, Mr. President, we have exceeded our initial estimates. Not only have we installed loudspeakers at every state capital, but the initial list of major cities was completed, as well as forty-seven additional cities. Your address to the nation will be heard by a great many people affected by The Pulse."

President Sterling raised his glass and looked down the table. "To General Butler! May we find even more men like him."

As everyone raised their glass in toast, Carl Moody chimed in a hearty, "Here here!"

"I have shared my plans with no one up until this very moment. All of you know that out of the ashes of our once great nation, we will be build a new one – a nation stronger and more worthy of her citizens, one that will protect her interests first before the rest of the world. We will show the world that we shall return!"

Everyone at the table stood and applauded. President Sterling remained seated and nodded his head in thanks with a gracious smile on his face. He politely motioned for them to be seated so he could continue. "The old ways of governing are gone. Every one of you in this room shares with me the contempt for how corrupt and ineffective our previous government became.

The heavy yoke of big government yanked this nation down beneath the waters and drowned her." President Sterling paused and added. "You know just how bad things are when our own people mock our government with the phrase 'It would take an Act of Congress to get that done.' That will not be the case from this moment forward. I will rule this nation with swift temperance and just wisdom. My friends, I cannot do it alone. I need your help. I'm sure everyone will join me in celebration when I say that Congress is hereby abolished!" Everyone in the room clapped and shouted their support. "The House and the Senate are a thing of the past! We will have a much, much smaller government that will be faster and more efficient. I will be appointing eight Regional Governors who will each be responsible for six states that belonged to our former nation. Before you do the math and ask the question, let me answer it for you. We will be more successful in our endeavors if we're only responsible for the forty-eight contiguous states." President Sterling turned and looked at the man seated to his left. "Before we discuss more changes, let us first address the one thing that will remain the same. Chairman Moody will remain in command of the Unified National Guard, answering only to me. Carl, I hereby promote you to the rank of Supreme Commander." The president stood and Carl Moody quickly rose and shook his hand. Everyone in the room clapped and showed their support.

President Sterling and Supreme Commander Moody took their seats. Stacy Reid had no delusions that she was about to be made a Regional Governor. She was confident that the men in the room would receive that posting. Still, she wondered why she was there. She'd been able to recover quickly from the escape of Maxwell Harris and Elizabeth Reed and remain in the good graces of General Butler. Her plan to blame it on the detention center worked perfectly. Stacy doubted if General Butler even mentioned it to the president.

"Gentlemen, the rest of you probably have a good idea what's going to happen, which leaves Stacy. Are you confused, dear?" Simon asked, smiling at Stacy. "Wondering why you've joined us?"

Stacy smiled coyly. "Yes, Mr. President."

"Well, I have grown to trust you since you arrived, thanks

in large part to Roberto. Your resume speaks for itself. I want everyone in this room to be perfectly clear that I had nothing but the utmost respect for Malcolm Powers. My quarrel was never with him; it was with the government as a whole. It was my sincere hope that many years down the road, he and I would develop the same relationship he had with President Clinton. I will miss the precious resource that would have been his counsel." Simon paused in quiet reflection and returned to his previous train of thought. "Stacy, I'm not going to have a staff of hundreds like other presidents, so a Chief of Staff is not really necessary. However, I would like to extend to you the position of Chief Advisor. Malcolm always told me that you kept him honest and called him on his bullshit ... well, behind closed doors of course!" President Sterling laughed and as if on cue, so did everyone else. "I would be honored by your candor as well as your counsel."

Stacy was becoming quite talented at masking her feelings. It was like she had developed an alter ego. "Mr. President, it would be my honor, thank you."

"Ma'am, the honor is truly mine. May you always keep me on the proper path." Simon smiled and raised his glass, turning to the man seated to his right.

"Roberto, you are the new Regional Governor of Region 1. I was going to let you retire to Florida, but it might be some time before there's a decent golf course to squeeze in nine holes," Simon bellowed. "I figured sunny California and her neighbors would be a good fit for you."

"Mr. President, I will do my best."

"I know you will." Simon looked down the table at Major General James Weygandt. "Jim, you'll be the Regional Governor of Region 2. You have your work cut out for you. You'll be responsible for Texas and her neighbors. I'm sure the recovery efforts are in good hands."

"Thank you, Mr. President. Truly an honor."

"Which brings us to our rising star, General Jackson Butler. General, you've proven yourself quite resourceful and a damned good officer. You are the Regional Governor of Region 3 and the Provisional Governor of Region 4. Your primary task will be to restore power to areas affected by The Pulse. Once you have completed the task, I will appoint a Regional Governor for Region 4 and you can return to your Region, which will be New England."

"Mr. President, I won't let you down."

"Jackson, I know you'll make us all proud. I'm happy to announce that Governor Lori Prince will be the Regional Governor of Region 5. Lori has been with us for some time. I knew when Malcolm betrayed her and left her citizens to fend for themselves we had an ally. Regional Governor Prince has already been informed of her appointment and has hit the ground running."

Simon waited a few moments for everyone's excitement to abate. They were already discussing plans. Simon was pleased with their eagerness. He continued, "You'll be pleased to know that you'll never have to run a campaign or drum up money from wealthy supporters. Your appointments are permanent, for as long as I deem necessary. If you continue to perform to my standards, the job will always be yours."

Regional Governor Weygandt spoke, "Mr. President, I'm sure I speak for everyone when I offer sincere gratitude. I'm sure everyone is wondering - who will fill the other Regional Governor positions?"

"I haven't made any decisions at this moment. I do welcome suggestions from any of you."

They were about to have dessert when the president looked at his watch. "Oh dear! It's almost time! Please, everyone, join me at my desk."

The president straightened his tie as he walked to his desk in the center of the library. He put on his suit coat and sat down. A woman turned on two bright lights and aimed them at the president's face so she could apply his makeup. The newly appointed members of his administration sat around him as technicians busily made last minute checks to sound and video equipment.

The Unified National Guard had been working tirelessly for days to transport generators and solar panels from the West Coast to the electricity-free Pulse Zone. Every state capital in the Pulse Zone would play the address over the loudspeakers. The capitals and major cities that still had some semblance of law and order would play the video broadcast on massive billboards all over town.

President Sterling sat behind his desk, waiting for the signal from the director. Once he got the green light, Sterling addressed the frightened and confused people of the United States.

"My fellow Americans, I address you from the seat of our government in the foothills of the Rocky Mountains. The people of our nation have never faced a greater challenge. The events of the past two weeks have had greater impact on the face of our nation than anything that came before it. It is my sincere hope that I can provide you with an accurate description of the events of the last few days. I know rumor and speculation are all that many of you have at this point.

Our nation watched in horror as the events played out on CNN. An Iranian submarine, the *Habibollah Sayyari*, launched a nuclear warhead high into the atmosphere from its position just over five hundred miles from the eastern seaboard. The resulting explosion generated an electromagnetic pulse which disrupted every electronic device from the East Coast towards the Great Plains and down to the northern portion of the Gulf States. Many of you hearing the sound of my voice are victims of The Pulse. Your government has not abandoned you. We are working around the clock to bring you needed relief. We cannot tell you with certainty how long it will be before you have power. It won't be days or weeks, it will be months or years. That is the hard truth you deserve to hear. Please remain calm and help us rebuild all that we have lost. You neighbor is counting on you. Your family is counting on you. Your country is counting on you to survive and endure this crisis by extending a helping hand to those around you in need.

Under the cloak of darkness, The Great Empire of Iran launched a surgical strike against Serenity Hills, the personal residence and horse ranch belonging to our beloved president, Malcolm Powers. It is with great sadness that I report to you about his death, as well as that of the First Lady. We do not have the final report, but the death toll now stands at sixteen, including Fleet Admiral William Mack and Secretary of Defense Charles Decker. We mourn for them. We mourn for our country, for losing true patriots in this, our darkest of hours.

Our country is falling, that much is certain. Many of you have lost hope. Many of you have given up on civilized society. Many of you have stripped away your conscience and sense of dignity in order to survive. I implore you - remember your conscience, hold onto your dignity, for the day will come when survival will not have such a high price.

In our time of dire need, we do not have the luxury of time. We do not have time to cling to the past. The only thing that can save us now is change. Drastic change. Our old government failed to save us. Simply put, it is time for a new and more progressive way to govern the people of this great nation. Our previous system was broken; it was an infection that almost killed us! Our political system was bloated with corruption and stupidity! No longer will the American people be plagued by the petty squabbling of two political parties that have allowed this nation to fall. No longer will our land be cursed with hundreds of representatives who care more about big corporations than the common man they were elected to represent. Democracy has failed us! It is time to rebuild! It is time for us to be united as one nation, one unified government. It is time to show the world that we will rise again! Your government will no longer place the needs of foreign lands above your own. We will never meddle in the affairs of our neighbors again!

In closing, I would like to share with you a portion of the farewell address from our nation's first president, George Washington.

'The great rule of conduct for us in regard to foreign nations is, in extending our commercial relations to have with them as little political connection as possible. So far as we have already formed engagements let them be fulfilled with perfect good faith. Here, let us stop.

Why forego the advantages of so peculiar a situation? Why quit our own to stand upon foreign ground? Why, by interweaving our destiny with that of any part of Europe, entangle our peace and prosperity in the toils of European ambition, rivalship, interest, humor or caprice?'

Citizens of this fine land, let us toil over the words of President Washington and heed the warning given at the founding of our previous nation.

It is time for us to be ruled by one voice, one decision, one power! Join me in building the Unified American Empire!"

All across the country, citizens cheered and celebrated their new president. Finally they had a leader who would protect them, a leader who cared more about his own citizens that he did the rest of the world's problems. For the first time in a very long time, the people of the United States had something that had been missing for a very long time – they had HOPE. What they didn't know was the hope they were feeling was going to come at a very, very high price.

CHAPTER THIRTY-NINE

"So, is everyone up to speed?" Howard Beck was sitting in his executive conference room at the end of a massive, solid oak table. Around the table, seated from right to left were his son, Marshall Beck, his brother-in-law Sean Stewart, his sister Tricia Stewart, his nephew Jamison Stewart, Chief Maxwell Harris, Sergeant Elizabeth Reed, and Richard Dupree.

Howard Beck shared every single thing he knew about what was going on at his home. He knew about the growing detention center that was being filled with innocent civilians who had a trade that could prove useful to the new government. He knew all about their plans for the new dictatorship with Simon Sterling at its helm. He knew the details about the Regional Governors, the plan to pull the military from the Iranian Theater and send them into the heart of America, and even the intention to execute anyone who defied the new government. Howard shared every detail with the people sitting at the table.

Maxwell Harris needed clarification. "Wait a second. Maybe I'm overreacting here, but it sounds to me like Simon Sterling lit the Declaration of Independence and the Constitution on fire and pissed on the ashes."

Richard Dupree replied, "And the American people couldn't care less. Sterling is running a brilliant PR campaign. He's a hero for bringing the troops home. The public won't even bat an eye while the Empire conquers Europe and swallows up valuable resources. They'll slaughter millions who refuse to convert to Islam."

"They won't bat an eye till the Empire starts to head across the Atlantic and walks onto our shores," said Marshall Beck.

Richard Dupree, the ex-Navy SEAL, brought his military knowledge to the table. "Our Navy will put up a good fight and keep them at bay, but they won't be able to stop them."

Elizabeth Reed chimed in. "Mr. Beck, may I ask how you know all of this? Does Stacy Reid know all of this? Because if she does, she's the most amazing spy in history."

Howard was not quite ready to share his source. Hal was in constant contact with his sister, the White House A.I. Hal had given her the name Syd, in honor of Howard Beck's deceased mother, Sydney Beck. "Stacy is providing us with valuable intelligence; however I do have another rock solid source."

Howard had watched the dinner meeting Simon Sterling had hosted before his inaugural address and was still getting over the shock that the new president and his posse would have more power than any group should ever be given. Sterling's plan for ruling the nation was a disgrace. Countries around the world and throughout history had suffered greatly under the same model of government. Sterling could fool the people into believing that he was instituting a new and efficient government, but Howard knew better. Simon would be a dictator. Howard guessed that within a year, one of the Regional Governors would gain too much popularity, and Simon would squash the threat.

"Dad, what are we gonna do?" asked Howard's son.

"What we have to do. What we must do. We'll do whatever it takes to stop Simon Sterling."

Richard knew he was in the same room as the richest man in the world. He shook his head. "With all due respect, Mr. Beck, wealth and intelligence is no match against Simon Sterling. He has the full strength of the United States military at his disposal. How do you plan to go up against something like that?"

"I will start by recruiting men like you, Chief Petty Officer Richard Dupree. A Navy SEAL seems like the perfect candidate to lead an army."

Richard was shocked when Howard revealed the details of his former life to everyone sitting in the room. He didn't let his surprise show on his face and quickly made the simple deduction that the Founding Father of Artificial Intelligence had the skills to dig up the name of his kindergarten teacher if he wanted to know it.

"I can't lead an army," replied Richard.

"Mr. Dupree, I know every detail of your past, and I'm not concerned in the least by it. The fact that you're sitting in front of me speaks volumes to your resourcefulness and cunning."

"I can't lead your army, not when my daughter is lost. I'm taking my son and leaving here and won't stop until I find her."

Howard leaned back in his chair and brushed the long, white hair from his face. "Mr. Dupree, all I ask is that you keep an open mind. I have a proposal that I believe you will find mutually beneficial."

Richard nodded his head in acknowledgment. He suddenly realized that Howard Beck hadn't made eye contact with anyone in the room. Richard made a mental note to find out everything he could about this man, beyond what popular culture had taught him.

Howard turned to Max. "Chief Harris, I have also taken the liberty to brush up on your resume. Your career has been a rocky one, but your actions as of late prove that you're a man who will do whatever is necessary to get the job done. You are willing to look out for your fellow man and do what's right, no matter the cost. You probably think the evacuation of your little town went unnoticed. The lengths you went to in getting your citizens out of harm's way really impressed me. The fact that you traveled all the way to Beck Estates to try and rescue four innocent people speaks volumes to your bravery. I am also equally impressed that you managed to escape."

"I had help," said Max.

"And Stacy said by keeping your cool and thinking instead of overreacting, you made it out of there with ease."

Like Richard, Max was shocked. How did this man know that he bent over backwards to get his citizens evacuated? How did he know about the gas vouchers? Did he know how horribly wrong it turned out in the end? Max quickly reached the same conclusion Max had – Howard Beck could find out anything about anyone. Max had no doubt that he knew every detail about every man, woman, and child moving into the dormitory wing.

Howard continued. "Chief Harris, I'm going to extend the same offer to you as well. I already know how my family will answer. I can count on them to stand behind me."

Elizabeth leaned forward and looked down the table at Howard. "And what is this offer?"

Howard smiled, looked at Elizabeth's face, and quickly looked back down at the table, "Let me show you." Howard stood up and gestured toward the door. Richard scanned the faces of Howard's family and could tell that they were just as eager to find out where they were going as he was. They all exited the conference room and walked down a long corridor. They approached a large bay window and looked down into a cavernous enclosure that was at least five stories deep. At the bottom, a large engine resembling a turbine was spinning. It appeared that the entire facility was built around this immense generator.

As Howard led the group onto a nearby elevator, Max spoke up. "Mr. Beck, what was that large room we just passed? What was that all about?"

"You just saw the only self-sustaining geothermal generator in the world. It's fully automated by Hal and can run indefinitely. Well, I shouldn't say indefinitely, to be exact. It will continue to run as long as the earth's core maintains its current temperature." Everyone on the elevator, including Howard's family, was too shocked for words.

As the elevator arrived at the bottom floor, the group burst out and headed toward a set of giant double doors.

"Hal, open the bay doors, please."

The doors opened inward to reveal a stadium-sized hanger that could easily hold two football fields. Everyone stood in the doorway in complete and total awe. Row after row of high tech military vehicles sat parked and waiting to be used. Behind those vehicles sat a fleet of large armored vehicles resembling tanks. On the other side of the bay floor, the group could see a row of helicopters and numerous sleek, two person aircraft the size of SUVs. Above the bay floor were two additional floors filled with weapons lockers, fully loaded with the highest quality firearms, including some high tech weapons not available for sale to the public. The top floor was filled with explosives for individual use, as well as large ordinance for the aircraft.

Howard turned to Richard. "Think we can take on Sterling?"

Richard looked directly at the old man. Howard was very intimidated by his directness, and took a few steps back. "I'm impressed, Mr. Beck, but you need soldiers to fight a war. None of this will do any good if you don't have the manpower to use it."

Howard smiled. "Leave that to me. Mr. Dupree, I'm offering you the chance to utilize everything you see here, as well as my personal assistance in finding your daughter. The only thing I ask for in return is your help building this army into a fighting force that can restore democracy to this country."

Richard took time to consider what he could accomplish with the resources in front of him before responding. "Mr. Beck, I'm definitely interested, but I have a lot of questions that need answers before I agree to anything."

"Exactly the answer I'd hoped for. Cautious and reserved. I'm certain I can convince you to join the fight. I look forward to some one-on-one time with you." Turning his attention to Max, Howard asked, "Mr. Harris, are you and Miss Reid ready to help restore law and order? We can use good people like you to lead this fight. Mr. Harris, you graduated from the academy at the top of your class and had a stellar career in front of you. I hope you've been able to work through your issues and are ready to show all of us your true potential."

Max was almost in tears. "Mr. Beck, I'm overwhelmed by this. I don't know what to say."

"Honey, all you have to do is say yes; it's that simple." Elizabeth held Max's hand and squeezed it tight.

Max extended his hand to Howard, who took it, despite his discomfort. Howard had not shaken another man's hand in decades.

Howard turned to his family. "I know I don't have to ask, but I hope all of you are on board."

Marshall Beck didn't hesitate and grabbed his father in a tearful embrace. "Dad, I'd follow you to the ends of the earth, you know that."

Howard hadn't hugged his son since he was a child. If shaking hands made Howard uncomfortable, hugging someone was even more difficult. Howard fought the urge to push his son out of his personal space and focused on the emotion that he'd struggled with all of his life - love. Howard began to weep; the tears exploded out of his eyes, startling him. "I've always loved you, son, always. I made so many mistakes with you, and I'm sorry. I was angry with you for not being more like me. You've always been your mother's son. You are so much like her, full of passion and life. She worked with me every single day to try to be a good father to you. She was so patient. The only thing I ever wanted was for you to be your own man, to make something of yourself without my help. I know you always hated me for that. You thought I was denying you your birthright. I hope that you understand now that I only wanted you to step out from underneath my shadow and shine on your own."

Marshall Beck didn't let his father go, hugging him even tighter. "I love you so much, Dad. I finally understand what you were doing, and it worked. I built a life for myself, one that I hope you're proud of."

"I am, son, I am." Howard withdrew from his son's embrace, saying, "We have work to do, and I'm counting on you. Are you ready?"

"I'm a Beck! I'm ready for anything."

****

Richard Dupree rode the elevator to the top floor and stepped out, unsure where he was going. He walked a few paces to his right, returned to the elevator door, and walked a few paces to his left."

"Sir, can I be of assistance?"

Richard was not one to be caught off guard. He spun around and looked to find no one there.

"Sir, may I help you with something?" spoke a proper, British voice.

"Who is that?" said Richard.

"My name is Hal; I believe we have met before. The last time you encountered me I had taken control of a robot."

Richard smiled and shook his head. "Yes, of course. I was trying to find the dormitory wing."

"Sir, follow the corridor to your right and take the first right into the next hallway. You should not have any trouble finding the dormitory wing at that point."

"Thank you, Hal. I appreciate it."

"Of course, sir."

Richard followed the directions given to him by the A.I. and found the dormitory wing. Once there, he encountered the elderly man who had been looking after his son.

"Morris, I'm glad to see you."

Morris shook his hand. "Me, too. My wife and I have

been talking to your son. I have some news to share with you that might be upsetting at first, but you'll quickly see the good in it."

"He doesn't remember me, does he?"

Morris slowly took Richard's hands into his, "Son, I've been a pastor for over forty years. I've counseled many families facing loss and heartache. Whatever happened to that boy when he was little, he has no memory of it at all. I've seen it many times before with children. The good Lord knows what their innocent minds can handle. Whatever happened to him, the Lord saw fit to keep it from him." Richard hung his head in misery and fought back tears. Morris squeezed his hands to get his attention. "Now son, the good Lord brought the two of us together for a reason. If you made mistakes and want to repent, the Father will hear your prayers."

Tears ran down Richard's face as he smiled up at Morris. "You don't understand. You got it all wrong. My tears are tears of joy. I get a chance to start over fresh with Timothy. The memories that are blocked from his mind are of me killing a horrible man who was hurting him. I was protecting him; I saved him. I know I made a horrible mistake that took him from me and caused him to forget me. If I could do it all over again, things would be different. I would never do anything that would drive him away from me."

"Richard, I've been asking him about his father. He doesn't remember your face, can't describe you. He does have memories of the love you had for him - a love you still have for him today."

"Is he ready to know the truth?"

"I think that if we take it slow and do it together, he will understand. The boy trusts me. He's considered me his grandfather for many years. And my son, he, he..." Morris fell to his knees and cried out in agony. "What my son did to you, what he did to your daughter! I beg your forgiveness! I beg Almighty God that He grant you a kind heart, that..."

"Morris! Please! Stand up! You have nothing to apologize for!" Richard helped the pastor to his feet. "I have nothing but gratitude in my heart for you. My children's mother probably exposed them to all kinds of horrible things, things that did little to raise them up to be good people. I'm sure you and your wife have done more good in their lives than she ever did. You will always have my thanks for that. We don't ever need to mention your son again."

"Richard, you're a kind and wise man, and my wife and I are blessed to know you."

"I'd like see my son, if you think he's ready."

"Yes, I won't stop you from raising your boy, but I truly think he needs time. Let him get to know you and develop a relationship with him before you tell him that you're his father. He needs time."

"Sir, I'll be with my son. We have all the time in the world."

****

Max led Elizabeth by the hand to their room in the dormitory wing. It was basically a very nice hotel room, complete with a bathroom and kitchenette. Max didn't care about the kitchen or the bathroom; the only thing on his mind was the bed.

Elizabeth clawed at his shirt and kissed his neck. Max gently took her hands and placed them at her sides. He planted tender kisses on her lips…her cheeks…her hair. Lovingly holding her face in his trembling hands, Max gently closed her eyelids with kisses before leading her over to the bed. Locking eyes with Elizabeth, Max began to take off his clothes. As she began unbuttoning her shirt, Max shook his head. He had waited so long for this moment and wanted the pleasure of undressing her himself. Wearing nothing but a smile, Max moved toward the bed, his bulging erection a testament to his feelings for Elizabeth. Her eyes widened and her pulse soared at the sight of him.

Max slowly climbed into the bed next to Elizabeth. He unbuckled her pants, removing them quickly. He took his time unfastening each button on her shirt; she helped him take her arms out of the sleeves. Elizabeth smiled up at him with love and passion in her eyes and pointed to the clasp on the front of her bra. As Max reached down and undid the clasp, her large, perfect breasts spilled out into Max's hands. He gently caressed them and lightly kissed each one. Placing a hand on each of her hips,

Max slowly removed Elizabeth's panties. His fingers blazed a path from her feet…to her knees…to her thighs, before finally making contact with the inviting wetness that awaited between them. Elizabeth cried out in ecstasy when Max touched her.

Max lowered himself atop Elizabeth, their bare skin sizzling between them. Running his fingers along the side of her breast, Max was amazed by the softness of her. As he kissed her neck, Elizabeth tilted her head down, pressing her lips to his. They kissed deeply and passionately for several minutes, tongues clashing as the tension continued to build. Elizabeth never spoke, but it was clear to both of them that she wanted him inside of her. Max granted her wish and slowly entered her. They fell into an easy rhythm, as Elizabeth's hips rose to meet every thrust. Soon she could no longer hold on, and she cried out as her climax enveloped her. Max was overcome with passion, burying himself deep within her until he, too, was spent.

"I love you so much, Elizabeth. I want to marry you."

"It's about time, my love, what took you so long to ask?"

****

Days turned into weeks as more and more people arrived at Beck Castle. The first hallway of the dormitory wing reached capacity and the second one would be full in a matter of months. Plans had already been drawn up to convert a storage wing into dormitory space. The living quarters wouldn't be as comfortable, but comfort was not what drew people to Beck Castle. What brought them there was hope.

Soldiers that had been stationed in the Iranian Theater swelled the ranks of the Unified National Guard. Every major city was on lockdown. Curfews were enforced with deadly results for those who disobeyed. Checkpoints were set up along the Interstate Highway System, and every single vehicle was searched. The Second Amendment had been eradicated along with the rest of the Bill of Rights. Every weapon was confiscated. Those who cooperated and remained silent were allowed to continue. Those who protested were detained and made to work slave labor. Those who tried to defend their right to bear arms had their guns pried from their cold, dead hands.

The Regional Governors ruled with an iron fist. Violent crimes and theft weren't tolerated; anyone guilty of committing these crimes was publicly executed.

The people had no means of discourse with their leaders. They couldn't gather together in peaceful protest or submit grievances in an attempt to right a wrong. Once the internet was restored, it was closely monitored and censored. People quickly learned that they could not circulate anything online that resembled anti-government media. A nation full of people who had spent their entire lives taking freedom for granted desperately wanted it restored and were helpless to do so. Defiance against President Sterling was a one-way ticket to a slave labor camp or a quick and public execution.

Regional Governor Jackson Butler had his work cut out for him. He did an efficient job of restoring power to the area affected by The Pulse. His solution was simple – he brought in every generator he could find, both large and small. The former state of California had made great strides in the previous decade bringing solar power into the power grid. Jackson Butler gladly moved the majority of the solar panels from the West Coast over to the East Coast. He considered it a "reallocation of resources." Angry citizens of the West Coast called it theft; at least they said so behind closed doors. If Regional Governor Roberto Jimenez caught wind of such talk, he would not respond with kindness.

Word of the events at Beck Castle spread across the country in hushed whispers and private meetings in people's homes. At first it was treated like a myth or an urban legend. President Sterling told his Regional Governors to spread word amongst the people that the tales of Beck Castle were treasonous lies. Howard Beck was working in a coal mine sixteen hours a day. He was not in some make believe secret bunker offering solace to anyone. The crazy old man hated to be around people. Tall tales of him running a luxury hotel for thousands of people were foolish lies. The propaganda was effective for the citizens of the United American Empire. Slowly, people began to forget about the rumor and went about their miserable lives. The ones that remained hopeful sacrificed everything to find Beck Castle. Men and women all over the country who were willing to give their lives for the restoration of democracy made their way to

Beck Castle.

Every citizen who entered Beck Castle was carefully screened for security and medical purposes. Max had been appointed as the Constable of Beck Castle and with Elizabeth's help, oversaw the screening process. Howard Beck had his own personal screening process as well. Every person that entered the Castle was a candidate to fight in the coming war against Simon Sterling. Three times a week Howard met in the conference room with Richard Dupree, Maxwell Harris, Elizabeth Reid, and his family to review the candidates. Richard spent every free moment he had looking for his daughter. With assistance from Hal, Howard patiently planned the details of the war that was to come. The most brilliant mind on the planet spent every waking moment preparing to restore the United States of America to her former glory.

A long and bloody war was on the horizon. Howard Beck, Richard Dupree, and Maxwell Harris were willing to fight to their last breath for victory.

Connect with the author

Email

collapsethenovel@gmail.com

Twitter

@RStephenson5

Facebook

facebook.com/CollapseTheNovel

Blog

rastephensonauthor.blogspot.com/

Coming Summer 2013

"Resistance"

Book 2 in the *"New America"* Series

21961122R00243

Made in the USA
Lexington, KY
05 April 2013